EVIL
NEVER
SLEEPS

K.G.E. Konkel

EVIL NEVER SLEEPS

HarperCollins*Publishers*Ltd

www.harpercanada.com

HarperCollins books may be purchased for
educational, business, or sales promotional use.
For information please write:
Special Markets Department,
HarperCollins Canada,
55 Avenue Road, Suite 2900,
Toronto, Ontario, Canada M5R 3L2

First HarperCollins hardcover ed.
ISBN 0-00-224366-0
First HarperCollins trade paper ed.
ISBN 0-00-648536-7

Canadian Cataloguing in Publication Data

Konkel, K. G. E.
Evil never sleeps

ISBN 0-00-224366-0

I. Title.

PS8571.O696E94 2000   C813'.54   C00-930096-1
PR9199.3.K66E94 2000

00 01 02 03 04 HC 6 5 4 3 2 1

Printed and bound in the United States
Set in Monotype Janson

For my dear mother Ann, who taught me the joy of reading and my lovely daughter Laura, who has quickly grown to share that joy. To Don Loney, my editor and friend who has been patient and probing and insightful throughout the process of creation. To Edward, my father and Lillian Grace, who remain always looking over our shoulder. And smiling. We'll also never forget Thelma Margaret Drouin who loved to sing and dance.

And now, always and forever,

To my wife Robin, who has been my constant companion and best friend when it really mattered.

And finally, for those people known only to me who have affected my life and made me what I am . . . God bless you all.

I hear a sigh across
the lands and the sea
and it is not a sigh, it is
that my son is going to wake

— José Martí

PART ONE
CORONADO

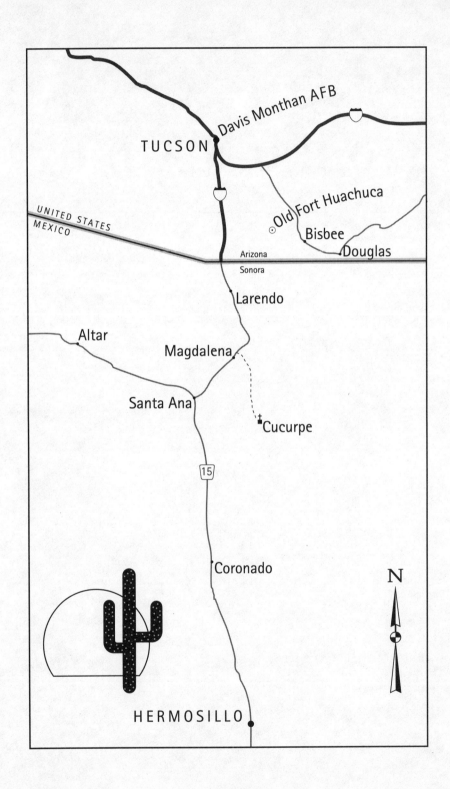

1 Highway 15, the four-lane toll road from Nogales to Mazatlán, cracked in places by the fierce coral sun, gamely connected Hermosillo, the capital of the State of Sonora, to Magdalena de Kino, before stretching across the border toward Tucson, Arizona, and a sunburst of points north.

This part of Sonora was nicknamed "El Zippo" by the *gringos* – American cousins who hauled basketball-sized melons across the Rio Grande in mammoth silver-sheen Fruehauf trailers. El Zippo. The Big Fat Nothing. And not without reason.

The moonscape of desert and mesquite was all but devoid of life – save for a rust-shingled gas station squatting in sagebrush, a tequila joint posing as a truck stop, a desolate tuft of abandoned hovels where long-forgotten *mestizos* clawed out what couldn't be called a living, and little else in the way of hope or humanity.

On the horizon, the car appeared as a pesky gnat, then grew swiftly larger as it lanced outward from Hermosillo: a Mustang GT, black-and-white police package, custom-fitted with tri-bar roof light, whiplash antenna, and deep-tinted windows. A tiny tarantula was stenciled to the driver's door just above the word POLICIA.

The car's occupant, a thickset male in his early forties wearing wrinkled khakis and a straw Stetson, absently thrummed his fingertips on the steering wheel to the beat of Gloria Estefan thundering from the radio. On such a fine May morning, Miguel Fuentes had placed himself on general patrol. As recently appointed *jefe* for the town of Coronado, he was getting acquainted with his territory, and, like most veteran police officers, he pounced on the opportunity to dodge paperwork whenever possible.

The buff-colored dashboard of the Mustang was grimy from abuse. It bore the scribbled traces of an infinity of useless phone numbers and the haloes of myriad bitter coffees – all in all, the grit and grunge of a faithful workhorse too much defiled and too little loved.

3

But Fuentes didn't mind, for the car was his and his alone. He coaxed the motor till it hovered near eighty miles an hour, luxuriating in the power of his most prized possession. The two hundred and twenty-five feisty horses under the dust-talced hood pounded a heady rhythm into the stifling midday air.

The unit was a five-year-old pursuit coupe that had begun life with the California Highway Patrol on the speedway between Barstow and the Nevada line. Three crashes – the last at a hairpin turn outside Needles – had severely cracked the frame and dissolved the optimism of the police body shop. The car was then lamely defaulted to the state auction block as surplus inventory.

Soon after, the Ford miraculously resurfaced as the newest addition to the stable of the City of Nogales Police. Fuentes inherited the vehicle over the clamorous protests of his frontier counterparts by shrewdly confronting an aide of the state's governor with certain irregularities he'd unearthed in the region's budget allotment for police training.

It might well have been a form of hush money to keep Fuentes silent, but the Mustang proved a distinct improvement over the vehicle of the previous *jefe*, a decrepit '74 Mercury Monarch two-door with chili-pepper upholstery and peach tassels dangling from its rearview mirror. The Merc had disappeared without a trace at about the same time as had Fuentes's predecessor.

"Tarantula" was the pet name Miguel had given the Mustang. He felt little remorse at the dubious circumstances of its acquisition. That was just the way it was. If he hadn't claimed the thing as the spoils of war, someone else would have.

Fuentes glanced out the partially opened window and felt the heat tingle his flinty face. Mirrored in the glass was a square jaw; broad, expressive mouth; nose broken in a Tijuana brawl a decade ago and never properly set; eyes perpetually hidden by Raybans; skin dried to a caramel hue; a trim pencil mustache.

He cut off the highway, waving to a drowsy ticket-collector as he did so. Swerving onto the red dirt road that started just beyond the tollgate and paralleled the highway, he continued northward, rapidly picking up speed as he went. The route was one of many that spread vein-like across the desert floor, connecting village to village, family to family.

He tried to stretch in the snug bucket seat, grimacing as he did so. The finely embroidered brown leather belt holstering a Corsair-blue Glock automatic had become a notch too tight. What had begun last night as a bona fide affair to honor a retiring school principal had soon degenerated into an endless gluttony of beef, sweet peppers stuffed with cream and nuts, giant enchiladas, and ice-cold beer. He felt a burning sensation deep in his guts.

The Mustang surged over a bend, then eased up as it passed the scattering of adobe huts, a stand of stunted brush, and the tiny cemetery that made up the dusty crossroads at San Cristobal. A shallow stream seeped up through the parched earth to feed a patchwork quilt of gray ash and jaundiced cinnamon that grudgingly bore crops. A trim pastel *casa* poised on a bluff overlooked what passed for the village.

Fuentes resisted the urge to stop and check on the place. Once again he was living alone, with only Salinas, a nine-month-old German Shepherd pup, for company. The Mustang accelerated, kicking up rooster tails of dust as it charged through. Salinas could wait.

Five minutes later, Fuentes passed the entrance to the Wal-Mart center, a spanking new, multi-acred expanse of asphalt and optimism bordered by coarse desert. He braked hard through a slalom curve before abruptly entering the outskirts of Coronado.

Named in honor of Francisco Vasquez de Coronado, who in 1540 became the first Spaniard to walk the plains of Sonora in search of a mythical land rumored to have seven cities of gold, the town was settled in the 1700s, soon after precious metals were actually found in the nearby mountains. In the uneasy times after Mexican independence, Apache tribes, forced from the north by avaricious American ranchers, constantly raided the village. Then, for a short interval in 1853, the area was an independent republic under the influence of the quixotic American adventurer William Walker – until he was roundly defeated by the Mexican military and fled to the relative safety of San Diego.

In the late 1940s, Coronado began the latest chapter in its sporadic history as a respite for foreign travelers en route to the resort beaches on the Golfo de California, the sapphire stretch of sea lying between the Baja Peninsula and the Mexican mainland. And when, in the early 1950s, copper was discovered in the nearby Sierra Madre range, the town's affluence was all but assured. Huge open pits clawed out of stolid rockface spewed forth half of Mexico's copper production. Coronado became home to hundreds of miners and their migrant families, many of them illiterate peasants from the troubled state of Chiapas in the distant south of Mexico, outsiders who mingled uneasily with the entrenched local population.

With just slightly over six thousand residents, the town was the self-proclaimed regional hub for northern Sonora, with all the pretensions to grandeur that inevitably came with such a claim. It had a grid of hard-angled streets, a courthouse, meeting hall, infirmary, and bus depot; eight churches, all Roman Catholic save one, which was Pentecostal; and an equal number of schools, all state-run, although Coronado's élite sent their children to the two private academies operated by the Church.

Miguel Fuentes was Coronado's police chief – *El Jefe* – a position he'd held for almost three months. In the primal rite of Mexican justice, the community of Coronado and its environs were his fiefdom and he its lord. But in these uneasy times, his tenure could vanish overnight.

There was increasing talk of streamlining emergency services, of declaring the Coronado police force – and countless others in the state – redundant, and of placing every municipality under the federal umbrella. And there was nothing Miguel could do about it. So he continued to perform his sworn duty to the best of his ability and to demand the same of his sluggish subordinates.

Sometimes he felt like the sergeant in the war movie *Bataan*, futilely leading a platoon against Japanese invaders in the Philippines in the dark days just after Pearl Harbor. All of them died, one by one, until the sergeant, the final defender, dug a grave by his comrades, knowing his body would fall into it as he fired a final shot and got a lethal rebuttal from the advancing enemy.

Fuentes liked forties' movies. He liked their pure messages; their tidier worlds of equity and respect; their celluloid universe of uncomplicated rights and wrongs that spoke of hope and direction.

He turned the radio off and became attentive once more to the dreary reality around him.

A girl played hopscotch near a scattering of rusty auto wrecks. Miguel sounded the siren as he whizzed past. The child stopped to peer at the police car. The image reflected in sunglasses was as hard as basalt. The siren's wail was lost under a sky the glint of polished sapphire.

Highway 15 arrowed straight into Coronado, and was pretentiously renamed Passeo Bolivar in the town proper, honoring the mythic Latin populist Simon Bolivar. The designation was surely meant to evoke the notion of broad, tree-lined boulevards and expensive cafés.

What Coronado offered instead was a potholed artery patrolled by mangy dogs and stinking of overripe garbage and diesel fumes. An army of creaking second-hand school buses served as the region's transportation system. The stench mingled with the piquant aroma of *tacos* and *frijoles* wafting from the sleazy bars that comprised Coronado's "entertainment district."

In the year preceding Fuentes's appointment, an ambitious state government had seen fit to speak of revitalizing the Passeo so that it might more adequately represent the "innate grandeur of the Common People of Mexico." Accordingly, millions of *pesos* were to be plowed into improving the roadway to ensure that it became an authentic boulevard. The resultant extravaganza along the Passeo – long banks of towering streetlights and regimented rows of parking meters – would assuredly harness the prosperity of the rough-hewn dynamo that was Coronado. The crowning glory was to be a magnificent park with a massive community center, complete with Olympic-sized swimming pool, auditorium, and fine restaurants.

Soon a veritable army of construction workers had descended on Coronado. Heavy trucks rumbled into town at all hours of the day and night. In swift order, deep exploratory ditches were dug into the red clay; gas mains were unearthed and capped for safety; rerouting signs were prepared and stacked by the dozen near a portable site-command trailer that was dropped on a side street like a beached whale. There was enormous activity, but very little real progress. The townsfolk expected nothing else.

Then, one morning, a tragedy occurred that marred the project and cast a pall on its future.

A monster tractor-trailer failed to negotiate a sharp turn in the old quarter of town. The twenty-five-ton Oshkosh transporter – a brutal centaur of the type that had conveyed Abrams battle tanks for the American army during the Gulf War – was towing a sixteen-wheel flatbed crammed with high-pressure canisters destined for the Bolivar site. One of the canisters broke free of its chain, careened off the trailer, and crushed a four-year-old girl playing on the roadside.

Fuentes inherited what had been, by all accounts, an indifferent investigation. There were rumors aplenty to contend with: tales of faulty braking systems and rusting mechanicals on the Oshkosh, and of substandard chains holding the canister in place. There were also whispers about the canister's contents, said to be deadly chemicals.

But no one officially reported such things to the authorities, and all the physical clues seized were smoothed over with extraordinary haste by the *federale* forensic lab. Inexplicably, the Oshkosh and its trailer weren't even impounded. On the very day following the mishap, the machinery was brokered by its owners to cart heavy equipment to oil explorations in the southern state of Oaxaca.

The torpedo-shaped canister was just as abruptly emptied and now lay abandoned and rusting in a transit lot off the Passeo. Evidence of what the canister might have contained was illegibly scribbled on an invoice seized by police. Investigators visiting the freight-forwarding yard – a place near the U.S. border called Larendo – were told it was propane, though substantiation was impossible.

The owners of the Oshkosh – a company with untraceable roots and a top Mexico City law firm running flawless interference – never showed a human face at any stage of the investigation. And no official voices were raised in protest.

Fuentes always suspected the truth behind the tragedy, although he couldn't prove anything. It was rumored that the unnamed consortium bankrolling the Bolivar project was controlled by the PRI – *el Partido Revolucionario Institucional* – the political regime that had run Mexico as a veritable oligarchy since 1929. The PRI and its supporters dominated many things nationally and most things locally, including dictating the hopes and dreams of Coronado's citizens.

In the end, the matter petered out. In Mexico, it wasn't healthy to talk about corruption, at least not openly, if one wanted to live in peace and feed one's family. It was said that those who knew the truth about the shipment had been muted by that most universal of all pacifiers – money. And so the investigation of the girl's death had been stalled in its tracks.

Entering the main thoroughfare, Fuentes eased the Mustang to a crawl. The way ahead was a sea of banana-colored *sombreros*. Pushcarts jammed full of produce crowded the curbsides. Women in their finest silk *rebozos* jostled each other at the foodstands, for today was Monday, when the town center became one huge and swarming open-air market.

A massive garbage truck inched through the throngs. The vehicle made only intermittent stops to pick up refuse, leaving drifts of stinking rubbish behind. Service had fallen off visibly in recent weeks as the town council struggled to make payments to the waste-management firm, a private-sector company contracted to do the work after a singularly dubious competition. A phone number was stenciled on the doors of the company's trucks. However, Fuentes knew from personal experience that anyone who actually took the trouble to call to complain would hear only a taped gospel hymn.

Miguel glanced up at a traffic signal dangling disconsolately from rusted guidewires. Shabby pickup trucks darted through the swelling confusion, charging the junction from all directions as if they were in a *charreada* – a rodeo. Horns blew and people clamored. No one paid much attention to his police car or the light. And, just as remarkably, no one got hurt.

At first, the sound was difficult to discern. It began as a low, sepulchral rumble, then picked up volume, surging like a tidal wave out of the bowels of nearby foothills before cascading down the crowded streets of Coronado. Then, suddenly, silence – a blank, white silence. People froze, shielding their eyes as they peered northwards to a heat-stirred horizon where a smudged cotton ball began to billow upwards into the sky. A baby wailed. A wind chime tinkled.

Miguel's mind raced. Was it an oil tanker accident on Highway 15? A ripened propane tank exploding in the peasant *barrio*? Perhaps a plane had crashed, one of the many overloaded DC-3 charters that carried tourists out toward Chihuahua and the fabled Copper Canyon.

His answer came moments later, called in on a citizen's band by a trucker en route to Yuma. An explosion at Zita's, three miles outside the town limit, near the first tollgate off Highway 15. Zita's was a fleabag motel run by a Hungarian spinster who told fortunes on the side. The time of the call was 13:36 hours – 1:36 p.m.

Fuentes reversed the Mustang off Bolivar and down a laneway, then ground his foot into the gas pedal. The car jackrabbited through the cramped back alleys, spewing rocks and debris as it careened back across the town line and out onto the desert. Above the frenetic wail of his siren, Fuentes demanded all available units. He was informed that the town fire department had been alerted; the regional air ambulance helicopter was on standby. He 10-4-ed acknowledgment.

As the Sonora desert blurred past, Fuentes mentally précised what he knew of the motel. Zita's loomed at the end of a serpentine dirt trail about eight hundred yards to the west of the tollway. In the time he'd been *jefe*, he couldn't recall a serious complaint, other than the occasional disgruntled *señoritas* angered by Zita's forays into clairvoyance. In his sporadic patrols by the place, he'd seen but a few patrons: *gringos* venturing off the beaten track in search of what passed for adventure, only to discover roaches in their Sperrys and bugs in their beds; teenagers sweatily groping for love, or what passed for it; and old *vaqueros* lost in a tequila daze, not really wanting to encounter anything.

As he approached, Fuentes eyed the billowing pall of smoke. He roared past the tacky neon sign resting on a U-Haul flatbed that advertised Zita's Motel:

> Color TV, Bottled Water
> Room rates 850 pesos ($12)
> Vacancies
> Major credit cards accepted

He plowed onto the newly graveled lot, vacant but for a tractor-trailer combo and several cars, all local, save two: one, a late-model Olds Cutlass with Arizona plates; the other, a Jeep Cherokee from Texas.

The motel was built along conventional lines, L-shaped with single-story units, management offices at the elbow, and angle parking at the entrance of each suite. The front of the motel looked untouched. But when Fuentes arced around to the rear he saw a maze of tangled girders and chunks of concrete framing a simmering hole in the desert floor where units 5 through 11 had stood only minutes before.

As he got out of the car, Miguel cautiously sniffed the air. The hot soot seared his lungs. There was no smell of gas or propane. Shocked survivors staggered about in smoldering rags, retching blood. The ambulance medics bandaged the worst of the injured, a badly charred male of indeterminate age and a young woman whose clothing hung in strips from blistered skin, her hair singed to her scalp. Her face had the rosy tinge of raw minute steak.

By the remnants of the motel office, a patrol officer interrogated Zita. Wearing a mauve Japanese kimono, the crusty Magyar sucked voraciously on a Benson and Hedges. Badly

stained false teeth clattered loudly out of a rouged face as she
rasped responses to the officer's questions.

The guest log proved to be surprisingly complete. A roll-call of
employees and patrons disclosed a pair of visitors and one staff
member unaccounted for: two single men occupying rooms 8 and
9 and the maid in section C. Eight guests and three staff, including Zita, were alive though badly shaken.

A police unit pulled up carrying a shaken youth they'd found a
quarter mile down the dirt path, mumbling incoherently about an
earthquake. He proved to be the occupant of room 9. That left R.
Palmer, section C, room 8. And Tina Arroyo, the chambermaid.

Fuentes exchanged a few words with the fire chief, whose
men were diligently dousing the flames. Then he returned to
the Mustang and slouched in the bucket seat, tipping the Stetson out of his eyes. He had the situation reasonably under
control: half a dozen units, scene contained, and the injured en
route to hospital.

He took advantage of the respite to update his diary, furiously
jotting down observations with a fountain pen. Fuentes intuitively knew that "R. Palmer" and "Tina Arroyo" were now just
so many willowy wisps of heat wafting off the rubble, and he
knew also that, as a consequence, he'd have to fully investigate
the reasons why.

The first thing Fuentes sensed about the unannounced visitor
was his cologne, a cloying fragrance of black dahlias that blew
through the half-open window long before a well-manicured
finger rapped on the glass.

"Miguel! *Mi amigo!*" a rich base voice pronounced. "It's been
too long!"

Fuentes turned his head. The newcomer loomed well over six
feet. A honey-hued Panama hat partially shaded dark, jeweled
eyes and thin lips worming their way to an emotion. He wore a
single-breasted silk suit, salmon-colored with a carnation bouton-
nière. The jacket was open, and Miguel spied a well-defined row
of speed loaders resting on an expensive notched leather belt.

"Obregon." Fuentes did little to hide his displeasure. He

reluctantly opened the door and eased himself out. "What are you doing here? This isn't a *federale* matter."

"Me?" shrugged Obregon, casting an indifferent glance on the nearby destruction. "Just happened to be driving through the neighborhood. Sight-seeing." His smile was a practiced opaque. "Nice explosion you have here, *hombre*. Quality work."

Fuentes stared up at his visitor. He did not match the smile with one of his own.

Obregon reached into his jacket pocket and took out a cellphone. He began to tap the digits. "You'll need a military bomb unit, Miguel," he remarked with sleek assurance. "Let me get one for you."

Fuentes grew testy. "Save yourself the trouble, Ramon. I'll see to a unit. Robbie Adalmo is the boss of the *Federale* Bureau in Hermosillo, and he's a friend."

Obregon continued punching numbers as if he hadn't heard.

Fuentes stared hard. "Enough! That call is my responsibility."

Obregon put the phone to his ear.

Miguel grabbed Obregon's wrist. The cellphone clattered to the ground.

The *federale* tensed. "You shouldn't have done that, *amigo*," he said coldly.

"Why, Ramon? What are you going to do?" Fuentes stood his ground. "Hold a public inquiry to shame me? Ruin my reputation? Have me removed from my position? You've already done all those things. Why don't you just stick to Mexico City? It's more your style."

A muscle twitched along Obregon's jawline. He began to say something, then seemed to catch himself.

Fuentes reached into the car and made a call to Hermosillo for the bomb team – urgent.

Suddenly, there was a clamor of frantic shouting. "Up here! *Jefe!* Up here!" A grimy figure gestured vigorously in their direction from atop the bombed ruins. "Hurry! We have bodies!"

Fuentes broke into a run. A compact man, he moved at a kind of loping gallop, an unsteady middle-aged gait.

A potbellied patrolman steered him to a grotto created by a profusion of fallen beams and concrete. The spot stank of cordite. The mutilated remnants of two human beings lay cloaked in debris. The first corpse, a fruity mass of blood and tissue and bone held tenuously together by a tattered yellow cleaning smock, was all that remained of Tina Arroyo.

The other body – a male – lay a few feet away in semi-fetal position. It hadn't been as badly butchered by the explosion. Its head and upper section were intact. The torso was of a Caucasian of muscular build, and its legs were truncated just below the kneecaps. From that point down, the cadaver had no limbs, just two pulpy stumps. A cowboy boot rested in rubble. Issuing from it, like a stalk of celery dabbed crimson, was a mass of gristle and blood.

Miguel peered at the carcass, banishing for a moment the vision of horror that was held for all eternity on that frozen mask: late thirties, clean-shaven, lacking tattoos, wedding ring, or other identifiers, attired in an anonymous khaki T-shirt and creased blue jeans.

He called for a pair of plastic gloves, snapped them on, and delicately patted down the exposed portion of the corpse, locating a soiled handkerchief, some loose change, and a motel key. The lettering on the key was pretty conclusive. It belonged to the missing tenant to room 8: R. Palmer.

An officer lurched through the ruins, breathless from exertion. They'd found Palmer's vehicle in the parking lot. Secreted under the passenger seat were two plastic bags containing a ruddy-brown substance.

"My, my, Miguel," offered Obregon, having caught up with Fuentes. "Aren't you suddenly the busy one? Suspicious deaths, one of them a *gringo* and a drug trafficker? Now will you let me summon an army bomb squad?"

Fuentes ignored him and sent a uniformed officer to investigate the other corpses.

Well?" Obregon became indignant. "I appreciate that, technically, this may still be your investigation, *Jefe*. But realize you will ultimately need us."

The *federale* adroitly removed the cellphone from his pocket. Once more he keyed in the numbers. "*Capitán* Torres?" he demanded in a caustic voice. "*Si.* Obregon here. Could you send your duty team north past Coronado? *Si.* Off Number 15. Go to the first tollgate then head west. A place called Zita's. Report to the local *jefe?*" He smirked. "No. To me. Who else is there that matters in this state?"

Obregon crowded Fuentes, then urbanely extended his right hand. "Perhaps, in all the confusion, I neglected to *formally* introduce myself," he purred with a sated smile. "In case you haven't heard, your man Adalmo has been reassigned. I'm the new *comandante* of the Policia Judiciale Federale in the State of Sonora." The slightest bow. "At your service."

After an unenthusiastic search that consumed two hours, Fuentes's constable found the tin hovel that housed the Arroyo family, etched into a prickle bush hillside a quarter mile from the district pumping station.

Perverse conjecture was raised as to who actually came to the realization first: Paco Arroyo, who, in a tequila-induced stupor, vaguely recalled that his two youngest children, five-year-old Willy and three-year-old Terese, had fled his drunken tirade to seek their mother's comfort; or the coroner's assistant, who compared the mangled remains attached to the toe tags of bomb victims #3 and #4 to the vague description of the infants provided by the father, and determined that Willy and Terese Arroyo were, in fact, now two young angels.

Monday, May 21, 5:03 p.m.
Coronado

2 Situated as it was, just off the intersection of Montoya and the Passeo, where it could soak up the poisonous fumes of the adjacent bus depot and the rank stench of an open sewer where the last municipal improvement contract had

abruptly terminated, the place might politely have been termed a garret.

Mule's anus, pigpen, she-devil's armpit – the room had certainly been labeled much worse and seen many far more unsavory uses in the past than the one that it now purported to fulfill.

Twenty feet long by twelve feet wide, with soiled boxes of bargain soda and gauze bags of rice pillowed to an uneven tar-papered ceiling, the loft was accessible by a trap door from the kitchen below. The more adventurous could use a rusted fire escape that resembled a comb with broken teeth, providing they could find their way through the debris-filled alleyway outside Eng's Chinese Takeout.

The chamber was as close as the air outside. A tiny electric fan stirred feeble wisps of stale air in the oppressive heat. Empty tequila bottles littered the bare wooden floor around a mini-fridge, the kind featured in cheap motels. The room had spawned a wrought-iron bed, an aged chest of drawers, side table, and high-backed chair draped with rumpled clothes. A cracked mirror was hung lopsidedly from a crossbeam. A pin-up calendar of a plump China doll wearing a garter belt and corset and not much else graced a space next to the mirror. Though it was daylight, the bulb dangling from the ceiling was lit.

A battalion of bugs beat a resolute path toward mounds of rice spread across the splintered floor. A pair of pink eyes blinked furtively in the darkness; a whippet tail flicked; an obese brown rat rustled about the rotting rafters. A mangy tomcat slumbered nearby.

A child's skipping rope was stretched across ceiling joists. From it drooped five mismatched socks, a set of stringy under-wear, a polka-dot handkerchief, two pairs of polyester suit pants, a plaid jacket, and an aqua-hued golf shirt – all in all, the yardarm of a professional bachelor. A basin with soapy gray water rested on a rotting crate; beside it was a bottle of dish-washing detergent.

Felix Maria Salvatore Asuncion had been born in Coronado, the sixth of nine children of a peasant family living within the echo of the church bells pealing the Angelus, in a part of the hamlet that then perched on the razor's edge between respectability and "the rest" and now sprawled firmly in the cesspool center of The Barrio de Santa Lucia.

Asuncion had been a mediocre student, a plodding oaf of a youth destined to a lifetime of manual labor in the nearby sesame fields. Still, in the dreamy summer of 1965, his prospects would dramatically change. One balmy Monday afternoon, he'd discovered Consuela Torres, a comely *señorita* of voluptuous proportions and allegedly insatiable desires, strolling on the town promenade beneath the statue of Pancho Villa. Asuncion was instantly smitten.

In an apparent burst of civic zeal, he decided then and there to help the local candidate for the PRI, a cross-eyed accountant named Simon Rios, with his campaign. In truth, the young field hand had been motivated far less by the lofty political evocations of the PRI cause than by the realization that the woman of his dreams was the man's personal secretary.

Simon Rios was moneyed; his parents owned several sesame fields, including the one that employed Felix. Rios had an annoying affectation that made him the laughingstock of Coronado and an embarrassment to his kin. Everywhere the young man went, he twirled a steel-tipped cane while affecting an absurd paisley ascot and stark white spats on patent leather shoes, like some English lord of the manor.

Partido Revolucionario Institucional had ruled Mexico for so long that the very words "democratic process" had become meaningless. For any political aspirant blessed by the PRI nod, ascension to the throne of resident power was a foregone conclusion, since it was generally only the PRI who ran candidates in the Mexican parody of "democracy."

Still, Coronado was distinctly different.

Rios's principal opponent, Chico Cordova, was a soured puritan with unruly hair and expired working papers retained from a memory-misted time he'd allegedly indentured as second mate on an Orinoco paddle-steamer. Spouting a cosmopolitan medley of Karl Marx and the American poet Rod McKuen to an indifferent populace, Cordova tramped Coronado's streets as a peppery-eyed Independent. Because of Rios's arrogance and the sullen backlash against his family's brazen power, Cordova, the babbling barge-master, acquired a following. The local election became a close one, watched throughout the nation.

Plotting a course to Consuela's heart via the ego of her employer, Asuncion volunteered to command a raiding party of boisterous men. Under the mantle of darkness, and suitably lubricated by tequila, they plastered all things stationary in Coronado with PRI campaign literature while gleefully shredding the pronouncements of any opponents to the PRI cause.

It had all seemed so much heady, innocuous fun – until the night before the election. PRI supporters, emboldened by liquor, converged on Coronado's union hall to strike a blow against the socialist Cordova. They painted *Viva PRI* over the billboards in front of the rickety edifice. Suddenly, they were confronted by a group of transport laborers leaving a strategy session held by the candidate.

An all-out brawl broke out in the town square, a disturbance that took overworked police three-quarters of an hour to quell. Several people from both camps were injured; one of them, an unemployed bus driver and virulent radical named Alzado, received a deep cut in the thigh. The local *policia* took eleven persons into custody.

As the morning sun rose sienna-red in the Sonoran sky, grumpy detectives prepared to lay formal charges against one of the arrested, Felix Asuncion, for grievous assault on *Señor* Felipe Alphonso Alzado, who lay heavily sedated in the town's hospital. But Asuncion didn't own a sword or bayonet, and he'd never resorted to using one during the grim confrontation. Only one individual, a nearsighted coward, had. Asuncion knew it, as did the victim. And the police. And the coward. Yet Felix said nothing in his own defense.

For nine hours he rested in a cell, made more solitary by police reticence to charge a PRI supporter and alienate their political masters than by any scheme they might have had to make Felix break down and volunteer a full confession in the interests of justice.

By two in the afternoon, a full half day before the polls officially closed and results were formally tabulated, word flashed through the *cantinas* and surrounding *barrios* like prairie fire: the PRI would once more secure the electoral seat in Coronado. Simon Rios would be elected by a landslide.

Fifteen minutes later, the doors to Felix Asuncion's cell clanged open and he was released. The youth was promptly driven to the paternal home of the Rios clan by the town's *jefe* and there, in the presence of the family patriarch, was fed a hearty meal.

The Coronado riot had shown that Asuncion was as strong as a bull and just as stubborn. It had also demonstrated to Rios the Elder that Felix was an individual capable of taking orders without questioning their validity, a man who could clasp the darkest whispers of a secret to his breast and not reveal their source.

Within three days, Felix Asuncion had gratefully accepted a recruit slot in what passed for the *federale* training academy outside Mexico City. The pay proved to be sixfold what he'd made as a field laborer. And he learned how to properly use a bayonet.

Felix never saw the lovely Consuela again. He heard rumors that when Simon Rios was anointed to the National Assembly, he'd taken the woman with him to be his secretary and companion. If such was the case, so be it, for Asuncion had found his true passion in the khaki uniform of a Mexican policeman.

Slightly less than a year ago, with a sparse pension and pocketful of tacky send-off cards, Asuncion had retired from his last post, as chief of investigations in a posh Durango suburb. Felix had traveled far afield in his career, from the Yucatan to Chihuahua, Guerrero to Nuevo Leon, but he was a homeboy at heart, and so it was only natural that he'd return one day to dwell in Sonora and, more specifically, his birthplace of Coronado.

Yet the indolent life of a retired civil servant in a small town was not for him. Three months of unmitigated boredom, split between tilling the powdery soil of an acre garden patch by day and watching Spanish reruns of "Gilligan's Island" on a flinty black-and-white screen every evening, and Asuncion had gladly accepted an offer to work for Miguel's predecessor, Mercedes Lopez. But, for all his convincing promises of meaningful employment, the best Lopez could offer Asuncion was an ill-fitting uniform, a rusting .38 with fake ivory grips, and assignment as special constable patrolling the town square on market days and ensuring that the traffic flowed. Felix had been many things in his checkered career, but he'd never babysat a bevy of parking meters. For a variety of reasons, it was a demotion he did not shoulder well.

The grizzled ex-*federale* was ready to quit for good when Lopez opportunely disappeared while responding to a mysterious phone call requesting his immediate attention. Shortly thereafter, Fuentes, a virtual unknown, was selected from among a field of nine candidates to fill the vacated position of *jefe* in Coronado.

While pondering his new boss's philosophies in a local bar, Asuncion had cautiously accepted a position, nominally as a working detective and then, as the economy soured and rapacious young bloods in the department elbowed their way past to nibble at the skimpy fiscal trough, as an "intelligence consultant."

Asuncion worked "flex time," the tender euphemism he'd adopted to mask the fact that the new *jefe* couldn't pay full wages for the few days he did appear for duty. Felix volunteered to become the officer in charge of Coronado's fragile intelligence service. Now, instead of checking for errant meters in the plaza, Asuncion shrewdly cultivated informants.

A car horn blew once. Twice. The walrus-like body in the bed remained motionless. Then came a dull, insistent thumping on the floor. In the kitchen below, Eng Chi Fai appeared to be sounding reveille with a broom handle. The body in the bed twitched in irritation.

The trill-like sound of flatulence. The car horn again, this time a long, wailing *beeeeeppp!* The lump in the bed lurched up, unsteady as a barrage balloon tethered in a gale. The figure settled itself on the edge of the mattress, winced, and peered groggily around, as if surprised to be in such circumstances. Then it gargled loudly, collecting a bountiful ocean of spittle in the folds of its cheeks before projecting the phlegm in an imprecise direction at the newspapers strewn about the floor.

He made his way unsteadily to a fissured mirror and contemplated the creature he encountered, the one with the bloodshot eyes of an Iberian fighting bull. Deep ridgelines were etched into a generous forehead. A lush Zapata mustache, stained yellow from tobacco, flared like an oxbow across his lower face. Patches of stubble flourished in the clefts of a ponderous chin. A pink T-shirt exposed a flabby, pear-shaped figure that did little justice to the wearer's claim to being as fit as a man half his age.

Around his neck hung a plain gold crucifix – the gift of a long dead mother on the occasion of his entering the police service as a callow youth of twenty-one, thirty-eight years ago. Though it now seemed improbable, there had once even been a time when the countenance in the looking glass had been judged quite handsome by local *señoritas*.

In this, the twilight of his fifty-ninth year, Felix Asuncion had to be satisfied with being considered a presence. But a presence he most assuredly was.

A rage of alabaster hair, matted from sleep, darted outwards from an oversized head. Slate-tinged beetle brows cambered across skin the color of salt-stained rawhide. Hazel eyes that looked out on the world were expressive, deceptively so, since only one, the right, was of any use whatsoever to its owner. The other, a glass ornament, was kept hidden behind a pair of tinted aviator glasses that had become his trademark.

Felix glanced at his wristwatch. He'd never owned an alarm clock in his life. Clocks were the bane of his existence, reminding him of deadlines he'd never adhered to and responsibilities he'd often chosen to forget. Asuncion had always preferred to live by his wits and witticisms. In his time, he'd acquired a highly developed instinct for trouble – he hadn't been called Felix the Cat for nothing. With some difficulty, he focused on the numerals. Shit! Only five-thirty. And work didn't start till eleven.

He padded over to the washbasin. Splashing cold water on his face, Asuncion considered for a moment whether he needed a

CORONADO

shave. He thought better of it; the grizzled look made him seem more rugged.

The banging on the floor increased in urgency. It was joined by an ungodly wail. "*Señor* Felixxx! *Despiertate!* Wake up!" Ascunsion winced at Ambrose Eng's horrible caterwauling.

The Engs – husband, wife, four offspring, and grumbling grandma – were originally from Macao, that decrepit Portuguese enclave that clung like a stubborn wart to the face of China. To expect them to have an affinity for the Latin tongue, thought Felix with some conviction, was as likely a prospect as finding a Chinaman in a bullring. Still, in a not-insignificant way, he'd grown accustomed to Ambrose and his brood. Felix Asuncion had lived in the storage loft of Eng's restaurant for a year and a half now, landing there on the first bounce of the proverbial jai alai ball, right after being kicked out of *Señora* Hurtado's boarding house after "the incident."

To this day, Asuncion swore it was a rat he'd seen skulking around his high-top sneakers. Swore it by all the saints! Even after he'd wildly shot up the floorboards and walls with his Magnum. Until Philomene, his defanged tomcat, had smartly trooped into sight, a stringy mouse in his jaws.

Asuncion's eviction by *Señora* Hurtado had been instantaneous. He hadn't even had the opportunity to make good, to patch up the drywall where the three bullets had left gaps as large as doughnut holes. He'd tragically become homeless. But as luck would have it, Eng's restaurant had been broken into that very night.

Felix held the grandiose title of Intelligence Officer and as such was on the scene within minutes, even before the uniforms had completed the desultory three-part criminal occurrence report. The crime? A till full of loose change and case of beer stolen from the restaurant. It was scarcely newsworthy, but since it had been the fifth in a lamentable series of petty thefts and bruised egos at the restaurant, the Engs had impressed upon Asuncion the need for intervention.

With the generous coaxing of a few ounces of premium tequila to fortify his decision-making process, Felix had offered to remain

22

overnight to conduct "observations." That night had stretched into days, weeks, and months, until now, like the creaky screen door and lavender neon sign out front that advertised "CHINE-E" cooking, Felix Asuncion had become a household fixture.

Ambrose Eng had cooked up a viable deal: room and board in return for the obvious presence he provided. In his modest opinion, Felix had become an extended, if somewhat unconventional, part of the family, like buck-toothed Uncle Wok from Acapulco or Cousin Han from Baja, California. Besides, he sort of liked the Chinese cooking.

Señooorr! The grating whine.

He picked up an old army boot and hurled it onto the floor. Silence. Good. Now he could collect his thoughts.

Beeeppp! The car horn persisted. The detective cursed under his breath, eyeing a half-empty bottle of tequila. He thought better of it. Felix espoused the self-discipline of a patient man, and patience was a virtue. But that wasn't to say he was always virtuous, or always patient.

He waddled unsteadily to the window and peered out to the source of his misery. An electric shock surged through his meaty two-hundred-and-thirty-pound torso. Damn! The boss! And he looked upset!

Felix stumbled over to the clothesline and hurriedly selected his ensemble for the day – a pair of polyester trousers and the wrinkled Madras shirt with the fewest stains. He tugged on a mismatched set of basketball socks and shuffled into high-tops, which he left unlaced. With dramatic flourish, Asuncion ran ham hands through an oily head of hair. He liked to think he resembled a mature Robert De Niro.

Asuncion snuggled into the old combat jacket that had become his unofficial trademark, 101st Airborne patches and all. With dramatic flair, he would tell anyone who'd ask that it was a memento from a wild and errant youth in service with the American military in Vietnam. In truth, he'd bought the gear at an army surplus store in Lubbock, Texas.

Oh, he'd almost forgotten. Felix darted to the fridge. From

among a forest of beer cans and rancid cold cuts, he took out his most valued possession, his police revolver. He fumbled with the frosty leather harness and with great effort strapped on the Magnum and handcuffs. Then he trundled out the window and down the fire escape to meet his boss.

Fuentes reached across to open the passenger door. "A moment of your time, *Sergente.*"

"*Si, Jefe.*" And with an almost supple bow, he slid into the Mustang.

They drove to the frayed edges of town. The traffic was heavy for a weekday. It was a surly evening brimming with bus vapors and grinding brakes.

Miguel pulled the car into a truck stop. He bought his passenger two steaming cups of black coffee; for himself he purchased breath mints. Felix swallowed the black mud in eager gulps. A silver mickey appeared from the folds of the combat jacket. Asuncion took a hefty swig. Fuentes did not remark.

There was one thing that Miguel had long ago learned about the *sergente.* With coffee in him, Felix was a relatively alert drunk; with a rash alcoholic jolt from the hip flask he perpetually carried, he was kick-started into remarkable lucidity.

In spite of his boozy tumble from grace, at his worst Felix Asuncion was still an improvement on most of Fuentes's motley crew. An ex-*federale* like himself, he was Miguel's confidant and, in some ways, his mentor. He was unique at his craft, a true original, married to "The Job" because no woman would have him, and because working for Fuentes was the only legitimate way he knew to pay for the tequila he'd grown to love. He was a man full of odd wisdom and hard counsel.

Miguel began to earnestly recount all that he knew about the bombing, rattling off the conventional investigative checklist for such matters: vehicle registration, Interpol name checks on all registered guests and employees, fingerprints to be run against the *Yanqui* AFIS system, border crossings to be electronically revisited using the TEX computer net. The obvious grocery list had been taken care of.

Then there were the sublime elements that only Felix could offer to enhance a criminal investigation: Lisa, the night cleaner at the bus depot, who might have noticed strangers milling around the terminal. Tino, the car jockey at the PEMEX gas bar on the outskirts of town, who would review all credit card invoices and had a knack for recalling out-of-state plates. Angelica, the lonely cashier at the Mexicali Rose diner near Carbon, who remembered strange males, if only as potential suitors.

"There were drugs involved in this one, *hombre*." Fuentes flipped over a mug shot of the deceased. "Find out who dealt with this man."

The portly detective grew thoughtful, wrinkling his massive eyebrows in exaggerated concentration. An unknown, for now. He kept the photo.

"I want you to tell me everywhere this *gringo* has been in the last hundred hours, Felix. Everywhere."

Asuncion brushed a bear-like forearm across a hoary face. "*Si, Jefe.*" His voice broke with melodramatic flourish. "Your request is my honored responsibility." He opened the car window and indifferently tossed the Styrofoam cup out into the desert, where it gyrated wildly in the wind before vanishing among the tumbleweed.

Miguel dropped his passenger at the bus terminal, right behind the evening Greyhound outbound for Tucson. He drove off with a single blast of his horn, leaving Asuncion lingering pensively at curbside. The detective peered up to the digital clock nestled in the highest rafters of the ramshackle building: 6:40.

Minutes later, Felix shambled up the fire escape to his quarters. The *barrio* beyond seemed reasonably serene. He'd have ample opportunity to dispatch his hounds later in the evening when the blood was rising.

Asuncion rolled into bed fully clothed and returned again to profound sleep. The guttural sound of snoring enveloped the room, punctuated now and again by the Engs' grating chatter downstairs.

3 The dawn sky strutted above Coronado like a peacock, lingering in shades of purple, profiling the stunted stands of tamarisk trees. A cloud of insects flitted about in the quiescent air. From the east came the hint of a bruised-nectarine sun.

Asuncion had risen early, purposely so. His trek to this isolated spot by the highway was made more resolute by a keen desire to be perceived as in control of events, just this once. Still, he needn't have bothered. The object of his pilgrimage was waiting patiently astride a Harley at their customary meeting place off the tollway.

The biker, although approaching middle age, was robustly athletic. He wore a flak jacket without patches and leather cutoffs over stone-faded jeans. Snake tattoos traced their way up muscular arms. He smoked a Tiparillo aggressively jutting from a vise-like jaw. But it was his hair, or lack of it, that was striking. An orange Iroquois cut traced a dramatic arc from the nape of his neck to his forehead. The rest of his tanned dome glistened like burnished redwood.

Foul-mouthed and ominous, notorious on the street for his short temper and long memory, the man was a handful for both his enemies – of whom there were many – and his friends – whoever they might be on any given day. He was also Felix's main snitch.

"You called for me, *Señor* Felix?" The stranger's voice was unusually polite.

"That I did, Papagayo. My apologies for the short notice." The name Papagayo, the Mexican diminutive for parrot, was a tag bestowed by biker peers, a tribute to the man's uncanny ability to disguise himself should the need arise and toe the party line whenever facing down the authorities, regardless of the depravity of his actions. He had parlayed a love of adventure and vicious capacity for violence into a formula for success.

"No big deal," the biker sniffed. "It was a nice ride from Ciudad Juarez." He calmly adjusted the wrist clasp to one of his gloves. "Two hundred miles, three hours. I needed the break."

"You been busy?"

"*Siempre.*" The forthright affirmation. "Always."

The grizzled detective knew better than to press. Cuidad Juarez, Chihuahua's state capital, was a bustling city of more than a million souls located on the Rio Grande abutting Texas. It was cosmopolitan – profoundly so by Mexico's standards – with four major schools of learning and a broad range of high-tech industries. Without asking, Asuncion appreciated that Papagayo had not attended an evening lecture on thermonuclear geophysics. He'd more than likely visited a *ranchero* bar on the wild south end of Avenue Juarez to dance to hard-edged Nortena music. And as likely as not he'd gotten into a fight – or gone looking to start one.

"I heard about the bombing, *hombre.* You want me to work on it?"

The biker's forthrightness made Felix uncomfortable. "Juarez is a long ride in, *amigo.* You need to rest."

Papagayo would have none of it. He cursed loudly. "If small talk is all you wish from me, I have other people waiting and better things to do with them, old man."

Asuncion fumbled about a baggy pants pocket and took out a dime bag of grainy reddish-brown powder. "You know who deals in this stuff?" he asked, his voice agitated. "The lab says it's good quality."

Papagayo considered the substance. "There's a price."

"We'll cross that bridge later," Felix replied, "if we have to."

The biker grew surly. "I won't cross that bridge until you cross this one." He held out an oil-stained leather glove.

Felix cleared his throat. "What do you want?" he muttered.

"The usual."

Asuncion reached into the breast flap of his combat jacket and removed a sandwich bag of rough-cut weed. He moved to hand it over, then hesitated. The biker laughed and gunned the Harley.

"Wait!" Felix howled above the revving bike.

Papagayo idled down. He snatched the plastic bag from the detective's hands, then raised an index finger. One more.

Asuncion fumbled about his shapeless pockets and brought forth a second bag. He meekly handed it over.

The biker beamed and cut the motor.

Felix reached into a pocket and retrieved a small snapshot. He thrust it into Papagayo's face. "Here's the photo of the man I need identified."

"Not a great haircut." The biker smirked. "Was he military?"

Asuncion hitched his rounded shoulders. "I don't know," he muttered. "That's your job to find out, isn't it?"

"Guess it is. Give me a week." He adjusted his riding gloves. "I'll need that much time."

The biker kick-started the Harley. Asuncion waved his hands in the biker's face to gain his attention. "The origin of the drugs?"

"What?" Papagayo yelled above the machined chaos.

"The origin! They want me to find out where the heroin came from."

Papagayo gave a thumbs-up. "A week." He shouted. "Then call." He snatched the photo and a moment later was roaring northward up the tollway. Soon the motorcycle melded with sunlight drifting idly at the edge of the sky.

Tuesday, May 22, midday. Coronado

Miguel Fuentes leaned forward in the swivel chair, toying with the tiny Mexican flag that adorned the pen-and-pencil set on his desk. The pole kept toppling from its pedestal and along with it, the fragile red, white, and green flag. He delicately paper-clipped the pole to its stand.

Except for two expensive ruby fountain pens that had been a graduation gift from his parents, a scuffed baseball was the desk's only other adornment. The baseball was a memento from a time when Miguel had been a sound Triple-A prospect, a hard-hitting third baseman for Los Venados with a bright future in the Big Leagues.

He'd broken his wrist and discovered that such dreams are for rich northerners, not a mechanic's son from Campeche province. He'd come to accept that he'd never realize the Great American Dream pursued through a Raleigh fielder's mitt.

A fly buzzed about his head. Fuentes brushed it away.

The door to his private office was propped open with a clay brick. A spindled barrier divided the adjoining room in two: on one side, a public reception area; on the other, what passed for the general administration area anticipating a community that never complained, where a uniformed *policia* slouched over a table, pecking away on a battered typewriter. A series of three holding cells loomed behind. They were empty. A water-cooler gurgled spasmodically from its spot next to the cells.

Although it was nearing midday, long, coarse curtains, with the brownish-gray tint of army blankets, were drawn over the gritty windows, opaquing a blazing light that seared the world outside. A primitive air conditioner seethed mist from its housing in one of the portals.

Fuentes's office was a crowded hush of redwood furniture, tawny vinyl, and moist darkness. The floor was chestnut tile and severely veined. An alarm clock ticked atop an open bookshelf housing law publications: the complete annotated edition of the 1978 *State of Utah Penal Code,* the whole lot bought for 6,500 *pesos,* and solely for effect. The clock was set at the wrong time. Next to it, atop a slim VCR, a portable television played an old movie: Greer Garson as Mrs. Miniver. A pile of film classics lay stacked against the base of the bookshelf like dominoes. Fuentes collected and played them incessantly. It was one of his few intellectual pleasures. The TV was on mute.

Bile-green walls held photos and certificates, uninspiring in their similarity. A uniformed Fuentes graduating from the Academy, closely cropped scalp, gleaming visor, severe with the trite determination of youth. Fuentes, a decade later, mugging it up at a steak barbecue, drink in hand, surrounded by a rheumy-eyed crew of bull detectives in Hawaiian shirts. And again, white-gloved and stern, inching irrevocably toward middle age, as he received a medal from an anonymous dignitary whose expression showed he had a million better things to do with his time.

And others. Certificates of learning and self-improvement.

Criminal Investigation Level One. Human Resource Management. Advanced Accounting. Cheap frames housing parchment, enduring testaments to tenacity.

Calmly surveying all from its resting place on one of the walls was a wooden crucifix. Fuentes, though not a religious man, was certainly a prudent one.

Unlikely companion pieces to the religious symbol on the wall were the two diplomas that had given him the most pride – and grief. One was a yellowing baccalaureate from the University of Texas, El Paso, his mother's hometown, where he'd resolutely completed a thesis on Pancho Villa, the *bandido* horse general from Durango who had became a hero of the Mexican agrarian revolution of 1910 with the battle cry *Tierra y Libertad* – Land and Liberty.

The other was a gaudy parchment from the Federal Bureau of Investigation Academy at Quantico, Virginia, where he'd been sent by a progressive superior, a protector who'd since prudently retired and left Fuentes to fend for himself. For, in spite of what Miguel preferred to call "integrity" and what others more highly placed in Mexican law enforcement labeled "obstinacy" or worse, his policing career need not have been so obviously deadballed in Coronado.

But it was.

And now, at forty-four, he seemed destined to finish his days amid dust devil storms and salamander sunsets, a disgraced *federale* on a flimsy municipal contract that could be instantly terminated, supervising corrupt incompetents in a town that boasted fifty-nine murders a year and the largest student *mariachi* band in the state. And there was nothing he could do about it.

Throughout his twenty-odd years as a *policia*, Miguel Fuentes had won awards for valor, dogged determination, and pure luck. But swatting flies in his shoddy office, he realized that all the decorations were nothing more than wall plaster.

Miguel was aware that the Coronado posting carried a hex. Both of his immediate predecessors had mysteriously disappeared. The first, "Peg Leg" Portillo, had vanished into thin air, widely rumored to have double-crossed *el Familia,* the mysterious crime syndicate controlling the seamier side of Sonora, to become coyote banquet somewhere between Magdalena and Nogales.

The most recent, Mercedes "Luppy" Lopez, had allegedly fled with a bagful of *mordido* – hush money – sufficient, it was said, to have instantaneously stilled his rising curiosity about the Bolivar Project. He had effectively quashed what was, at best, a lukewarm investigation into the truck fatality involving the young girl.

For his part, Fuentes drew grim satisfaction from the fact that increasing numbers of people in Coronado had grown to love and respect him. And that the local PRI bosses and their toadie didn't.

He took a healthy gulp from a bottle of Doctor Pepper and savored the wetness. His forehead had fine beads of sweat on it, his thick black hair was damp. His underarms were drenched. He eased back in the chair against a protest from the springs.

Fuentes glanced over his shoulder to a huge wall map that outlined his realm in shades of crocus-yellow and plum: the town proper with its twenty-nine square miles, and the general administrative territory of "Greater Coronado" with roughly 120 square miles of scrub brush, devil cactus, cordon, and gila lizard. A patrol unit operated in each of four sectors, two uniform cars cruised the downtown, three plainclothesmen currently conducted surveillance on a cocaine-smuggling operation in among the hills and abandoned mines out by Querobabi, and a chain-smoking, bleached-haired civilian dispatcher named Stella inhabited the tiny Communications Center, the Comcen, located to one side of the general office.

"Comcen" was too grandiose an expression. With its microwave and coffee machine, and a television console constantly tuned to Spanish soap operas, the room was more an informal rendezvous for the town's womenfolk on nights when the bingo wasn't on in the church hall than a proper dispatch facility. Still, it was here all incoming calls were received, logged, and routed on the ancient Westinghouse Radio system, so Communications Center it had been christened by Miguel, and Comcen it would remain.

A force of twenty-six functioned fitfully under Fuentes's command – seventeen uniform, six investigative, and three civilian. And for the most part he wouldn't trust them as far as his shadow at high noon. Was it any wonder there was talk that the *federales* were taking over the entire region?

In the short time he'd been their chief, his people had found new ways to redefine both the words "corruption" and "incompetence" and their application to the profession of policing. Thus far, Fuentes had fired six of his staff and endured only one less that number in SSG shotgun volleys aimed at his hillside home.

He sighed. There'd be more firings, and probably more damage to his stuccoed walls, until he succeeded in solidifying his grip on this sorry lot. The prospect didn't worry him, though it was getting somewhat tedious patching his home after each succeeding fusillade. It was no coincidence that in the local community, the *jefé's* place by the crossroads had quickly acquired the nickname *El Presidio,* the Little Fort.

Fuentes finished the soft drink and tossed the empty bottle into a garbage pail, where it landed with a hollow thud. He opened the interim report and began to reread it yet again.

Just over one day old, the murder dossier was growing exponentially and taking on its own unique character. Eighty-six pages of foolscap, and a pocket sleeve in the binder containing over two hundred and fifty black-and-white photos of the bombsite, the deceased, the car, and its contents.

Fuentes reviewed the evidence index. There were more than thirteen hundred items, from the obvious – tattered remnants of clothing, chunks of bomb shrapnel, glass shards numbered in magic marker – to the frankly intriguing – a plastic pocket calendar with the aquamarine motif of a chess knight on one side and several dates blacked out on the other, a crumpled parking stub, and a credit-card receipt for gas purchased somewhere outside Coronado.

Whatever Miguel's personal feelings about his federal counterparts, Obregon's people had been meticulous and quite proficient; he'd grudgingly grant them that. Fuentes felt the urge to sneeze and caught himself. The damn air conditioner was giving him a cold. Or maybe it was his allergies acting up again. He carefully resealed the exhibits.

As of this morning, Felix's crew of street snitches, his "fleas," had achieved results that could be considered, at best, mediocre. The seized heroin had been purchased locally, but that tip was hardly profound. Heroin was as prevalent in Coronado as *ajonjoli* – sesame – the legitimate cash crop of Sonora.

As to the truly critical questions – the identity and motive of the murderer – there was nothing. And the identity of the victim? Also a giant *nada*. Not known by whores or druggies, a man without vice or venom.

Perhaps, Fuentes thought forlornly, that's why Felix spent much of his time of late chasing strays instead of foxes. Maybe his people had become too soft, scenting only lap dogs. Miguel could have been more demanding of the old detective, even torn a strip off him. But he knew that would not have produced a more satisfactory result. You play the hand you are dealt in this contest, he mused gamely. He just was not certain these days whether to consider Asuncion a trump or a joker.

Fuentes resolutely retraced his mental road map. The motel maid had simply been at the wrong place at the wrong time. The positioning of the body, physical evidence derived from her autopsy, her personal history – all these removed thirty-four-year-old Tina Arroyo from suspicion and made her a classic victim of circumstance.

The two dead children? Ditto for them. After the hellish life they'd lived on earth, they were assuredly with their mother in heaven – or whatever passed for it. Three more little ones, all under ten, would learn endurance under that burbling, useless mess of a father. Elderly grandparents resided on a sharecroppers farm up the road apiece near San Xavier. That left *Señor* R. Palmer as the only object of Miguel Fuentes's attention. And an increasingly fascinating object he was most assuredly becoming.

Room C-8 had been registered as a single and pre-booked by phone twenty-four hours before Palmer's demise with a forged credit card most likely produced in Canada, one of thousands flooding the southwest United States and Mexico.

The Cutlass belonged to a leasing company in suburban Tucson, rented on the same day as the hotel space and with the same bad plastic. The description of the driver was identical to the antiseptic cadaver now lying in Coronado's tiny morgue. The Arizona callback number for the signer of the lease agreement had been fictitious.

Border records showed that the Olds crossed into Mexico early on Monday morning, May 21. The deceased had arrived at Zita's shortly before nine-thirty. After signing in, he'd gone straight to his room. According to the motel laborer, he'd left in the Cutlass an hour later with no luggage, save a gym bag. It was the last time "Palmer" had been seen alive.

The autopsy was more revealing. Contrary to Fuentes's first premise, it wasn't an explosion that had killed the mystery man. Instead, the deceased had been injected with a mixture of high-grade heroin, 72 percent pure, enough to ensure he'd be extinct before the blast eviscerated him. There were also old tracks on the dead man's arm, the kind one got from needle injection. But his blood work did not indicate that he'd been a heroin addict.

The stash found beneath the seats of the rental represented two kilos with a street value of $300,000, from the same batch that had killed "Palmer." Nothing else from the Cutlass seemed to be helpful to forensics.

The deceased's stomach held a partially digested egg sandwich. Caffeine remained in the urinary track – coffee, black, no sugar, by the looks of the analysis. Fingernail clippings showed traces of salt inside the cuticles. The coroner recorded that his heart had been strong and that he'd been neither a smoker nor a drinker. Not that such caution had prolonged his life, Fuentes reflected with palpable irony.

He pondered the snapshot, absently brushing at his mustache. The killing had all the appearances of a professional hit. Fuentes's instincts told him that the murder was a drug rip-off gone sour. In addition to those he'd given Asuncion, Fuentes had passed photos of the corpse to his narco squad to spin past their druggies. He did not have high hopes.

As expected, responses to date from the local riffraff had all been the same. The deceased was no one they knew or admitted to knowing. For his part, Obregon had faxed a mug shot to American authorities with special attention: Tucson. Their reply would be coming soon.

Fuentes moved patiently to a different section of the file. The bomb fragments found at the blast site intrigued him. The military had consulted with the laboratories of the American Bureau of Alcohol, Tobacco, and Firearms in West Virginia.

According to their findings, the splinters were consistent with those of high-grade U.S. military ordinance – nothing that Mexican crime syndicates used, or had ready access to. It was too hard to get, too sophisticated to prepare. There were certainly other and easier methods to deliver so absolute a message. A bomb of this category drew too much attention.

But what if the dead man wasn't the intended victim? What if this "Palmer" had been on his way to kill rather than be killed? What if he'd planted the explosives and been cheated by the Fates? Miguel Fuentes was not naive. In the dark and tawdry world of a small Mexican town, anything was possible.

The desk phone trilled. It was Obregon calling from Hermosillo and he was conciliatory to a T. Had Miguel had a chance to review the file sent down by motorcycle courier? Did he need anything to further the investigation? Personnel? Equipment? If so, he need only ask.

Fuentes declined. He was all too familiar with the formula. When he'd worn the finer cloth of a national police official, he'd often chanted a similarly insincere mantra himself.

Nothing? Good. Obregon's patronizing manner left no doubt as to what he thought of Miguel and his true place in the scheme of things. As *jefe* of Coronado, Fuentes was technically in charge of the murder investigation, but it was clear that Obregon viewed him as so much window dressing.

Still, the *federale* didn't seem prepared to have his people take over the case. Not yet. Fuentes recognized Obregon's cynical cunning in holding back. As surely as the morning sun would rise fiery ochre over the Aztec ruins in his native Campeche, the degree of *federale* interference in the case would increase in direct proportion to the crime's solvability.

Fuentes knew that as *jefe* of an insignificant town eight hundred miles away from the epicenter of the political universe, the *Distrito Federale*, as the capital region of Mexico City was known throughout the nation, he could do little or nothing about it.

Obregon invited Miguel to join him for a late lunch in Hermosillo. "For old times' sake. We can drink white wine like we used to and reminisce about the good times we had as partners in the DF."

"The DF" – Fuentes winced. He made a lame excuse, but Obregon was unrelenting.

"Come on! Consider it an olive branch. I owe you this much after our misunderstanding at Zita's. Cafe Angelica. Ascension Plaza. Two o'clock."

Silence.

"Fuentes! It's only a lousy fifty miles! That's no more than an hour's drive. Even for you. Or don't you have a fuel allowance?" The new *federale* chief at Hermosillo couldn't resist. "It's not like government auditors are going to check your odometer reading every time, is it *hombre*?"

Miguel sighed.

His urbane contemporary offered a chuckle that found no echo. "If it's the cost of a meal that concerns you, I'll buy. I know how tiny your budget is." The laughter faded. "Oh, and Miguel? Don't forget to bring the entire file with you. We wouldn't want it to go missing in your custody, would we?"

Fuentes resisted the temptation to respond in kind. He clung to his pride. Between wolves, as between princes, there was room only for treachery. *Click.* Obregon had hung up.

Miguel edged his chair from the desk. It was something that Obregon had said. Something that suddenly made such sense . . .

Perplexed, Fuentes ran his fingers through his hair. *Caramba!*

That was it! He took a scratch pad and pocket calculator from a desk drawer, drew a pen from its ornamental setting, and then hurriedly leafed through the dossier until he found it, the photocopy of the gas receipt. In the top left-hand corner were five figures, nothing more. Just five figures.

He tapped the pen impatiently on the desktop. The first steps toward the solution to this conundrum lay in a series of numbers written by a dead man's hand. Miguel flipped the file over to the seized property section.

After preliminary forensics had been completed at the scene, the Cutlass had been towed first to an underground garage at the *federale* lab in Hermosillo, then to a nearby compound, where it now securely rested. Miguel's index finger ran methodically down the impound slip.

Slowly, then with ever-increasing confidence, he scribbled down figures, worked the sums with a calculator, glancing alternately at his wristwatch and over his shoulder at the wall map of the Greater Coronado jurisdiction and its adjoining territories. It wasn't much, but …

There was one more thing he needed. Flipping to the Exhibit section of the dossier, Miguel located the plastic property bag with a rumpled parking stub in it. Monday, 21 May – 11:22 a.m. entry and 12:50 p.m. departure. The fee? An indecipherable amount. The specific location in Mexico was smudged beyond legibility.

Fuentes tore the scribbled sheets from the pad. He neatly folded and tucked them into his shirt pocket. Humming to himself, he strode over to the shotgun rack and lifted the straw Stetson from its resting place, flicking its brim low over his eyes as he put it on.

He peeked into the Comcen and told Stella he was going for a little drive. He'd be taking one of the unmarked Caravelles. "If *Señor* Obregon should call, tell him he'll get his file tomorrow. And also" – a shrewd smile traversed his face – "wish him a fine lunch."

"Sir?"

"He'll understand, " Miguel winked. "I can survive on a taco and a Doctor Pepper to go. *Adios*."

4 Fuentes's calculations proved to be remarkably accurate. Journeying up Highway 15 for eighty-four miles, he came upon Larendo, a town slightly less than halfway between the figures scrawled on the gas receipt and the mileage registered on the odometer of the Cutlass now resting in the police pound.

Larendo had had its origins two hundred years before as a Franciscan mission post on the northern circuit, an insignificant rosary bead mischievously tossed to earth. The town reached its peak growth during the American Prohibition, when it boasted two *cantinas* and a whorehouse. But the booze eventually lost its allure, and the whores had long since withered to dust. For nearly a century, Larendo had been a place in name only, with more inhabitants in its hilly cemetery than living on the thirteen gritty streets that had, until recently, defined it.

Now that the North American Free Trade Agreement had bound the United States, Canada, and Mexico in an unholy and unequal trinity, *maquiladora* boom towns like Larendo, with their plentiful supply of non-union labor for low wages, had had new life and luster breathed into them. In four short years, Larendo's population had exploded a hundredfold. As a consequence, the street grid had matured from a feeble arrangement of crisscrosses until it now resembled an Etch-a-Sketch pad left too long in a monkey cage.

The highway ran arrow-straight through Larendo. The downtown covered four blocks, a heady mix of takeout and *salsa*. In the unpaved driveways of one-story *haciendas* that leached off it on all sides, chrome-heavy pickups crowded pastel-colored muscle cars. The reek of fresh drying cement was everywhere.

Fuentes stopped for a red light, carefully checked the odometer, and estimated that he had ten miles to go. He entered the manufacturing area on the northern stretch of town out by the new ball diamonds. Six miles to go. He slowed down. Three. What? He glanced around at the open spaces. He was beyond the factory zone. His premise seemed shot to hell.

As he came over the crest of a hill, however, he knew he was on to something. In front of him a new industrial park surged out of the sweet-potato-orange earth. Miguel pulled onto the shoulder, crushed gravel popping under the broad tires of the Caravelle. He counted five principal buildings the size of zeppelin hangars, each with massive sliding doors, multi-port loading docks, and walls the color and texture of buttermilk. To the side, corporate headquarters was a profusion of azure-tinted glass and clipped shrubbery where a pride of executive Mercedes and BMWs lay nestled.

The entire facility was ringed by a chain-link cyclone fence crowned by a triple sequence of barbed wire. A uniformed guard in a sentry box stood sentinel to the one road leading in. Curiously for such a grand complex, it was unnamed but for a sign at the fence giving its address: Six Tampico Court.

Immediately north of the property line, an old clapboard bar sprawled in the dust. A sign proclaimed in sloppy magenta letters:

Happy Hour – 24 hours a day – All Day
Every Day!
Pizza and Steak Burgers
Takeouts to order: dial 905 4444
Truckers welcome!

A mangy bull crouching in a stand of mock sagebrush gave the place its name, El Toro. The pounding bass of a jukebox cranked to full volume insulted the desert calm. Willie Nelson was singing "The Ballad of Poncho and Lefty." A large "P" scribbled on cardboard directed patrons to the rear of the building.

The dusty lot held a half dozen passenger cars, some pickups, a few long-distance transports. A sheet-metal enclosure housed the parking attendant. Miguel pulled up to the kiosk and peered inside. A rail-thin youth draped in faded denim and sporting a San Jose Sharks cap that failed to cover a crop of unruly hair intently watched "The Jetsons" on a black-and-white portable.

"You pay to park here?" Fuentes called.

The attendant turned up the volume of the TV. He hadn't noticed the Caravelle.

Fuentes sounded the horn.

The noise drew the youth's attention. He squinted in Miguel's direction, visibly irritated. "What?"

Fuentes repeated the question.

The boy shrugged. "A security deposit to get in. A fee when you leave. Park your car on the highway and someone will probably trash it."

"Is that so?" Fuentes's jaw firmed.

"My patron believes in free enterprise." The kid smirked as he snared Fuentes's accusing stare. "He also respects my initiative."

It was then that the attendant spotted the police flashes on Miguel's shoulder and the tasseled Stetson resting on the passenger seat. His face paled. "I'm only doing my job, *Señor*," he stammered. "You – you can get in for nothing."

"Good. I'm glad we understand each other." He took some three-inch by five-inch glossies out of an envelope and passed them over. "See if you can help me, eh *amigo?*"

It never ceased to amaze Miguel how a citizen's memory could be prodded by the smallest thing. The parking attendant was no exception.

The man in the photograph had been there only yesterday, a little before noon. A pause. Come to think of it, the attendant did remember something about the car! It was purple. A late-model four-door. Upscale. A General Motors car. The guy had scraped the left front fender when he rammed the fence in his rush to park. The kid pointed past Fuentes to a dent in the mesh.

Miguel pulled the car ahead and parked. He strolled over to the spot. The wire bore traces of burgundy fleck. The chips were the same color as the Olds in the police pound in Hermosillo.

What urgency had driven him to this flea-bag bar? Then again, what sort of person would put his odometer reading on a gasoline chit? En route, Miguel had nursed the theory that Palmer had been a meticulous sort, an accountant, journalist, or the like. But that now seemed unlikely. Fastidious people park inside the lines, even when there aren't any. They don't generally leave pieces of General Motors brand Madeira maroon, paint style number 2b22556, on the mesh of a parking lot fence in Mexico.

So suppose Palmer had been in a field of work where record-keeping was a necessary evil. A traveling *Yanqui* salesman check-mating the American IRS? Perhaps. A disgruntled government employee? Curious.

Moist waves of air engulfed Fuentes as he entered the strip club. It took some time for his eyes to adjust to the dim indoor lighting and billowing haze of cigarette smoke. The roadhouse was big, a large rectangular room. Disco globes were suspended from the ceiling. A sagging dance floor was surrounded by a labyrinth of circular tables and folding chairs. A stand-up bar ran the length of one wall; at the far end, a narrow runway protruded from stained lavender drapes that only partially hid washrooms, kitchen, and storage area.

The jukebox was now silent. Brassy music suddenly blared out of box speakers. On the runway, a flabby peroxide blonde in her late forties stormed out from behind the drapes. Foregoing erotic preliminaries, she was quickly down to a G-string, indifferently jiggling siliconed breasts into the bloated, beery faces of a trio of hydro repairmen. Fuentes counted a dozen customers: truckers, farmhands, a rumpled-suited traveling salesman or two.

Buxom waitresses plied the room serving drinks, the occasional daily special of house draft and chili burgers. Miguel was certain they offered more discretionary favors for an inflated price. The women wore heavy mascara and pouting Barbie doll expressions. They couldn't have been older than eighteen but collectively sported the hardened look of someone whose psyche was jammed into neutral.

The barman, a beetle-browed troll with a luxuriant mustache and the fleshy arms of a longshoreman gone soft, idly wiped the countertop with a ragged towel. A farmhand guzzling a vodka straight was his only customer. Fuentes eased himself onto a barstool and removed his Stetson.

The barman scrutinized him with mute unease.

"What's your pleasure, *Jefe?*" he shouted above the music.

"Coke. A Coca-Cola, please," Miguel replied in a raised voice. "Just a little ice."

"Anything to top it off?" The slick smile and a wink.

"No." Miguel glanced at the charge listed on a chalkboard and reached into his pocket, rummaging for spare change. "Just a Coke."

As he brought over a large, cool glass, the barman motioned with his free hand. "No. It's on the house, *Señor.*"

Fuentes tossed the necessary *pesos* into a half-filled ashtray where they lay with other tips, untouched.

The strip show ended to tepid applause. No one moved to the jukebox. The audience seemed content to amuse itself with food and drink.

"I've never seen you before," the barman ventured. "What's the occasion?"

"I'm from Coronado." Fuentes took a tentative sip. "Could I have more ice?"

The barman opened a martini shaker and plopped shaved ice into Miguel's drink.

"Nice place." The barman spoke with practiced enthusiasm. "I went through there just a few weeks ago. A nice place," he repeated to himself. "Not like here."

He leaned forward, so close that Fuentes could smell the man's chili-pepper breath. "Some say Larendo's nothing more than a one-horse town. But I know where they store the hay to feed that horse." The man's chuckle was mirthless. "If you know what I mean."

Fuentes nursed the Coke.

The barman flung the filthy towel over a shoulder and cruised down the bar. After pacifying the farmhand with a vodka refill, he ambled back past Fuentes, a wad of bills in his hand, whistling buoyantly as he counted them. He then drifted to a cash register located in the farthest corner of the bar area, his back to Fuentes. Miguel heard the till open, the jingle of loose change, the sound of paper bills being secured in the cash drawer.

The barman readjusted the belt of his pants. He glanced

around, then shut the till. His eyes caught Miguel's in the full-length mirror. He grunted.

"Another Coke?"

Fuentes declined. He took the photographs out of his shirt pocket and propelled them across the counter. "You ever see this man here before?"

The barman picked up the snapshots and considered each with exaggerated care. After a few moments, he placed them back on the counter.

"Well?"

"Maybe. Maybe not. I meet lots of people in my line of work."

Fuentes's patience was thin. "What would it take to refresh your memory?"

The barman's eyes sharpened. "How long you been a *policia*?"

"Long enough."

The barman brushed his chin with a hairy hand. "Then you should know what it takes to refresh someone's memory.

"How much?"

He scratched something onto the back of a cardboard beer coaster and tossed it over.

Fuentes sighed wearily. "I was hoping you'd be more community-minded than that."

The barman inched forward, his voice a hostile whisper. "Well, how much will you offer to teach me civics, Professor?"

"*Nada.*" Miguel placed the empty drinking glass onto the counter.

"Nothing?" The man roared loudly. "You want something for nothing?" He shook his head in disbelief. "You're very humorous, *Jefe*. Very humorous." The laughter stopped. "But not very practical."

The barman reined his apron tightly over a mammoth stomach. His countenance turned serious. "I got work to do," he grumbled, briskly wiping the melamine clean where the glass had been.

"Does your boss know you double-till?"

"Pardon?"

"I saw you take that fellow's money and split it, some to the till,

43

some to your money belt." Miguel gestured to the bartender's midriff, where a leather wallet inched above his filthy apron.

The man blanched. "You can't prove it," he rasped.

"No," Fuentes allowed. "But I can certainly make things uncomfortable for you until then."

"It's my word against yours, *Jefe*," the barman blustered, then stormed away.

For a few minutes he went through the motions of cleaning dirty shot glasses in the sink, casting the occasional sullen glance in Miguel's general direction. Then, grudgingly, he slinked back. "What do you want from me?" he muttered.

"The photos," Miguel pressured. "Tell me about the man in the photos."

The barman sighed. "I have seen him here before. Once. Yesterday toward noon," he allowed reluctantly. "He had a fight with a woman at one of the tables in the back. A noisy fight."

"Describe her."

"Red hair. Mid-twenties. Short – only five feet or so. Maybe a hundred pounds, though I'm not good at guessing weight. I remember she wore jeans, a T-shirt, real expensive boots." He sighed, as if the effort of recollection was overwhelming.

"Did they argue in English?"

"Yes. She spoke it very well."

"Why would you say that?"

"Her face, her eyes." He shrugged. "You know, everything about her looked Mexican, *Señor*. But no *chiquita* I know speaks *Yanqui* like she did."

"Where did you learn to speak English?"

"I worked in Phoenix. Gardening. Till I got caught by U.S. Immigration. Also, I have two brothers in Chicago, one in – "

Miguel interrupted, tugged him by the wrist and gestured once more to the photo. "This woman. She could have been Mexican-American, no?"

The barman agreed with a nod, crestfallen that his American odyssey was not of greater interest.

"You said the boots were expensive. How do you know?"

"The leather. It was soft like silk. A beautiful cut, the kind they sell to rich tourists in the hotels in Acapulco."

"What else?"

"The hair. Her hair. It wasn't real."

"She wore a wig? How do you know?"

"Come on, *Jefe*. When you work with women like I do, you know what's real and what isn't – if you know what I mean." The leer quickly disappeared before Fuentes's frigid gaze.

"Do you remember what they fought about?"

"Look, boss. I serve drinks. Clean the bar. Try to look busy. Anything else" – the bartender shook his head emphatically – "anything else is not my business."

A waitress came to the counter, ordering three Buds, two daily specials and a side order of *fajitas*. She offered a smile to Fuentes. He did not return it. The barman acknowledged her as Dolores and got beer from the fridge. He barked the order back to the grill. The *fajitas* and specials would take ten minutes. Dolores left with the bottles and frosty glasses, but not before giving a parting wink to Miguel.

Fuentes waited until the woman was out of earshot. "Do you know the *gringo*'s name?"

"Until Monday I never saw this fellow," the barman replied with great solemnity. "On my mother's grave." He crossed his barrel chest with a greasy thumb. "And never since."

Fuentes took the photos and placed them back in his shirt pocket. "Why didn't you tell me this before?"

"*Jefe*," the barman answered, with what he imagined passed for sincerity, "I can't be talking to the police about everything I see here, you know. I have a reputation to keep."

The farmhand brayed for another vodka. The barman moved to serve him, then halted in his tracks. He turned one last time to Fuentes with a sharp, pitiless gaze. "Where'd you say you were from?"

Miguel eased himself off the barstool. "Coronado."

"Nice little town." He eyed Fuentes's departing figure, then spat venomously on the sawdust floor.

* * *

After the caverned darkness of the El Toro, the relentless sunlight pounding the northern Sonora caused Miguel's eyes to ache. A car alarm bleated in the nearby industrial park. Fuentes turned to the sound, shading his face with an upturned palm. A flustered, cursing male of bull-like proportions, wearing a lime-green leisure suit and designer sunglasses, wedged himself into a crimson Jaguar XJE. The alarm stopped. As the sport coupe came quietly to life, the driver glanced up from the dash. For a split second, his eyes met Fuentes's gaze. Then, in a cloud of bronze dust, the Jaguar was gone.

Fuentes thought he recognized the driver, then swiftly dismissed the notion. "Fast Eddie" Bono? Here? Impossible. Eddie was more apt to be flouncing about the dance floor of an Acapulco nightclub, or lazing at the poolside of a Cancun villa surrounded by blond bimbos, than to be here in the barren back reaches of the desert. A punch-drunk ex-boxer with a row of gold teeth and a reputation for a short temper peppered by stupid indiscretions, he was an adviser, some said bodyguard, to Hector Rivera, the taciturn investment banker and PRI strong man who ruled Sonora.

Miguel started to maneuver out of the parking lot. The attendant flagged him down. The boy was nervous. He turned off the portable TV.

"May I have your parking voucher, *Señor?*"

"What?"

"Your voucher," the attendant repeated, his throat constricted with anxiety.

An infinitesimal tilt of the head. Miguel understood. After rummaging in his glove compartment, he found a business card and handed it over.

The boy took the card and scrupulously compared it against a fee schedule taped to the rear wall of the hut. "Your *gringo* was with someone else," he said without looking up.

"A woman?" Fuentes asked quietly as he made a great show of going through his wallet for money.

"No. Him." The boy gestured faintly to the departed Jaguar. "My *padrone*."

"Your boss? Bono?" A slight nod. "When?"

"Yesterday. They both went into the El Toro around eleven-thirty in the morning. A good half hour before the woman came."

"How did they seem?"

The kid shrugged. "Like guys goin' into a bar," he remarked in the absence of anything else to say.

"Was Bono still around when the woman arrived?"

The boy's face screwed up in deliberation. "No," he said finally. "Bono was gone before she got here."

"Did my man leave with her?"

"Nope. She stayed maybe ten minutes, then left. The guy in this picture waited around an hour or so."

"You remember what she was driving?"

He shook his head. No.

"You ever see this *gringo* before?"

"Nope."

"And Bono?"

The boy fixed Fuentes with an incredulous glare. "Shit yes. He owns the flippin' place, don't he?"

Fuentes sat mulling over the improbable. "Eddie Bono owns the El Toro?"

"Ya. And the slimy bastard cut my salary in half for watching television."

"When?"

"Just now. When you were inside."

"A last question. What do they do in that plant over there?"

"Six Tampico?" The youth glanced at the industrial park gleaming boldly in the desert sun. "It makes electronics for helicopters."

"Like?"

The kid scrunched his eyes. "I don't know," he admitted. "They say it helps pilots find their way."

"Radar?"

"Ya. Radar. And stuff to find oil in the ocean," the youth added.

"They got a lot of technical shit inside. I should know! My fifteen-year-old sister had a job as cleaner on the night shift." A sly smile. "'Til she got pregnant."

"Do you know what the company's called?"

"Called? My sister only worked there, Boss. She didn't own the place. I never bothered to ask her."

Miguel scratched his chin. "How much did you say parking was?"

"Ten *pesos* an hour."

Fuentes handed the kid a hundred-*peso* bill. "Keep the change. You may need it."

Tuesday evening, May 22.
Coronado

5 The summons to see Obregon came shortly after six that evening, while Miguel was polishing off the house special at El Loco's, a cozy diner just outside of Coronado. He drove the thirty miles into Hermosillo at a leisurely ten miles below the posted limit, down Via Prosperidad, a rugged switchback road that the locals called *El Espinazo del Diablo* – the Devil's Spine – because of its unrelenting potholes. He arrived just before nine.

Located a stone's throw from a new Ford factory, the federal police building was virtually deserted. Fuentes parked in the compound. After having his credentials scrutinized at the security booth, he was escorted by a police sentry into a huge suite fully the length and breadth of an entire floor of the building.

Works of art decorated soft plum walls. Large Mayan area rugs covered waxed hardwood floors. Lilac scent teased the air. A Toshiba television nestled in a teak wall unit, part of a luxurious entertainment system that featured a micro-stereo system. Framed photos, some of them portrait-quality, rested on various tiers within the unit. An enlarged photo of Ramon Obregon as point man chatting comfortably with Bill Clinton during a semi-official state visit to Acapulco – earplug and wraparound sunglasses and, to complete the effect, a gun grip revealed by a flapping suit jacket. Another with the *federale* standing on the running board of a Popemobile, talking animatedly to His Holiness John Paul II during his visit to Mexico. Yet a third, as a member of a golfing foursome with a former Mexican president, grandiosely signed "To Ramon from *El Aguila*" – The Eagle, the security designation for the chief executive officer of that nation. Several other photos had similarly coy salutations. All prominently featured Obregon in the company of important Mexican officials or foreign dignitaries.

The remaining shelves were overflowing with computer manuals, including books on programming and encryption, for Ramon Obregon had a well-deserved reputation as a computing genius.

A choral recording wafted gently through the office, and Fuentes tried hard to place the composer:

> *The people that walked in darkness*
> *have seen a great light;*
> *They that dwell in the*
> *Land of the shadow of death,*
> *Upon them hath the light shined . . .*

The *comandante* sat behind a desk hammering at a computer keyboard. An electric piano rested on a chrome trestle in a corner of the room, linked to the computer tower by a long, coiled chord. The new head of federal police in Sonora was inspired by music and evangelical about technology.

Obregon wore a button-down shirt and British regimental tie. A charcoal-gray suit jacket made of the finest silk was draped over a chair.

"I called for you over three hours ago, Miguel." The *federale* scowled. "I'm a busy man."

"There was no urgency in your message, *Señor*. I stopped for dinner."

"Miguel, Miguel." A meager smile progressed along Obregon's

tanned face. "Remember what old Flores taught us at the academy?" he scolded gently. "Policing is a science of precision and efficiency."

"He also liked his *tacos* and *siestas*," Fuentes countered.

His host chuckled in agreement, then motioned to one of two leather captain's chairs in front of the desk.

Fuentes made himself comfortable. Obregon made innocuous small talk as he adroitly played on the computer keys, turning every so often to consult a large black binder. He spoke fondly of his most recent posting before Sonora, when he'd been the leader of all federal forces in the neighboring state of Chihuahua. The *comandante* was charming, but Miguel had learned to be circumspect.

After a time, Obregon was done. He swiveled the monitor around so that it faced his visitor. Miguel watched as textured cubes briskly filled the screen.

"It's a graphic for my spreadsheet," the *federale* stated with obvious pleasure. "We have to submit our annual budget to headquarters by the weekend."

"Pardon?"

"Here." Obregon directed a manicured finger to a descending echelon of rectangles. "Do you see the green boxes?"

Fuentes nodded.

"That was overtime last year. Yellow – the year before. Blue – the one before that. And here," he tapped a crimson icon, "this is our projected overtime budget for the coming year."

"Projected? For your civilian staff?"

"No," Obregon expounded. "Much more. It's the overall forecast for all my people: investigators, uniformed officers – everyone. All *federales* in Sonora State."

"You can predict this total with such a high degree of accuracy?"

"I can create a rational estimate based on past history." Obregon assumed a smug mien that Miguel found unsettling.

"But what if things change?" Fuentes asked. "What if you have a serial killer? A major heroin investigation? How can you accurately integrate unexpected crime into your financial projections?"

"What if? What if? What if tomorrow we were to suffer the devil as *delegado* of Sonora? Come on, Miguel! Let's face it, after all's said and done, some things never change. Least of all career criminals and their ways."

Fuentes could not let the observation pass unchallenged. "Ramon, you're telling me you can accurately forecast crime?"

"To a large extent," Obregon answered, with the lithe polish of the newly converted. "Contemporary policing is a process of letting people see what they want to see. Like this." Multihued helixes filled the monitor, taking on three dimensions, then two, then one, and back again. "What you see is what you get."

Fuentes watched, entranced in spite of himself.

"Perplexed?" Obregon asked. Fuentes nodded.

"Good. I'm now going to teach you Ramon's Theory of Relativity. It's simple, really. The bottom five percent of the world we know is composed of naive fools and do-gooders. For them, the police are nothing but bloated fat cats. Incompetent and overpaid for what we purport to do and overvalued for whatever we might have actually accomplished in the past to protect the public. For these people we are worthless, now and always, no matter what our stipend. No matter what our successes.

"Then there's the top five percent – people who are willing to pay us to do their bidding rather than society's, without compunction, without restraint. These we call organized criminals. They've figured us out. For them, money is no object, for they have far more wealth and far more tricks up their sleeve than we could ever dream of." An unrestrained chuckle. The *comandante* seemed quite pleased with his premise. "And ultimately, it costs so little to keep us under heel."

Obregon observed Miguel's disapproving look. "Miguel, you cannot pretend naiveté. Organized crime can influence the police to leave it alone using incentives and disincentives far more powerful than the money that honest citizens can pay us to oppose it. This is done openly through bribes, corruption, and kickbacks. And more subtly, by creating systems that are intentionally exhaustive and not very productive, grinding investigators down with the help of high-powered defense lawyers and mind-numbing procedures."

"The courts?" Miguel gambled.

Obregon nodded agreement. "In part." And by using expensive stables of lawyers that can outlast a prosecutor – even a diligent one ..." He reached for a pack of cigarettes and offered one to Miguel, who declined. Sofia, a rare Bulgarian brand, Fuentes noted.

The *federale* took a cigarette and lit it with a silver monogrammed lighter. He continued.

"But, the top and bottom five percent don't factor into my hypothesis. Instead, it's the remainder – the dull, plodding ninety percent of what passes for mainstream society, the ones who recognize us as the anointed enforcers of law, that count. It's for them that we perform, and in an unpredictable economic climate, we must make certain our cost of doing business is just right.

"And what is that cost?" Obregon inhaled deeply. "Our role is to keep the community safe and stable and to do so at a reasonable return on investment. To give that ninety percent a sense of well-being, the expense should be something predictable. It should be bedrocked in a perception that the police are in control of crime – and that the public, in turn, is in control of us."

Fuentes counterpunched. "Perception? What's perception got to do with policing, Ramon? A gun jabbed in a victim's face isn't perception. Neither is the bomb at Zita's that killed four people. That's not perception. That's reality."

"Let me explain," Obregon said, leaning forward. "Then maybe you'll understand." He took another puff of the Bulgarian cigarette. Smoke blurred his face.

"If our costs are reasonable when balanced against outcomes, Julio in the local *cantina* will pay his taxes and assume he's protected. But if we become too expensive a government operation, he'll become indignant and complain. Like everyone in today's world, he'll demand we do more with less. And naturally we'll accommodate him because we are, above all, dutiful civil servants."

Obregon crushed the cigarette in an ashtray. "You see," he concluded triumphantly, "as time goes on, our capacity to effectively function in that imprecise region existing somewhere between Julio's willingness to pay and his anxiety about crime will become the final measure of our success as professionals. That and nothing else."

Fuentes shook his head. "I thought our professionalism was gauged by our capacity to catch criminals and keep the public safe. Not by our ability to come in under budget. Or by our talent for making people think everything is okay when it isn't . . ."

Obregon smirked. "Remember what the Bible said: 'The poor you shall always have with you.'"

"And?"

"The same holds true for criminals."

The *comandante*'s shirt was well starched and, for that late hour, remarkably free of perspiration stains. Miguel noticed the enameled cufflinks on his sleeves, emblazoned with the crest of Mexico.

"My friend, it's the appearance of security that counts these days. Perception. Image. Not reality." Obregon gestured around the office. "Clothes. Cars. Computers. The world is appearance."

Obregon clicked off the computer program. The screen turned black, but for the large revolving icon of a musical note.

"As far as our own bosses are concerned, I predict that in future years the appearance of safety will increasingly come to define our level of civilization as a nation. Why? Because it's that appearance that ultimately nestles in the vague chasm between a citizen's fear and his shrinking wallet. And it's that appearance that ultimately counts over all other possible criteria – that, and not the number of *bandidos* who might actually exist out here in the big, bad world."

Fuentes felt the plush leather engulfing him. He caught himself. He knew that with the growth of NAFTA and a greater exchange of trade and people – both legal and illegal – between the United States and Mexico, hyper-aggressive, business-minded officials like the *comandante* had proliferated in the landscape of Mexican government like barrel cacti in the desert, forever "managing earnings" in defiance of the cold light of reality. Critical thinkers, they liked to be called. Pragmatists. Though Miguel had other, more pithy terms in mind.

"Interesting theory, Ramon. But do you really believe it?"

"What I believe doesn't matter." Obregon halted for effect. "It's just the way life is, a checklist of costs and savings. Expenses and results." His eyes hardened. "Why should policing be any different?"

Fuentes was pensive. "So you're saying that money should determine our capacity to serve people?"

"Serve?" Obregon laughed. "Miguel, don't play me for a fool! Money makes the world go round! Without it you wouldn't be able to motivate a jackass, let alone one of your 'highly skilled staff.'" Obregon lit another cigarette. Distractedly, he said, "Not that it's likely to matter for much longer."

A wall clock chimed the half-hour. Fuentes let the comment pass. Obregon seemed impervious to discussion as the wall of pungent tobacco smoke.

"Anyway," the *federale* continued, "we're not here to discuss modern criminology or how to change policing standards for the State of Sonora. Would you like a coffee?" He motioned to a carafe shaped like a silver bullet. "It's excellent Colombian."

Fuentes declined.

"Perhaps something stronger?" Miguel noticed a recessed setting in the wall unit, brimful of brand-name liquors, soft drinks, and pure spring water bottles.

"No, but thanks."

Obregon stretched his lanky frame, got up and went to the bar. He poured bourbon straight then added ice shavings. He sank back into his chair, crossing his legs as he did so. Miguel detected the hint of an ankle holster peeking out from beneath the *federale*'s pant cuff.

The *comandante* became very businesslike. "I have good news about the bombing. But before we discuss it, I've got a rather delicate, but temporary, situation. An unofficial one." He blew a trail of smoke through his teeth.

Fuentes tensed. He knew enough about unofficial discussions to realize that they didn't exist. He hoped his discomfort did not show.

"I've received a written report that you were seen today in Larendo." He tapped the shiny lighter with a trim forefinger. "As you are aware, Larendo is clearly outside your jurisdiction."

"I was conducting an investigation," Miguel answered truthfully.

Obregon continued as if he hadn't heard. "It's alleged in this document that you extorted money from a barman at the El Toro Roadside Café."

Fuentes jerked upright in his chair. "That's a lie!"

Obregon's expression was stolid. "We have a handwritten statement here that you've been squeezing this fellow the last two months."

"Bullshit!"

"I have a written report that reads otherwise." The *comandante* took an extra long drag from the Sofia, filled his lungs, then exhaled. "A signed one."

Fuentes vigorously shook his head. "That's not evidence! Words without corroboration are empty. Nothing."

Obregon fingered the rim of his glass. The action made a faint, trilling sound. "The person pressing for this investigation is pretty powerful, Miguel." He stopped. "Don't make this harder than it is."

Fuentes's eyes narrowed. "His name."

Obregon pursed his lips as if he'd swallowed something distasteful. "At this stage of the inquiry, I don't know if I can give it to you."

"I'm not corrupt," Miguel fumed. "You of all people should know that! What is this man's name?"

"I have a duty to perform," the *federale* noted delicately. "A citizen's complaint has been filed. Political figures are aware of its existence. I must investigate."

Fuentes fought to control his anger. "You were my partner in Mexico City. What happened to me there, and whatever might have come between us, isn't important now." He looked hard at Obregon. "Name him and I'll prove how absurd this allegation is!"

The *federale* sipped the bourbon. "It's your political boss. Hector Rivera."

Fuentes felt blood rushing to his head. Anger gave way to panic. He sensed that Obregon was attentive to his every move, watchful for a sign of weakness.

The *comandante* finished the drink. He reached over to pluck a steno pad from the in-tray on his desk. He flicked it open.

"Rivera says that today one of his staff leaves a business meeting at a factory in Larendo when he sees you exit the El Toro. At three o'clock, my people get a phone call from the barkeeper. A detective takes his declaration. I have it here, if you wish to see. It clearly implicates you."

Miguel took the notes. He glanced at them briefly, then flung the pad onto the floor where it landed with a hollow clatter. "That lying bastard!" he hissed. "With what I've unearthed today, Rivera might have some serious problems of his own to contend with before I'm through with him."

"Pardon?" Obregon leaned minutely closer.

Miguel caught himself. "Nothing," he murmured. "It's nothing . . . I'm upset. That's all."

"Certainly. It's understandable. But there is something about Rivera, isn't there? An indiscretion, perhaps? Maybe an investigation you're opening up?"

Fuentes shook his head.

"Good. I'm glad you understand my position." The *federale*'s manner was silken. "There's no point in going after Rivera. He's just a politician. And we all know they have dog piss for brains. It'll blow over before you know it."

A pager beeped. Obregon reached to his belt, glancing down at the display. "Excuse me. I have to take a call."

The *comandante* was out of the room only a few moments. On returning, he went to the bar for a refill, then made himself comfortable once more at his desk.

"That was Rivera. He was asking about you." He paused, then clarified. "Actually, he was asking about your case."

"And?"

"I told him that you were here. That we'd talked about the matter."

"And?"

"And that the allegations are being probed."

Fuentes sat up and was about to say something. Obregon stilled him with a breezy wave. "It's politics, my friend," he remarked blithely. "Politics, plain and simple. To the *delegado*, it's important that his officials appear above reproach. Whether they are or not is another matter, entirely. In the end, you must resign yourself to the fact that you can't avoid an investigation."

"Even though there's no truth to the charges?"

"These things take time," Obregon observed with toneless distraction. "Even when we all know what the outcome will be." That vapid, insincere style that irked Fuentes so whenever a bureaucrat lapsed into it. "After all, we're professionals. At the very least we must give the appearance of going through the motions." Obregon eased forward. "I know there's been tension between us – unfortunate rumors that did us both a disservice. But understand that's all they were. Rumors."

"Like the ones Rivera's spreading about me now?"

Obregon avoided the point. "The *delegado* isn't pleased with your work." He eyed Miguel over the edge of the glass. "You know he wants *federales* to replace your people in Coronado."

Fuentes could barely contain his frustration. "What do you want me to do? Stand by idly as this man takes my force apart?"

Obregon sighed wistfully. "His son is Mexico's justice minister, *hombre*. Even a blind man should see the writing on the wall."

Fuentes sank back in his seat.

"Leave the complaint with me," Obregon purred with stately poise. "I'll look after you. I promise. But you'll have to be patient. Unless . . ."

"Unless?"

"Unless you have something that can turn the tables on Rivera."

Fuentes hesitated. "I have nothing."

"You admit being in the bar?"

"*Si.*"

"On this investigation?"

Fuentes remained expressionless.

"Come on, Miguel ..." The fawning, disingenuous tone. "You can trust me. What was it? A gambling debt? A quiet place to have a beer? A woman?"

Fuentes briskly made up his mind. "It was a girl," he murmured. "A girl named Dolores."

Obregon guffawed. "You're a crazy *hombre*, Miguel!" A lascivious wink. "Was she any good?"

Fuentes gave an exaggerated shrug.

Obregon continued to laugh, louder and longer as the liquor took hold. "And here I was worried about you!"

He turned to the computer and clicked the icon. The screen filled with sheet music. Obregon's fingers nimbly played the portable keyboard. Chords, single notes, then more chord – Fuentes couldn't discern a pattern.

After waiting a few moments, without further comment from his host, Miguel got up to leave. "We're finished our business?"

"Sit down! Sit down!" Obregon gestured breezily. "There's more. I called you here for a reason, you know!"

Fuentes did as he was told.

"There's been a breakthrough." The *comandante* beamed. "Our American brothers have positively identified Palmer!"

Fuentes held his emotions in check. He searched his host's face for clues.

"They didn't say much on the phone. They want a meeting in Tucson tomorrow."

"So, you're going ..."

"No, my friend," Obregon laughed, once more the bon vivant. He finished his bourbon, then gestured with an impish wag of an index finger. "*We're* going. After all, this is still a joint investigation, is it not?"

"*Sí*," Miguel replied, his guard up. "It is that."

"Good. Then I'll pick you up at your place. Eight forty-five. Be ready. You're sure you don't want a drink to celebrate our good fortune?"

Fuentes declined and asked again if the audience had ended.

"Certainly." The *federale* turned speculatively to the portable keyboard. "You are free to leave."

Fuentes started for the door. Obregon began to play, then hit a key on the computer keyboard, activating a compact disc. Miguel stopped to listen:

> *The people that walked in darkness*
> *have seen a great light;*
> *They that dwell in the*
> *Land of the shadow of death,*
> *Upon them hath the light shined ...*

He faintly recognized the harmony from his days at university: Handel's *Messiah*. Except that Ramon was performing an orchestral background an octave higher and with slight melodic differences. To Fuentes the music sounded far more intricate.

> *For unto us a Child is born,*
> *Unto us a Son is given:*
> *And the government shall be upon his shoulder:*
> *And His name shall be called*
> *Wonderful,*
> *Counsellor,*
> *The Mighty God,*
> *The Everlasting Father,*
> *The Prince of Peace*

Obregon clicked off the CD. "A moment, Miguel."

Fuentes looked diffidently to his host.

"The complaint with Rivera? It'll be all right. You can trust me." He turned back to the keyboard.

Miguel had been thinking something over, uncertain if he'd do it. The *federale*'s parting comment made his decision for him.

"You won't mind if one of my people comes along with us?" he asked.

Obregon stopped playing. "Who?" His manner was again imperious.

"Felix Asuncion."

"I'm sorry?" Obregon spluttered.

Fuentes repeated the name. He could see Obregon try not to wince.

"That old goat? Why?"

"To begin with, he's familiar with the case, and" – Miguel savored the next moment – "sometimes even an experienced investigator like me needs a second 'qualified' opinion."

If Ramon Obregon had caught the affront he didn't let on. "So long as you pay his way."

"Of course," Miguel responded with a charm to match the *federale*'s. "As you've said, I'm on a tight budget. But, I'll find the money."

Fuentes reached the door. "It'll be all right, Ramon," he parroted. A smile. "You can trust me."

Cruising up the tollway toward his home by the San Cristobal crossroads, Fuentes radioed a final detail to the station. He advised that he'd be out of town for the next twenty-four hours. In the meantime, he wanted checks run on an industrial property near the border. In Larendo. A new factory next to the El Toro, one that made radar equipment for aircraft and ocean vessels. And range-finders for drilling oil.

He told the duty officer it was merely "professional curiosity" on his part, but the exhaustive list of dictated demands – company records, town taxes, registered vehicles – all but telegraphed the true pedigree of his concern.

A cacophony of half-baked excuses. A swirl of irritation passed over Fuentes's features like a dust cloud. Yes, of course he knew it was another jurisdiction! Still, the *jefe* in Larendo could be persuaded to be accommodating, no? A garbled transmission. Repeat? Miguel pursed his lips in irritation. Yes, it would be worth a few hours' overtime in the book to complete such a task. Then, it would be so? Good. And while they were at it, the usual stuff on the El Toro. Ten-four? Roger. He returned the mike to its cradle before there was opportunity for more grumbling.

Rivera! Complaint or not, anything that involved Hector Rivera now acutely interested Miguel. On principle. He was damned if he was going to run, tail between his legs, at the insinuation of a complaint, even if Rivera the Younger – the arrogant and ambitious Hippolito – was the federal minister of justice.

He wanted a signed statement from the young carhop specifying that he'd seen the *delegado*'s flunky with Palmer on the morning of his death. Then he'd target Rivera's involvement in the El Toro, where the complainant was employed. He'd wipe the smirk from Hector Rivera's features, no matter who his son was.

Fuentes allowed himself a slight smile, then gunned the Mustang up a steep hill and round an S curve, where it was soon swallowed up by the vast and brooding landscape of northwest Mexico.

Wednesday, May 23, after midnight.
San Cristobal

6 Late that night, after ironing three shirts and packing a change of clothes, Miguel fell asleep on the sofa while watching an old Andrews Sisters musical on television. As he dozed off, he could hear the comforting rumble of thunder in the far-off mountains.

Shortly after one, the phone rang. It was Obregon, sounding perplexed in that artificial way he had when he wanted information quickly but didn't want to forego the niceties.

A traffic patrol unit had come across a hit-and-run victim on the tollway, a mile or so out of Larendo. There wasn't much of the victim left. A crushed skull had put an end to any hope of meaningful discussion. The deceased – "name of Chico, Chico Alomar" – had been a parking attendant at the El Toro Roadside Café.

The body had been identified by squatters who lived nearby through a baseball cap Alomar had been wearing: San Jose

Sharks. What the kid had in his pocket was curious, though – the *federale* probed transparently – Miguel's card and his unlisted phone number, handwritten.

"He wasn't an informant for you, was he?" Obregon asked. "No? Just a screwed-up kid you were trying to help out? Okay." The *federale* boss sounded disappointed not to hear more. "Just being helpful. Goodnight."

Fuentes stumbled groggily into the bedroom and fell onto the unmade bed. After the call, he didn't rest at all well. The air in the tiny room felt oppressive.

His alarm clock ticked on without conscience, the lime-tinged luminescent dial penetrating the dark. Outside he heard the feeble swish of vehicles on the distant highway, the yipping of a lone coyote, the dry rush of a hot-breath wasteland breeze. The tinkle of a wind chime. Rain splattered on the clay rooftop, slowly at first, then, as the storm closed, harder, and with more persistence. Lightning etched the windowsill. Miguel's dog, Salinas, lay at the foot of the bed, ears perked, his fox-like eyes scanning the shadows.

Fuentes lapsed into fitful sleep.

Near three, he awoke. Changing into track pants and sweat top, and shoulder-harnessing his weapon, he took the Mustang out for a run on the tollway. The shepherd pup curled up in the passenger-side bucket seat.

The storm had spent its electric blue fury. The night sky was clear for miles around, the stars high and fulsome, gossamer clouds traced the horizon toward the west, off into the mountains. The road stretched before him like soft gray velour.

As the miles passed one by one, his mind drifted. He considered the motel bombing and Palmer's murder and wondered if one had led to the other, or masked it. Then there was the meeting that Palmer had with Eddie Bono at the El Toro, a rendezvous Miguel knew he'd now be hard pressed to prove had ever occurred, especially with the kid dead. Oh, he could canvass the staff and patrons, all right. But he had as much chance of getting anyone to admit they'd seen the two men together as he did of winning the California State lottery.

He thought of that remote stretch of four-lane road up by Larendo where trucks geared down in the hairpin, where earlier this night a teenage boy had been ground into so much bone and tissue. How much, Fuentes wondered, had Chico Alomar really known?

Inside the darkened car, the dash cast an eerie crimson pallor. Miguel turned the radio up a few notches to drown his thoughts. Yet the nagging torment remained.

In his youth, Miguel Fuentes had played all the right games. As a rookie *anti-narcotico* in the Matamoros general squad along the Rio Grande, he'd made his initial mark with a four-kilo seizure of top-grade *polvo blanco* – cocaine – and the subsequent capture and conviction of six *contrabandistas,* petty smugglers who were willing flunkies for the local drug family.

In six short years, he'd quickly advanced to squad supervisor by maintaining the same high arrest-conviction ratio, much to the shocked relief of his jaded Drug Enforcement Agency counterparts in neighboring Brownsville, Texas, who'd grown accustomed to the more laid back – almost prone – approach to enforcement customarily exhibited by the Mexicans.

From Matamoros, Fuentes had been moved to general investigations in Acapulco. There he'd assiduously honed his craft on international credit card rings that preyed on the local hotels, and he'd successfully convicted several dozen felons.

As with all police officers, worldwide, what followed was a time wandering in the proverbial wilderness, as Miguel was dispatched to a number of postings throughout Mexico, situations that added exponentially to his portfolio but did nothing to further his career.

A near-decade later, Fuentes was promoted to a senior detachment commander in the Yucatan near the ruins of Izamal, hurtling over a generation of aspiring compatriots. Within the ensuing months, and under his active direction, a sting operation resulted in the capture of three German businessmen for the attempted theft of local antiquities – a number of seventh-century jade masks and a 1,300-year-old ceramic pot depicting the howler monkey, patron of writers in the Mayan pantheon of gods.

In the xenophobic police hierarchy that was the *Federale Judicio* of Mexico, such activity against the *gringo* was as significant as a huge heroin bust. Once more, Fuentes's star began to rise fast and furious. He soon acquired a "rabbi" – a protector – to clear his way up through the quagmire of *federale* politics to yet another promotion and then the National Academy course at FBI Quantico. Eleven weeks in the misty Virginia countryside served to further solidify Miguel's reputation: an individual, outspoken, but loyal to "the cause."

His next assignment – a stint as section head in the Commercial Crime Section, Mexico City – was meant solely to showcase Miguel Fuentes to the brass. His short time in the paper chase was relatively uneventful, with just enough spice and sacrifice in his caseload for his portfolio to remain sparkling. There was even talk that he'd reach the hallowed rank of *comandante* by his twentieth year of service.

Then, without warning, it happened. With the indictment of several close relatives of a powerful PRI senator in a stock-manipulation scheme that exposed the seedy underbelly of the Mexican Stock Exchange – the *Bolsa Mexicana de Valores* – Fuentes's career burst like a giant piñata.

His active partner in the investigation, Ramon Obregon, had been an academy classmate. Handpicked by his bosses, Obregon was the son of a wealthy Acapulco real estate developer, a person far shrewder in the guileful ways of Mexico's moneyed élite than Fuentes could ever hope, or wish, to be. He also possessed one of the finest computer minds in the *federale* organization.

With Fuentes's intuitive policing instincts and Obregon's obvious fiscal sensitivities, they seemed a perfect team, charging bull-frenzied into the corrupt arena of Mexican commerce. They worked together on the stock manipulation file, assessed documents, interviewed sources, sharing dangers and successes and even the inevitable failures that to the uninformed might be labeled an injustice.

After a time, Obregon became his shadow, his confidant, a

person Fuentes entrusted with the two most precious things a police officer could ever hope to possess: his judgment and his integrity. And that, in twenty years of policing, proved to be the biggest mistake Miguel Fuentes would ever make.

The subject of the inquiry was a company called NEDEROIL, a Dutch-Mexican joint venture that wanted to drill in the Pacific in the northern sectors of the Mar Muerto off Chiapas State, while it traded simultaneously as a speculative on the Bolsa Mexicana.

NEDEROIL had entered into negotiations with the Mexican government to obtain the necessary approvals to assess and drill the coastal area. The process had been a long and tedious one, for such exploration was the legal monopoly of PEMEX, the Mexican state oil firm. But because of unease about the extent and forcefulness of the emerging native land claims in Chiapas, even PEMEX had not, as yet, ventured to obtain permits to fully drill the region.

Insiders smiled a knowing smile. It was highly unlikely that a foreign firm would ever be granted something so potentially lucrative, even a firm with intimate connections to one of the world's oil giants and the state-of-the-art technology that went with it.

Yet miraculously, late one Friday morning in January, at a time when most brokerage houses were gearing down for the weekend, a drilling permit was indeed issued. The word seeped out and became a giant magnet greedily attracting filings. The market was flooded with investor capital, all targeting NEDEROIL. Included in the hopeful thousands offering their money were relatives of the powerful in Mexico's ruling party, the PRI.

That very afternoon, without apparent reason, the permit was rescinded. But not before tens of millions of shares had changed hands. And millions upon millions of *pesos* had been made. And lost.

In short order, the Mexican Ministry of Justice received a phone call from a distraught Dutch principal in NEDEROIL – one Joachim Van Deenst – who intimated that there might have been an insider fix on the stock, a fix generated from high within the ruling Mexican government. Van Deenst didn't want to complain formally, mind you. Not just yet. He just wanted someone to know that what had transpired was a most unusual turn of events; certainly his own shares had peaked and troughed in the span of five hours. He had also received certain information – disturbing information – which he chose not to speak about over the telephone.

Fuentes and his partner were ordered to commence a discreet investigation into alleged insider trading concerning NEDEROIL. They scheduled an interview with Van Deenst in Holland and booked a KLM flight to Amsterdam for the coming Monday morning.

Late Saturday night, Fuentes got an urgent call from Dutch authorities. The plan had changed. Van Deenst was being taken to a "safe house," a dairy farm outside of a place called Hilversum, southeast of Amsterdam. He'd received an anonymous threat to keep his mouth shut. Or else.

Fuentes was given detailed instructions. Upon their arrival at the huge Schipol airport located in the dank Dutch polderlands outside Amsterdam, he and Obregon were to proceed immediately to the police post to arrange transport to the farm where Van Deenst would be ready to give a full statement. The Dutch investigator gave his name as the security check. He also gave Miguel a secure number to call before Monday should they need further information. Fuentes wrote the digits down in his working notes and locked the file in the safe.

But he and Obregon never got to see a windmill. They never even reached the tarmac at Mexico City International Airport.

Late Sunday morning, Amsterdam time, Van Deenst was found floating in a canal opposite the Central Railway Station. The autopsy showed he'd been killed by a heart attack. The profile fit – mid-fifties, stressful occupation, a history of heart disease in the family. But Joachim Van Deenst had been a jogger, a teetotaler, a vigorous man who looked to be thirty-five. Perhaps, most pointedly, he'd just had his annual physical checkup a week before, and his heart had been fine. A short phone call from a senior Dutch official: they were treating the matter as highly suspicious. A formal Interpol request was being drafted, asking for the assistance of Mexican authorities.

An affluent businessman found dead while dabbling in megabucks. In the scheme of things, it was certainly good for a few minutes' conjecture over morning coffee, or perhaps a news-bite on a national broadcast, or even CNN. If unsolved, it might have a media shelf life of three days, nothing more, nothing less. And there the matter would have ended.

However, Joachim Van Deenst had also been a respected member of a venerable, moneyed family, cozily related to the House of Orange, the ruling house of the Netherlands.

Pressure was brought to bear on the Mexican ambassador to The Hague. His Dutch counterpart in Mexico City also beat a path down a series of increasingly plush ministerial hallways. Still, Miguel caught none of it. After all, Amsterdam was an ocean away, and he could deal only with the reality at his fingertips, not some bleached corpse lying in an ivory-tiled morgue.

Fuentes focused on his principal investigation. Over the ensuing days he made slow and steady progress. Petty kickbacks, dubious phone calls, and signed statements from underlings in brokerage houses all too ready to point the finger of guilt elsewhere. The noose was quickly tightening around the corpulent neck of a Mexican senator, first cousin to *el Presidente* and his circle.

And then the kicker – a voice-mail recording dropped off to Fuentes in a brown paper bag by a disgruntled maid tired of being used as a mattress by her employer, the senator. A tape advising him to buy into NEDEROIL on Friday morning – "big time" – and sell everything just before one o'clock that same afternoon, "before the sky falls." An archive ending with the words: "Your friend always. Humberto."

"Humberto." It was a male's voice with an asthmatic gurgle. Miguel recalled that it belonged to a stock promoter he'd inter-viewed about NEDEROIL, a nervous man with dandruff shoulders and bad breath named Guzman, who'd invented a boiler-room scam aptly called Cheetah Enterprises.

Cheetah had been a viscous entity with neither principle nor principals, possessing a microscopic life expectancy, with corporate headquarters first in Belize and then in Panama City.

As Fuentes was preparing to execute a criminal warrant at the senator's residence, while simultaneously having a second team primed to bring Guzman in for questioning, Mexico's largest tabloid printed a "stop the presses" exposé. An anonymous tip had given the news editor the telephone number to Van Deenst's safe house outside Hilversum, stolen from an impregnable *federale* vault, and supposedly obtained on the black market for $25,000 U.S. and offered to the paper for a slightly larger sum as "a public service."

A reporter at the tabloid dialed the number. When a startled Dutch detective answered, it didn't take long to draw a crude mental image of what was said and what the consequences of that discussion might be. While word processors in the newsroom furiously composed the article, the newspaper judiciously doled out the money, to be picked up at a mutually agreed drop-off spot. Payment for services rendered was, after all, the honorable thing to do.

As he found himself cannonading down to the cavernous headquarters' property vault, newspaper clenched in hand, Fuentes already knew what he'd find – and he was not disappointed. Critical case files were missing. They included original, highly incriminating statements taken from stock traders who held among their portfolios those of senior PRI members, including the president's closest relations.

The detectives detailed to raid Guzman's arid abode briskly determined that he'd skipped town that very morning. The Cheetah offices had been hurriedly vacated. As a consequence, potential criminal proceedings against the senator were stayed, and the investigation effectively stopped dead in its tracks.

It didn't take long for the media to begin howling.

And when they did, Fuentes's orderly world turned madly upside down. The Dutch government was furious at what they believed to be Mexican complicity in the death of a royal. The international press went berserk. In Mexico, opposition politicians made fodder of the PRI, and a *federale* police hierarchy that had, until that moment, trumpeted its every move as a triumph, swiftly disowned both Fuentes and Obregon.

The man on the street shrugged and smiled a world-weary smile. Was this any different from so many other police investigations in Mexico, be they about drugs, prostitution, corruption, or gun smuggling? Nothing had changed. It was always the same. Nothing would be done, because nothing could be. And nothing could be done, because nothing would be.

And for a time, it seemed that the man in the street was right.

When it became eminently apparent that too many influential international investors had lost money, and that certain critical government insiders hadn't obtained their piece of the action before the alarm bells sounded, boisterous demands were made for an Internal Affairs review of the investigation itself, with its results to be made public.

And for once the demands were heeded.

Though Obregon – and who knew how many others – knew the combination to the vault, the ensuing internal investigation placed the blame squarely on Fuentes's shoulders. He'd been the senior investigator. He'd held absolute responsibility for the security of exhibits and the physical safety of the Dutch informant.

It was fully expected that, as the designated sacrificial lamb, Miguel Fuentes would give his evidence at the public inquiry with professional politeness and later submit to his disciplinary action in a similar manner. That was the way of such things, in all places and in all times. That was how ethical institutions survived.

But Fuentes was anything but meek and mild as he entered the witness box and, for six solid days, he spoke the truth as he knew it. He testified to unsanctioned and illegal actions by parties privy to the inquiry, from *federale* associates, to powerful bankers, to government mandarins, and even higher.

It was truly a pity, then, for Fuentes that his "friend," Ramon Obregon, marched to a very different drummer.

For, when Obregon rose to take the stand, he was the epitome of sanctimonious solidarity with his superiors. He couldn't recall the things that Fuentes vehemently asserted: statements people had made in the presence of the two of them, exhibits they'd seized in tandem, investigative chronologies they'd developed through their inquiries together. Obregon was walking a verbal tightrope, balanced by both ambiguity and ambition. He crossed to the other side, unscathed.

At the conclusion of the hearings, the people in the *cantinas* and *barrios* sided with Miguel. It was glaringly apparent to the common man that Obregon had prostituted himself and his beliefs. Unfortunately for Fuentes, with vapid stonewalling by his partner and without the comforting corroboration afforded by the missing files, even his own evidence proved more titillating than decisive.

When his time in the box ended, so, it appeared, did his tenure as a valued member of Mexico's national police organization. By going public with allegations of insider incompetence, if not outright corruption, he'd left his superiors temporarily vulnerable. Miguel Fuentes's vulnerability was anything but temporary.

Within the *federale* bureaucracy, middle-ranking heads rolled by the plateful, Fuentes's first and foremost among them. Ramon Obregon deftly distanced himself from his former colleague and remained untouched by an infamy that effectively blitzed Miguel's career.

The media were onto Miguel like a gaggle of hyenas. There were offers for his story in ghosted form. Several journalists ambitiously promised American cable network rights. Some of the submissions were quite lucrative; all carried the implicit recognition that his would probably be a posthumous memoir. Miguel stayed sensibly silent.

One muggy morning, a mere three days after the hearings ended, he was ordered to Personnel to confront a brooding tortoise of a man respectfully known throughout the organization as *Señor* Ernesto. His official title was Director – Personnel and Human Resources, but he was known colloquially as "The Fixer." His posting lists created instant millionaires and paupers.

For such beneficence, Ernesto demanded only what he felt was his due: a cut of the action, a slice of the proverbial pie.

Ernesto's previous posting had been drugs. He'd been the senior operational *anti-narcotico* in Mexico for nearly as long as snow had nestled on Mount Orizaba in Veracruz. He knew the drug families, their trading territories and shipping routes, had been invited to the baptisms of their children, broken bread at their daughters' weddings, and imprisoned those who wouldn't pay for the right to be rich.

It was said behind his slightly hunched back that the *Señor* was one of the old *federale* pedigree – a man who feared no one, not even *El Diablo*. That meant he was extremely wealthy and supremely ruthless. No one dared ask him where he got his money. Even the *Yanquis* from the agencies he'd occasionally dealt with deferred to Ernesto in his territory – that is, if they wished to survive, with their investigations intact.

A *federale* agent posted to the State of Guerrero had allegedly disobeyed the *Señor's* dry admonition and neglected to cut him a finder's fee for a shipment of cocaine seized at the Acapulco navy yards. Taken up by helicopter, the young agent learned all too abruptly that flying didn't require a pilot's license – just wings – which the *Señor* had, somehow, neglected to supply. The agent disappeared into the shark-infested waters.

The police funeral was closed-coffin. Representing the senior command, *Señor* Ernesto delivered the eulogy about sacrifice for the common good. The drugs vanished from the *federale* property vault later that week, never to be recovered. Soon after, Ernesto's daughter purchased a forty-five-foot sailboat and refurnished her seaside villa. The pilot and crew of the helicopter died in a training incident in the Sierra Madre at just about the time *Señor* Ernesto was promoted to his present preeminent position.

When Fuentes went in to see him, there was a single sheet of paper on the table. He was given five minutes to consider it. The ultimatum proved disarmingly straightforward: it was an imperative disguised as a choice.

There was an opening for a chief of police in the State of

Sonora, in a medium-sized northern town offering no great import or potential for the successful aspirant. Except for longevity. A place called Coronado. On the balance of probabilities, Miguel deemed it not such a bad deal after all.

He heard, sometime later, soon after the hearings had ended and the harsh light of public opinion had dimmed, that oil explorations had indeed actually commenced in the Mar Muerto. NEDEROIL had first quietly dropped its claim and then declared limited bankruptcy. PEMEX instead had been assured its rightful place in the food chain with a legal drill permit for the offshore site. And the same investors who'd anxiously scampered for cover in the face of the police probe were now openly working subcontracts through PEMEX. They were, in the process, being well rewarded.

Fuentes never questioned his truth – or regretted the telling of it. But if only he hadn't trusted Obregon. If only he'd listened to that inner voice of caution … If only … And now, of all people, his destiny would once again be resting in Ramon Obregon's hands.

Fuentes gunned the Mustang over the crest of a hill. It was almost dawn. They'd be leaving soon, driving the 150 miles to Tucson. Miguel turned the car back toward Coronado, back to his responsibilities and his fate. He opened the window a crack and let his consciousness drift out among the mesas and scrub.

Wednesday, May 23, dawn.
Coronado

7 Obregon picked up Fuentes promptly at 8:45. On their way through town, they stopped at Eng's restaurant. Felix was waiting outside the shuttered eatery, dressed in an ill-fitting salmon-hued suit over a pair of crocodile-skin cowboy boots. He sported a pink and green candy-striped tie that had gone out of fashion and a button-down shirt with a wrinkled collar. He wore an expression of strained discomfort. A faint film of perspiration already nestled on his skin. Asuncion was strangely subdued.

The day was already warm, in the low eighties, with the promise of wilting heat to come. Filigreed wisps of cloud hung in the morning sky.

Obregon drove a government vehicle, a Buick Regal with a midnight-blue interior and a digital stereo system tuned to symphonic music. Miguel was quite impressed with the vehicle and said so. He was surprised when the *federale* told him the car was only a pool vehicle he'd taken for the day. Ramon purred that he preferred something more substantial, in keeping with his rank, something with presence and panache – like the Land Rover he'd had in Chihuahua, or the white Lincoln he used to maintain in Mexico City as his personally assigned unit. For now, funding restraints had prevented it from being so. But that might soon change. Fuentes didn't ask how; he knew only too well the machinations of government budgets.

Obregon turned the air conditioner on full blast. Fuentes watched the desert shimmer past. Felix fell fast asleep, snoring, in the back seat.

The border crossing at Nogales proved a starchy formality when a crew-cut Customs officer with a Midwestern drawl searched their trunk for contraband, Obregon's *federale* badge and mild protest notwithstanding. There was unquestionably no bootleg; there was no apology, either.

They made steady if unspectacular time into Tucson, arriving shortly before noon. Fuentes never failed to be impressed by the sheer bloated pleasure of this place called America, with its mindless miles of concrete and neon. It was a seamless consumer nirvana of car washes and take-outs, discount malls and gas bars, motels and drive-through banks, stretching across a crayoned desert vista.

Just outside the city, Obregon handed Miguel a tour book map and directed him to find their destination, a place called Davis Monthan United States Air Force Base.

After a short drive due north, a seemingly endless stretch of wire-mesh fence paralleled the highway. Fuentes whistled under his breath, for although he'd heard the United States Air Force had chosen this vastness to store its military inventory, trusting in the suffocating dryness of the northern Sonora to preserve the testament to its supremacy in the air, nothing had prepared him for the sight now rushing by.

Row upon row of silver warplanes stretched as far as the eye could see and probably beyond: canopies sealed, wings barely touching, once proud war paint dulled by all-purpose coating. Thunderchiefs, B-52 bombers, Phantoms, Sabres, Wildcats, Orions – a veritable history of martial aviation lay sequestered on the desert floor.

The stenciled sign at the main gate identified the Elite Gate Guards as Trish Anne Smith, hometown: Slidell, Louisiana, and Tyrone Baxton Smith, hometown: Brooklyn, New York. The bereted female corporal who came out of the guardroom to direct them was coolly efficient and quite attractive. A passing glance into the guardroom revealed a six-foot-four behemoth rested in a chair leafing through a dog-eared edition of *Sports Illustrated*.

They drove down Craycroft Road and turned right onto Madeira where they parked outside a stark three-story facility adjacent to the Base Law Center. An armed MP took them onto the top floor and to the rear of the building. They halted in front of an unmarked door. The guard knocked. A muffled reply, and they were escorted inside.

The man who confronted them was in his late forties, short, stocky, and serious, possessing a suppressed tension that was the inevitable by-product of a lifetime of discipline. He wore pressed khakis and officers' tabs on his epaulets, though Miguel couldn't make out the rank. His hair was stiff, colorless, and crew-cut. Stress lines etched a tight web around his mouth.

"*Señors?*" The American looked quizzically at his guests, through strident eyes dappled a cornflower blue, perplexed as to whom to address first.

"*Comandante* Obregon." Ramon glided forward and with counterfeit solemnity shook his host's hand. He spoke in an unaccented voice, the culmination of expensive Berlitz courses in his youth.

"And these gentlemen are?"

"Miguel Fuentes, police chief of Coronado," Obregon offered glibly. "And his escort." The *federale* didn't bother to introduce Asuncion, nor did their host respond with anything beyond the faintest flicker of acknowledgment.

"A pleasure to meet you, sir," Fuentes declared. It was only after doing so that he realized he'd come to full attention. Ascunsion seemed overwhelmed by it all.

The American's features inched their way toward a smile then retraced their path to sober neutrality. "My name is Colonel Joshua Bragg, officer in command of Detachment 217, U.S. Air Force Office of Special Investigations, here at Davis Monthan." He gestured to a set of overstuffed chairs and a sofa arranged in a half circle.

He and Obregon reclined in the chairs. Fuentes eased himself into one corner of the sofa, and Felix meekly inhabited the other.

Miguel sized up the office. The room was rectangular and decorated in functional military, circa Cold War. In addition to their seating arrangement, a conventional desk, an ensemble of table and chairs, an upright uniform locker, and two columns of olive-drab filing cabinets completed the quartermaster's inventory. A framed illustration of a P-38 Lightning in combat with Japanese Zeros relieved one gaunt wall. Much of the opposite wall was covered by bulletin boards featuring two items: staffing allocations – hours worked, overtime, and callback, in pie-chart form – and a tricolored topographical map of Arizona.

The desktop was bare save for a reading lamp, coffee mug brimful of magic markers, and a scale model of a Voodoo fighter-interceptor in Arctic ice camouflage. The venetian blinds were closed.

"Gentlemen," Bragg pronounced in a resonant baritone. "The FBI section head in Tucson told us you'd be coming. The United States Air Force is at your service."

Fuentes responded with a quizzical stare.

"You have a problem, sir?" the American rasped.

Miguel hesitated. "It's just that I'm more accustomed to working with the FBI."

The air force colonel clasped his hands together in the manner of a priest, then opened the palms expansively. "Then you're in for a uplifting change, *Señor*," he declared with the aplomb of a heat-seeking missile zapping its target. "The Office of Special Investigations is responsible for all major criminal inquiries in the air force. My operational control comes direct from Washington. Bolling Airbase, District of Columbia to be precise. Realize that we also handle counterintelligence and counterespionage. I would think somehow that we're competent enough to handle a small case of homicide, wouldn't you, *Jefe?*"

"The government of Mexico is most appreciative of your generous offer of assistance," Obregon interceded, with the bravado of a petty man in the company of his betters.

Bragg accepted the cloying compliment with the slightest tilt of an eyebrow. He turned to a telephone located next to the sofa. Without asking their preference, he ordered coffee for his guests and a bottle of mineral water for himself. "In training," he commented to no one in particular.

After refreshments arrived, Bragg allowed them a few moments to make themselves at ease. The coffee was weak and instant, the cream slightly off. He fashioned small talk about their drive from Mexico and the fine spring weather that Tucson was experiencing. Obregon responded in kind. It was an unctuous nicety that civil servants seemed universally adept at, a form of decaf diplomacy that set the stage for the hard-edged discussions to follow.

Fuentes nodded occasionally to show he was conscious of what was being said. He observed his host's hands. The cuticles were manicured and the nails scrupulously clean – the instruments of a rigid perfectionist, an individual who would not consider for a moment expending energy on superfluous things, even a chat over coffee, without design. The colonel was about as malleable as fire-hardened brick.

It was Obregon who finally brought up the subject. "As you well know," he began civilly, "we're investigating a serious incident that occurred at Coronado, one surrounded in most suspicious circumstances."

"Yes," Bragg replied with bulldog bluntness. "An American citizen was murdered."

Miguel felt compelled to interrupt. "As were three Mexicans. Two of them children."

Obregon cast an austere glance in his direction. Fuentes took a long sip of coffee and placed the cup on a side table.

"Of course," Bragg answered with feeble sincerity. "A great tragedy for all concerned."

"I believe you have information concerning the American?" the *federale* requested cordially.

"We do," Bragg replied, reaching for an item on his desk. "Your government has provided us with duplicate field reports." He drew out a plain manila folder, removed two prints of a passport-sized photograph and handed them to his guests. "Is this the party in your morgue?"

Fuentes looked down at the photo. He nodded.

"So." Bragg paused to sip some mineral water. "If that's the case, the deceased was Captain Wickham Everett Chandler. Age thirty-nine. A bachelor, born in Tuscaloosa, Alabama. Recently transferred from Griffiss, a B-52 base in upstate New York." He took another sip. "He was last seen by the gate guard exiting camp to take annual leave."

Bragg spoke in a disinterested monotone. His answer was textbook, the kind Fuentes knew was meant to placate yet leave no ambiguity as to its overbearing intent.

"And what date was that, sir?"

"May twenty-first. At 6:09 a.m."

"Does base security normally record people exiting?"

Bragg was prepared. "Not usually. But both guards remember talking to Captain Chandler. He was a gregarious fellow. Quite well respected by the rank and file."

"Did they recall the car he was driving?" Fuentes probed

"His private vehicle, a Mazda sports coupe. Tucson authorities found it in their pound, towed in as 'abandoned' from a parking spot on the same street as the rental agency that owned the Olds you found at the motel." He completed the thought. "The

Mazda's been checked by our Ident. section and its contents compared against what you have. There's nothing suspicious."

"Can you think of a reason the captain would change vehicles?"

"You tell me," Bragg countered with a sharp tongue.

A clumsy stillness filled the room.

Obregon spoke first. "Did Chandler return to Davis Monthan after departing?"

"No. Our entry log would have disclosed it. There's no record of the Mazda or the rental."

"What exactly did the captain do here?" Fuentes asked.

"His posting at Davis was in Ordinance. He was one of our senior supply and inventory officers; our only experienced one, I'm told, since his counterpart was on extended sick leave with ulcers." Bragg paused. "Your coroner states he died of a heroin overdose?"

"Yes." Obregon nodded. "The autopsy indicates the presence of a fatal level of heroin in the deceased's system."

Bragg impatiently thrummed his fingers on the chair's edge, then stopped. He structured his next response with evident care. "We're deeply distressed about the mode of death." He stared at Fuentes as he made the comment. Fuentes parried the look, but detected no emotion in the colonel. At all.

"There's nothing in Chandler's service record to suggest a substance-abuse problem. He was churchgoing, a Methodist. Past financial secretary of the Officers' Club and a member of the base outreach program – volunteer work with inner-city kids." A wan smile. "We encourage our staff to be community oriented." The last words flowed over them all with the insincerity that characterized their host. "As I said, he was starting his annual leave when this happened."

"A tragedy for us all," Obregon minced. "We will do our utmost to see justice is served."

"I'm sure you will." Bragg barely succeeded in masking his derision. "And you, *Jefe*?" He looked at Fuentes. "I gather this thing is your investigation. Have you determined a motive?"

"No," Miguel admitted. "We were hoping to find something here."

"Yes, of course," the American tut-tutted. "Well, you might well discover this case isn't going to be easy. Drug-related murders never are."

Fuentes had given up trying to stomach the coffee. The large office had become suddenly quite confining. The tenacious roar of a jet engine in the distance like pregnant thunder. A phone ringing in another part of the building. A door shutting with a resounding thud.

"Let's cut to the chase, shall we?" Bragg suggested tersely. "We're all busy people." The colonel got up and crossed to his desk, relieving a drawer of a number of files. He returned to his chair.

"Last week," he began soberly, "we conducted a random audit of BFL 430s – air force administrative ledgers governing fuel expenditures. There are a number of active combat units here at 355 Operations. Demand for fuel is high. Our supply squadron handles over 45 million gallons of aircraft grade, about sixty-five thousand transactions annually. We conservatively value this account at $35 million." The American let the figures sink in.

"My people compared the 430s that Chandler kept with comparable tallies from the ordinance squadron at Williams Air Base in Phoenix. Both units use virtually the same suppliers. Yet the disparities are very disturbing.

"For the last four months, Chandler's numbers have been much too tidy. Not a single item isn't rounded off to a five or zero digit. In the fuel business that just can't happen. Not with the price fluctuations we've experienced the last few years.

"Admittedly, there are cases where his ledgers record amounts lower than the bills submitted by suppliers. But in most, the final sum is rounded off a few cents upward from the statement tendered to Base. When this occurs, a notation 'BFL 430 – 9 overage' appears in the remarks column."

Bragg stood up, smoothing the pleats of his trousers as he did so. He began to pace the room.

"Lieutenant Maria Donovan is second in command at Ordinance. We interviewed her yesterday. Donovan is new, less than two years out of the Academy, less than three months here, but she's reasonably competent.

"She noticed unusual sums in the books a while back, but only established a pattern last month. She immediately confronted Captain Chandler. He became uneasy, and then he stated that he'd developed a new budget procedure to deal with what he called 'contingencies.' He said there were nearly always market fluctuations in the wellhead price of oil that neither he nor his suppliers could foresee when they negotiated purchase orders for delivery at a later date."

Fuentes inched forward on the sofa. "And that's where this accounting practice would kick in?"

"Yes." Bragg considered his audience with a patronizing stare. "Chandler told Donovan he'd devised a method to guard against billing surprises. He called it the Dash 9. He said the system was good for Uncle Sam because it'd protect the taxpayer from gouging by suppliers, and that his sources preferred it because round-offs made for tidier bookkeeping." The trim airman recommenced his methodical journey across the breadth of the room.

"Chandler said that, at year's end, he could average out all the monies so that no one would lose. The air force and ultimately the taxpayer would benefit because they couldn't be held hostage by dramatic market fluctuations. Dealers would be happy because they were now guaranteed business. In addition, dealers would never be denied government contracts because of market variations, nor would they suffer cash-flow problems caused by tardy check-cutting practices."

Obregon's brow furrowed. "But there must have been someone who didn't benefit?"

Bragg nodded. "That's precisely when the wheels fell off the wagon." He started pacing again. "A week ago, the base commander got a phone call from the president of Luther Fuels here in Tucson, wondering why our Base Supply never called any more for business. Yesterday, a small company in Green Valley that has dealt with the airbase for years complained. Then a third called from over in Casa Grande. Same criticism."

The American stopped. "The fact is, gentlemen, that Wickham Chandler committed a major fraud while extorting decent citizens in the process. The way he structured his accounts had the effect of making legitimate companies pay for the privilege of dealing with the United States Air Force. Or else."

"Or else?" Asuncion blurted.

"If they said anything, Chandler let it be known informally but firmly that they'd forfeit the right to any future contracts from Davis Monthan."

The colonel sat on the edge of his desk, arms crossed, a look of grim resolve on his features. "Chandler was on leave so we couldn't confront him with our findings. In the interim, we've identified all beneficiaries of his unique 'Commercial Code.' The results?" Bragg took a binder from the pile on his desk. He opened the book and began to read. The folio appeared crammed with computer printouts vigorously red-circled and yellow-tabbed.

"Over $187,000 in government money went into Chandler's cookie jar as forward averaging. Of that, $120,000 is adequately reconciled in accounts of oil companies granted subsequent business. The remainder?" He closed the jacket with a loud thud and placed the binder before Obregon. "More than $67,000 is missing, not counting interest."

Fuentes shook his head incredulously. "Yet no one protested until last week?"

The American emitted a chuckle that sounded like the rasp of dry cornstalks breaking. "If you're an outsider, you wouldn't even know it was happening. And, if you're in the loop, are you going to admit you were part of an illegal scheme to defraud the Government of the United States?"

"Do you have any idea where the money went?"

"No," Bragg replied with ponderous resolve. "My investigators tried to unearth where it might be hidden. They found that, from the time bills were submitted to the time they were paid, there was no legitimate place the surplus could go to be domiciled."

"Could one of the disgruntled suppliers have killed Chandler?" Fuentes speculated.

Bragg appeared startled by the question. "Certainly not. The public contractors who deal with Davis Monthan are small businessmen, sir. Not murderers."

"Money makes strange bedfellows, Colonel," Fuentes said.

Bragg countered, "We've checked everyone we think was on the Dash 9 list, and any individual who might have lost contracts because he refused to be. They all seem to have legitimate alibis."

"Has anyone made a formal complaint about what Chandler has done to them?"

The colonel shook his head. "Other than the Government of the United States, you'll be hard pressed to find someone who might help your investigation from this end – certainly not the local American suppliers. Especially now, when there's a corpse lying in a Mexican morgue. From here on in, they'll all be kicking and bucking like mules before you get them to admit to anything.

"I would suggest that whatever Chandler was doing in Mexico is integral to this scam," Bragg opined darkly. "Find out where he converted the funds and you'll find out why he was murdered."

Obregon nodded. It was left for Fuentes to broach the inevitable question.

"Do you have a drug problem on Davis Monthan?"

The American didn't flinch. "A small one," he acknowledged "Certainly. I'd be lying if I said we didn't."

"Heroin?"

"No." Their trim host tartly dismissed the word. "The usual. Soft drugs. Enlisted man stuff. A little cocaine. Nothing involving the officer cadre. And certainly nothing involving Wick Chandler."

"Could he have dealt off base, Colonel?"

"No. According to the Tucson drug squad, he was an unknown."

"But he could still have brokered narcotics without getting his hands dirty, couldn't he?" Fuentes pressed.

Whatever room for cooperation Bragg might have pretended to leave open, banged shut like a trap door. "That's for you to find out," he snapped. "The murder happened in Mexico, not in Arizona."

The colonel tersely gathered the remaining folios and handed them to Asuncion. The binders were heavy. The old *sergente* grunted with exertion. The room was so still Miguel could hear the air-conditioning unit drip moisture.

"You may have the investigation brief. It goes without saying that I retain the originals."

"Of course," Obregon agreed, not smiling. They looked at each other a moment in uneasy repose.

The American broke the spell. "How long do you expect to be in Tucson?"

"It depends," Obregon responded. "Two days, maybe three."

"We could put you up here at the base," the colonel offered without enthusiasm.

"No." Fuentes thanked him. "We have hotel rooms."

"Good." Bragg seemed genuinely relieved. "Feel free to drop by and see me if you want clarification of anything. Some of the documents are quite challenging, especially the supply sheets. Depot has codes to confuse Confucius." He laughed at his own joke. "Naturally we'll do everything to assist you, in the spirit of mutual cooperation."

"*Si*," Obregon echoed. "In the spirit of mutual cooperation."

The Mexicans stood up and mumbled thanks for their refreshments. They moved to the door, guided by Bragg's not unsubtle gestures.

"One last point." The American imperiously raised an index finger. His guests stopped in their tracks. The colonel's eyes compressed to slits. "You're not at liberty to carry weapons or conduct any independent police investigations while in the United States."

Obregon gathered his self-importance around him like a *serape*. "I'm well aware of diplomatic etiquette," he huffed. "I am, after all, an official of the Mexican federal state."

"Fine," Bragg replied with raw finality. "I'm glad we understand each other."

The door closed in their faces.

"Bastard," Obregon muttered under his breath as they strode
from the building into a searing noonday sun.

"Pardon?" Fuentes turned.

"Oh, nothing." The *federale* straightened his tie, then smiled a
glassy-eyed smile. "I was just commenting on the case. I found
the colonel was most helpful, Miguel, didn't you?"

"*Si*," Fuentes responded laconically, winking to a bemused
Asuncion as he did so. "Most helpful. A truly sincere *Yanqui*."

Wednesday, May 23, morning.
Tucson, Arizona

8 They ate lunch at a nearby greasy spoon and spent the next
hour driving idly around Tucson, killing time, the binders
nestled in a box in the trunk.

Fuentes didn't relish for one moment the thought of plowing
through the government double-talk he knew he'd find lurking
between the blue jacket covers. And he was certain Obregon
felt likewise.

The two men didn't talk much. The awkwardness of actually
working together again after so many years, in light of what had
transpired between them to cause the rift, had created a palpable
tension. When they did discuss the murders, it was with the
obliqueness of fencing partners striving to score a touch without
surrendering one.

Fuentes still bristled over the recent accusation that he'd
engaged in improper conduct in Larendo. He distrusted Obregon
and sensed that the *federale*, despite his syrupy protestations to the
contrary, would use anything, including false allegations, to have
him removed as chief of police in Coronado. Anything to score
brownie points with the *delegado*, Hector Rivera.

For his part, Felix Asuncion kept a respectful silence in the presence of his betters. After a time, he dozed off in the back seat. The only indication of the sergeant's presence came when he occasionally broke wind.

Shortly before four, with the temperature hovering in the high nineties, Obregon reined in the car and turned back toward their lodgings. En route, he stopped at a 7-Eleven to get cigarettes. Disappointed that they didn't carry his favorite brand, he settled for Marlboros. While Felix seized the opportunity to buy three six-packs of Colt 45, a few bags of tortilla chips, and dip, Fuentes remained seated in the Buick mulling over the work ahead.

When they arrived at their hotel, an "urgent" phone call awaited the *comandante*. He took it in the lobby, out of hearing of his associates. As he spoke, his face mirrored a myriad of expressions. The call was lengthy. Obregon seemed drained when he hung up. There were pressing issues back in Sonora, he related vaguely on his return, investigative matters unconnected to this one. He'd require some privacy to resolve them.

He assured Fuentes that they would get together for supper to discuss the day's events. He tossed Fuentes a spare set of car keys so he could retrieve the air force files from the trunk of the Buick.

Their hotel room was a chilled igloo, the air-conditioner unit frothing a dank smog. After loosening his tie, Asuncion tossed his suit jacket onto one of the beds. He closed the drapes with a dramatic flourish and, from the plastic bag, he stocked the fridge with beer, leaving four bottles on the table.

"Come on, *amigo*," Felix invited between gulps. "Have one. You might as well be comfortable."

Miguel appreciatively accepted the offer and sat on the bedside.

As he munched chips and sipped his beer, he opened the first binder. The documents were quite exhaustive, containing statements from everyone who'd had even the remotest contact with the deceased man in his final hours: from a guard who had watched Wickham Chandler leave Davis Monthan the final time, to the rental agent who had leased the Olds, and even to a woman at the base PX who had sold him toiletries on what was destined to be his last journey. A photocopied credit-card receipt was affixed to her statement listing the mundane items that marked the journey of a life: Arm and Hammer toothpaste, Right Guard dry stick deodorant, Gillette shaving cream, disposable razors and an anonymous numbered item marked "sundries" and valued at $4.93 – small change spent on an item not identified on the PX's computerized inventory.

Asuncion switched on the TV and settled down to take in a baseball game televised from the west coast, the Montreal Expos playing the Los Angeles Dodgers.

Fuentes cracked binder two. What he found wasn't entirely unexpected: quasi-obituaries, bland statements from associates and friends attesting to the captain's work ethic and integrity. The chaplain commented on Chandler's Christian generosity; commissioned officers on his professionalism and esprit de corps. Enlisted men attested to his compassion in handling their personal problems.

Chandler had numerous citations for good conduct, including one for expediting a load of essential foodstuffs to American Forces in Operation Desert Storm, acquired when he was temporarily stationed in the Canary Islands. With typical military thoroughness, the base commander had even affixed a photocopy of stores cargoed: canned tuna, beans, peaches, ration packs, iodine, and toilet paper.

That said, his career history was meticulously uninspiring. At first blush it appeared that Chandler had been aptly mated to the uneventful life of a military supply officer. But what could one expect from someone who had received an official commendation for shipping a cargo of two-ply toilet paper to the Saudi desert?

Born thirty-nine years before, in Tuscaloosa, Alabama, the only son of a retired air force colonel who'd specialized in the creation of quick-response air bases in combat zones before he'd retired at full pension, Chandler had graduated from the USAF Academy in Colorado, where he'd finished in the top third in his class. His scholastic attainments had been pedestrian in nature – he showed a marked aptitude for mathematics and astronomy – with prosaic hobbies like Civil War history, stamp collecting, and chess to spruce up the bland mix. Cerebrally fit, his stamina was somewhat wanting, as his poor physical training scores bore out. Though he'd aspired to assignment to aircrew as a navigator, his career counselor had wisely slotted him for the more common-place, but certainly essential, tasks of quartermastering and supply, where a natural aptitude for numbers and attention to commonplace detail could be more aptly applied.

Throughout his career, Chandler's proficiency ratings had been superb. Over time, he had become a masterly manipulator of materials and personnel and had excelled in that function with the same zest he'd demonstrated as the Academy chess champion.

The captain had spent fifteen years in ordinance, with post-ings in Spain, Japan, and England to complement his dossier. He'd taken eight staff courses and placed well in each. He'd even presented the Pentagon with a working paper outlining a revolutionary concept that would use computer graphics to redesign the inside of a C-130 transport and increase its cargo load by 29 percent. Granted, the man was never to be a legend in the combat arms department, but Wick Chandler still appeared to have been a legitimate – albeit unheralded – cog in the American war machine.

Fuentes briefly examined the remaining evidence. Binders three through five would prove laborious: supply sheets and documents involving what seemed to be more technical aspects of the dead man's work.

Miguel glanced over to his roommate. Asuncion lounged snugly on the bed, seated upright, his head resting on a pillow as he coaxed another beer into his mouth. The Dodgers were losing 5 to 1. It was the top of the sixth inning. Felix watched intently.

"What do you think happened to the *Yanqui?*" Fuentes asked. "What got him murdered?"

Asuncion offered an imprecise nod of his head. Miguel wasn't certain if the gesture was meant for him or for the Dodger reliever, who had struck out his first batter.

"Felix?" Fuentes prompted. "Are you listening to me?"

The pudgy detective pushed himself off the bed and grabbed a handful of tortilla chips. "What got him murdered?" Asuncion munched loudly on the chips. "The guy was playing out of his league. Like the pitcher that L.A. started tonight." He smirked at his little joke.

The next Expos batter hit a two-run homer. "*Manoooo . . .*" Asuncion shook his hands wildly in the air in frustration. The next batter walked on four straight balls. The Dodgers' pitching coach strode quickly to the mound. Asuncion groaned and turned his attention from what appeared to be a hopelessly lost cause.

"You really want my opinion, Boss?"

Fuentes nodded.

Asuncion cagily began crafting his theory. "We know three things: Wick Chandler fiddled the books where he worked, he had drugs in his rental car, and he overdosed, right? But the money taken from the airbase wasn't nearly enough to buy the stuff we found in the Olds. It wouldn't have got Chandler much more than a box of quality syringes."

Fuentes rubbed his chin thoughtfully. It made sense.

Asuncion perched on one elbow. "Face it, Miguel. The *Yanqui* had the perfect 'in' at the base. It's almost certain the money he pilfered from accounts wasn't bankrolling his drug buys. For all we know, in return for the heroin, he was supplying all of Mexico with Hostess Twinkies.

"No, seriously," the detective continued, his speech slightly slurred. "The more I think about it, there's quick and easy money in this. In food. In commodities. In supplies." A loud belch. "And once it's out of the government warehouse, it's not like bank notes." His eyes shone. "It's untraceable."

He paused. "Maybe," he added thoughtfully, "maybe Chandler committed the cardinal sin of all independent businessmen. Maybe he double-crossed his dealer network by skimming from both ends."

Fuentes disagreed. "People don't blow up supply officers over toilet paper, tacos, or toothpaste."

"They do if a big order has been screwed up." Asuncion's face was dead serious. "Or if what they get isn't what they asked for. "

"You have a point, *mi amigo*," Miguel conceded.

Asuncion scrunched his features into a mug. "And you thought I was just a pretty face . . ." He suddenly gave a triumphant howl. "Double play!" The inning was over. A car rental commercial came on.

Fuentes opened the third binder. He sifted through documents, working patiently for a few more minutes. In the background he heard the announcer commenting on the game. The Dodgers had opened with a lead-off single and had just gotten another hit.

"You know, there's something to what you said," he mumbled, as much to himself as to Asuncion. "I've gone through the supply printouts several times. The base fuel account isn't the only one that seems kind of funny . . ."

"Funny, *Jefe?*" the detective replied with mock seriousness. "Funny is the Expos not tagging the runner. Look," he gestured, laughing uproariously. "Just look at the replay!"

Fuentes politely turned to the television. The screen showed the pitch in slow motion: down and in. A fleet Dodger outfielder named Highsmith connected, gracefully swooning the ball into the gap between short and third. The action cut to the force play at second: a dust storm of activity as the lead-off hitter slid into the bag and the Expos' third baseman confidently brushed his glove across the base runner's body. And then – the fielder's face showed visible surprise as the umpire motioned "Safe!"

"See!" Asuncion hadn't stopped chortling at the absurdity of the act. "The crazy *gringo* went to the man. He should've gone to the bag. *Loco!* Miguel! Those Canadians are all *loco!* They should stick to chasing a rubber thingy on ice and leave this game to people who can play it – Latinos."

"They're mostly all Americans," Fuentes calmly corrected.

"What?" Asuncion screwed up his face.

Fuentes repeated himself. "Except for a few Cubans, some Dominicans, and a Japanese or two, the ballplayers are all American."

"That's my point!" Asuncion countered with a look of victory.

"*Loco Yanquis.*"

Miguel turned back to the binders. He wanted to share his latest observations with Asuncion, but his roommate was totally enthralled by the TV. The Dodgers went on to score six runs in their half of the ninth. The game was tied.

Fuentes took out his notepad and jotted down some words, sufficient to jog his memory, but cryptic enough to be innocuous should someone else see them.

The game went into extra innings. An American playing for a town in a French province called Quebec in a country called Canada hit a home run that stood up, clinching a victory for the Expos and causing Felix to gleefully throw his pillow at the television. They watched the post-game highlights, news, and weather. Asuncion offered his roommate a beer. Fuentes accepted. At midnight they went to bed. Miguel kept his conjecture to himself. It could wait till daybreak.

He was disturbed from a sound sleep at two o'clock by a hollow thud. Asuncion was sitting in the chair, his face haloed by a night-light. He waved a contrite hand in his boss's direction as he lifted a binder off the floor. "Get some rest, *amigo*," he whispered. "In the morning. We discuss it then."

Shortly before five, Fuentes awoke. His partner was snoring, fully clothed, in the chair. The reading lamp was still on and all the binders were neatly stacked on the floor. There was a notepad atop the pile. Miguel leaned over to look at it.

In scrawling longhand, Felix had generated several pages of his own findings. He had highlighted a number of points, quite consistent with the conclusions Miguel himself had drawn from the evidence given him by the military.

Before going back to sleep, Miguel carefully placed a pillow behind Asuncion's head and turned off the lamp. Obregon never did call.

9 They woke early, only a few minutes past seven. While Fuentes briskly donned a clean cotton shirt and pressed pants, Asuncion dressed in the wrinkled suit he'd worn the day before. They met Obregon in the hotel restaurant. He was attired in an expensive beige business suit, summer weight, an Italian cotton, which he'd complemented with a flowery peach and periwinkle tie. His manner was collected.

Over an overcooked breakfast and black coffee, the *federale* asked what Fuentes might need from the Americans to further his investigation. On a scratch pad, Miguel outlined his requirements. They came to five pages of scrawled notes covering three principal issues: motive, opportunity, and outcome.

Obregon offered an astute observation or two, but no more. He ate little. "It's still your case, *hombre*," he remarked airily, cufflinks glistening in the honeyed morning light. "You have a good handle on it."

A telephone call ahead to Davis Monthan firmed up the necessary arrangements. Promptly at ten-thirty, the Mexicans arrived once more at the airbase. A transformed Joshua Bragg awaited them. He apologized for his earlier curtness and then invited his distinguished federal counterpart from Mexico to be his guest for the day. The general commanding the 355 Operations Group would be host. *Señor* Obregon would receive a strategic briefing on Latin Affairs, a private brunch at the Officers' Club, and a leisurely "training flight" in the base's VIP Sabrejet. Obregon basked in a self-important glow. Bragg excused himself to make arrangements.

He was gone but a moment. Upon returning, he begged Obregon's indulgence, then beckoned the others to follow to a sparsely furnished anteroom located off the main hallway.

A lieutenant rose from a hard-backed chair as they entered. In her late twenties, she had a well-rounded figure that her blue summer kit did little to hide. She was slight – only an inch or so over five feet – and her regulation low-cut shoes didn't help. Her jet-black hair, gathered in a bun and collected under a uniform cap, was obviously long.

Sparing them a formal introduction, Bragg explained her presence with staccato brusqueness. Because of her knowledge of supply functions performed by Chandler and her "cultural sensitivity to the issue" – an expression that initially befuddled Miguel – he'd made "this particular officer" available to guide the Mexicans through the remainder of their stay at Davis Monthan.

"Gentlemen," he nodded in her general direction, "Lieutenant Maria Donovan."

"*Señors.*" The young officer smiled primly. Her teeth were white and even.

"Good day, *Señorita* Donovan." Asuncion waddled forward and tendered a genteel handshake.

"Lieutenant Donovan," she corrected, her smile firm.

Donovan shook Miguel's hand with a secure grip. Her fingernails had the faintest gloss on them, a suggestion of rose. Freckles sprinkled high cheekbones, framing eyes that were deep chestnut and expressive. Fuentes sensed the subtle insinuation of perfume in the air. It seemed like lavender. Coming from this precise young woman it was quite pleasant, almost exhilarating.

Miguel's first request was a logical one, a visit to the deceased's home. That would be no problem, Donovan replied affably as she guided them out to the parking lot. A few paces behind them and striding in step, Bragg and Obregon appeared to have become the best of friends.

A Crown Victoria, buffed to a glistening black pearl, a single star pendant attached to the front fender, waited to whisk Obregon and his American host away. Fuentes watched them depart, Obregon comfortably ensconced in the back, the colonel beside him, obviously enjoying a joke.

Donovan started toward a yellow Hummer with personalized plates and a panel painting of a Navajo warrior raiding party riding its sides. She stopped and laughed aloud before heading instead toward a gray government-issue station wagon of uncertain vintage. "Sorry." She opened the doors for her guests. "Almost took you to my new truck by mistake."

As they rumbled out of the lot, Miguel noted the personalized plates on the Hummer: PALOMA. He glanced at his petite host – "dove." How eminently fitting. Fuentes asked affably about her unconventional choice of personal vehicle.

"The four by four?" He caught the reflection of a broad, high-cheeked grin in the rear-view mirror. "I've started to go into the Baja. It's in my blood."

"You like cross-country?"

"Let's just say I like challenges," the young woman replied enthusiastically. "I bought the thing only two days ago."

Asuncion had been peering intently out at the scenery. "Lieutenant?" He was decidedly changing the subject. "Your statement says you last saw Chandler on May 21?"

"Yes. On Monday." Donovan stopped at a school crossing to allow a junior class the right of way. "I met him near the main gate while I was jogging. It was the captain's first day of leave. He was taking the week off."

"What time was that?"

She thought a moment, then replied, "Early. Maybe six. Maybe a little after. We spoke for a few minutes. He'd been very busy on annual inventories and seemed happy to be taking a break from work."

"Do you recall what he was driving?"

"His Mazda. He told me he was heading up to the Grand Canyon to do some hiking. Said he'd never been. He liked hiking. Just last year he went into Mexico, to the Sonora desert, with his dad. They backpacked for two weeks solid."

"And from there?"

A military combine loomed ahead on the narrow road, inching along at ten miles an hour, squat as an armored tortoise, a rotorless Huey helicopter securely battened down with heavy cable onto its flatbed. Donovan expertly weaved around the lumbering rig.

"He didn't say," she answered as she completed the maneuver. "We weren't that close."

"You went on leave soon after that?"

"Yes. Last week. My family lives in Houston, my parents and four brothers."

"Is that where you are from?" Asuncion continued. "Houston?"

"Yes."

"You found nothing unusual about the captain's mood?"

"No. Wick Chandler was always polite. Always pleasant . . ."

"Of course," Felix answered, as if it were a given.

The woman spoke in a melodic voice, striving to be businesslike, with a familiar accent that Fuentes could almost, but not quite, place. Cordoba, perhaps Monterey, pure Spanish at its root but altered somehow, enriched in cadence by its exposure to the American Dream. Whatever it was, he found the timbre quite pleasant.

They pulled onto the gravel roadside at Base Security. A rather young master sergeant named Ticonan had been assigned to accompany them. Blue beret smartly canted on his shaved head, the airman darted out of the blancoed building, hobnailed boots crunching on loose shale.

As they drove off, the topkick outlined arrangements he'd put in place for Chandler's residence. With the captain positively identified as a murder victim, an Ident. team had conducted a full forensic workup. They'd been on-site for nine hours. When they'd finished, an armed guard had been posted overnight at the apartment door. This morning it had been pulled. The deadbolt and alarm system that Chandler had possessed in life would have to suffice to protect his personal effects in death.

And what precisely was included in such a workup? The usual, Ticonan responded with a youthful enthusiasm: video, still photo, print dust. Nothing omitted. When would the results of the tests be made available to them? Ticonan hesitated. They should speak to Colonel Bragg about that particular issue.

They headed into Greater Tucson. At first, the city thoroughfares were teeming bazaars of bargain gas stations, sprawling plazas, and a seemingly infinite variety of fast-food take-outs. But by the time they'd traveled a half hour, the cityscape had subtly transfigured itself into something serenely middle class. Fuentes gazed out at a bland profusion of low-slung ranch houses. Children's toys were strewn about manicured lawns like brightly colored flotsam in a languid emerald sea. A cadmium sun was cemented against a sapphire sky. The car's air conditioner struggled to keep them cool. It was well on the way to becoming a brutally hot day.

Wickham Chandler had lived in a luxury condominium on Sunrise Drive near the Coronado National Forest, precisely three-quarters of an hour's drive from the base. A Tucson police car was parked outside the lobby of the high-rise. Ticonan, vaguely troubled, left to investigate.

After exchanging mandatory courtesies with the two officers, he returned, presumably satisfied that the local presence was purely coincidental. "Just a car trashed in the underground."

Fuentes politely commiserated. It seemed no one was safe any more.

"The boys tell me this place has had a real problem over the last month. Nothing big, though." Ticonan added. "Chickenshit."

"Chickenshit?"

The topkick smiled with artificial politeness. "Smashed car windows. Graffiti on paint jobs. Busted aerials. The usual small stuff."

They exited the station wagon and walked briskly toward the condo. A tow truck labored up the underground ramp and blocked their way. On its hoist was a late-model Cadillac. Its windows had been shattered, its doors and trunk bashed in. Some attempt had been made to torch the vehicle: its front end was charred black around the engine block. Chrome around the grill had bubbled and discolored, and long, oily streaks were traced along its sides. Fuentes checked the rear of the car. The license plate was missing. The initials "VV" had been carved into the paint. There was a decal identifying a dealership in Huachuca City, Arizona.

"The usual small stuff?"

Ticonan shrugged. "Well, maybe a bit more. Youth gangs," he added uncertainly.

He ushered them through a sumptuously appointed lobby and

into a glass-walled elevator. The apartment was located on the sixth floor at the far end of a long, broadloomed hall. Strips of bright yellow crime tape hung from the door frame. The topkick fidgeted with a set of keys until he found the right one. He turned the lock.

A huge living room greeted them, dominated by a central fireplace made of sculpted granite and a rock garden complete with miniature waterfall. Silken-pillowed sofas and massive armchairs drowned in opulent Hopi Indian rugs, while dramatic shaman masks dangled from creamy stuccoed walls.

The design flowed on several levels connected by circular stairs. At one end, immense windows afforded a panoramic view of far-off woodlands; an ultra-modern kitchen occupied the other. Fuentes ruminated. For someone who'd been a champion of ergonomics, Chandler's residence was flamboyantly large. He estimated the place in excess of four thousand square feet, furnished in earth tones cleverly accenting the mock witch doctor façade.

A pile of correspondence lay bundled on a table adjacent to the door. Fuentes picked it up. Nothing out of the ordinary: gas bills, a coupon from a local Thai restaurant, a teaser campaign from a publisher's clearinghouse, membership renewal from *Sports Illustrated*, and a postcard of the Alamo. The card featured a romanticized depiction of buckskinned frontiersmen and troops of the Mexican army of General Santa Anna in their Napoleonic uniforms – snowy cotton fatigues and black shakos – locked in mortal combat atop the crumbling mission walls. On the back was a jotted notation: "If the worst happens …"

It was signed "J.J. Bramble" and postmarked May 17 from Mexico. Fuentes contemplated the message for a moment before he tossed the card back onto the table.

He moved to the kitchen. A microwave, matching dishwasher, and electric oven nestled around a portable television. The fridge held everyday staples: milk, eggs, yogurt, two bottles of Coke, processed meat and cheese, all in sealed packets. There were no fresh foodstuffs, no fruits or vegetables. Miguel considered that a person on vacation wouldn't bother to stock up on perishables.

He opened the larder and found two loaves of whole wheat and a dozen hot dog buns, all untouched. The expiry date on each bag was May 25. The bread appeared to have been recently purchased. Going to the pantry, he found it well provisioned with can upon can of soup, prepared macaroni, and sardines. He checked the electric can opener on the countertop; the blade was clean.

The medicine cabinet in the bathroom provided additional insights. Shaving cream and balm, unscented soap, and a straight razor. Chandler had been a traditionalist in more ways than one. Medicines? Aspirin and off-the-shelf remedies. All the items were sealed. In a corner almost hidden from view he found something intriguing: an empty insulin bottle and a bag half filled with disposable needles. The pinprick scarring on the cadaver and an absence of sugar in the kitchen fit into place. Chandler might have been mildly diabetic.

The study was quite different. It was dark, broadly masculine, with mahogany trim and rich accents; its traditional look had perhaps made it the captain's favorite room. An oak bureau rested atop a flaring red Persian rug. A bust of Lincoln and an oblong glass paperweight accentuated the desk's smooth surface. A bronzed U.S. Army scepter was captive inside the ornament. A pen-and-pencil set and green-domed reading light, the kind found in the chambers of litigation lawyers, completed the effect of diligent precision. The walls held a number of parlor prints – English fox-and-hound scenes bordered in carmine – which accentuated the mottled paisley wallpaper. A vase with moribund roses rested on a three-legged table by the entrance to the room. It seemed the only intrusion into masculine domesticity.

A bay window offered an Arizona sun treakling flaxen onto a ceiling-high case of leatherbound books. Fuentes heard the faint trill of classical music drift through the room. Chopin, if he wasn't mistaken. A mazurka, to be precise. He glanced at the unit. A laser-like light radiated from a micro-stereo. It was probably on a timer. The piece ended. A Spanish announcer came on, asking for musical requests.

The other shelves held a variety of hardbound books. Beyond the predictable Shakespeare and Churchill were more fascinating items – McLuhan and Muggeridge and Camus. All in all, Chandler's reading had been quite eclectic.

Fuentes paused, looking for something he couldn't quite place. He opened one of the texts. The spine made a healthy crack. The pages themselves had a crisp, virgin feel. He glanced at a few others. None had Wickham Chandler's signature in them.

"There aren't any works on the American Civil War," he mused aloud.

"Sorry?" Ticonan said.

"We were told the captain was a Civil War buff. Yet nothing on the topic appears anywhere in his quarters. Don't you find that unusual?"

Donovan suddenly appeared. "Captain Chandler kept all his other effects in a basement storage locker. Now that you mention it," she remarked with practiced charm, "there were some hardcover texts on the subject. We can provide you with an inventory if you want, can't we, Mr. Ticonan?" An abbreviated nod. "The captain always talked about southern battlefields," the lieutenant continued pleasantly. "He planned to go through Georgia this fall."

"I see." Fuentes glanced at Asuncion, who was lingering beside the table with a setting of once-fresh roses. Ticonan hovered. Miguel had had just about enough of this boy scout.

The minutest nod. With exaggerated clumsiness Asuncion tipped the vase over; water and wilted flowers gushed over Ticonan's lustrous boots. A harsh obscenity rent the air. Felix mumbled profuse apologies and offered a handkerchief.

In the commotion, Fuentes was momentarily freed of his unwanted guardian. He walked down the hallway and came upon a closed door. He opened it.

The room was square and painted mauve. The walls held a number of charts. Some were professionally drafted, others mere pencil sketches. A telescope occupied a bright space by the window. Next to it, an artist's tripod held a single sheet of foolscap. A squat teakwood table and black folding chair were the only other furnishings. A small assortment of books were strewn idly atop the table. Fuentes looked at them. A Spanish–English dictionary. A cheap detective thriller. A publication on the grapefruit diet. A pamphlet on U.S. Customs regulations. A PEMEX roadmap of Mexico with the northern states of Sonora and Chihuahua marked with dog-ears.

The foolscap on the tripod was littered with a flood of dots. A series of algebraic calculations were jotted in black marker to one side. The writing was precise. Restrained. The hallmark of a measured man.

A number of the points were more pronounced than the others, like cat's-eye marbles in a sea of pebbles. These formed two discernible shapes: one, a stark five-dotted cross tilted leftward; the other, flowing down from the uppermost tip of the image, a nearly perfect isosceles triangle, highlighted by slashes of red and green.

Fuentes heard the door open and then sensed perfume, that agreeable hint of lavender that reminded him of spring. He became aware of Donovan standing beside him.

The young woman tapped the triangle with an index finger, glancing to the wall maps as if for confirmation. She gestured to the bottom left of the three triangle points. "There's Altair." Then to the tilted cross formation. "That's Cygnus – the celestial swan. And at the apex," she pointed to the upper right, to a circle whose core was furiously accented with lime marker, "is the brightest of the three and fifth-most-luminous star in the summer sky, Vega."

"These figures relate to constellations?"

Donovan nodded. "They seem to." Her fingers dwelled on the limed circle. "It appears the captain had a fascination with Vega, the Lyre Star."

"I'm sorry?" Miguel asked, perplexed.

"It's a tale from the Greeks, from the time of the philosopher Pliny."

"Go on," he coaxed. "I'm intrigued."

"It is said that Orpheus possessed a lyre, which he acquired from the God Hermes. The instrument cast a spell, charming everyone who heard it. Its music persuaded the Guardians of the

Underworld to let Orpheus rescue his wife from the Land of the
Dead. He was warned not to gaze upon her until they reached the
earth's surface. But at the last moment, he broke his word . . . ."
Donovan hesitated. "His wife was pulled back into the Underworld. He was never allowed to see her again."

"And so the story goes." Fuentes smiled.

"And so the story goes." She matched his smile with hers.

"Sad."

"Yes. Most of the Greek myths tend to be."

"Only there's something more." She gestured to a corner of the
sheet, to a small penciled-in item with the numbers 112-
625232329051 and digits 17-05 written next to them. "This doesn't
make sense." Her brow furrowed. "At least not yet."

Fuentes pondered the woman now standing silently next to
him. He found himself wanting to know what she was thinking,
then, in turn, thinking himself foolish for having such a thought.

"You know Greek mythology quite well," he chanced.

"I liked to read it in my spare time at the Academy."

"And astronomy?"

"What else is there in a Texas night?"

Fuentes shook his head in grudging admiration. "I'm
impressed, Lieutenant. Quite impressed."

A blush rose to Maria Donovan's face. She excused herself and
left Fuentes standing alone.

Miguel poked around a bit more, then entered Chandler's
sleeping quarters. It was scrupulously maintained. A bed, corners
tightly tucked, military-fashion, rested beneath a sealed window.
A chest of drawers, full-length mirror, and writing desk with
nothing on it. An exercise bicycle and two sets of weights
completed the effect. Pepper-grained black powder, the kind
police forensic teams use, was everywhere.

"Negative on prints." Ticonan gruffly countered Fuentes's
query before he could form it.

The side table held a functional reading lamp but no books. A
telephone, but no address book, just the base directory. Miguel
picked it up. There were no scribbled notations inside, not even

an underlined phone number. The room suddenly seemed disturbingly sterile.

"May I?" Fuentes held his palms out in practiced anticipation.

Ticonan shrugged and provided a pair of surgical gloves. Miguel snapped them on. "And my partner?" He motioned to the pudgy detective who'd discreetly rejoined them. The topkick tossed Asuncion a second set, then watched with ill-concealed boredom as the two men began to comb the room, starting at opposite corners, working methodically toward its center.

Felix checked the bed. Miguel opened the dresser drawers, one by one. Inside, rows of socks were stowed like tidy hand grenades; shirts, evenly ironed and starched, underwear likewise. There were no T-shirts.

Fuentes entered the walk-in closet. Garments, uniform and civilian, hung crisply pressed, shortest on the left, longest on the right. Mess kit, dress uniform number-ones, daily working gear. A wardrobe of blue and gray business suits sans pinstripe, conservative ties, blazers, and slacks in traditional tones of matte blue and charcoal.

Miguel nimbly ran a gloved finger over the fabric of one of the jackets, a double-breasted gray flannel. The dead man would never have been mistaken for a clotheshorse. His personal livery ranged from drab to two-tone drab. His casual apparel was some-what more adventurous, but only somewhat. It ran to the upscale range of designer golf shirts in traditional colors and chinos, rather than blue jeans. In fact, there were no jeans to be seen.

Fuentes found something else tucked behind a laundry hamper at the rear of the closet: expensive cowboy boots, lavishly embroidered and quite petit – a woman's. The intricate pattern matched the footwear Chandler had been wearing when he died.

He called Ticonan over, asked for the apartment inventory and, receiving it, quickly perused the list. Investigators in their search of the premises hadn't itemized the boots. He drew this discrepancy to the master sergeant's attention. The young man was more than mildly chagrined. He would send someone over to take additional photographs.

"And check for scrapings, would you?" Felix interjected curtly as he rummaged behind the doorway.

Ticonan nodded with barely suppressed anger. It would be done.

Fuentes was silent. "Chandler didn't have a sister, did he?" he wondered finally.

"No," Ticonan mumbled.

"Well," Fuentes's voice rose a notch, "nowhere in the documentation we received is there the remotest mention that the captain might have had a female companion."

"We have no record of a woman's friendship," Ticonan replied timorously. "Really."

Fuentes stared long and hard at the airman. He wanted to say something, then thought better of it. Lieutenant Donovan had entered the room.

"They look like they'd fit you, *señorita*." Miguel gestured to the footwear.

Donovan gave an apprehensive smile. She avoided his eyes. "They're not my style," she responded. "Too *gaucho*."

Fuentes chuckled. "I understand, Lieutenant."

The rest of the condominium didn't take much longer to search. It was tidy to a fault, almost as if someone had been anticipating them. They returned to the living room. The young master sergeant kept glancing at his wristwatch. He seemed anxious to leave.

"You've reviewed his net worth?" Fuentes asked distractedly.

Ticonan stiffened. His face contorted into a large question mark.

"Come now, Top-kick." Miguel's voice carried a tone of irritation. "The dead man's assets. Bank books. Accounts. Sources of wealth. You know," he continued sternly, "something routinely checked in situations like this."

Ticonan remained silent.

"It doesn't matter." Fuentes sighed. "It's probably somewhere in our files. If not, it should be. You can make this very easy, or very difficult. Either refresh my memory on this specific point, or we stay on the base a few more days." A false smile. "And I imagine we all know how Colonel Bragg feels about having us here, don't you?"

The last observation evidently struck a nerve. "The deceased had $19,000 cash in an account at the base branch of the Bank of America," Ticonan said flatly. "The account has been frozen. The captain did his banking by direct deposit. There were no sudden withdrawals."

"But were there any recent cash infusions?" Asuncion interjected. "Say, of the $67,000 variety?"

"None."

"You are certain?"

Ticonan shook his head.

"I beg your pardon?" Fuentes snapped.

"No sir," the master sergeant mumbled.

"Is there anything more?" Miguel pressed. The senior NCO reluctantly obliged.

"The captain had a quarter-million-dollar life insurance policy," he parroted. "His father was the sole beneficiary. The policy hasn't been cashed."

Fuentes peeled off the gloves and pitched them into a garbage pail. "There are no personal photos anywhere. Don't you find that unusual?"

"Captain Chandler was a very private man," the MP replied in a clipped tone.

"His file gave every indication he was close to his father," Fuentes countered.

"Different people show that in different ways." The master sergeant bristled. "Sir." He peckishly mouthed the last expression.

"Certainly." Fuentes smiled without sincerity. "And where does the elder Chandler live?"

"Travis Chandler? Here in Arizona. A town called Benson."

"You've contacted him about the death?"

Ticonan hesitated.

It was left for Lieutenant Donovan to explain. "We haven't been able to find Mr. Chandler Senior yet. He left home last Monday – the fourteenth – and hasn't been seen since."

"Isn't that unusual?"

"No." Donovan spoke with a surge of confidence. "The authorities in Benson tried to reach him. His neighbors said Travis Chandler left for Europe on an extended vacation. German authorities confirm that he rented a car at Dusseldorf International. We don't know exactly where he is at this point. There's a trans-European alert on both car and driver. Compassionate grounds."

"Hummph." The expression on Fuentes's face showed quite plainly that he wasn't convinced of what he'd been told.

Ticonan made to leave the room when Felix halted him in his steps. "One last thing, *amigo*. Before we go."

"Yes?" Ticonan asked sharply.

"Does the air force issue supply officers with a weapon?"

"No. Not generally."

"Did Chandler have an issued firearm?"

"No."

"Was the *capitáno* then a member of a gun club?"

"No." Ticonan searched for footing. "Not that I know of."

"Was a gun registered to his name in any of the United States?"

"No," the master-sergeant answered with swelling annoyance. "Why?"

Asuncion held up a dark windbreaker with a U.S. Air Force crest on its left breast and opened it to expose the inner liner. A faint spray of dark powder speckled the material. "Gun blue," he remarked, with a practiced eye. "Can you think of any reason it might be there?"

"It's possible Captain Chandler was duty officer," Ticonan conceded grudgingly.

"Possible?" Asuncion arched his back. "'Possible' doesn't show anywhere in the notes we received." He toyed with the coat collar. "An essential item of clothing for such a decisive man. Yet, curiously, something he never dry-cleaned. Even though his entire wardrobe looks like it's ready for morning inspection." The detective's countenance curled to a sour sneer. "Help us with this one, *amigo*."

Ticonan's face drained to ashen white.

Fuentes took up the thread. "Given the desert climate, an educated guess would be that Chandler wore this at night." His eyes narrowed in thought. "Correct me if I'm wrong, but don't duty officers pull twenty-four-hour stints?"

"Yes, sir. You're right, sir," Ticonan answered numbly. "He was base duty officer. In April this year. Sir."

"And the coat?"

"That would be issue," Ticonan replied.

"Yet we have no record of Chandler as duty officer on our reports."

"It may have been an oversight." Ticonan paused. "Sir."

"Another oversight," Felix grunted. "Like the boots?"

Donovan placed a hand on Ticonan's arm, directing him to another part of the apartment.

"My apologies for the master sergeant," she whispered. "He's doing his best. This wasn't intentional. It's just that we've been under enormous pressure from Washington to ensure the investigation is done promptly. And comprehensively."

"No apologies required." Fuentes turned toward the airman and granted him a fleeting smile. "The last few days have been rough for all of us."

Their search of the bedroom was at an end. Ticonan phoned forensics and arranged to have them revisit the condominium later that day to photo and inventory the boots. He also requested that heel scrapings be taken for analysis.

After double-locking the door, they returned to the elevator bank. Fuentes pressed the "down" button. The center doors opened. A well-dressed woman in her sixties emerged, leading a miniature poodle with a diamond collar. Fuentes saw a flicker of recognition as she passed Donovan.

The woman appeared to want to say something, then changed her mind. She entered an apartment opposite the one they'd just exited. Fuentes knew that look. It had tentative warmth to it, a metered expression of social acquaintance.

Road traffic was heavy on the return to Davis Monthan. Donovan concentrated on driving. There were junior schools in the neighborhood, it was nearing one in the afternoon, and youngsters were everywhere. Not a word was spoken by anyone. Ticonan, seated in the front passenger seat, gave every indication of wanting to be anywhere else.

As they pulled up to Base Security, they found their path blocked by a parked black Yukon. The afternoon sun faintly outlined wire mesh on smoked windows. An MP hopped out the escort side, pried open the rear doors, and led a handcuffed male in green coveralls into the brig.

"Mr. Ticonan?" Fuentes leaned forward from the back seat. "Did Chandler charge anyone with a discipline offense in the last six months? Sleeping on duty? Insubordination? That sort of thing?"

"We reviewed that possibility," the topkick replied. "The closest incident occurred in February. The captain went after an airman named Buscom for making a false entry in the duty ledger. It seems he'd fudged overtime while working as a senior clerk at Supply. Chandler was his boss."

"What did Buscom draw for punishment?" Felix piped in.

"Two weeks in April. Night picket at AMARC."

"AMARC?"

"The Aerospace Maintenance and Reclamation Center," Donovan explained. "It's the big skeleton fleet you probably noticed as you entered the base."

"Where was Buscom four days ago? When Wickham Chandler was killed?"

"On a training exercise over the North Pacific," Ticonan explained.

Donovan intervened. "You've confirmed that?"

"Affirmative, ma'am." Ticonan gave a vigorous nod. He suddenly seemed quite anxious to show some professionalism. "Accurate to within minutes. The airman was onboard a Charlie 130 transport as the relief cargo-handler. We estimate he was twenty-four thousand feet above the Aleutians at the precise time the explosion happened in Sonora."

"And just where is Airman Buscom today?"

"In Alaska, sir. Elmendorf Airbase. He transferred in the second week of April, right after completing his punishment detail. The C-130 was from that base."

"Did he go of his own accord?"

"No. He was ordered out."

"Any specific reason?"

"I understand Captain Chandler didn't particularly want Buscom around any more," Ticonan commented dryly.

Miguel ruminated over the new information. "Thank you, master sergeant. Your candor has been most enlightening."

"We investigate every scenario." A stubborn pause. "Sir." And the young man's face turned to stone.

Thursday, May 24, midday.
Davis Monthan Airbase, Tucson

10 After dropping off the MP, their next stop was Chandler's office, with the 355th Supply Squadron. The unit's home was a mammoth facility, a melon-yellow hangar over a city block long, with endless rows of transport rigs parked outside enormous delivery bays waiting patiently to be unloaded or filled. Donovan escorted her visitors to a motorized golf cart. The cart transported them at a healthy clip down a passageway under a canopy of cool neon, crammed with cargo pallets, fuel drums, and multi-sized tires, all neatly stacked in elevated bins and held in place by seeming miles of gleaming green steel pipe. The tour took the better part of half an hour and was, at best, superfluous.

They'd been back in the office less than a minute when the door opened. An enlisted man entered, carrying a tray that he placed on a side table. On the tray were three glasses, a tumbler of iced tea, and a side dish of muffins with pats of butter.

"Gentlemen," Donovan cooed. "Refreshments?" She poured the liquid into the glasses. The lieutenant plopped three sugars into her drink. "A sweet tooth, I'm afraid," she remarked with a slight giggle. "I'm lucky my metabolism allows me to splurge without showing it."

Fuentes selected a single cube that fizzled merrily at the bottom of the glass. For his part, Felix passed.

They sat down on the sofa and lounge chairs. After the obligatory small talk, Fuentes began.

"This is where the deceased did most of his work?"

"Yes, this was Captain Chandler's spot. Security's gone over it with a fine-tooth comb," she hastened to add, clearly mindful of her guests' unfortunate discovery at the apartment.

"He had ultimate accountability for all inventory in this building?" Miguel continued.

"Yes."

"I take it that Unit policy has work files backed up on the computer?"

Donovan nodded.

"Copies of which we have from the military police?"

Donovan nodded again.

Felix glanced at Fuentes. Their eyes met.

"There's a question I've always wanted to ask about government warehouses like this one," said Felix.

"Go ahead."

Felix had an angelic expression and looked every part the befuddled country bumpkin. "It would seem relatively easy to misplace something in such a large building. How do you keep track of all the items?"

"You mean, how do we make certain someone isn't stealing from under our very noses?" Donovan responded frankly. "Certainly, after what happened to Chandler, the idea of internal theft entered my mind." She gave a resolute toss of her head. "But I dismissed it outright. Reviewing our system, I'm convinced we would have caught any stealing or attempts at it."

"No matter how small?"

"No matter how small."

"How can you say that?" Felix asked.

"Let me show you." Donovan pivoted her chair so that she faced a computer monitor on the corner of the desk. She turned the machine on, punched in a few characters, and allowed the microchips to do their magic. Within seconds, an olive-green background laced with fine yellow grids dominated the screen.

"Supply operates a computer interface called CAMS/SBSS," she explained. "The Core Automated Maintenance/Standard Base Supply System. CAMS allows technicians to order spare parts and stock replenishments without going through cumbersome red tape. It clarifies accountability at the front end instead of having it hidden behind fifteen copies of carbon-papered signatures."

"That's aircraft-related inventory only, though, isn't it?"

"No. That was before. The expanded system reviews the availability of all stock – not just obvious assets like airplane parts and ammunition. In fact, it houses data for anything you might remotely think could be required in an air base this size: baby talcum, magic markers, car cushions, triple-A batteries, you name it. Constantly."

"But you're primarily a military establishment – not a department store – aren't you?" Miguel chided.

Donovan bristled. "We like to think so."

Miguel continued the line of inquiry. "In the process you've outlined – this 'one-stop shopping' – you could theoretically steal something really dangerous or valuable. And no one would know about it for quite some time."

Donovan frowned, finished her drink, and placed it back on the tray. "That's virtually impossible. Checks and balances exist everywhere in the network. Inventory is programmed so that no person has sole authority to remove critical items, like ammunition, for example. There's always secondary approval somewhere down the line."

"No matter what the rank?"

"No matter what the rank."

Miguel took a lingering sip from his cup. "How can you guarantee it?"

Donovan seemed to anticipate the question. "For starters, at entry level each person has a unique password that's theirs alone."

"As senior base supply officer, didn't Chandler have access to passwords of all the staff, especially his subordinates?"

"No. The captain was very ethical about that point. Five months ago he created a computer protocol to neutralize just such a scenario, one in which individual codes were maintained at arm's length. He said it was better that way, so that no one had complete autonomy within the system."

"So?"

"So, the only person with that information is the system operator for the net."

"Who is?"

"Colonel Bragg. "

"Ah," Felix commiserated. "The mighty Colonel Bragg."

Maria Donovan laughed – a highly pleasant trill that caught Fuentes off guard. "Yes, one and the same. You look troubled."

"It's nothing." Miguel consulted his notes. "Could we see Chandler's last entries again?"

With rapid keystrokes Donovan pulled up the screen. "The very last was on May 20 at 1538 hours – shortly after three in the afternoon. The day before the captain left the base for his holiday."

"What did it involve, Lieutenant?"

Donovan jotted something onto a piece of paper, then turned to a large binder that she removed from a shelf. She leafed to about the center and ran a practiced finger down the page. Her suspicions apparently satisfied, she closed the book and faced them with renewed confidence.

"Nothing dramatic. The code is for floppy disks. Captain Chandler co-authorized the shipment of a quarter-pallet of floppy disks to the base's accounting department."

"How large is a quarter-pallet?"

Donovan pondered for a second before answering. "About the size of a fridge."

"That's a lot of floppies." Fuentes chuckled.

"It's a computer world, gentlemen."

"The person initiating the paperwork?"

"An airman named Moffatt. Damien Moffatt."

"And it was keyed for approval by Chandler, am I right?"

"Precisely. We used a computerized counter-signature for

verification. Floppies, in bulk, are worth a large amount."

Fuentes nodded in agreement.

"That was all?"

"'Fraid so. Scarcely national security, is it?" Donovan smiled.

Fuentes returned to his notes. "Could you tell me what inventory code AC 3382-44 stands for exactly, Lieutenant? It appears here in one of the printouts your colonel gave us."

"Alpha Charlie 3382-44?" Donovan typed the cipher on the keyboard. "Computers. And I can even tell you the exact particulars of the shipment in question." Faint worry lines suddenly creased her brow. "Impossible," she whispered, gazing at the screen.

"I beg your pardon?"

"Impossible," the supply lieutenant repeated in a firmer voice.

"What's impossible?" Fuentes coaxed her.

"Our records show on May 21 at 0303 hours there was a correction overriding the original order that sent the floppies to accounting. The amendment authorized the immediate release of a single computer from our in-transit warehouse to accounting, instead."

She read further. "Later, at 0938 hours the same day, there's an urgent departmental minute indicating that nothing was ever ordered by accounting at all." The worry lines grew pronounced. "And all items were to be returned to stores that date."

"Who authorized the amendment?"

"That's what's impossible, *Jefe*. According to our records, it was Captain Chandler."

"Who was on vacation."

"I saw him leave the base," Donovan stated uncertainly.

"Who paperworked the altered shipments?"

"Airman Buscom."

Fuentes tentatively articulated a misgiving he'd first crafted in the hotel restaurant earlier that morning. "By that date, your people have told us Buscom was in Alaska, so he couldn't have done the paperwork, could he?"

"No," she whispered. "No, he couldn't have."

Donovan turned on her heel and grabbed the nearest office phone, punching the numbers with feverish urgency. Within moments someone was on the depot floor checking the containers in question.

When it finally came, the response was anticlimactic. The amazed look on the airman's face said it all. The pallet that had been returned from base accounting held two full loads of unused computer disks. The pallet that was assigned to the computer was empty – the instrument itself – missing.

"What is the mainframe in this specific instance?" Felix wondered.

"It's a VAX 10-790 micro in transshipment to Fort Huachuca, an army facility just east of here," she explained guardedly. "Near Tombstone."

"Is it valuable?"

"Probably worth $20 million. Maybe more."

Asuncion whistled softly.

"Are there inherent uses to this VAX other than the obvious?" Fuentes asked.

"I beg your pardon?"

"Does it have military applications of a sensitive nature?"

"I don't know," she stumbled. "I can't say." Lieutenant Maria Donovan suddenly seemed very vulnerable.

"I see." Fuentes navigated warily through the awkwardness. "One last question, Miss Donovan. Who was the base duty officer on the dates that Dwight Buscom drew his punishment detail?"

Donovan reached for a clipboard dangling from the side of the desk. "There were two. In the first week it was Lieutenant Steven Lammers. In the second" – she flipped to a new sheet – "Captain Wickham Chandler."

"Were other people on the punishment detail?"

"Just one. Airman Damien Moffatt." She peered disconsolately up from the roster. "But I don't think . . . "

Asuncion emitted an involuntary grunt. Fuentes was more subdued. "I wouldn't be one to tell you your responsibilities," he remarked sincerely. "But I'd carefully review your inventory. You may find you have some serious unfinished business."

The young woman paled. "There's got to be a logical explanation."

"I think you should call Colonel Bragg, Lieutenant."

Donovan appeared not to have heard.

Fuentes repeated his inquiry more forcefully. "Colonel Bragg?"

Donovan excused herself. She stepped to a phone out of earshot and placed a call. The conversation was one-sided; Donovan barely spoke. The exchange ended abruptly: "Yes, Colonel. Immediately, sir."

When she rejoined them, Maria Donovan was visibly shaken. So it didn't shock Fuentes one iota when she asked their indulgence and suggested that they might see themselves out, candidly pleading that "to clear this matter might take some time."

Thursday, May 24, afternoon.
Tucson

11 By the time they'd departed the building, Fuentes had already formulated a plan. It wasn't profound, but neither was their predicament. It was clear now that the United States Air Force, rather than acting in a forthright manner in the murder investigation, had diligently adopted the position of the turtle that does nothing but hunker down in the mud at the first hint of trouble.

For starters, Chandler's condo had contained a veritable treasure trove of untapped evidence, yet no one in authority had seized upon the items until the arrival of the two Mexican policemen. And even then, the authorities had acted with only grudging accord. To be fair, errant boots and windbreaker did not of themselves a murder case make, but they did give a seasoned investigator like Fuentes pause to ponder.

To compound this, Ticonan, the air force sergeant assigned to oversee the crime scene, had either been overly sloppy or sullenly selective in portraying the deceased's life and work. Beginning with his sketchy recall of any person with a possible motive – like enlisted personnel who Chandler might have alienated in the course of his duties – and moving on to his reluctance to discuss the deceased's banking habits and the whereabouts of his blood relatives, there seemed to be momentous gaps in what was passing for an investigation.

Finally, the seemingly respected Captain Chandler had somehow managed to steal a valuable computer from a high-security installation within hours of his untimely demise. Yet no one had noted its disappearance until they'd come knocking. Literally.

Fuentes knew that they needed to find out answers to some, if not all, of these riddles. And soon.

Whoosh! He glimpsed skyward, shielding his face with a forearm. An F-18 darted past at barely a thousand feet, followed in close pursuit by another. And yet another. The sound waves ruffled his hair. The air was dry as sawdust, the mid-afternoon sun an unforgiving fireball in a turquoise sky. In the distance was the brutish growl of heavy hardware revving on the flight line.

They exited at Craycroft Road, accepting a stern once-over from the sentry because of their pedestrian mode of departure. From there, they boarded a city bus, and five stops later they walked into a Tucson police station. After showing their identification, they were ushered into the glassed-in cubicle of the officer in charge.

That individual, a surly six-footer named Matty Greco, was professionally tolerant off the start line, but only just. Fourteen years on the job, and Greco had stomached more than his fair share of Mexican authorities – from their sloppy investigations to their outright belligerence in dealings with Tucson PD. His icy gaze spoke volumes.

However, the Tucson native became eminently more sympathetic – and inestimably more proficient – when Fuentes explained the purpose for their inquiries. The words "murder investigation" had that palpable effect on most people, especially those who liked to call themselves police.

Five minutes later, the three of them were seated around a functional metal desk, the kind that usually graces rural morgues and office furniture auctions, analyzing a printout of calls for service to the Villa Grande apartments – the slew of opulent condos at 500 Sunrise Drive, the last known residence of Wickham Everett Chandler, deceased.

The reporting sequence was in reverse chronology, starting with the most recent contact and backlogging to January of the current calendar year. The first few pages seemed to validate all that Ticonan had told them. Although there had been the expected number of noise complaints, various tenants arrested for driving while under the influence, and a "visitor" to the building taken in on a domestic assault, mostly the police had responded to incidents of petty vandalism.

Then they reached page nine – the month of April – and Miguel began to believe his silent prayers might have, indeed, been answered. For there, in the evening hours of April 12, between 7:05 and 10:23 p.m., were four instances of harassing phone calls, all directed to one party – the occupant of apartment 603, Wickham Chandler. The police attended after the third call at 9:16 p.m. and returned for the fourth and last time shortly after 11:00 p.m. The incident was marked NFA – no further action. Cleared through investigation.

"Did your people know Chandler was an air force officer?" Fuentes asked.

"No. There's no mention of it in the occurrence reports."

"Would your procedures have been different had attending police units known?"

Greco nodded. "We customarily notify base security when it involves service personnel." He reflected on the data sheet. "It seems, in this instance, the complainant was satisfied to have the matter handled by us."

"And?"

"We determined the caller's identity and advised Chandler accordingly. He declined to press charges." The desk sergeant paused to gauge the impact of his words. "We also cautioned the originator of the harassing calls."

"Just who was that person, Sergeant?" Asuncion asked respectfully.

"A man named Moffatt. Damien Moffatt."

"Does your printout list Moffatt's occupation?" Asuncion continued.

"Beg your pardon?" The policeman became oddly obtuse. He sat back in his swivel chair. The seat squeaked.

Asuncion repeated the question.

Greco hesitated. "It states he's self-employed. A car mechanic."

"Was Moffatt known to you?" Fuentes interjected.

A quizzical look.

"Did he have a criminal record?"

"That's restricted information," Greco replied abruptly.

"And we're investigating the murder of an American citizen, *amigo*," Asuncion stormed. "You can help us or jerk us around, *mi amigo*, but murder is murder."

The two sergeants glared balefully at each another.

Fuentes intervened. "Look, Sergeant Greco," he remarked affably. "I respect your position here, but you must also respect ours. Murder is the most serious of crimes. This might be the very lead we need."

Greco seemed to consider the matter. "All right," he conceded. "Damien Moffatt has a sheet. A misdemeanor conviction for possession of cocaine in February of this year."

"The location of the arrest?"

"Los Lobos. It's a bar on Pantano Drive."

Fuentes sensed a certain reluctance in his host's manner. "Anything else?"

"There was a second party convicted with Moffatt. A fella named Buscom. Dwight Buscom."

"Occupation?"

"It doesn't say."

"Figures," Asuncion muttered petulantly.

"I beg your pardon?" Greco snapped.

Felix shrugged. "Nothing."

"Where does this Moffatt live?" Fuentes probed.

Greco looked away. "I gave this information to the people at Davis Monthan already. To Phil Ticonan."

"I'm certain you did," Miguel agreed with a glib nod. "We probably already have that information on the reports Colonel Bragg gave us." He paused. "But don't you think it'd be easier to explain, in the context of everything else in the file, now that we're here, rather than having us come back to trouble you a second time?"

The uniform sergeant briefly considered the Mexican's statement, then scribbled something on a scrap of paper.

"You mentioned Phil Ticonan, *Señor* Greco," Fuentes continued. "You know the topkick?"

"Phil Ticonan? Known him for at least five years. We play squash twice a week at the base's fitness club."

"Oh. I'll give him your best when I see him later today. He's a nice young man. Very competent."

For the first time in their conversation, the tension eased ever so slightly in the desk sergeant's face. "You need this guy's address?" Greco waved the scrap of paper in the air.

"Sorry?"

"You going to check him out?"

Miguel took the paper, pondered a moment, and then handed it back.

"No. I don't think so. Do you, Felix?" Fuentes looked to Asuncion whose expression betrayed nothing. "We'll leave this to base security. They seem to have a solid handle on the file."

"That's a good idea." Greco sounded relieved. "You got wheels?" he inquired. "Or do you need a lift back to Davis?"

"No." Miguel grinned with shallow politeness as they rose to leave. "We have our own transportation, thank you." He hesitated. "One last thing, though, speaking of wheels .... There was a car towed from the underground at Sunrise while we were there. A Cadillac."

"The Caddy?" Greco seemed genuinely surprised. "Didn't Phil tell you? It's registered to Travis Chandler in Benson, Arizona."

"The captain's father?"

"Yes. According to the building super, Chandler usually kept the car in safekeeping for his dad when the old man traveled." Greco shook his head in dismay. "It's too bad some pukes did this."

"So you don't think there's a tie-in to the murders?"

"Nah. Believe me. Scratch marks on the hood? It's the usual. Local punks from the project. There've been six other cars trashed in the past two weeks, all with the same M.O. Not to worry. We'll have a neighborhood meeting or two. Get some community input. Involve our stakeholders."

"And the problem will go away?"

Greco looked at his guest as if he were drunk. "Does it matter? It's a victimless crime, bud. Insurance will cover it. Besides," he observed, "small stuff only ties up our people when they have more important things to do."

"Like towing vandalized cars out of undergrounds?"

Matty Greco pretended he didn't hear the comment.

"Can I have a copy of the damage report?" Fuentes asked.

Greco appeared quite surprised by the request. He hesitated, then went to the photocopier. "Here." He handed Fuentes a duplicate. "Don't know what good it will do you, though. It's just another crime stat."

With that, Miguel's better judgment disappeared. He'd heard the line from Obregon. It didn't sound any more credible coming from this robust cop. "I like to collect them." He smiled with pointed innocence. "It's better than stamps." He winked at the American as they left the station.

As soon as they'd rounded the corner and could be certain they were out of sight of the police station, Fuentes flagged down a Checker taxi. As best he could, he repeated the address he'd gleaned from the scrap of paper. The cabby recognized the location, even with Miguel's broad mispronunciation.

It wasn't far, a fifteen-minute ride to a townhouse in a low-income development on the fringes of the city. A camper-trailer blocked the end of the driveway. Its hitch rested on a cinder block.

A straggly-haired elf of a woman with the temperament of a thirty-year-old stressed past her fifties confronted them behind a rusty screen door. The woman's face was a splotchy cream and coffee color. She wore bargain-basement cutoffs and a faded halter-top and held a two-year-old in pencil-thin arms. Miguel could smell freshly soiled diapers. In the background, the sound of a television blaring and the screeching of youngsters.

"Mrs. Moffatt?"

"Who wants to know?" she muttered, skewing dishwater-gray eyes.

"Police." Fuentes vaguely flashed his wallet identification. The woman seemed weary and disinterested, as if such visits were not unusual.

"Is your husband home?"

"What's he done this time?" The woman hesitated, mustering a façade of self-esteem from what was obviously a depleted reservoir. "Look, he's at work, all right?"

Though it really wasn't necessary, Fuentes pressed. "And work is what? The airbase?"

The woman screwed her face selfishly tight and smirked. "I guess it's for you to find out, isn't it, Spic?" She moved away from the door.

"Listen missus," Fuentes challenged. "I guess all these kids are in your care too, then — aren't they?"

The woman stopped.

"You got a license to provide day-care?"

"You wouldn't."

Fuentes didn't reply. Then he spoke. "So I take it the old man's at Davis Monthan right now, is he?"

The woman mouthed an obscenity.

"Beg pardon?" Fuentes resisted the temptation to answer in kind.

This time she uttered the words with remarkable resonance. Her fierce eyes bore holes into the darkest reaches of his skull.

Miguel placed a finger to the rim of his Stetson and tapped it. "Why, thank you, ma'am," he said with exaggerated politeness. "Thank you kindly."

12

Miguel and Felix returned to the airbase shortly after four o'clock in the afternoon and, before venturing onto AMARC territory, sought out Maria Donovan. The lieutenant seemed gratified to be of service. In fact, just then she seemed gratified just to be doing something – anything.

After they'd left to drive into Tucson, Donovan had met with Colonel Bragg at great length about her discoveries and, in so doing, borne the brunt of his anger. There'd be serious crap to pay for this one, she plainly told her visitors. And without saying another word, Miguel could guess quite accurately where Donovan stood – on the receiving end of that commodity.

Donovan escorted them to her personal vehicle, the yellow Hummer. Fuentes climbed into the front passenger seat. The apple-scented interior of the all-terrain seemed as expansive as an airport control tower. The windscreen was split. Each frame seemed as large as the bay window in Miguel's modest home. A sticker with a vermilion flamingo resting inside a gold circle graced a corner of the front window.

The console housed a stick shift, coin tray and refreshment holders. A plastic Mickey Mouse rested in one of them. The transparent toy was filled with blackball candies. Donovan palmed one and started to suck on it before clicking on the ignition.

The vehicle, in the lieutenant's deft hands, dashed down winding base roads. Suddenly, Fuentes sneezed.

"My cats," the woman apologized as she lowered the passenger-side window. "I have two Siamese. Had them at the vet this morning for their annual shots. You must be allergic."

Fuentes nodded, his face scrunched as he barely managed to control another hearty sneeze. Donovan offered a kleenex. The irritation subsided. He felt the air hot on his face.

The AMARC boneyard was a giant preserve of glistening metal. Tidy files of dust-canopied warbirds stretched along a pancake-flat desert toward infinity. Fuentes contemplated what tales the giant bombers and rafts of missiles might tell if they could, and how they still held the resident power to end the telling of all tales, forever. It was a supremely disquieting thought.

They found Damien Moffatt where his supervisor had said he'd be, slaving with studied indolence to plaster gray sealant onto the wings of an ancient Liftmaster cargo plane. The markings of its new owner – the Paraguayan Civil Defense Force – were freshly stenciled onto the aircraft.

Moffatt proved to be a slight, angular man in his late twenties who wore oversized coveralls that billowed in a skittish wind. On his head was a grimy, duckbilled cap with the words AIR FORCE emblazoned on it. The letters I and F were missing.

The lieutenant beckoned. The airman leapt from the wing onto the baked desert surface. He had ballpoint-blue eyes, a small head with protruding ears, and wore a caustic countenance.

Moffatt slouched before his visitors, nonchalantly wiping grime from stubby fingers onto a filthy towel that he drew from the back pocket of his coveralls. He shambled to a semblance of attention only when ordered to by Donovan. And only just.

The lieutenant was coolly methodical as she introduced her guests as "Mexican authorities who'd like to ask you a few questions."

"'Bout what?" the airman demanded guardedly.

"About you." Fuentes brushed the Stetson back on his head and took off his aviator glasses. "And about Captain Chandler."

The man's eyes narrowed. To Fuentes, Moffatt looked like a trapped lizard.

"I got nothin' to say to these people." He gave a contemptuous sneer. "They ain't got no authority. They're foreigners." He spat the last phrase.

"Airman!" The lieutenant bristled. "You will cooperate. That's an order."

Moffatt shuffled his feet in the sand, kicking up little volcanoes of dust. "What would you do in my place, ma'am?" he challenged pointedly.

Donovan took the airman over to one side, out of their hearing.

They exchanged words. Miguel saw that the enlisted man was becoming quite uncomfortable. The discussion came to an abrupt end. For a time Moffatt stood alone, facial expression mercifully hidden by the bill of his grimy cap.

Fuentes walked over to him. "You worked for a period of time at 355 Supply?"

"I did," the airman replied laconically.

"On May 20, you authorized the shipment of a computer and a quantity of disks to the base's accounting department?"

Silence.

"A $20 million piece of hardware has gone missing, signed out under your authority," Asuncion interjected.

"I did no such thing," Moffatt retorted, squinting under the cap. "Ask Chandler."

"The captain is dead," Miguel observed with brutal candor.

"I know," Moffatt droned with a graceless sneer. "Go figure."

"We're investigating his murder."

"Big deal." Moffatt snickered. "You want me to do handstands for you?"

Miguel let the comment go. He tried a different tack. "Do you know an airman named Buscom? Dwight Buscom?"

"Never heard of him." There was naked defiance in the voice.

"You pulled picket duty with Buscom in April. Wickham Chandler was one of the duty officers."

"Buscom?" Moffatt rubbed his chin. He repeated the name. "No. Can't say as I know him."

"That's funny," Miguel replied with unnerving calm. "In December you were both arrested outside a bar in Tucson. A place called Los Lobos on Pantano. Possession of cocaine. You were convicted this February."

Moffatt hesitated. "Never been there . . ." He cleared his throat.

"Really?" Fuentes pressed. "Well, maybe you're right and we're all mistaken, eh, airman?" A pause. "In April, Tucson police investigated four harassing phone calls to 500 Sunrise – the Villa Grande apartments. Wickham Chandler's place, to be exact. You never told them you were military."

"You got a complainant on that?" the airman answered. "Hear no evil, see no evil," he smirked.

"Point taken," Fuentes conceded. "But your name is on a government supply document involving you in a multimillion-dollar theft."

Moffatt rummaged through coveralls until he found what he was looking for. "You want something else, buddy?" He forced a crumpled business card into Fuentes's palm. "Go call my lawyer. I got nothin' to say till then." He paused. "Better still," he said, motioning to Donovan, "ask her."

Fuentes let the card tumble limply to the ground. He stood so close he could almost count the stubble on the airman's jutting chin. "I have a better idea." He peered icily into the airman's torpid eyes. "Have your lawyer call me – *buddy.*"

Damien Moffatt didn't flinch. "Are they finished, Lieutenant?" he snarled. "'Cause I got a deadline to meet and an airplane here to get ready for export."

Suddenly, three Hummers, painted in dappled cream and beige camouflage, groaned down on them from the distant hard-tack roadway, brewing up a storm of saffron dust in their wake. Activated bar-lights twinkled blue from their rooftops. The vehicles skidded to a halt. Security personnel bounded out carrying submachine guns.

Bragg clambered down from the lead truck. "This area is off limits to civilians!" he roared. "I want you out of here!" He gestured to Moffatt with furious thrusts of his finger. "Him! Take him for questioning. Now!"

The security teams moved in. The airman was trundled into the last Hummer.

"Lieutenant Donovan," the stocky colonel growled. "You'll be in my office in fifteen minutes with a full explanation for this serious breach of regulations!"

The two Mexicans began to stride toward Donovan's truck. A hulking sergeant blocked their way. "This way, sirs," he commanded, motioning to the second Hummer with a combat rifle. Fuentes and his partner were brusquely hustled into the back seat. They were greeted by the sound of an automatic door lock and the company of Ramon Obregon. The truck started with a jerk and butted its way into the center of the tiny procession.

Fuentes had never seen Obregon so agitated. "You went over the line, *amigo*. You had no right to be here without their knowledge."

"I was conducting a simple inquiry," Fuentes responded in an even whisper.

"Without their permission!" Obregon's voice rose an angry octave and drew the driver's attention. The airman peered suspiciously into the rearview mirror, then regressed into practiced indifference.

"I called for you, Ramon," Fuentes deftly lied. "You were unavailable. So I had the lieutenant accompany us."

"She has no authority in this matter, Fuentes," the *federale* chided. "She's only a supply officer. And you? You have no business whatsoever on this part of the base."

Miguel turned to his accuser. "How was I supposed to know?"

"Come on!" Obregon, incensed, gestured out the window. The fence line separating AMARC from Davis Monthan stretched to a far distant horizon. Hitched on the wires with bureaucratic repetition were signs with "RESTRICTED AREA. NO ENTRY TO UNAUTHORIZED PERSONNEL" stenciled in bold black letters. "I wasn't born yesterday!" Obregon thundered.

A long, brooding silence. "Who did you think 'unauthorized personnel' referred to?" Obregon grumbled, sarcastically, after a time. "Armadillos?"

Fuentes could smell peppermint. He knew the *federale* had been drinking.

"Not only did you bluff your way in," Obregon stormed anew, "but you also conducted illegal inquiries and abused our mutual agreement with the Americans!"

"I prefer to say I used my initiative to confirm some facts," Fuentes responded defensively.

They neared the junction connecting AMARC to the main base. The driver negotiated a downgear and the Hummer screeched reproachfully.

"All right!" Obregon smoldered with thinly disguised rage. "Play word games with me! Call it what you will! You haven't done me any favors with the *Yanquis!*"

Fuentes was beside himself. "Doing you favors?" he blurted. "I don't see how that matters! Frankly, there's much more to this than meets the eye. Drug smuggling! Secret computers! It's all here at Monthan, if you'd just take a moment to look around. "But then, it's like the NEDEROIL inquiry all over again, isn't it?" Miguel pressed bitterly. "You don't like offending powerful institutions or people, no matter what the price. After all, Colonel Bragg is such a wonderful host, isn't he? That's what makes you the perfect *comandante* for Sonora, Ramon. You're too busy jetting over Arizona with an air force general to care any more what real crimes are."

A taut silence filled the back seat of the Hummer.

For the first time in their conversation, Obregon smiled, and Fuentes realized then that he had gone too far.

"You have such a perverse hatred for me, Fuentes, that you've lost your objectivity." he glowered. "You have no sense of what really matters. No sense of place. No sense of time. Certainly no sense of purpose. And that's why I'm taking this criminal matter out of your hands."

"I beg your pardon?" Miguel mumbled, in shock.

With a terse movement Obregon reached into his suit jacket and thrust a flimsy sheet of paper into Miguel's lap. "As the senior *federale* in Sonora, I'm taking over command of the inquiry. Read it!" he demanded. "You're being placed on notice effective this minute! Ninety days and you're history."

Fuentes glared at his tormentor, then skimmed through the message. There were three pages. The first was a communication to the Ministry of Justice in Mexico City requesting the replacement of Coronado's municipal police force with *federale* personnel. It was signed by Hector Rivera, the *delegado*, titling himself somewhat fatuously "a concerned citizen," written on PRI stationery.

The other sheets were pro forma reply. Full-fledged approval for the takeover from on high, with all the gaudy seals and mastheads that went with it. But it was the last page that was most disturbing, for it appointed *Señor* Ramon Obregon, provincial commander, as the future regional Director of Policing for Coronado.

His companion couldn't resist a smirk. "It's a done deal, my friend. After ninety days your town goes *federale*."

Miguel seethed. "The date on the fax from Justice approving the turnover? It's four days old."

For a split second Obregon's eyelids flickered.

"You knew about this before we came here, didn't you?" The Hummer slowed for a stop sign. A platoon of military personnel jogged across their path at the double.

Obregon quickly gathered his composure. "When we spoke several days ago, you had a reasonably important role to play in this investigation. It's now patently obvious that you can't conduct an inquiry of this magnitude." The glacial smile. "It's clear that if I don't remove you from this matter right now, you'll hang yourself out to dry once more with your big mouth and conspiracy theories. Just as you did with NEDEROIL!

"In spite of what you might think, I've tried to be decent, tried to give you a chance to redeem your career." Obregon sniffed with practiced remoteness. "And you blew it!"

Fuentes felt a discreet tug on his arm. From the corner of his eye, he caught Asuncion's subtle hand gesture. He wisely acquiesced.

The Hummer pulled onto Madeira and stopped in the Law Center parking lot. The driver motioned them out.

"Fuentes!" Obregon commanded bleakly as they strode toward the entrance.

Miguel halted. "*Si.*"

"In future, you'll report everything you or your people do in furtherance of this matter. It will be submitted by six each morning. To me. On *federale* format and in triplicate." The sun reflected off Obregon's dark glasses. "Have I made myself clear?"

Silence. A rude gust of wind flung dust into Miguel's face. He nodded.

They followed the guard at a brisk pace, the sounds of their feet reverberating down the vacant hallway like a fusillade. It was an inevitable and unavoidable issue of protocol that they visit Bragg one last time.

The colonel kept them waiting in an antechamber for twenty minutes. Obregon was allowed in first. After a further eternity spent cooling their heels, the door opened and Fuentes and Asuncion also entered the office of the American official. There was another person in the room, a mousy individual wearing a rumpled brown suit and cherry bow tie that Bragg identified as Homer Styles from the Reconnaissance Bureau in Washington. Fuentes was never told what the Bureau was. He assumed it had to do with military surveillance.

The meeting was strained, but that was to be expected. With a bleak smile, Bragg formally accepted Obregon's apologies on their behalf for what he termed a most regrettable faux pas. As a token of reconciliation, the colonel presented each with a matching pen and pencil, cast in Air Force blue.

Obregon gave his host an ashtray that he removed from his briefcase with the flourish of a magician taking a rabbit out of a hat. It was made from potter's clay and stippled in red and green pastels. It bore a vague resemblance to an eagle rampant – the seal of Mexico.

Then it was his turn. As Bragg waited irritably, Miguel fumbled about his lapel. He offered the American a tiny enamel pin with the town seal of Coronado and the words *"Jefe de Policia"* scripted on the base. The colonel's face was like stormhewn granite as he thanked them.

Before they'd crossed the threshold of the door to leave, Styles had moved behind the desk and was on the phone, his back to them, whispering angrily into the mouthpiece. It was as if he owned the place.

They departed Davis Monthan. Fuentes suggested a stop at the Base Exchange to get snacks for their trip back to Coronado. He told Obregon they were hungry, since he and the detective sergeant hadn't had an opportunity to have lunch. Obregon pulled the Buick into the parking lot, then snapped the car into park as he turned off the ignition. With a dismissive flick of his hand, he motioned for them to be quick.

The confectionery section was nearly empty. Fuentes went to a cooler by the magazine stand and selected a pre-wrapped roast beef sandwich and a quart of two percent milk. Asuncion, as was his habit, plucked a large bag of salt and vinegars from the chip rack to go along with a large bottle of diet Coke.

The girl behind the cash was *Chicana*, pretty and bored.

"Miss?" Fuentes asked after paying for his purchases. "Could you possibly tell me what this is?" He foraged in his pants pocket and removed a photocopied credit-card receipt. The words "Base PX" were at the top of the sales slip with the date, May 20. The initials of the seizing officer and property tag number were scribbled to one corner in black ink. Miguel skipped the items readily identified and drew the cashier's attention to an anonymous numbered purchase – one valued at $4.93.

"It's from our store," the girl said in a flat voice. "From the candy aisle."

"Could you be more specific, please?" Fuentes spoke in Spanish. He showed her his badge.

As she peered at the peculiar identification, the cashier's reluctance melted into curiosity. She opened a drawer beneath the register, took out a logbook, and opened it. "We ran a special a few weeks back," she replied after scanning a list. "A Mickey Mouse character with candy inside."

"What was the candy?"

"Blackballs."

"Pardon?"

She gestured to a display where a shimmering mountain of charcoal-colored candy rested.

"Are they sweet?"

"Try for yourself."

Fuentes took one, rolled it about his mouth, then bit into the hard surface. He grimaced as the sugar trickled around his gums, then spat the remains into a handkerchief. "Do you sell many, *señorita?*"

"Only for kids. And anyone with a sweet tooth."

"Not a diabetic, then?"

The young Chicana dismissed the thought with a resolute shake of her head.

Fuentes thanked her and moved toward the exit. His eye caught something plastered to the windows. Next to a promotional display for suntan lotion was a poster for the Pima County General Hospital Building Fund. It offered a new car as grand prize, an all-expenses-paid holiday to Britain for two for the runners-up, and membership in a luxury fitness spa for a year as the third and final prize. The trademarks of all sponsors were prominently displayed: General Motors, British Airways, and the donor of the last prize – the club membership – a vermilion flamingo inside a golden circle.

"A last question, *señorita?*"

The cashier was balancing the till receipts for her relief. She turned to him. "Yes?"

"What's this company?" He motioned to the flamingo.

"That? Kachina Village. They own the club."

"Where is it located?"

"Across the street from the base." The girl was in obvious haste now, her manner harried. It was after four o'clock and she had a date. "Above their condos."

"Lots of air force types live in Kachina?"

"Only those with money," she groused, as she divided receipts into tidy little mounds. "Officers, mostly." She turned her back on this abrasive stranger, hoping he'd go away.

"On second thought," he gestured to the blackballs, "can I have some of those, please?"

"How many?"

"A dozen."

She mimicked his words in disbelief. Miguel seemed perplexed. "Is that too many?" He didn't hear the murmured response, but he would have easily understood the utterance. It had nothing to do with candies. Or sweetness, for that matter. The total came to eighty-five cents.

Before leaving the store, Fuentes placed a phone call to an old friend from Brownsville in days gone by, now posted to U.S. Customs at Nogales. He suddenly knew with remarkable clarity the license plate that he wanted run on the computer. It would have crossed into Mexico within the past few days and returned to the United States within hours of the explosion at Zita's. Taking a healthy bite of roast beef, he returned to the Buick.

Thursday, May 24, night.
Coronado

13 They arrived in Coronado at twilight. A lingering film of pollution, the texture of heavily iodized gauze, clung to the town. From a distance, the buildings were stippled as though with washed inks.

Traffic muddled through narrow streets like a gaggle of old women trapped in a funeral procession. Obregon negotiated a series of red lights to hasten their progress back into the downtown core.

The *federale* dropped his passengers in the town square and drove off with the car stereo oozing Brahms from the public broadcasting station beaming out of Phoenix. He couldn't take them to the police building, he said without apologizing; he was late for an appointment. But Miguel knew better. Ramon was still fuming about Davis Monthan. The thought of that discomfort brought the vestige of a smile to Fuentes's tawny face. Perhaps there were small mercies after all.

Miguel and Felix wandered down Avenue Valencia in the general direction of the faltering brownstone that housed the *policia*. The structures along the avenue were fairly modern, built in the Forties from a mottled stucco design that quickly weathered. Ground-floor businesses had full-length grilles to protect against break-ins. These were parted on many, revealing the cluttered shops inside. Nearly all the windows above street level had shutters, their original pastel veneer now largely faded to anemic shades of mango and plum. Potholed sidewalks teemed with people going home and refuse going nowhere. A municipal garbage truck inched down a squalid back lane. The sky turned milky gray, the air grew increasingly muggy. Fuentes tasted the gritty tang of road dust on his lips. It was an evening that would bring thunder near midnight.

They reached the office. Asuncion held the door open, then followed in his *jefé's* wake. Fuentes sighed as the cool air surged damp as a burst watermelon onto his body. He could feel his underarms moisten with the chill.

There was only one person in the place, Pluto Velas, one of the older uniform types. Slab-featured, broad as an ox and not nearly as bright, Velas had been a *policia* for thirty-six years. He performed this work because he lacked the skills to make it as a criminal. He'd earned the nickname Cement Head from his contemporaries – and not without reason. Miguel had it on good authority that on attaining adulthood Velas had tried to join one of Coronado's many street gangs, but had been unable to pass any of the initiation rites. So he'd reconciled himself to the lower pay and diminished social prestige of the police.

Velas lounged in Miguel's armchair in semi-slumber. His puffy face slumped forward onto an avalanche of chins. Curly tufts of hair sprouted from beneath a stained open-necked shirt. Pants soiled from a generous feeding of fried beans draped his gargantuan form. On his feet, Pluto wore a pair of green sneakers that would have seen better days on a corpse – and that, Miguel reflected cynically, is probably where he'd stolen them from. A filthy cross-strap tried to hold in his stomach. A pager was attached to the webbing, a device with a read-out option that seemed out of place, but Pluto paid for it out of his own pocket.

Pluto said he needed it to keep in touch with his informants, of which there were assuredly many. Yet in all Fuentes's time in Coronado, Velas had yet to receive a shred of criminal information from one of them. It was more likely that the pager allowed Velas to receive point spreads from his bookie.

Prior to Fuentes's appointment as *jefe,* the Coronado force had, by ethical attrition, annually churned through half its complement, yet Pluto Velas had always managed to keep a chunky toehold on his job. Some in the community said he'd accomplished this by liberally bribing his previous bosses – including personages as powerful as the *delegado* himself – with a cut of the action. Others were more humane in their estimation of his dubious talents. To them, he was merely a profoundly incompetent ignoramus who'd evolved into the perpetual object of supervisory pity.

Initially, Fuentes had accepted this rudimentary explanation for Velas's continued existence on the force. With his ponderous girth and convoluted blend of gullibility and guile, Pluto personified all that was wrong with Mexican law enforcement. He was an offensive boor in a town that had accepted that as the standard of its policing for far too long.

But there was more. Guardroom gossip quickly fingered Velas as the number-one contributor to Hector Rivera's "fink file," with the new *jefe* openly identified as the *delegado*'s principal target for destruction. It was rumored that Velas would sell his soul for promotion to *sergente* and the cash cow that he assumed went with those elusive stripes, and that he'd do anything to destroy Fuentes to achieve the rank.

In Miguel's initial month in Coronado, several allegations were made about him: foggy whispers of kickbacks extorted from tow truck-operators, pilfered prisoners' property, and padded investigative expenditures. All such rumors were unsubstantiated and all seemed to have their genesis when Velas was on duty.

A week after the first of several fusillade incidents had Swiss-cheesed the walls of Fuentes's *casa* an anonymous caller had pointed the accusatory finger right at Pluto. Miguel had thought little of it.

But while he was out walking Salinas, he'd chanced across Pedro, the retired accountant who also lived at the San Cristobal crossroads. The accountant had reluctantly described a man who "could have done" the deed – someone in green sneakers, heavy-set, driving a car that looked remarkably like one of the town's marked patrol units. Thereafter, the die had been cast.

Corruption and disloyalty were pervasive within Mexican policing circles. Miguel could cope with such traditional demons. What truly troubled him about Pluto were the latest batch of rumors, suggesting that Velas was no longer "quite all there," that he'd begun to dabble in the occult, the Dark Side. Corrupt cops were one thing; *loco* ones were yet another.

A portable television droned from atop the bookshelf. The news announcer jabbered on about the current unrest in Chiapas, where a regional bus had been ambushed outside the town of Arriaga. Rebels had murdered five passengers. That made a total of eighty-nine deaths in the past four months.

President Estrada had hurriedly called a press conference in Mexico City. The army was being sent in to restore order. The last time that had happened was in 1995. Estrada had been in office less than half a year and had already been losing his grip. But had not been unexpected.

He'd been an unpopular compromise candidate selected to replace Ernesto Zedino, who'd suffered a massive stroke five days after the NEDEROIL investigation had gone public. There were leaks about palace revolts in the federal cabinet, attempts to have Estrada replaced by a stronger figure. And like all Mexicans, save the occasional village idiot, Fuentes knew that in the lexicon of the PRI "stronger" meant someone more acceptable to the thirteen ruling families who ran the nation as if it were their private piggy bank.

The television showed dead Zapatistas left behind by their peers in the aftermath of a village ambush; stickmen stained crimson. Some wore jungle khaki, others the battle dress of the revolutionary: blue denims and cheap sneakers. Most wore the telltale orange-and-white polka dot bandanna of their movement knotted around their necks.

The newsreader switched to a looming crisis in Tajikistan, poorest of the former Soviet republics of Central Asia, where, after a four-year UN-brokered truce, the Taliban, an Islamic revivalist movement that had previously captured most of neighboring Afghanistan, threatened the Tajikistani capital of Dushanbe. Russian paratroopers had been invited in by the ruling Tajik regime, and twenty-five thousand now uneasily patrolled the troubled area. The camera switched abruptly to a guerrilla camp somewhere in the mountains abutting Afghanistan as Taliban rebels, clenching captured Kalishnikovs and SA-7 Grail shoulder-fired, surface-to-air missiles in their callused hands, smiled bashfully out at the universe.

The next story concerned a major devaluation of the ECU, Europe's new common currency. The run on European money markets – the third in under a year – had begun innocently enough, but now resembled dysentery. The closing story was a short documentary on the upcoming visit of the Pope to the American Southwest. Parade routes and mass at Sun Devil Stadium in Phoenix were going to require elaborate security.

Fuentes loudly cleared his throat. Velas started with a porcine grunt. Seeing the *jefe,* he shambled to the vaguest semblance of attention, stumbling to switch off the television as he did so. After a shabby greeting, the patrolman grudgingly departed the cool of the office for the muggy evening outside, straightening a grime-encrusted forage cap on his matted red hair as he did so.

In the ComCen, Stella sat engrossed in a glossy romance magazine, unaware they'd returned.

"*Jefe!*" she sputtered as she spied his frame looming in the doorway. "You're back!" She thrust the periodical under a pile of knitting. "Did you have a good trip?"

"*Sí,*" he replied with a canny smile.

"A full record has been kept," she gushed, handing him a plain diary. But her demeanor changed abruptly as Fuentes examined the journal, creasing his brows occasionally as he tried to decipher the haggard handwriting. "Don't blame me, sir," she stated accusingly. "It's Velas's work."

Fuentes couldn't be bothered with such pettiness. He skimmed through the notations. There were several pages of them. As he'd already suspected, there were no new leads in the homicide investigation. But life went on, even if death didn't.

An arrest outside the PussyKat bar had led to charges of possession of a switchblade against a migrant Honduran. Three break-ins had occurred. In the most enterprising, someone had stolen an ancient six-foot by four-foot ice cooler from Conchita's Diner by entering through a skylight in the roof. The exit was presumably the same. The cooler's contents, forty-three bottles of beer, were also missing.

Federales who claimed the play as their own had ordered off the three-person town *anti-narcotico* squad doing cocaine "obs" out by Querobabi. Fuentes could read only too well between those lines. It wasn't worth arguing about to Obregon.

There'd also been a suspicious death the previous morning: the raw bones and ashes of a body found in a farmer's clearing, five miles east of the town limits. Little was known about the deceased – even the gender was amorphous. An empty jerry can and a short note tipped the scales toward suicide. But Fuentes was disinclined to accept the obvious.

The suicide note was typed in a jumbled mix of upper and lower case, clinically brief and singularly unhelpful: "I CanT LIvE aNY loNGeR. Im SORry. GoODbyE." It was unsigned. An autopsy underway in Hermosillo might narrow the investigative variables, as would analysis of the note by forensics. That was about it – for now.

Nine property-damage accidents and a stray cow left for a vulture's banquet by an unknown transport on the southbound tollway completed the police blotter. In every other respect, Coronado appeared to have survived quite nicely in Fuentes's short absence. As it would continue to do – at least for the next thirty or so days until Obregon inherited the flip-charts and crayons.

Fuentes returned the logbook to Stella. Handing her a slip of paper with a series of letters and digits scratched on it, he requested that a registration be run through the American NCIC system, and the results be checked on the forty-eight-hour no-hit file.

The figures he provided were from the impound sheet Greco
had reluctantly surrendered. They corresponded to the Vehicle
Identification Number of the car towed out of the underground.
The forty-eight-hour file would record all instances in which the
Caddy had come into contact with authorities in the past two
days – anywhere in the United States or Canada – provided that
the license data had been recorded at the time. Much as he
trusted the accuracy and integrity of law-enforcement types like
Greco – which wasn't a lot – Fuentes had long ago learned the
number-one dictum of his profession: check everything, even the
patently obvious. Yourself.

He had a nagging suspicion about the Cadillac, a tiny molecule
of doubt that a vehicle so superficially clean, albeit bruised, could
have been stored underground for so long without a speck of dust
on it.

As they left the room, the dispatcher rummaged feverishly
through her knitting. Within moments, she was once again
devouring the latest gossip on the British Royals. The vehicle's
particulars could wait until she'd finished the article.

Miguel went to his desk, plopped into an armchair, and
reached out to grab the baseball trophy from its mount. He
plucked at some loose stitching, then began tossing the ball idly
into the air. Asuncion went to the watercooler, took a paper cup
and filled it. The cooler gurgled. The detective sat down on the
sofa, which sagged noticeably.

"You seem preoccupied, *Jefe*."

"A little." Miguel twirled in his chair. "I have to wonder why
Bragg didn't tell us about the airmen."

"Buscom and Martin?"

Fuentes nodded. "Regardless of what the colonel has stated, the
American military must've known what those fellows were up to.
I can't believe they didn't." He pitched the baseball in Asuncion's
general direction.

The detective snatched it with a ham-handed grasp. "Those
two? I'm certain the U.S. Air Force has its own reasons for keeping silent."

Fuentes cupped his hands behind his head. "A murder investigation is not a good reason."

His portly subordinate toyed with the ball. Grinning, he tossed it back to Fuentes, who caught it with his fingertips and held it motionless in the palm of his hand.

"It is, if this is more than an uncomplicated drug murder." Felix absently brushed his forehead. "As I said before," he continued, "we must find everyone and everything that Chandler dealt away. And why."

The detective inched forward on the sofa. The springs groaned. "With a multimillion-dollar computer missing from the warehouse, it isn't illicit drugs alone that we're looking at. And speaking of alone," he sniffed, "I believe the *capitano* had accomplices other than the airmen." Fuentes contemplated what his traveling companion had said. He flipped the baseball back to Asuncion, who dropped it. "And you told me the *Yanquis* were poor ball players?" he contested in mock derision.

They laughed. Then Fuentes turned suddenly serious. "Why do you think there were others?"

Asuncion shrugged. "It's just a thought I have, a sense that Chandler needed the cooperation of someone very trusted to enable him to do such things and for so long a period without official detection."

"I agree with you."

"Is that why you used the pay phone at the Base Exchange?"

"You knew?"

"Naturally," the detective chortled, his vast stomach heaving. "You'd check out Saint Peter at Heaven's Gate, *Jefe*."

"And you wouldn't?"

"What do you think?" Asuncion's face was unexpectedly somber.

"I think we may be on the right trail with this one, Felicio." Asuncion stood up and stretched. "And I think I'm hungry. How about Eng's for some Chinese?"

A *federale* motorcycle bearing an enamel-helmeted cop roared up just as they were about to close the office door. Overtly in love with himself and his Harley, he saluted sprucely, took a lean folio from a shoulder pouch, and was gone before Fuentes had time to ask any questions.

The document was addressed to Miguel. It profiled autopsy results on the death in the farm field and, stapled to them, forensic findings that confirmed the obvious. The suicide victim – a male, white, in his early thirties – had died from burn wounds. He'd had gold-capped teeth and a bad liver. His nose had been broken several times, as had three fingers on one hand and two digits on the other. The breaks were old; rheumatic swelling had set in. There was also a large quantity of heroin found in his system.

A copy of the field report was attached for ready reference. There were no syringes found around the body, no overt evidence of violence at scene. And there the trail might have ended.

Fuentes flipped the page and found what he needed. The charred husk in the candid photo didn't look at all like the inso- lent mugshot affixed to the folder. But then, he mused wryly, it only confirmed what he'd long suspected – that beauty was only skin deep, after all.

The forensic lab positively identified the corpse on the coro- ner's gurney. Prints on the suicide note matched those from a two-year-old minor assault charge. In addition, a dentist in Acapulco had kept thorough records. The X-rayed rear molars were a neat match to the corpse's teeth. The human ashtray had been Eduardo "Fast Eddie" Bono, age thirty-four. Listed occupa- tion? Personal escort. Hobbies? Predictable for someone in his profession: sex, booze, and violence. Ambition? To live to thirty- five, only he hadn't made it.

In some respects, this new information proved revealing, disturbingly so. But in too many others, it left Fuentes howling in the wind, no closer to the truth, whatever that was. He handed the file to his detective. Images of Fast Eddie Bono in an absurd lime leisure suit and a smartass kid strewn lifeless on a midnight highway raged uneasily within.

14

The restaurant was empty, but Asuncion and Fuentes slipped into a booth at the back. After ten minutes, which Felix spent in the kitchen rousting his informants by phone, they ordered "the usual." Over a bowl of Singapore noodles and lukewarm beer, served in a chipped pitcher, the detective briefed his boss about what had been accomplished by his "fleas" to unearth possible suspects for the bomb murders.

"I can assert that my people have fanned out over the countryside," the *sergente* intoned augustly between mouthfuls of noodle. "All is being well looked after." The vigorous wave of a fork-filled hand. "They have many leads. Many ideas."

"You mean they have nothing to report," Fuentes countered with stark frankness. He picked at a bit of curried shrimp on his plate.

"Yes . . ." the detective stumbled. "Well, no . . ." Asuncion retraced this now-familiar path with a flustered smirk. "No, not yet. But soon." He nodded, generous jowls quivering with emphasis. "On the drugs. I have a good man who'll get me a definite answer on their origin. And *pronto.*"

"Soon isn't good enough." Fuentes nibbled at a prawn. "I need this bombing solved and quickly. I need results, Felix. Not leads. Leads are for cub reporters."

"Right." Felix briskly downed his third beer. He pushed the tumbler to the center of the table. "They have many leads," he muttered again, vaguely.

Miguel caught the unsubtle gesture. A nod in the direction of the kitchen. Within seconds, Eng had refilled the empty glass.

Asuncion took a toothpick from his combat jacket and pried it in his teeth. "Are you going to surrender control of the inquiry to Obregon as he demands?"

Fuentes patted a paper napkin across his lips. "No, Felix," he said with quiet conviction. "As long as I'm *jefe* of this town, it is my right and responsibility to investigate."

The sergeant shook his head. "But you can't go behind Obregon's back!" he warned. "You've been expressly forbidden to do so!"

"Who says I am?" Fuentes replied slyly. "I was given a direct order to report my findings daily to the *federale* head in Hermosillo. This I intend to do. At no time did Obregon tell me to cease seeking the truth."

Asuncion belched. "This is important to you, isn't it, Miguel?" he chanced.

"It is," Fuentes answered in a sober voice. "Trust me, it is."

"Why?" Asuncion asked, a look of practiced innocence in his eyes.

Fuentes sighed. His tormented mind lurched back to another time, to a raucous hearing room in Mexico City.

"Because I sense there are secret things at play here, *hombre*," he remarked finally. "Unpleasant things happening, undercurrents. And I mean to discover what they are."

"Even if it means your job?"

"They have my job," Fuentes replied with grim resolve. "They'll never have my integrity. And that integrity means I shall remain *jefe* in Coronado until the very last second of the ninetieth day." Fuentes smiled then, a tired smile.

Asuncion crunched the toothpick to pulp and spat it out. "Then I shall see to it . . ." He excused himself and disappeared back into the kitchen.

In a minute the detective returned. "We meet my man at two this morning," he whispered. "He swears he'll have an answer for us."

"And where do we encounter him?"

"The Barrio, *señor*. We rendezvous just outside the Barrio."

They spoke little for the balance of dinner. When they'd finished eating, Fuentes filled their glasses and toasted their good health. The bill arrived on a cracked tea saucer. As always, Fuentes paid. And as always, Felix Asuncion mumbled his thanks.

On the way out, Fuentes called his office to inquire about the NCIC vehicle check. Stella answered the phone, her voice deceitfully melodic. The American system was down for maintenance. She expected results after midnight. She'd make certain the night dispatcher paged him immediately when these came in.

Two in the morning was not a time for an old man to be in the Barrio, Asuncion thought to himself, not even with a handgun and eighteen rounds. Ahead, he barely made out the orange plumage of his guide and the sheen of an expensive leather bomber jacket. Behind, he sensed his chief's calm, measured footfall.

The Barrio was built on a rank, clay floodplain several feet below the main highway. Sheet-metal cages masqueraded as dwelling places and shimmered eerily in the moonlight. The site was a patchwork quilt of corrugated zinc roofs and walls made of cigarette cartons, cardboard, and black plastic wrap. Naked electric wiring stretched from hovel to hovel, attached precariously at various junctions to slivered bamboo poles. The cables sparked in the damp night air. There were no defined paths to follow. Canted duckboards made of rotten wood covered a muddy slop of human sewage and the remnants of garbage. The planks wound veinlike into the heart of the settlement, connecting what passed for civilization to this shriveled appendage of humanity. A baby wailed; mariachi music from a portable radio lingered feebly in the inert air. A human cough ratcheted into the pitch black.

The air reeked of fecal droppings and deep-fried beans. Other than the loathsome smell, the thing that Asuncion noticed each time that he chanced into this wretched place was the charged closeness. Everywhere it seemed there were witches' eyes peering at him. Creatures slunk about in the shadows, some human, some not. Rats. Dogs. Other things.

They walked for ten minutes in seemingly endless circles accompanied by the eerie jangle of a strand of chains suspended from the biker's jeans and the firm crack of his hobnailed boots on the planking. Papagayo led them ever inward into the bleak heart of the Barrio of Santa Lucia.

Fuentes had never met the biker before. There'd just been time enough for rushed greetings on the gravel shoulder by the tollway before they'd descended into this seventh circle of hell. But he'd taken an instant dislike to the man and sensed the feeling was mutual.

The hut was single-story and located at the confluence of several trails. Mountains of empty oil drums and shipping crates were its only immediate companions. The premises were ingeniously constructed of rusting billboards. Images of Burma Shave and 7-Up collided with Colgate Toothpaste and Oscar Meyer Wieners. A dull hum emanated from a wooden pallet that served as the entrance. The hum had a calypso beat.

The biker pulled back the pallet. It took Miguel a few moments to grow accustomed to the raw dimness. The impotent bluish glow of a computer screen constituted the only light source within. His eyes strained as he gazed around the chamber. Vegetable crate and *serape* partitions formed a sleeping area, sitting room, and kitchen. Snapshots of male children adorned what passed for walls. The earthen floor was littered with refuse: candy wrappers, beer cans, old chicken bones, grit-encrusted cutlery. A cheap tape recorder rested on a three-legged table. It played Belafonte.

A laptop computer rested on a fruit crate next to the table. The screen was set to a CD-ROM war game, one with jet fighters swooping about in simulated combat.

In the light cast by the screen, Fuentes could make out a vaguely human form huddled in front of the computer. The face was a mass of scar tissue zippered together by staples and sutures. It was wrapped in filthy towels. A crippled foot emerged from swathed layers and kept time to the music.

A foul odor Fuentes could not immediately place permeated the room. He abruptly realized that it came from decaying skin, and gagged.

Papagayo spoke a few words to the specter, arms confidently folded across his chest. "Gentlemen," he offered gently, "this is the one who is called The Gatekeeper. His name is Felipe."

Fuentes gritted his teeth and mumbled hello, but Asuncion was virtually fawning in his attempts to be friendly. "Good to see you, *señor*," he gulped, bobbing his head in greeting. "A true pleasure."

The creature spat a wad of bloody phlegm onto the floor. His full attention was on the computer game. An American F-18 had just downed a MIG-21.

"He can't talk," Papagayo whispered for their enlightenment. "You see, his windpipe was damaged in an accident."

The biker turned to their macabre host. "Our friends are very interested in the photo I showed you yesterday, Felipe. They want to know if you've met that man."

The cripple remained motionless. His chest gurgled. His eyelids blinked languidly like a reptile's. A second MIG-21 tumbled from the electronic horizon.

"I brought you a present," Papagayo remarked enticingly. "The one you asked for."

Felipe suddenly turned from the screen and beamed like an excited child, smiling hideously. With hands flapping about, he merrily urged them closer.

"If you help us a little . . ."

Felipe shrank visibly. He brought the towels like a monk's cowl back over his head. More Belafonte spilled into the room. Miguel knew the melody. He vainly tried to remember the words:

Yellow Bird, high up on banana tree . . .
Yellow Bird . . .

A full minute passed, then a second. The body shuddered under its wrappings. Fuentes prepared to leave. The blanketed apparition rustled.

The thing called Felipe painfully eased the towel back from a hideous face and sat sphinx-like in repose. From the folds of his mantle he brought forth a slate board and piece of chalk. He clawed two characters onto the slate. "OK."

Papagayo took out the snapshot. "Have you seen this man before?"

A nod.

"Where?"

An expansive gesture. Here.

"Often?"

Wag of the head.

"When did you see him last?"

The troubled cast in the misfit's eyes as he searched for an answer tucked somewhere in the recesses of a frayed memory. A grunted expression.

"Pardon?"

He paused. On the slate tablet he eked out the letters "M A Y O."

"*Mayo* – in May?"

Felipe shook his head in the affirmative.

"In the past week?"

Another shake. Firmer this time. Yes.

Fuentes took up the questioning. "What is this man's name?" He motioned to the photo.

A dumb animal shrug.

"Who was with him?"

The number "2" was stroked on the chalkboard. Beside it, Felipe scrawled a stickman and another figure with a skirt.

"Describe them."

Felipe tapped the female image, then gestured with his hand. Small. He turned to the male form and thrummed his chest – strong – the hand shot upwards – and tall.

"The woman?"

Felipe wavered. With pitiful exertion he wrote the word "Rosa." Then the beggar did a curious thing. He tweaked his nose.

"Smell?" Fuentes offered on impulse.

Felipe nodded emphatically.

"Perfume?"

A furious wagging of the toweled head. Felipe drew a tiny flower on the board. Beside it he sketched a smiling face. A pleasant aroma.

"And the man?"

Felipe jabbed a filthy stub of a finger onto the male icon, tapped the top of his own head, then made the motion of someone cutting scalps.

"Short hair!" Fuentes interjected. "He had short hair!"

Felipe nodded again. He sketched a cap onto the caricature and painfully wrote the letters A R O R C E inside it.

Fuentes looked to Asuncion, who seemed perplexed.

"What does *that* mean?" Miguel jabbed a finger to the board. It glanced across the cripple's hands. The skin felt brittle.

The creature skewed his eyes in pain.

"Were they *Yanqui?*"

Felipe winced, a mewing sound like a puppy yelping. He nodded.

"What did they want from you?"

A cadaverous groan escaped the cripple's lips. He gazed up to the biker. The subtlest nod coaxed him on. With a palsied hand, Felipe gestured to a stack of folded cardboard leaning against the far wall.

Asuncion picked through the pile. The cardboard had manufacturers' serial numbers. The labels were in English. Microwaves, televisions, stereos – an appliance heaven of brand names. In each instance, shipping particulars had been torn off.

"These people," Fuentes pressed, "they smuggled things into here?"

An expression of abrupt alarm slashed across the misfit's face.

"And what did they get in return?"

A cough – torturous, sordid. The breathing became hurried. Spittle flecked with blood trickled from the edges of a wretched gash of a mouth. A sullen foulness pervaded the room.

Felipe convulsed then curled up, cocoon-like, into a ball.

Papagayo inserted a needle into the cripple's emaciated arm. Within moments, the wretch's eyelids fell back, his mouth gaped open and he dropped off to a restive sleep.

They lingered on the pathway; portraits in troubled indigo. A whisper breeze came from nowhere, then was gone.

"Why did you call him 'Gatekeeper'?" Asuncion whispered

The biker took a cigarette from a patch pocket in his jacket and jammed it into his mouth. He struck a match on the sole of his boot.

"Because of what he does for his bosses." Papagayo exhaled the rank tobacco. "He's the go-between."

"And who are his bosses?"

"Let's just say a major employer in the community, shall we?"

"Like drug dealers?" Ascuncion challenged. "They're always drug dealers, aren't they?"

"I prefer to say they're customer-driven businessmen," the biker sneered. The tip of the lit cigarette danced as he spoke.

Fuentes shushed Asuncion. "Tell us more about Felipe," he asked.

The biker complied. "Felipe Mitchell was born to work the fields, planting cotton. I knew him before he became addicted, when he had a large family – a wife, five children. He was a party animal. But he had mouths to feed, and piece-labor doesn't quite cut it. He went to work for the *Familia Sonora*. Two-bit courier runs, hanging six as lookout for ten-bag dealers, stuff like that."

A ravenous drag from the cigarette. "Felipe liked to gossip. One of the dealers was caught by anti-*narcoticos*." A pause. "The *Familia* solved that predicament quickly. Felipe paid big time." Papagayo exhaled languidly, letting the smoke trail a capricious path into the blackness. "They took him drinking one night, passed him tequila laced with lye. It tore out his guts – and tore apart his family."

Papagayo finished the smoke.

"What you see is what's left of his system. The doctors gave him six months."

"When was that?"

The biker shrugged. "About half a year ago."

"What did you give him just now?" Fuentes demanded

"Morphine."

"From where?"

"None of your business," Papagayo hissed. "It was good quality, and he's resting now. That's all you need to know." He peered into their eyes, a cold, stark stare. Fuentes detected nothing but contempt.

15 The night was sultry, the moon ripe and full, stars shining high above the town like an ocean of rough-cut diamonds. The streets of Coronado were nearly deserted. Rats slunk through open sewers. Young punks lurked outside an all-night *cantina* by the bus terminal. A drunk vomited loudly into a garbage bin.

After dropping Asuncion at his apartment, Fuentes drove back to the office. He hadn't been paged, but he instinctively trusted American technology over the dubious efficiencies of his own force. And he was right. The NCIC system was up and running; Stella was snoring at her workstation.

He let the dispatcher sleep and did the check himself. The ownership was registered to T. V. Chandler from Benson, just as the impound sheet had indicated. And that's where the similarity to truth ended. As Fuentes suspected, the Cadillac had been far more than an expensive dust-collector abandoned in an underground Tucson parking lot. According to the NCIC, an Arizona Department of Public Safety unit had checked it less than a week ago, at 11:00 a.m. on May 20. The origin for the query had been a detachment just outside of Bisbee, in the southern region of the state, abutting Mexico.

Intrigued, Fuentes was on the line to the Highway Patrol before the printer had stopped clattering. Fortunately, the officer he needed was on duty and refreshingly obliging. He'd stopped a Caddy for speeding heading south on Route 80, fifteen miles from Tombstone. Registered to a Travis V. Chandler, resident in Benson, Arizona. He remembered the driver well. Sole occupant, a man in his mid-fifties with a snow-white crew-cut and sideburns. Quite pleasant and apologetic for going too fast. So much so that he'd let him off with a caution.

Anything else?

No. Nothing to add. The condition of the vehicle? A long interlude at the curious question. Nothing apparent. It looked to be top of the line.

Fuentes hung up. The physical description seemed a good match to the elder Chandler. But the information did something else entirely. It placed the Caddy seventy-eight miles away from the underground garage in Tucson where it had supposedly been stashed from May 14 onwards. It also placed Chandler in the United States, not in Europe.

Ten minutes later, while pecking away on an old Olivetti to complete an overdue report to Obregon, which required paragraphs to reveal nothing, Miguel received an abrupt call from the night duty officer at Davis Monthan. He was being notified that the U.S. Air Force could now confirm Travis Chandler's location. As per Colonel Bragg's categorical instructions. With one hundred percent certitude.

Eighteen hours earlier, the elder Chandler had been pulled over by German police on the eastbound autobahn near Hanover. He'd suffered a minor heart attack upon hearing the distressing news of his son's murder and was currently resting in the intensive care unit of the U.S. military hospital in Frankfurt.

Fuentes completed the summary and placed it in the "Out" tray for the morning courier to Hermosillo. The phone rang again. Bisbee Detachment. Only this time it was the shift supervisor, awkwardly contrite. There'd been an unfortunate error in the details Miguel had been given in the earlier phone call. The vehicle in question had indeed been a Cadillac, but the officer had made a mistake keying in the license plate number. Properly input, the registration would have showed a car registered out of Yuma – not Benson.

The erroneous NCIC data would be amended immediately. Certainly, the driver of the Cadillac had been in the right age group, but that was mere coincidence. The supervisor hoped the blunder hadn't caused any great problems. He apologized once more and explained he was in a real hurry. They had a drunk driving spot-check to man and, one boss to another, he knew Fuentes would understand that orders were orders. You know? He scrupulously repeated the expression. Orders were orders. The line went dead.

Fuentes sat still, contemplating what he'd been advised. Something told him that the first call hadn't been a mistake; something instinctive and foreboding told him that Travis Chandler wasn't in a semi-private hospital room in Germany, but rather was floating out there in that bleak wilderness that embodied the borderlands, and for mysterious reasons that Bragg didn't want him to discover.

He rose to leave. It was then that he saw the manila envelope stuffed into a mail slot. Inside, on three typed sheets, as he'd requested, was an investigative work up on the El Toro Tavern and a detailed review of Number Six Tampico Court, the *maquiladora* plant next door, its principals, and operations.

The tavern had been owned for the past year by one man – a clean, cash-down, no-mortgage purchase. And that man would certainly be hard pressed to help now, even if he wanted to. Cinders don't solve crimes, Fuentes mused cynically. Especially those with the name of Eddie Bono.

Yet, the probability of Bono ever possessing the intellectual assets needed to purchase even a flytrap like the El Toro was minuscule. Eddie couldn't collect his thoughts, let alone sufficient coin to own a *cantina*. So, there had to be others. Still, fronting a business for silent partners, however dubious they might be, wasn't a criminal offense. If it were, then most money-making establishments in Mexico would be boarded up. Anyway, Fuentes wasn't on a morality kick. He was after a murderer, and researching the El Toro was a bum steer.

The *maquiladora* at Six Tampico Court was a more complex affair. It had been federally incorporated as a numbered company two years ago in Mexico City. The identity of its officers was patently irrelevant; it was a standard legal ploy to use the names and particulars of junior partners and secretaries from whichever law firm forged the deed of incorporation, rather than those of the real owners.

Fuentes read on. In addition to manufacturing radar components for helicopters and geological seismographs for commercial exploration, the company also umbrellaed a heavy-parts wing that owned a vehicle fleet and oil rigs involved in offshore drilling. That side of the firm was independently incorporated. All its units – transport trucks, executive-driven Mercedes and BMWs, and, interestingly, a crimson Jaguar XJE – were registered to an office in the upscale Zona Rosa district of Mexico City, while the oil rigs had maritime designations with an address of registration care of a post office box in Panama, a place called Miraflores.

Miguel reflected on the farmer's field and the fried remains that had once been Fast Eddie Bono. There was something about the oil rigs and the postal address that intrigued him, some link that he couldn't quite put his finger on – yet. He scribbled a notation on a blank sheet of paper and, yawning with fatigue, placed it in his breast pocket.

On the way home to his place at San Cristobal, Fuentes stopped near the intersection of Montoya and the Passeo and shoved the note through a mail slot that led to the landing of the second-floor garret at Eng's Chinese Takeout. Felix Asuncion would discreetly check it out, and not ask for the world in return.

Saturday, May 26, morning.
Coronado

16 The funeral service, a Catholic High Mass, was held later that morning in the Basilica of the Virgin of Guadaloupe, the largest church in Coronado. It was nearing the half-hour, the time in the ritual when, in the minds and souls of believers throughout the millennia, leavened bread and wine were transformed into something miraculous.

But miraculous was not how Miguel felt as he pulled his Mustang to a screeching stop in the rectory parking lot. His alarm had failed to go off and he'd slept in. He was too late even to be respectable, let alone party to the stuff of which miracles were made.

As he dashed up the stairs, fidgeting with the cross-straps of his chocolate-brown dress uniform, he caught a glimpse of two of the uniformed officers assigned to traffic points in the procession. They were shooting craps in an alcove of the church.

"Hey! *Hombres!*" he yelled in a voice that resonated angrily across the plaza. "*Atencion!*" The men lurched to attention, but not before stuffing the money into their pockets. The dice tumbled down the steps.

The church was dark, yet inviting. A baroque glow radiated from the votive candles, blending delicately with the gilt-edged paintings and varnished pews that accentuated this House of God. It was packed with mourners and the tangy musk of incense.

Miguel slid into the last bench, next to an elderly usher. The slumbering man started, then gave him a disapproving glance. He wasn't certain if the look was because of his tardiness or because he'd interrupted the old man's sleep.

Fuentes had ordered a large floral arrangement for the grave-side and provided a four-member uniformed traffic escort – symbolic gestures that seemed only fitting. Out of reverence, he didn't take communion, one of the few people in the church who abstained. He didn't bother kneeling but sat, eyes shut, contemplating the stark sadness of the event. A widower left with four children under seven.

At the end of the mass, the caskets were escorted out of the church behind a phalanx of altar-servers and a trio of white-robed priests mumbling hymns, off key. The organ in the choir loft boomed as the congregation screeched a peasant chant.

In the street, the pedestrian cavalcade shuffled into line behind the clergy: the husband, heavily sedated by prescription or design, the remaining children bewildered as sheep, the stolid quadrant of grandparents in funereal black, a bevy of aunts and uncles and ever-present "friends of the family." And there in the center, rigid as a cigar store Indian, stood the *delegado,* Hector Rivera.

Despite the intense heat, he wore an impeccably tailored morning coat and a refined air of overt power, which he carried with the same ease as the gray gloves he'd folded in his clasped hands. He spotted Miguel and inched toward him through the milling crowd.

Fuentes extended a hand in greeting.

Rivera did not respond to the gesture. Instead, his eyes housed a cold hatred. "The crimes you seem unable to solve," he hissed, "involve the murders of a woman who once worked for me as a maid and her children. I greatly respected *Señora* Arroyo."

"I . . . I didn't know," Miguel stammered.

"That's precisely my point," Rivera muttered. "There are too many things you don't seem to know. No matter. You have fewer than thirty days left as *jefe*. Don't bother following to the cemetery, Fuentes. You're not welcome."

"It's a gesture of respect from my office," Miguel replied evenly.

"Respect?" Rivera snorted. "You were late coming to the church. You don't even respect the dead."

"Like some people respected Eddie Bono?" Fuentes shot back. "And that kid at the El Toro?"

Miguel thought he saw the glint of something in Rivera's eye. Then it was gone.

"Bono?" Rivera brooded over the name, then answered with languid ease. "Eddie Bono made some very unfortunate choices in his personal life. He just dealt once too often with unsavory characters." The *delegado* smiled balefully. "I think you'll find we dispensed with his services, in writing, two days ago."

Fuentes was unrelenting. "Bono was found dead around that time."

Rivera shrugged indifferently.

"And the kid? Alomar?"

"I know nothing of him."

An usher discreetly tugged at the *delegado*'s sleeve. His presence was required at the head of the cortege. The procession was beginning to move off.

Rivera cleared his throat. With the deft whisk of a glove, he flicked imaginary dust flecks from his shoulder. Without another word he moved toward the street.

The *delegado* walked a few paces, then turned. He seemed to ponder the town police chief standing before him. His face was unusually serene. "I'd tread carefully, Fuentes," he remarked, not unkindly. "A carhop and a petty hood? Some people aren't worth the effort. Even your thick predecessor Lopez finally came to realize that." And then he was gone.

In the broiling heat, the crowd surged around the coffins. Fuentes returned to the Mustang. His uniform stank of body odor. He flicked off his tie and loosened the top buttons of his dress shirt. He flopped into the front seat and tossed his Sam Browne and holster onto the console. He adjusted the rearview mirror and caught his reflection. Worry lines that he hadn't noticed crept around the face. A graying at the temples, a pinched look around the eyes. Whether he realized it or not, he had begun to look terribly old.

Stella's voice came over the radio. Could the *jefe* see Manny the florist – something about payment. The Town of Coronado check for the floral arrangement had bounced. Fuentes glumly acknowledged the call, telling Stella he was ten minutes away.

Manny Truscon owned a little florist's shop in the gentler part of town, propped between a dressmaker and child's toy arcade. He had a reasonable trade in eucalyptus and yucca and specialized in hybrid cacti, which was not unusual for a town in the middle of the desert, and in long-stemmed tulips, which was.

Truscon was an insincere beetle of a man with a walrus mustache and face moon-cratered by the ravages of a childhood illness. He was given to wearing striped shirts and coordinated bow ties and suspenders. He also wore bright lime rubber gloves whenever he put his hands in water, which in a florist shop was often, so often that they never seemed to be removed. The penchant, he said, was to preserve his delicate skin.

Truscon was a typical Coronado businessman, a man of single purpose and double-talk. He paid taxes faithfully and, in the practical way of all merchants, conspicuously supported the *policia* by displaying a bumper sticker to that effect on his Jeep Cherokee. He was also a vice president of the service club that supplied baseball caps to the local Peewee team. Still, he never volunteered information or support to the police, except when it suited him.

That was not to say that the florist was in any way a problem for Fuentes. Far from it. His premises had never been burglarized. He'd never been the victim of a bad check or credit card. Armed thugs had never crashed through his display of azaleas in search of a safe. Then again, Miguel couldn't imagine a self-respecting thief surreptitiously entering the premises. To steal what? A display of mums? A fleuret of red ribbons? A flowerpot shaped like Mother Goose?

Fuentes parked his Mustang at the rear of the store. He patiently re-holstered his gun, fastened his tie, and made himself respectable.

The high-pitched tinkling of a bell atop the front door. Sickly sweet nectar oozing from the profusion of flowers inside. There was no one in, save Manny, busily cutting stems from marigolds in the work area at the back of the shop. With calm deliberation, the florist completed his task before coming forward to greet his visitor.

Fuentes apologized profusely for any difficulties he might have caused and volunteered to pay for the memorial wreath out of his own pocket. Truscon, ever pragmatic, accepted the offer without hesitation. For him, charity began and ended at the service club.

The bi-focaled storekeeper puttered about the cash register, preparing an invoice for the flowers Fuentes had ordered for the church. Miguel glanced at a poster stapled to the wall next to a Florist International fee schedule. It was a sampler created to assist merchants in identifying the faces of legitimate credit cards. Miguel's eye caught something that intrigued him. Lodged amid the flurry of customized designer graphics – the dramatic desert vistas, coastlines, and canyons – was the sculpted image of a chess knight colored a brilliant aquamarine, and at its base, in Gothic print, the initials "B. B."

The florist was actually quite helpful. "It's a new one," he explained as Fuentes wrote out the check. "Bank of Bavaria. Been in the state six months. They use MasterCard for credit. I get some customers out here," he beamed proudly. "They like my stunted peyote – buy them by the dozen."

Truscon made a patently insincere comment about the tragedy that had befallen the Arroyo family, then heaved the cash register shut and smiled a fixed and frozen smile. As far as Manny was concerned, this audience, too had ended.

Saturday, May 26, afternoon.
Bahia Kino

17 The nearest branch of the Bank of Bavaria proved to be an hour away in the coastal town of Bahia Kino. Miguel headed down the tollway in the direction of Hermosillo, then west toward the Pacific and his destination on the Sea of Cortez. He knew the place well. A five-mile-long beach boasting spectacular sunsets and overpriced tourist lodgings were the town's principal claims to fame.

As Fuentes tried to avoid the worst of the potholes, his mind wouldn't let go of the aquamarine image on Manny the florist's poster. It kept merging, hand in glove, with the icon etched on the pocket calendar found in the car Wickham Chandler had parked at Zita's.

The bank, a creased and dirty little building, was on a side street off the main avenue. Built in 1916, the institution had once allegedly held the personal accounts and much of the treasure of the famous revolutionary Pancho Villa. Legend had it that Villa had stored gold bars in its cramped vaults. In the summer of 1923, he'd ordered the bars moved to a more secure location. Then, during the transfer, his black Dodge had been ambushed by gunmen, who peppered one hundred and fifty shots into the roadster in less than two minutes. Villa had sensibly died and the bars mysteriously disappeared, as had all records of his business transactions in Bahia.

The bank had since changed hands, often and predictably. It had survived for a time as head office for a small mortgage and loan company, then as a credit branch for a fishermen's guild that went belly up when the bottom fell out of the spiny lobster market. Colorful posters from Lufthansa and Volkswagen featuring Rhine castles and blonde *frauleins* now adorned the crumbling walls. The new owners were expatriate Germans hedging their bets on the tourist trade.

The interior was high-ceilinged, a large, impersonal chamber bedecked with chunky brass railings and weathered oak. Long lines of raven-garbed widows patiently lined up in front of teller cages as harried clerks doled out huge Mexican notes with falsettoed officiousness. The odor of strong disinfectant permeated the air, mingling with cheap talcum and red peppers.

Miguel's cavalry-cut boots cannonaded on the scuffed marble flooring. He approached the nearest wicket and, still wearing his sunglasses, loudly demanded the manager. The startled cashier scurried apprehensively to a frescoed door marked *Gerente* and disappeared within. The patrons shuffled uneasily.

After a moment the door opened. A wasp-waisted young man with harried eyes and a crop of strawberry blond hair badly in need of trim came to the counter. He mumbled something in Fuentes's general direction. Miguel didn't quite catch the words.

With ponderous resolve the man repeated himself. "*Señor* Gordon – Maximilian Gordon." He extended a limp-wristed hand, then withdrew it before Miguel could reciprocate. "I am the manager."

In heavily accented tones, Gordon explained that he'd been brought in from head office in Mexico City to organize the new branch, with all of a week to make the place viable. One hoped the local police understood the primacy of such mandates. The banker left no doubt that Fuentes's presence was an intrusion.

So? The insincere smile. Was there an urgent matter he could assist the authorities with? Otherwise, he'd gladly give the *jefe* the number for head office security. The smile stayed frozen on his face. He could even provide a telephone at no cost. The banker glanced along the countertop, selected a deposit slip, took a gold pen from his breast pocket, and jotted down some numbers.

With an adroit motion, he handed the completed slip to Fuentes. "Again," Gordon said, wrapping his voice in ersatz innocence, "a pleasure meeting you." A slight nod of determination, not deference. He began to stride back to his office.

"*Señor?*" Miguel chanced. The man had reached the door. He wasn't listening.

"*Señor* Gordon?" Miguel repeated, his voice rising. "This has to do with murder."

The people in the lineups perked their ears; the shuffling of feet stopped. A teller coughed.

Maximilian Gordon froze in his tracks. He turned back to the counter. "What?"

Fuentes took off his sunglasses. "Murder."

The policeman was promptly ushered into an office.

Fuentes didn't waste time. Before the door closed behind him, he'd thrust the photo into his host's flustered face. "This character," he demanded. "Know him?"

Gordon hesitated. Then he nodded. The man had an account. Was it a joint one with a woman? A redhead? Now how did the *jefe* know that? A limp smile. Yes. And she was a fiery one to boot. *Gringo?* No, she'd been Mexican: olive skin, petite, five foot two or so.

Their names?

The banker didn't have the information at the tip of his tongue. A moment. He minced away and returned with paperwork. "You're sure you need these?" he asked, flickering his eyelashes in the harsh light.

Miguel nodded.

"Well, I suppose if there's been a murder . . ." Gordon yielded grudgingly. "It wasn't gruesome, was it?" he wondered, curiosity getting the better of him.

"As gruesome as it gets, *Señor,*" Miguel replied, effectively silencing the man.

Maximilian Gordon wilted visibly. He ran nimble fingers through his fine-stranded hair. With obvious and exaggerated effort, he composed himself, then shuffled through the pages until he found what he wanted. "Mr. W. and Mrs. H. Clinton," he remarked. "That's how we knew them."

"An address?"

"Number 11467 on the Via Prosperidad in Coronado."

"Anything else?"

The banker gamely tendered the remaining details on the account. It had been opened three months ago and until Monday held slightly over $67,000 U.S. There were two signatures on the specimen card – one male, one female. But both held independent signing privileges, including those of withdrawal. The amount appeared to have grown in dribs and drabs over a period of time. It was always bills – large denominations – and always deposited by the male.

"And last Monday…?"

"It was all taken out near closing time. Every last cent."

"By the woman." Fuentes had intuitively completed the equation.

"You knew?"

"An educated guess," Miguel replied dryly. "Their occupations?"

A meek shrug. Notwithstanding the banker's initial bravado, Fuentes realized that money talked, and very few ever dared to ask why.

On his way back into Coronado, Fuentes resolved to check the address he'd been provided. Situated on Prosperidad, the number sounded vaguely familiar. It was only when he pulled up that he recognized the vacant lot next to the El Loco diner. It seemed that, in between defrauding the United States Air Force and dealing hard drugs, Chandler and his lady friend liked to enjoy the house special as well. With the last piece of the puzzle falling neatly into place, Miguel Fuentes had pretty much made up his mind whom he wanted arrested for the murders at Zita's. He went to the pay phone outside the diner and dialed Obregon at his office.

The *federale* was unavailable. He was at budget meetings and might be tied up for hours. An underling grudgingly took Miguel's message and in a testy voice assured him that the *comandante* would return the call.

"Oh? And *Jefe*?" The assistant caught Fuentes as he was hanging up. The Querobabi drug investigation? The one the *federales* had just taken over from the locals? It was expanding in scope and severity. Selected military personnel were being airlifted into foothills around the *pueblo* to create a cordon in support of federal *anti-narcoticos*. If the *jefe* could keep his men outside a fifteen-mile radius of Querobabi unless otherwise ordered – just to ensure a clean line of authority? Paperwork would be sent to him via courier to formalize the matter. The project was now classified as Top Secret. It even had a name he could use, if need be, to refer to it in any future discussions he might have with the *comandante*. It was now being called Project Phoenix.

"*Si*." Fuentes grimly acceded to the request. Such options were not his to exercise. And if the military wanted in on a gravy train? At least his men weren't being tempted.

He emerged from the phone booth and glanced at his watch. It was a little after two o'clock. His dress uniform was becoming quite unpleasant in the sultry afternoon heat. A cool shower and change of clothing seemed in order. Then he would deal with Obregon.

Sunday, May 27, afternoon.
San Cristobal

18 "Hello?!" The front door rattled. "Hello! Is anybody home?"

Fuentes briskly toweled his damp hair as he brushed past a howling Salinas to the source of the commotion. He flung the towel onto a chair, opened a sidetable drawer, and took out a snub-nosed revolver. Concealing it in the pocket of his tattered housecoat, he walked to the door.

A man was peering through the mesh of the screen door. Miguel liked to let what breezes existed waft up the bluff from the dusty crossroads below. The stranger was a well-dressed individual in a seersucker suit with expertly trimmed white hair and a face made lobster red from either too much sun or too little tonic water.

Rimless designer glasses dangled on a chest the girth of an Okto-
berfest beer keg. The stranger pounded on the door once more,
aggressively, as if he had far better things to do with his time.

"Hello!" With the peculiar slant of the late-afternoon sun he
couldn't yet see inside.

"*Sí?*" Miguel inched closer to the entry. He kept one hand in
his pocket.

"Are you Fuentes?" The man chewed gum loudly and spoke
with a drawl Fuentes could only place as north of Texas.

"Who's asking?" Miguel stayed back from the door. He'd never
liked people who chewed gum and didn't much care for arrogant
Americans in seersucker suits who affected dangling sunglasses.

"The name's Firestone," the man offered between chews.
"Seymour Firestone."

"And?" Salinas nuzzled up to the screen door and growled.
Miguel tightened his hand around the pistol grip of the snub-nose.

The man on the veranda seemed honestly perplexed. "You
don't know me?"

With a polite smile, Miguel indicated that he didn't.

"I'm an attorney. I represent Damien Moffatt – you know, the
enlisted man from Davis Monthan. I believe he gave you my
card. May I come in?"

Miguel hesitated. "I'd prefer that you stay outside, Mr. Firestone." His mouth sloped in an awkward grin. "My place isn't too
tidy right now."

Firestone gave an understanding nod. "Your choice, Colonel."

"*Jefe,*" Miguel corrected him.

Firestone sniffed. "Whatever."

Fuentes eased the shepherd pup away from the door and
stepped outside. The air was hot and stale. He took the offered
card. Firestone had come from Phoenix. Accepting his credentials at face value, he appeared to be a senior partner in a large
firm and he practiced criminal law.

"You want to speak to me?" Fuentes asked.

"Yes, I do. My client indicated that you wished to discuss
certain things with him."

"Things?"

Firestone swallowed the gum. A translucent smile came to his face, then faded as he saw it had no effect on the Mexican. "My client has information that could prove useful to you . . ." He paused. "But he'll need protection."

Fuentes handed back the card. "I don't quite understand who your client needs protection from."

A seam of sweat, thin as a knife cut, trickled down Seymour's ruddy forehead. The lawyer impatiently brushed it away. "Well," he chuckled, "Mr. Moffatt can't tell you that right now, can he? And I reckon I'd be a bit reluctant to do the same. It just isn't something you volunteer on a front porch." Firestone's dreary eyes narrowed. "Let's just say for the right deal my client can remember lots of things."

"Such as?"

"Colonel . . . general . . ." The man mumbled.

"*Jefe*," Miguel corrected.

"Ya, sure." The impatience was quite naked, like the gaudy ring on the man's finger. "This is the picture. Moffatt can reveal everything about the mess at Monthan, but he's got to get an honorable discharge from the air force."

"That's not mine to give," Fuentes responded candidly.

Firestone shrugged. "Then you can go on guessing who stuck Chandler and where the Semtex came from . . ."

The lawyer strode to the end of the porch. Miguel noted that he took calm, measured steps as if he, and not Fuentes, owned the place.

Firestone brought a hand to his eyes to shade them as he gazed at the far-off mountains. "Nice view," he remarked affably over his shoulder.

Miguel agreed.

The American moved to where Miguel stood. A mild wind brushed the scent of sagebrush through the air.

"Funny how the light plays tricks in the desert, though, ain't it?" Firestone commented. "So you see only part of what's out there to see. Mirages we call 'em back home."

"*Si.*" Fuentes nodded. "In Spanish the word is *espejismo.*"

"Face it, *hombre,*" the lawyer observed discerningly. "You need the Mexican end of the smuggling scheme, and you need a motive for Chandler's death. My man can give you both. Either that, or you're whole file is full of 'ee-space-moes,'" he stumbled over the word.

Miguel corrected him.

"That's it," Firestone smiled. "Spay-zeee-moos." He cheerfully mangled the term once more.

Fuentes opened the screen door. "Come in." He palmed the revolver in his free hand, taking care to keep it hidden. "I think we can talk."

The meeting lasted less than half an hour. Firestone did what lawyers do best: he waffled. Miguel hadn't expected much, if anything, else. But in the verbal fencing he did accede one point, and at the end of it all, as the screen door creaked open in the faint breeze and a black BMW roared off into a tawny cloud, he'd created breathing room for his client and provided the motive Fuentes was seeking.

The call that night came from his contact at the U.S. Customs post at Nogales. Miguel was expecting it. The times and dates matched, as did the description he'd provided, right down to the designer boots, cats curled up on the rear bench seat of the truck, and toy dispenser on the console, a plastic Mickey Mouse crammed with blackball candies.

Fuentes hung up the phone and calmly dialed another number. This time he got through to Obregon.

Monday, May 28, morning.
Davis Monthan Air Force Base, Tucson

19 The digital radio kicked in at 5:55, as it did every weekday. That left her ample time to listen to the early news over breakfast and slip into a cotton track suit for her morning run. It had been a restive weekend. She'd been expecting company and had become anxious and troubled when her guests hadn't arrived at her doorstep. Stress of this sort was the last thing she needed, particularly now. For the moment at least, she'd allow herself the predictable comfort afforded by routine, for routine had become a source of solace and stability, like the uniform she proudly wore and the profession she espoused in defense of her nation.

Breakfast was blandly domestic: a slice of grapefruit, two pieces of dry toast, coffee black, and an egg, over easy – a meal that usually took fifteen minutes.

The training regimen that followed was equally predictable, a disciplined routine she'd observed without alteration since coming to Davis and had practiced in all the places she'd called home before. A windsprint from the condo onto the base proper and then, starting at the main gate, a three-mile perimeter jog at an average clip of nine minutes, forty-four seconds per mile. All this and she was easily at her office reading briefing notes by 0715 hours. She finished her warm-ups, adjusted her headphones, and set off.

Discipline. Its roots were set in the years when she was growing up with four siblings in a working-class family in the inner city. Discipline – a welcome sinecure against shock. And shock there had assuredly been in her young life. Rico, the eldest brother in the family, had been arrested for robbery and the murder of a cornerstore clerk; Ignacio, the second, was a petty car thief who hung out with a gang that terrorized the neighborhood; her two other siblings were more interested in impregnating the local *chiquitas* than improving their station or that of their family.

Unlike his male offspring, Virgilio Donovan had been a proud man, a first-generation Mexican-American who'd seen combat in 1966 as a Marine gunny near Cam Ranh Air Base in Vietnam, a man who stood to rigid attention, ball cap over heart, at Oilers football games, until even he came to realize that this brand of loyalty had gone out of vogue in every possible way – that, like discipline, and his beloved Oilers, who had cavalierly moved off to Tennessee, it wasn't considered important any more.

Her dad had the heart attack just days after Rico was committed to life in prison. She'd been there when it happened, an eleven-year-old watching helplessly as he'd collapsed in a lump on the kitchen linoleum.

Virgilio had never been the same after that. He surrendered active partnership in the thriving brake shop he'd set up twelve years before with $400, a set of mechanic's tools, and a dream, to a cousin, who promptly declared bankruptcy and fled to parts unknown with what remained of the investment.

While Virgilio sat at home doing crosswords and watching old George Raft movies, the three remaining brothers begged, borrowed, stole, and only occasionally labored for the bread that made its way to the dinner table. Maria's mother, Inez, cleaned doctors' offices and car showrooms to make ends meet. In the face of all of this, her father preached what he believed. Loyalty and Discipline.

So Maria joined school clubs and studied vigorously to stay on the principal's honor role, where she soon became a fixture. Three nights a week and every second Saturday, she worked as a supermarket cashier, even after she'd been held up at gunpoint twice in the course of a year and seen a dairy clerk knifed in the groin during a robbery.

In her senior year it came time to chart her future. Finishing first in Texas in her academic field, a hardworking, popular student, and from a minority group to boot, she was a sought-after commodity for university recruiters. Then she'd gone and surprised everyone but her dad with her choice. She could do no other. She'd live what he preached. Loyalty and Discipline.

She went from an inner-city *Chicana* to Air Force Academy freshman. In her four years at Colorado Springs, she held the same position she had in her middle schooling: third in a class of two hundred and sixty-six, bested only by a physics genius from Los Angeles, the progeny of a Rhodes scholar and a resource librarian, and a letterman linebacker on the Falcons football team. Her graduation from the Academy was a proud moment for Virgilio, the old Corps gunny. An enlisted man with a commissioned officer for a daughter. And an air force one at that!

But the comfortable routine she so assiduously embraced was

a veneer. Beneath the surface, she was as fragile and lonely as the little girl who'd looked helplessly on that day when her father almost died.

She gave a friendly wave to the gate guard as she entered the base. She turned onto Arizola and broke into a heady pace, lost in the rhythm of the music in her headphones. One mile. She noted the markers along the road and glanced at her watch. Better than average time. One and a half. Another turn and …

A dusty Intrepid came alongside, then slowed almost to a crawl, pacing her. Inside she recognized base security – Cullpepper, Grant, and one person she didn't know, a stranger in civvies wearing a cherry bow tie. She waved to them but her greeting wasn't returned.

Suddenly, a Taurus pulled past the Intrepid. It darted to about a hundred feet ahead then spun inward, blocking her path. Two uniformed airmen bounded out. The front passenger door burst open. Out stepped Colonel Bragg, his expression austere.

"Lieutenant Donovan."

"Sir?" she replied, startled at the formality. Still breathing heavily from her exertions, she came to attention.

"Maria Victoria Donovan," the colonel continued flatly, "I'm placing you under arrest for the murder of Wickham Chandler. Security, read her Miranda. Then take her away."

The air gushed out of the young woman's lungs. Drivers in passing cars, some of whom she recognized, slowed down to gawk. For a moment, just a moment, she saw, too, her father's tormented face and asked his forgiveness for what now appeared to be happening.

Twenty-one minutes later, a phone trilled inside the hillside *casa* at the crossroads of San Cristobal. Fuentes stumbled out of bed to take the call, eyes slow to adjust to the blind-shuttered darkness.

It was the FBI lab in Phoenix confirming what Fuentes had suspected: that the woman's boots in the apartment closet and the item of footwear found on the dead captain were of the same manufacture, from a specialty leather shop near Cochise. The lab also made a one hundred percent match in heel scrapings from the apartment to the soil type found in Zita's parking lot.

Most important, technicians had located traces of dried blood in the footwear, a minute quantity consistent with a mosquito bite, but sufficient to compare to DNA samples obtained from Maria Donovan as part of the air force's compulsory personnel identification process. Like the soil, the DNA was a perfect match. The boots belonged to Donovan and could now be tied directly to Zita's.

The information had been passed to air force investigators at Davis Monthan. Colonel Bragg had suggested that Fuentes be informed, as a courtesy. Miguel was suitably appreciative.

Not more than a moment later, he fielded a second call, from an old university pal who now held a senior position in the American Department of Veterans Affairs, a friend with a tantalizing morsel about a Marine veteran named Virgilio Donovan who'd been a demolition specialist in Vietnam. He had an only daughter, Maria, who'd excelled in chemical engineering at the U.S. Air Force Academy, completing her thesis on plastic explosives and their applications in counterintelligence and terrorist warfare. Her peculiar specialty was Semtex and its properties. The discreet voice at the other end had just about filled in the last piece in the puzzle.

By then it didn't much matter any more. Lieutenant Maria Victoria Donovan was already being processed into the brig at Davis Monthan for the murder of a United States Air Force officer and was surreptitiously being profiled by a team of clinical psychiatrists as the principal suspect in the bombing deaths of a Mexican woman and her two young children.

Tuesday, May 29, morning.
Tucson

20 Dunc Wooster was eleven days past his fifty-seventh birthday, and it was not being very good at it. He was tired and nearly broke, which was not an advantageous thing for a criminal lawyer to be. The tired part wasn't that unusual. In these days of flagging economies and flailing fists, most defense counsel in Pima County were run off their feet just keeping up with their caseloads.

Dunc Wooster was not destined to be one of them.

And that made for the self-fulfilling prophecy in his personal finances. While his more professional peers were profiting from crime in ways that made their accountants swoon, Wooster, who'd hustled for nearly thirty years, still fashioned only a semblance of decorum, scavenging legal aid cases outside courtrooms that went about as far as a piss-poor plea bargain.

Yet he somehow managed to acquire sufficient retainers to keep gas in the aged Ford Fairmont, the semblance of food in his stomach, and perhaps, just perhaps, a minuscule sum for his monthly bloodletting – the alimony check to his ex, the Beloved Isabel.

He was sitting in the car across from the Pima County courthouse, drinking a coffee and listening to the world news on a cheap portable suspended from the rearview mirror. An apartment arson in Potsdam, the new chichi suburb of Berlin, had claimed the lives of seventeen Auslanders from Romania and Vietnam. With Teutonic assertiveness, a government spokesman dismissed any rumors that the incident might have been racially motivated. A second piece summarized a brutal maritime tragedy in Bangladesh, where two hundred peasants had perished when a Taiwanese freighter struck an overcrowded ferry in the Bay of Bengal.

The final story was a detailed item about Mexico – something about the peasant struggle in Chiapas province and efforts by the Mexican military to put a lid on it, efforts that the reporter indicated were proving futile. Intriguingly, according to the commentator, the true flash point lay not, as one might expect, in the area of human rights, but in a simmering controversy over oil.

In recent months, it appeared that exploration teams in the southernmost part of the Mar Muerto had done preliminary drilling into the spine of the continental shelf within sight of the Chiapas town of Arista. The results were tentative at best, but analysts were already predicting a find that could well develop into the world's largest reserve of untapped oil. The rebels had quickly laid claim to the enormous wealth by virtue of their aboriginal rights. The Mexican government seemed just as determined to assert that rights to the field abided in the hands of PEMEX, the national energy conglomerate.

Ultimate ownership of the dormant black gold was proving a costly and divisive issue. In the past week, eight soldiers had been killed in clashes with insurgent Zapatista rebels. Sixty-two innocent civilians had also died in crossfire. The Mexican army was sending six thousand troops into the region to supplement twenty thousand already there. There was no telling when, or how, the dispute would end.

Domestic instability on such a scale had put tremendous international strain on an already weak *peso*. Moreover, the PRI policy of military intervention was meeting with growing international censure. As a consequence, there were unsubstantiated rumors of secret negotiations between rebels and government, talk of a settlement being hammered out somewhere in northern Sonora, an accommodation brokered through a most powerful intermediary whose word was sacrosanct and whose identity was, as yet, a closely guarded secret.

A quick voice-cut to a man speaking heavily accented, though quite articulate, English, in what appeared to be a hurried interview setting. The man spoke volubly of the need for reconciliation with the rebels, for greater understanding among the various regions and peoples of Mexico, for a lasting peace above all lesser needs. Given the extent of civil unrest and attendant dislocation to that nation and its people, Wooster was somewhat taken aback to hear this individual identified as the new president of Mexico himself, Emilio Estrada.

Wooster paid scant attention to the closing analysis. For him, most elements of Mexican politics were eminently predictable. Those in power were corrupt and making money while those in opposition weren't and wanted to be. He was more interested in the ball scores and climate.

After hearing that his beloved Orioles had won, the weather forecast captured his undivided interest. The mercury would rest in the low nineties, and his Ford had no air conditioning. He grimaced and resolved to stay in the courthouse for the foreseeable future, where he was guaranteed to be cool at least, if underemployed.

A shrill *beeeep!* Wooster felt along his waistband. Damn! Not there. He turned to rummage furiously about the back seat. His mobile office definitely needed renovating. A portable typewriter and box of cheap stationery sat atop a bench seat cluttered with expired court briefs and dog-eared legal texts. A notary seal clamped a cold pizza rind in its metal jaws. A spider crept across a photocopied page of *The Annotated Criminal Statutes of Arizona*. Wooster found the pager under a weeks-old *USA Today*.

The driver's door didn't work and hadn't for nearly four years. Wooster lurched out the passenger side. He waddled over to a pay phone, jammed a quarter in the coin slot, and dialed the answering service. His nemesis, "Nasal" Hazel, answered. Yes, he had one message. What had taken him so long? "Did ya get the names, Mr. Wooster?" He scribbled the particulars of the communication on the back of a pack of Camel filters. "I ain't givin' 'em to ya again."

She'd given Wooster two names. The first was unfamiliar. But the second – now where had he heard it? Where?

Snapped out of his apathy, he called the first name, which carried the prefix "Reverend." The military chaplain stated, with a certain amount of genteel awkwardness, that Wooster had been selected by the "person in custody" solely because his surname was at the top of the last yellow page in the phonebook.

The minister or "Captain whatever" wasn't all too sure about how Wooster would get paid. But he'd spoken to the prisoner and she did have some money set aside. How much, the Reverend couldn't say. But surely, given her obvious state of distress, Wooster as an ethical man could at least meet with the woman, could he not? Right away?

Wooster gazed across the street at the gleaming chrome courthouse. He knew the trial judge assigned to Room 204 was one Bufford Smithers. His Honor was a stickler for precision, a magistrate who assessed each defendant according to the shine on his lawyer's shoes and the tightness of his Windsor knot. Wooster peered forlornly over his stomach toward a pair of scuffed brown loafers. The stitching was coming undone, the sheen, once bright oxblood, was now a dull pounded liver. He shrewdly weighed his options.

Today Wooster had Mina, a veteran prostitute, for a client, and a "Proceed" sticker on a dope sheet resting somewhere in the pile atop the District Attorney's desk in Room 204. Mina was a court regular who would invariably plead not guilty on blind principle. Dunc knew that if he didn't show and she did, he'd be up the creek with the Criminal Lawyers Association – not to mention His Honor, Judge Smithers, who'd surely blow a gasket.

But Mina, though principled, was also unpredictable, and had the dubious distinction of having been issued the most bench warrants for non-appearance in the history of Pima County.

Wooster peered at his watch. A little after eight. A half-hour travel time each way. A half-hour to converse with the client. And then? Oh, what the heck! Mina? So what if he was held for contempt for missing another trial date? If he was late, he might yet catch Smithers, smoldering and fuming in all his Vesuvian glory. And the worst that could happen? A few days in the bucket, regular meals, and a built-in list of potential customers. Besides, the weatherman had just predicted four more days of this heat wave. What the hell! If worst came to worst, the jail was air conditioned.

After their confrontation outside the cathedral that Saturday, Fuentes hadn't expected to meet the *delegado* again, so he was quite astonished when he received a phone call ordering him to appear immediately at Rivera's hillside villa.

"Rancho Rivera" was a new split-level located in the exclusive part of greater Coronado known as Isadora, a gathering of foothills five miles from the outskirts of town. Built along California lines with a tennis court, Olympic-sized indoor swimming pool, and six-bay car park, to complement an interior of twenty thousand square feet, the *rancho* easily matched the grandeur of its neighboring homes.

Miguel had never been to the mansion on business or otherwise. It wasn't his way. Yet he was neither shocked nor daunted by the magnificence of the place. He'd expected nothing less. This was, after all, the residence of the PRI boss for the State of Sonora.

He pulled his Mustang to rest by the car park. Two cars sat idly in the driveway: a 1998 Mercedes hardtop and an antique pink-and-gray two-tone, a vehicle that Miguel vaguely recalled from his father's days, a Kaiser American. A pair of workman's legs stretched out from under the Kaiser.

As Miguel passed the two-tone, he heard the unmistakable voice of the *delegado*. "Fuentes, come here."

A figure in grimy dungarees rolled out from underneath the chassis of the Kaiser. It was Rivera himself. Miguel waited as the huge man eased himself upright to his full six-foot frame. His eyes were hard as burnished steel.

"Fuentes," he scowled, "I've reconsidered your future. I'm letting you stay on in Coronado. When the ninety days run out, you'll revert to patrol officer. For now, you'll report to Obregon. Do as he sees fit and only that. Do any more and I'll personally see you locked up without a key. Understand?"

Miguel felt a confused jumble of emotions. "Thank you, sir," he offered with what he hoped would pass for sincerity. "Whatever you wish."

Rivera spat on the cobblestones. "No need to bow and scrape, Fuentes," he snarled. "Before you think anything's changed between us, it hasn't. Obregon put in a word for you, said you'd be invaluable at the trial in Hermosillo. If I had my way, you'd have been history long ago."

The *delegado* strode resolutely up the sloped walkway toward the residence. With a precise thrust of his thumb, like a master bringing a dog to heel, he motioned Miguel to follow.

Fuentes did as he was told.

"I'm only keeping you because you lucked into the *Yanqui* murderess. And that's good for the town." Rivera rummaged through his pants, found a filthy cloth, brought it to his nose and blew heartily.

He reached the ornate doorway to his mansion. It was clear from his posture that he wasn't in the business of entertaining strangers to his realm, least of all soon-to-be-redundant police chiefs.

"Now," he barked, "go find some parked cars to ticket. The town needs the cash." And with solemn finality, the *delegado* entered his mansion and banged the door shut.

21 Major Bartholomew "Bart" Sloane was a seasoned press officer, a carrot-topped career type who'd shrewdly discovered early in his professional life that the key to survival in the modern air force was not so much in knowing what to *do* but in knowing what to *say*.

Sloane had made his mark in the Kuwaiti war, guiding smart-bombs to the streets of downtown Baghdad from the safe and sanctimonious vantage point of a press room monitor hundreds of miles away in Riyadh. He'd served in western Europe during the B-52 bomber downsizing and Stateside when the latest Cuban crisis had erupted and died a quick death. He'd stood at the podium for a slew of base closings and farewells and, in each, he'd faithfully toed the party line.

Sloane had earned the rank of major half a decade ago – the Pentagon's reward for his fluid media stonewalling of a potentially damaging scandal. The major's pending retirement was only two years away and Sloane was doggedly determined that he would still hold the position of Base Press Officer when that day came. From his reserved parking spot immediately next to the commanding officer's, to the annual charity foursome with the boss and base chaplains, Bart Sloane knew all the angles and all the players. And he was going to keep it that way, despite the fiasco he now had on his hands.

A young, female – and minority – commissioned officer charged with murdering her superior. And three Mexicans killed as a consequence of her actions, two of them children. Mix it all up with drugs and the blemish of a broader corruption? It didn't get much better. Or worse.

The major's closest army buddy had adroitly handled damage control for a multiple rape in Nagasaki. A navy friend had successfully diluted the press sludge around a nuclear spill caused by a Triton-class sub off the coast of Wales. So when he'd read the in-house briefing, Bart Sloane guilefully called around and had some sense of what to expect in the way of incoming artillery. Or so he thought.

Nothing could have fully prepared Bart Sloane for the spectacle that greeted him in the enlisted man's cafeteria of Davis Monthan Air Force Base at one o'clock that afternoon. The room held over eighty reporters and their equipment – boom mikes, cameras, recorders, klieg lights. It was filled with a blue haze of spent cigarette smoke wafting at eye level. The atmosphere was charged with the pervasive distrust and creative tension that came when deadlines collided with the stolid demeanor of the military.

Time and *Newsweek* had tentatively scheduled the story for their covers. The major American newspapers were carrying it under banner headlines. The evening news on all television networks had it as a lead. "60 Minutes" had sent an investigative team for the long haul, as had CNN. The BBC was intrigued enough to detail its North American correspondent to cover the piece between snippets of another equally tantalizing piece involving kickbacks in the international oil industry. Even Japanese television had sent a stringer.

Sloane bounded onto the podium, smartly attired in his dress uniform, campaign medals glistening, eyes sharp as a falcon's seeking its prey. He tapped the mike head. The commotion around him diminished. He opened a black binder, cleared his throat for effect, then started to read:

"Ladies and gentlemen, at 6:35 a.m. this date, Lieutenant Maria Victoria Donovan, United States Air Force, age twenty-five, stationed at Davis Monthan Air Force Base as a senior supply officer, was arrested by personnel from the United States Air Force Office of Special Investigations. She has been charged with the murders of Captain Wickham Everett Chandler, United States Air Force, age thirty-nine, Tina Arroyo, age thirty-four, William Arroyo, age five, and Terese Arroyo, age three. The latter three are Mexican citizens. The killings occurred on Monday the 21st of May this year in the Town of Coronado in the state of Sonora, Mexico.

"Miss Donovan is being held in custody without bail. Mexican authorities are seeking her extradition to face these charges. The United States government is currently in the process of expediting that request. Are there any questions?"

The room exploded as if it had taken a direct hit from an Exocet. Sloan zeroed in on a petite brunette sitting in the third row, waving a pencil over her head, steno book balanced in her lap. He acknowledged her with a darted finger and a nod, and she responded with the standard preface – name and agency.

"Maria Luisa Sanchez, Telenews Mexico . . ." the brunette began sonorously and then lapsed into Spanish.

Sloane turned to the side of the podium where a civilian interpreter, standing with a gaggle of brass, translated the question. "Miss Sanchez would like to know if the American government is going to compensate the survivors of the Arroyo family for their victimization at the hands of the American military."

"These issues will have to be determined after the trial . . ." he started. Miss Sanchez did not look amused, but Sloane didn't much care. "Lieutenant Donovan, who is of Mexican-American descent, is innocent until proven guilty."

The reporter frowned and launched into a second question, but Sloane moved on. "Mr. Meyer?"

Lou Meyer was a Tucson radio reporter and golfing buddy of the major's. His question was a plant. It required that Sloane outline the duties and responsibilities of the Air Force Office of Special Investigations. It also required little intellectual effort and effectively killed six minutes of the scrum. The information was readily available in the bound briefing notes stacked on tables at the rear of the cafeteria.

The next dozen queries fell into a predictable pattern and gave Sloane valuable respite. He strung out the answers for all he was worth. The multiple killings at the Mexican motel were not common knowledge, and what little information he possessed became highly precious collateral.

Sloane paused to straighten his tie. He would permit one more question. He peered across the forest of raised pencils before settling on a somber-faced, middle-aged male standing erectly off to the side. Tweed tie, powder-blue button-down shirt, sensible shoes, white skin, a conservative law-and-order type by the look of his gray flannels. Sloane didn't quite catch the man's credentials as reporters protested being overlooked.

"Will the government of the United States allow an American citizen to be tried for murder knowing that the penalty on conviction in Mexico is forty years without benefit of parole?"

Sloane began to answer. The speaker interrupted. He was not done with his query.

"And more importantly, knowing that Mexico has a civil rights record that is highly suspect?"

Sloane gritted his teeth and gave the set-piece response reserved for just such occasions. "The Mexican government is fully committed to justice. As are we. Senior officials of Justice, State, and the Secretary of Defense are all working with their Mexican counterparts to – "

The man in the gray flannels grew impatient. "Will that translate into a show trial in Mexico, or will Lieutenant Donovan be arraigned in the United States?"

"I hope you aren't questioning the integrity of Mexican criminal justice for persons awaiting trial?" Sloane countered. Then he drew in his sword. "If the issue in your mind is one of a Mexican system which you feel lacks rectitude or even-handedness . . ." He paused, calculating that the show of solidarity with the Mexicans was not lost on the audience. "It is my understanding that

Lieutenant Donovan can either fight extradition or waive that right."

"And she realizes the consequences of her actions in a Mexican court if she waives her right to fight extradition?"

Sloane's anger was rising. "Lieutenant Donovan is fully cognizant of her rights under law."

"And you feel she'll be properly protected by the Mexican authorities if she's tried in Mexico?" The man was shouting now.

"Sir," Sloane bulldozed into the thick of it, "we have great faith in the integrity of the Mexican judicial system. We've had assurances from the Mexican government that this trial will proceed according to the best traditions of justice." He made a point of closing his binder.

"Are you able to protect her?" the man demanded.

"I'm sorry?"

"There are rumors that the murders have something to do with Mexican politicians."

The room quieted.

"Will you be able to physically protect Lieutenant Donovan?"

Sloane's reply was cold. "There is no substantiation for any such rumor."

"But I'm in possession of certain information which indicates …" Reporters began to surge around the speaker. What remained of the man's statement was drowned in the commotion.

"Could you please repeat that?" someone yelled from a far corner of the room. "Louder!" someone else shouted. "I can't hear you!"

Sloane's nemesis stood on a hard-backed chair to be heard. "I've received a phone call from a source I believe to be reliable, who states that Lieutenant Donovan's life may be in grave danger should she face trial in Mexico."

Sloane glared at his support staff, furious to be standing alone on the high wire on this one. His survival instinct kicked in. "There is categorically no danger to Lieutenant Donovan's person. But I invite you to speak with one of our officers." Sloane had regained the floor. All eyes were on two military police making their way to the man in the gray flannels. Seconds passed, only seconds. But by the time the focus switched back to the speaker, he had somehow disappeared.

Bart Sloane advised the room that the press conference was at an end. He immediately demanded the credentials of the speaker from an aide. He was informed that no one knew the man in the gray flannels. He wasn't properly accredited. He'd somehow managed to sneak into the media briefing. In effect, in media jargon, he was a non-person. He just didn't exist.

Thursday, June 11.
Tucson

22 The windowless interview room was spartan, ten by fifteen feet, with fluorescent lighting, a square field table, four folding chairs, and two doors – one through which Dunc Wooster was allowed entry, and another, iron and grilled, which remained shut until he was seated and the door locked behind him.

The woman was brought in under armed guard. She wore oversized prisoner's fatigues of a brilliant Seville orange with a jet black "P" on the back. He was told bluntly: ten minutes.

The iron door crashed shut. The key turned, ratchet-like, in the tumblers. Then they were alone, sitting opposite one another.

Pale, delicate as a ballerina, she didn't look at all like the photo in *USA Today,* Wooster mused. But then, how was an accused murderess supposed to look?

"You know who I am, I suppose?" she asked plainly.

Wooster nodded.

"And you know what I'm accused of?

"Yes."

"Have you ever represented a murderer?"

Dunc Wooster's lips were suddenly as dry as prunes. "No," he croaked.

Maria Donovan got right to the point. "I'm prepared to pay you a handsome retainer. But I have two questions that must be answered. One. Do you have a legal contact in Mexico?"

Wooster paused. "There is someone I use regularly, a very competent professional," he lied. If she could use the phone book to advantage, so could he. "Next question?"

"Have you ever done an extradition hearing?"

"Fought one?" he asked, putting on a show of bravery. He hesitated. For once, good judgment would supersede facile valor. "No." He shook his head. "Can't say as I have. Not 'fought' ..."

Maria Donovan interrupted. "You may have misunderstood me." She smiled. "Not fought. Surrendered."

Wooster crinkled his forehead. He wasn't certain if he'd heard right. "I beg your pardon?"

"You know ..." The young woman hesitated, searching for the word. "I believe the legal term is 'waived'?"

"I beg your pardon? I'm afraid I do not understand."

"I wish to stand trial in Mexico," Donovan declared, as plainly as if she were describing the color of the sky beyond the jail window.

"You don't need me for that," he said. "You can waive the hearing yourself."

Maria Donovan had a most serene look on her face. "But I do need your assistance."

"Why?"

"Let's just say it would be better if I had some pretense of legal counsel in the United States. And in Mexico ..."

Pretense of counsel. The words hurt. But Wooster had learned long ago that words don't pay the bills. Cash does. "You'll pay a big chunk of it up front," he commented matter-of-factly.

"Yes," she agreed.

"Ten thousand retainer, twenty-five thousand to follow."

Donovan nodded.

"Cash?"

Another nod.

"I can have the documentation done in a day, Miss Donovan. You'll be in Mexico within forty-eight hours."

"You may call me Maria." She smiled a little-girl smile. "One more thing." And the smile disappeared from the angelic face. "You'll stay with me in Mexico."

"It will cost . . ."

"I will pay you handsomely, Mr. Woolster."

"Wooster," he corrected.

"My apologies. I didn't get the name quite right from the chaplain."

"That's okay." The attorney smirked. "You can call me what you want."

He got up to leave, but now he felt sullen, disdainful. He adopted the tone he reserved for the misfits who bankrolled the gas tank of his Fairmont. "I won't insult you, or the video-monitoring system they have set up in here, by asking if you really did it."

"And I," she countered, not batting an eyelash, "won't insult you, Mr. Wooster, by asking if you're really capable of defending me."

PART TWO
HERMOSILLO

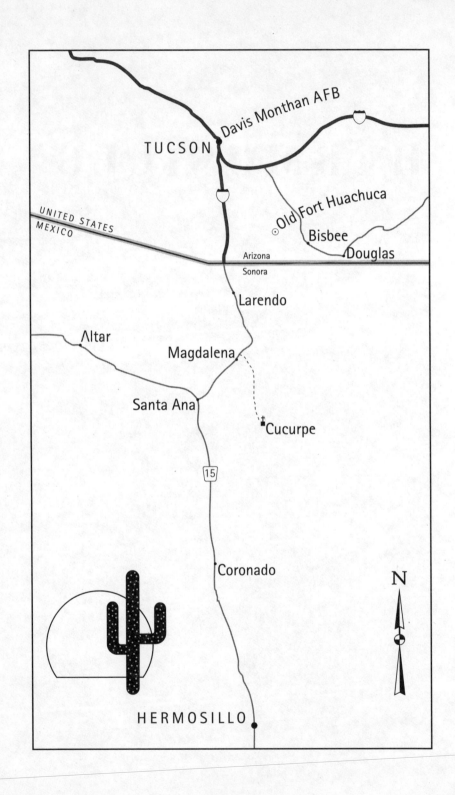

TUCSON

Davis Monthan AFB

Old Fort Huachuca

Bisbee

Douglas

UNITED STATES

MEXICO

Arizona

Sonora

Larendo

Altar

Magdalena

Santa Ana

Cucurpe

15

Coronado

N

HERMOSILLO

23

Fuentes flashed a building pass to the guard, a tall *federale* with an attitude and a submachine gun. Fuentes noted others of his ilk at attention in the lobby.

A reptilian flicker of recognition, a confirming glance at the sheet on the clipboard, and a nod. He could enter. Day nine of the trial, and no lapse in security. This was not characteristic, he mused. Even though he'd paced down this same corridor at the same time and seen this sentry each and every morning for more than two weeks, the ritual never changed.

In an unprecedented exhibition of Mexican judicial efficiency, though perhaps not respect for the rights of an accused to mount a proper defense, formal proceedings had commenced within three months of Lieutenant Donovan's arrest and extradition. Surprisingly, neither she nor her counsel had challenged this alacrity.

The hearing chamber was large, with a series of French doors extending along one side. Intricately laced portals overlooked a plaza and the *Catedral de l'Asuncion*, a dazzling white building with twin towers filling the azure sky like marzipan crowning a layered wedding cake. In the distance, beyond the diesel pollution and far beyond the green-tufted hills, Miguel could see the filmy, serrated peaks of the Sierra Madre.

The general public who now fought for a seat here, the hottest ticket outside of the bullfights, took their chances when the doors opened at nine every morning. Lineups extended around the block. Outside, in the searing heat, the taco venders and palm-readers did a roaring business.

The room was bathed in placid morning light. Motes of dust danced lightly on slanted sunrays. Downtown traffic droned outside the windowpanes – a faint, not unpleasant hum, like a hive of sated bees.

Fuentes seated himself to the right of the judge's raised bench at the end of a long table. As case exhibits officer, he was responsible for tracking evidence to ensure that it was ready for introduction at the wave of the prosecutor's hand. The work was precise to the point of tedium. To date, he'd handed over more than a thousand items of varying size and importance, each of which ultimately found its way to the court clerk to be registered as material testimony.

Understandably, his effectiveness as *jefe* had swiftly diminished, for the court proceedings had demanded considerable time and energy. In any event, there wasn't much happening in Coronado proper during the high summer heat. The only action was out near Querobabi, where the top-secret *federale* drug project was still active. And still without apparent result.

At Obregon's insistence, Miguel had just deputized a subordinate. The man selected, Emilio Commacho, was both able and respected by those of his peers who worked, and scarcely tolerated by the remainder. That, given the sorry state of the Coronado police force, was the best that could be expected. The appointment had been formalized over the past weekend.

Fuentes hadn't asked Asuncion if he'd be interested in the position of interim *jefe*. The portly detective would have agreed as a favor but, after thirty-eight years in harness, neither his heart nor stamina was up to it.

When not ferreting out meaningless snippets of *cantina* gossip in his nominal role as an intelligence operative, Felix now whiled away his considerable free time playing horseshoes in a pitch agreeably nestled in the town square, halfway between a stand of *palo verda* and a likeness of Pancho Villa slouching for all eternity astride a stallion tinged cullpepper-green by acid rain. It was his right. Fuentes knew he'd earned it.

Besides, according to their last conversation, eight days earlier, Asuncion was still discreetly digging into the convoluted roots of the enigmatic company at Six Tampico Court, with little success.

A month earlier, Fuentes had taken receipt of thirty volumes of binders, replete with identification photos and forensic notes belatedly forwarded by the U.S. Air Force Office of Special Investigations at Davis Monthan. They crammed a fridge-sized crate to overflowing and profiled in every conceivable way the contents of the Sunrise apartment and the assorted minutiae of Chandler's domestic life. After a pointedly short session with Miguel, the prosecutor's office had pragmatically concluded that their inclusion, en masse, in the trial would only decelerate the state's case from its current relatively tart pace to one of languid monotony. Fuentes had agreed. With enough testimony to hang Donovan from a dozen yardarms, he neither needed, nor wanted, more rope.

Still, he spent long nights at his *hacienda* poring over the binders, one by one, until, slowly but surely, he'd begun to find himself exploring an investigative path that he was loath to share with any living soul, except Felix.

He eyed his watch. Eight twenty-five – perhaps half an hour before the side door opened and Judge Herzog stormed in. He unrolled the newspaper he had brought with him.

A lead story outlined the Pope's recent trip to a small Navajo settlement in Arizona, part of a Vatican initiative to bolster the relevance of Christianity among aboriginal peoples. The elderly pontiff was on the eighth day of what might very well be his last visit to the New World. He was scheduled to spend a while longer in the U.S. Southwest before heading to Mexico, where he'd perform mass in the north, followed by stopovers in several of the largest Mexican cities. Fuentes was far from pious, but the theme of the papal tour – the need for justice for indigenous communities – was assuredly topical and not without controversy. Miguel languidly browsed through the paper before setting it aside and preparing for what the day would hold.

The judge, Esubio Herzog, was a bachelor from Acapulco with a reputation for fast living and faster women, a brilliant legal mind, and an even more consuming ego. He'd made his first millions as a nimble-witted defense counsel and counted among his closest personal friends some of Mexico's most notorious drug lords and high-ranking *federales,* some of whom were identical.

A stylish dresser given to elevator shoes and flowing judicial gowns, Esubio Herzog bounded into courtrooms with a theatrical flourish and a bullfighter's energy, diminished only slightly by a permanent limp, caused by a fall from a polo pony. He walked with the aid of a silver-tipped cane. His proceedings were electric and unpredictable.

Herzog was nearing retirement. The beckoning assurance of an ambassadorship in Costa Rica awaited him. He shrewdly parlayed this potential by showing fiscal loyalty to PRI coffers and by making judicial pronouncements on contentious cases that could have been dictated at the desk of the president of Mexico – and probably were. He ruled his court with energy and élan – and the public loved him.

The prosecutor was a brilliantined young blood with a bristle mustache named Diaz. He'd been especially assigned from Mexico City. When introduced, Fuentes had made the blunder of inquiring what the man's first name was and had been met with a cold response: "*Señor* – to you." It was only later he'd discovered that the pompous fool was called Adolpho. It made sense. The prosecutor was a martinet who twirled and danced and spoke on cue. He was good at it. Thereafter, Fuentes spoke little, and only when necessary, to "*Señor*" Adolpho. With their starched attitudes and monogrammed shirtcuffs, he and Ramon Obregon had a lot in common.

Miguel peered at the defense table and the toothy giant who loomed there, casually perusing some notes. Fiodr Zenin – "*El Loco Serb*" – the Mad Serbian – six-foot six and kneecap bald, was a most unusual man in a nation of unusual people. With his hunched shoulders and shining pate, Zenin looked like a brooding vulture. He'd even shaved his eyebrows to complete the grotesque effect.

The son of Balkan intellectuals who'd piously followed Trotsky to Mexico and remained true to "*la Causa*," even when it had been blunted by a madman's icepick, Zenin had inherited the trial as the result of an unusual phone call he'd received one sauna-hot weekday afternoon when he'd decided to stay at work rather than *siesta*. He didn't know the caller, but what he heard intrigued him, as did the promise of a healthy retainer, paid up front in American dollars.

The Mad Serb had acquired his unusual nickname as a consequence of constantly taking on seemingly hopeless causes, from peasant land claims against the Mexican military to privatization challenges at the Vera Cruz Port Authority. But his reputation as a man of integrity and determination was clinched by his greatest victory – a Pyrrhic one against car manufacturers who'd come to proliferate the *maquiladora* lands bordering the United States. With the active support of the PRI, the transnationals ravaged salaries, broke unions, and fired employees at will.

Zenin took on the manufacturers, one by one. He challenged them at arbitration boards, in the media, and in the streets. His actual successes were negligible, but considering the corrupt system he opposed, his proponents were forgiving. The same could not be said of the opposition.

When the car windows of his tangerine VW Beetle were blasted out on a main thoroughfare in Mexico City, with him still seated in the car, bemused police put it down to kids playing with pellet guns. When his apartment was broken into and its contents trashed, it was a case of an overexuberant amateur.

But when he was confronted in a dark alley by three punks who pummeled him to within an inch of his life while cursing him by name, police reluctantly admitted that Zenin might have some very serious enemies. They hinted darkly that "for health reasons" he should take on less contentious legal issues. If anything, the attacks made Fiodr redouble his labors.

While Obregon and other federales detested Zenin, Fuentes was more accepting. He'd never crossed swords with the Mad Serb, and as a matter of course, he drew no conclusions without experience.

A rumpled-suited gnome named Wooster completed the defense team. Early in the trial, Miguel had heard through the grapevine that Wooster was an eccentric intellectual who'd terrorized the Arizona courts, criminal division, with his brilliance. But that rumor had quickly gone the way of the Maria wind, as the American religiously nodded off daily by two-fifteen and did *The New York Times* crossword and little else for what remained of his waking hours in the courtroom.

At any trial presided over by Esubio Herzog, the jury members were present only for window dressing. Miguel knew that, in the end, they'd listen to Herzog's charge and do his bidding. The judge was a man who lectured loftily about principles but acted clearly in his own interests.

In the center of it all, seated behind bulletproof Plexiglas, sat Maria Donovan. Miguel had seen her in Tucson shortly after her arrest, and the ensuing spate of media attention had featured her comely image. A week had passed, and then came the news that she had waived extradition and would stand trial in Mexico.

When Fuentes had actually seen Donovan enter the courtroom in Hermosillo, he was shocked by the deterioration in her appearance. She'd lost weight and looked wan and dispirited. The luster was gone from her hair. It was now tied in a utilitarian ponytail. She wore formless prison garb of bleached cotton and was guarded by a slew of female prison officers, even though she was shackled hand and foot whenever she left the box. Maria Donovan averted her gaze, as if she could withdraw from the room.

The prosecution's opening address to the jury took the better part of the first day. It was a spirited defense of the Mexican family and its values that awed Miguel, despite his personal misgivings about Diaz. The prosecutor had shrewdly downplayed the fact that, by his involvement in drug dealing, Wickham Chandler had been as instrumental in laying the foundation for his own death and the ensuing tragedy as was the woman facing four counts of murder. Diaz skillfully played every emotional chord, short of taking the gory crime scene photos and passing them out to the jury. This he wisely left for later.

For six days, a cavalcade of prosecution witnesses passed in ponderous procession, unchallenged, but for the most basic and innocuous questions as points of clarification by the defense.

In sequence, Adolpho Diaz brought to the stand individuals who could place the deceased at the hotel before the blast, then those who'd arrived immediately after it had happened, including police officers and civilian volunteers who'd dug out the site in the trying time that followed to unearth the horrific remains of four human beings.

Central to the prosecution's foray was the role Fuentes had played as senior local official at the disaster scene. By his own recollection, and Diaz's grudging public admission, Miguel had acquitted himself well, both at the site and in the subsequent retelling under oath.

With Donovan's whispered prompting, the defense asked only one thing during cross-examination, a curious query that had also secretly troubled Miguel throughout his investigation. How was it that *Comandante* Obregon happened to be at Zita's so promptly after the explosion? Judge Herzog ruled the question out of order and beyond the scope of competence of the witness.

Ramon Obregon took the stand immediately after Fuentes. He proudly recounted a litany of *federale* efficiencies in the inquiry, glibly explaining away his own peculiar presence at Zita's as a coincidence of the highest order. And there it remained.

The next witness was a paunchy Mexican army officer, a bomb-disposal expert seconded to the *federale* detachment at Hermosillo for the investigation. He laboriously explained the evidence of blast damage he'd observed at the demolished hotel suite, the high heat, distorted metal, and tracings he'd located at the blast seat and removed from the crater to be sent out for analysis.

He was followed into the box by a specialist from the Explosives Technology branch of the American Bureau of Alcohol, Tobacco, and Firearms, a dour New Englander who prosaically outlined the science of gas chromatography – a chemical process used to separate the compounds that make up all explosives.

Soil samples from the Coronado site had been carefully analyzed in the West Virginia lab. Each in turn was vaporized and sent down a tube of inert gas. All the compounds separated, and each settled in the tube at a different monitored rate, which was called its retention time. The times were then compared to parameters already known at the ATF facility. Traces of RDX, PETN chemical compound, and plasticizer were verified.

Five hours after its initial receipt by ATF staffers, the explosive used to blow a gaping thirty-by-twenty-foot hole in Zita's motel had been accurately identified. The signature composition was unmistakable. It was of Czech origin – Semtex.

Was he certain?

One hundred percent.

He was not rebutted.

Midway through the witness list, the prosecution called on a drug expert, a sallow-skinned Mexican from the Central Government Labs, who glumly confirmed that the heroin in the two bags found in the Oldsmobile had tested seventy-two percent pure and that it had a street value of more than $300,000 U.S.

Immediately following him, a *federale* fingerprint technician explained that six latent prints had been lifted from the surface of one of the bags, and that they belonged to the accused before the court, Maria Donovan.

Thirteen witnesses later, the prosecution had successfully established that there had been an explosion caused by military-grade Semtex explosive and that four people had died violent deaths. It had also introduced the drugs and painted a reasonably successful portrait that connected the accused to the vehicle and its particular contents at the time of the blast.

By this time, Miguel Fuentes had doodled his way through five scribblers and checked off slightly more than one thousand of the exhibits.

It was then that Adolpho Diaz went for the jugular.

Shortly after two o'clock this particular afternoon, with buffed cobalt thunderclouds muttering in the far-off mountains, he called his next witness, Dr. Lexor Smit, chief coroner for the State of Sonora.

Pince-nezed and sporting a bow tie with saffron polka dots on a cranberry field, Lexor Smit was intent on bringing sobriety and somnolence to the proceedings. He stubbornly responded to the prosecutor's questions at his own pace and stayed in the box for the next three days.

Much of Smit's evidence was corroborated by video footage of the bodies. Smit sequentially outlined various injuries the deceased had suffered, in dispassionate detail. The footage of the two children proved the hardest to bear. Three jurors blanched visibly, one fainted outright, and more than a handful of spectators had to be escorted out of the courtroom threatening vengeance against the prisoner.

In the late afternoon of Smit's second session, in the midst of the videotaped autopsy of the girl, Terese, the courtroom staff approached Obregon to report that they had received their first serious bomb threat. The next morning, five huge and cumbersome metal-detectors appeared at the courthouse entrance. Thereafter security became airtight.

It was just before noon, after an army metal-detector had swept the room, that the state completed its questioning of Dr. Lexor Smit.

Then, after a short break, it was the turn of the defense.

Fiodr Zenin was an imposing figure with an ego commensurate to his size. But the gods had played a mean-spirited trick on him. He stuttered.

"Doctor," the Serbian émigré began, speaking in a gratingly slow cadence, "the prosecution has indicated that three persons were killed as a consequence of blast trauma. The fourth, Wickham Chandler, expired of a heroin overdose."

"Correct."

"What specifically caused Captain Chandler's death?"

"It's as you have said, counselor," the coroner commented dryly. "A heroin overdose."

"What was the purity of the heroin recovered from Captain Chandler's car?"

"Seventy-two percent."

"And you testified that the purity of heroin found in the body of Wickham Chandler was – how much?" Zenin asked once more with a diffident smile. He began to approach the box.

"Seventy-two percent. As you implied with your previous question," he added impatiently, "enough to kill him."

"In your professional opinion, do you believe that Captain

Chandler was, in all likelihood, already dead when the bomb exploded?"

"Yes," Dr. Smit said testily, "I believe that is so."

"Is there any indication as to who might have injected the heroin into the body of the deceased?"

"No." The doctor gazed uncomfortably up at his accuser. "Of course not."

"Why are you so sure of this?"

"Because," Smit declared, "the blast destroyed much of the evidence."

"Such as?" Zenin eased away from the witness box.

"A needle," Smit smirked.

Zenin turned on his heel, interrupting Smit's musings. "A good point, Doctor. Did anyone have a needle? No, let me rephrase that. To the best of your knowledge, did anyone find the needle – or for that matter any syringe – at the crime scene?"

"No."

"Was any syringe introduced to you by police for purposes of comparison in relation to this tragedy?"

"No."

"So you have no way of knowing who injected the drug into the deceased party?" A pause. "Or when?"

"No."

"Do you believe Wickham Chandler was a heroin addict?"

Smit glanced to the prosecution table. "No," he replied finally, in a less-than-firm voice. "There was no metabolic evidence of previous usage."

"The accused before you, *Señorita* Donovan? Do you know if she might be a heroin addict?"

"No."

"Have you ever tested her to see if she was?"

"No."

The titanic Serb pressed. "Has any person in the Mexican prison system?"

"Objection, Your Honor," Diaz intervened politely, straightening a pleat in his trousers as he rose to speak. "This goes beyond the scope of Doctor Smit's experience. The good doctor is coroner for the State of Sonora, not a general practitioner in a federal prison treating inmates for their addictions."

"Sustained," sniffed Judge Herzog, twirling a pencil about a legal pad as if it were a spinner on a game board.

Zenin scratched his bald pate and smiled, showing a battlement of bad teeth. "Doctor Smit," he began, "two kilos is a lot of heroin, don't you agree?"

"Yes," the coroner snapped.

"Assuredly an amount that would give rise to serious questions if you found it in someone's possession?"

"Yes."

"You can't inject heroin that you don't possess, can you, Doctor?"

The coroner's eyes narrowed at the curious question. He fumbled with his bow tie. "I beg your pardon?"

Zenin shrugged as if what he'd noted were patently obvious. "Logically speaking, Doctor, you can't physically inject heroin if you don't first physically possess it? Am I right?"

"Yes," Smit conceded, "I don't suppose you can – "

"And the only types of people that illegally possess heroin are those that inject it for their own use or those that traffic in it for profit?"

"Yes," the coroner harrumphed. "Of course, that goes without saying."

"And it also goes without saying," Zenin continued, his voice rising, "that the police do not have any real evidence that would lead them or you to conclude that Wickham Chandler himself physically possessed the bags of heroin found under the seats of the Oldsmobile parked at Zita's Motel, do they?"

"No, they do not."

"Or that Wickham Chandler was an addict?" A pause. "Or that the accused, Maria Donovan, had injected him? Because if any of these possibilities existed, you would have utilized the syringe as a test sample against the quantity found in the victim's system, am I right?"

Despite his better impulse, Smit agreed. "Yes, you are right."

"You don't know if the accused was a heroin addict do you, Doctor?" Zenin pressed on. "Or if she could even obtain a supply of heroin?"

"Your Honor!" Diaz leapt up, beside himself with exasperation.

Herzog dropped the pencil from his hands. It clattered onto the floor. He glared toward the gangly defense attorney.

"*Señor* Zenin," he remonstrated, "you'll refrain from badgering the witness. Doctor Smit is a well-respected physician in this community."

The defense lawyer bowed in deference to the judge's pronouncement. The honor of his witness satisfied, Adolpho Diaz sat down.

"Let me summarize the evidence for you, sir," Zenin began anew. "We have a man found dead of a heroin overdose, a man who'd apparently never taken heroin. And we have no drug evidence to link his death to any living person in this courtroom. Does that about summarize it, Doctor?"

Diaz darted once more, whippet-like, out of his seat. "Objection, Your Honor!" he pronounced wearily. "The question calls for speculation on the part of the witness and goes far beyond his realm of expertise. Doctor Smit has been called to testify as a medical professional, a coroner, on the status of the bodies he autopsied. We are not indicating that he has anything else to offer this court. And neither should the defense."

Zenin didn't wait for the judge's pronouncement. "My apologies," he conceded, placing his hands together, lotus-like, at the palms and bringing them dramatically to the tip of his nose. "Doctor Smit," he plodded on, "let me rephrase the question. You are not *personally* aware of any medical evidence that would link the tragic drug overdose of Wickham Chandler to my client?"

"No."

The Serb canted his gleaming head to one side. "Repeat that, please?"

"No," Smit stormed, exasperated. "I have nothing."

"Thank you, Doctor."

Adolpho Diaz stood up with quiet and controlled grace. "Doctor," he began pensively, "I have but one question. In your vast experience as a coroner, is the amount of heroin you discovered in the system of the deceased, Wickham Chandler, the customary dosage one might attribute to an addict?"

"No sir," the coroner replied, caution scribbled like graffiti over his features. "It was between ten and twenty times as potent as what addicts generally use in Sonora."

"Would it be potent enough to kill?"

"It could do nothing else."

"So you'd agree," Diaz continued, a sanguine smile on his face, "that whoever did this to Wickham Chandler clearly intended to commit murder?"

Lexor Smit demurred. "There is no other plausible explanation."

"No further questions."

The next witness was an impeccably dressed Asian by the name of Lilly Truong. Of Vietnamese origin, she was a university-trained pharmacist who worked at a drugstore in suburban Tucson. After having the witness describe her professional credentials, Diaz began his examination.

"Did you know Wickham Chandler?"

"Yes. He was a regular customer at our pharmacy."

"Could you indicate to the court if he ever required needles?"

"Yes," the woman chirped. "He was diabetic. He needed needles for his insulin. He got that through our pharmacy, too," she added by way of illumination.

"When did you last see him?"

"Several weeks ago. On April 28. He bought insulin and a box of needles. I filled his prescription for the drug."

"How long would that amount of insulin last?"

"About four weeks."

"So he would have needed insulin after that date?"

"Certainly. He couldn't do without it." She nodded for emphasis. "He was diabetic, as I said."

"Yes," Diaz commented dryly. "You did tell us that, Miss Truong." He perused his notes. "And to your knowledge, did anyone fill Wickham Chandler's prescription for insulin after that time?"

Lilly Truong nodded. "I did."

"Did the captain bring that prescription to you at the pharmacy?"

"No."

"Who did that, may I ask?"

"Miss Donovan. Maria Donovan."

"And is that person in the court?"

Lilly Truong nodded once more. She timidly pointed to the individual in the prisoner's box.

Diaz went back to his desk and returned with two pieces of paper stapled together. He handed the witness the items. "Is this the prescription you refer to?"

The tiny pharmacist peered intently at the document as if committing it to memory. "Yes," she replied, "that's it."

"Please read the details," Diaz commanded.

Lilly Truong did as she was told. "A box of one hundred ROY cc insulin syringes, twenty-nine gauge, with a capacity of fifty units, at a cost of $23.60."

"How were these items paid for?"

"By credit card," the woman answered, flipping to the second stapled page. "There's a credit-card carbon attached to the prescription. And here are my initials, next to the authorization number."

Diaz enthusiastically leaned forward into the witness box. "What is the name on the credit card you accepted as payment?"

"Maria Donovan."

Diaz passed the pages to the court clerk, who gave them to Judge Herzog to peruse. They were then introduced and recorded without defense challenge as exhibits 1136 and 1137.

"Did Miss Donovan often come into the pharmacy to get things for Captain Chandler? Prescriptions and the like?"

"Occasionally."

"And did he do the same for her?"

"Yes," she whispered.

"Would you say Wickham Chandler and Maria Donovan knew each other on a more than professional basis?"

"Objection." Zenin half stood in his seat. "That calls for speculation on the part of the witness."

"Sustained," Herzog yawned.

"Let me rephrase that question, may I?" Diaz deftly back-tracked. "Miss Truong, did you ever see Maria Donovan and Wickham Chandler together?"

"Yes, often."

"Describe those meetings."

"I beg your pardon?"

"Well, did you ever see them holding hands?"

"Yes."

"Did you ever see any overt gestures of affection?"

"Certainly." She nodded her head with vigor.

"Why do you say that?"

The woman in the witness box blushed ever so slightly. "Because . . ." she began, hesitating to go further. "Because, since they lived together, I just assumed that . . ." The words trailed off.

"I beg your pardon?" Diaz interrupted. "Speak louder."

"I said that since they lived together, I just assumed . . ."

Diaz raised his hand to interrupt. "Lived together?" he uttered. "How do you know that?"

"Well," Lilly Truong replied, "I also prepared medication for Miss Donovan. The prescription was for the same condominium address in Tucson: 500 Sunrise Drive, apartment 603."

"During what time period would this have happened?"

"At least through April and May of this year."

"You are telling me that, for the months of April and May of this year, Captain Wickham Chandler and Lieutenant Maria Donovan shared the same address: apartment 603, 500 Sunrise Drive, Phoenix, Arizona?"

"Yes."

"No further questions." With an exaggerated flourish, Diaz sat down.

A wave of brisk chatter quickly engulfed the courtroom. Judge Herzog allowed it to flow, then ebb. After a finely measured moment, he tapped his gavel. Briskly. Once. Twice. The commotion ceased.

When his turn came to examine the witness, Fiodr Zenin for a moment chose to stay seated. "You're a very precise woman," he lauded, "a pharmacy graduate –"

"UCLA, cum laude," Lilly Truong interrupted with obvious pride.

"Congratulations. A marvelous accomplishment! I'm certain you're quite diligent. Thorough. You pay attention to every detail."

"As a professional, it is my duty."

Zenin paused; with a beckoning hand he coaxed her on.

"You see, competence is critical for a pharmacist. You can't afford to make mistakes with prescriptions and the like."

"Certainly." Zenin smiled a honeyed smile that showed nothing behind it but teeth. "So you feel you must pay attention to detail. Dosages. Expiry dates. The color and shape of things – pills. And the like."

The witness gave a vigorous nod.

Zenin rose and the grin disappeared abruptly from his face. "Can you describe a single item in the apartment of Wickham Chandler and Maria Donovan, Miss Truong?" he asked, his six-foot-six frame approaching the witness box. "The apartment you're so certain that they shared?"

"No," she stammered meekly.

"Can you describe their living room?" He glowered down at her. "No."

"Have you ever actually been to the apartment at 500 Sunrise?" "No."

"Yet you assert that these two individuals were living together." "I assumed . . ."

"But you have no proof of familiarity other than an address on a prescription receipt and some visual observations you made about their 'apparent' familiarity?"

"I may have been mistaken – "

"Mistaken?" Zenin tut-tutted. "Isn't it a fact that all that you saw were public gestures of affection that could be interpreted in many ways? In truth, isn't it fair to say that you don't know anything about the lives of my client and the deceased, Wickham Chandler, either public or private, beyond the fact that they bought certain items from your pharmacy?"

"Yes, I suppose that is so," the woman whispered.

"No further questions."

Diaz was rapier-short and to the point in re-examination. He asked but three things. Were the needles sharp? Could they be used to inject prescription drugs? And finally, could they be used to inject illicit drugs? The answer to each query was an unequivocal affirmative. Then he sat down.

Zenin became confused as to where this particular line of examination was heading. But then, he wasn't in the business of shoring up the state's case, he thought with guarded optimism. He let the matter rest.

The session was brought to a close on a more positive note for the prosecution with a plenum of witnesses provided courtesy of Obregon's investigative teams. Evidence adduced from these people appeared irrefutable and quite damaging to the defense.

The bartender from the El Toro recalled the scene between Donovan and Chandler in evident detail. They'd been at a table by the front door, arguing in urgent whispers. He'd overheard much of the discussion.

She was overwrought. Chandler appeared equally agitated. The barkeeper heard her say she was tired of the game, that the project was too big and wouldn't go for much longer, that they could move shipments efficiently across the border but needed each other to make it work. He countered that she was jeopardizing the whole thing. The woman said it was Chandler; that if he didn't trust her, she'd do something about it and soon – before the border guards lost their nerve and did them all in. She left visibly agitated. He stayed a while longer then left alone.

The next witness, a plumber sent to upgrade sinks at Zita's, had passed a vehicle in the motel parking lot when he'd arrived at a little after ten on the morning of the explosion. The truck was big, bright, and yellow, the kind the U.S. army drove in all the TV commercials. He remembered the license plate – "PALOMA" – and the sole occupant, a petite, pretty woman. He fingered Donovan from the witness box as that person. She'd looked really worried that day. A while later, at maybe 11:15, he'd gone outside to get tools from his pickup. The truck was nowhere to be seen.

He'd had to return to his vehicle a few times because the plumbing job was a complicated one and he needed special wrenches. On the last occasion, the mysterious yellow truck was parked on the perimeter of the lot, its motor running. The woman was still inside. She was still alone.

Two minutes later, maybe three, tops, the explosion happened. The plumber spent a short time trying to help victims. When he left to move his own vehicle to safer ground, the yellow truck and its female occupant were gone. Disappeared. He'd never seen her again, until today. When asked about the woman, he pointed directly to Donovan.

A handwriting expert flown in specifically from the FBI forensic laboratories in Arlington, Virginia, compared specimens of working files at Davis Monthan seized under warrant with the signature of the mysterious "Mrs. H. Clinton" found on the Bank of Bavaria client card and determined that they were written by one and the same person – the accused, Maria Donovan.

The bank manager, Maximilian Gordon, identified Donovan instantly and placed her in his bank on the day of the bombing, despite the fact that she had been wearing a red wig. He also recalled that Donovan and Chandler had opened a savings account that ultimately held $67,000 U.S. And that on the date of the murders, at about 3:40 p.m., Donovan, red wig and all, had been to the bank and, without explanation, withdrawn the entire amount, asking that it be given to her in $100 bills.

The next witness called by Diaz was a bucolic car dealer from Tucson by the name of Aristotle Giftopolos. In addition to a hamburger and souvlaki joint, Giftopolos owned a used car lot with the improbable title of Nick the Greek's Flagship Auto

Sales. He moved all sorts of items, quickly, with an inventory and sales hook that ran the gamut from "just like new" rentals to "little old ladies from Palo Alto."

Under examination, Giftopolos bragged about his latest acquisition – a troop of slightly used army Hummers. The car dealer remembered the accused. She'd leased a Hummer on the very day it arrived on the lot. A $55,000 price tag, and a bargain at that. How had she paid? Monthly payments of $1,000 and an option to purchase. He'd accepted the first installment with a personal check. She was creditworthy – an air force lieutenant. Aristotle Giftopolos was proud to be an American and supported its military.

Giftopolos apologized vaguely to the court when it was brought to his attention that he was in Mexico and not the United States of America. And further payments? Well, that was rather fascinating. Donovan came in about a week later and paid it all off. In cash. Fifty-four thousand. In crisp $100 bills.

The sturdy Greek businessman had the bill of sale with him. Her signature was on it. He thrust the document into Judge Herzog's hands. See? Maria Victoria Donovan. The lieutenant's own signature as new owner. The date? May 24. Was she driving the Hummer that day? Sure was.

"Could you describe the vehicle?" Diaz continued.

As he could his first date, Aristotle Giftopolos burbled. Brilliant lemon color. By then she'd gotten personalized plates and put custom panels on the sides – a bunch of Indians racing around in the desert. The license she'd purchased? He remembered it, too. Like the Bobby Vinton song, you know? "PALOMA."

The last witness summoned was a U.S. Customs agent at the Nogales border crossing, who produced a printout for the month of May. It recorded a license plate "PALOMA" entering Mexico at 8:19 on the morning of May 21 and leaving at 8:57 that same evening. The female occupant, an American citizen, had nothing to declare on reentry into the United States.

Fuentes sensed the dampened mood of the defense counsel. But Zenin knew better than to dig his own grave and that of his client at this point in the trial.

24 "Sir! Sir!" A young court officer hovered over Fuentes. "Court's beginning soon." Fuentes roused himself from his seat. He hadn't realized he'd been daydreaming.

He glanced around. The wall clock showed 9:30. The courtroom was full. Zenin and the American lawyer sat huddled on the defense side, plotting strategy. Diaz, wearing an expensive charcoal suit, confidently strutted up the center aisle toward the prosecutor's table, carrying an armful of papers. Obregon followed at a respectful pace carrying a trim briefcase and his ever-present cellphone. He seemed preoccupied as he spoke animatedly into the device.

Diaz sat next to Miguel without even a customary nod of greeting. Obregon remained standing. He had a troubled look on his face. Miguel overheard the expressions "secure escort" and "risk" frantically whispered. He tensed, for he knew who the next scheduled witness would be.

Obregon hissed something into Diaz's ear, then glanced in Fuentes's direction. The *federale*'s face gave away nothing. With a laconic nod, he signaled to the guards. A door opened and the prisoner was escorted in.

Given the circumstances, the accused appeared quite calm. She wore the standard-issue drab prison garb. Her hair was tied in a bun on this occasion, emphasizing her high cheekbones. The guard removed the wrist shackles and escorted her behind the bulletproof glass of the prisoner's box. Donovan was surrounded by a phalanx of armed police. She chatted amicably with one of the female guards.

The clerk entered from a side door, followed by Judge Herzog. The tenth day in the trial of Maria Donovan had begun. Court was once more in session.

"I'd like to call the first witness, Your Honor," Diaz opened in an imperious manner. "Airman Damien Moffatt, United States Air Force."

The rear door of the courtroom opened ever so slightly. Miguel caught a brief glimpse of federal guards surrounding a tall, spindly individual in a U.S. Air Force dress uniform. The guards wore berets and combat fatigues. The submachine guns they carried at the port position appeared more menacing than usual.

Moffatt walked to the front of the courtroom, flanked by two men in business suits who made no pretense of concealing the awkward bulges in their jackets. The airman's straw-colored hair was shaved to recruit length. His ears protruded even farther than Miguel remembered. He moved cautiously. Fuentes thought he looked pale and scared.

After the oath-taking and ritual identification of the witness, Diaz began.

"Airman Moffatt, how long have you been in the United States Air Force?"

"Three years, sir."

"And where have you been posted in that time?"

"Davis Monthan Airbase, Tucson, Arizona. That's the only place. I'm with AMARC."

Judge Herzog interrupted the prosecutor. "What is AMARC?" he demanded in stilted English, waving off the interpreter with a jaded flick of his hand.

"The Aerospace Maintenance and Reclamation Center."

"Where you now work?"

"Yes, sir." Moffatt turned to face the bench. "It's where we mothball our old stock."

"Such as?" Herzog peered over his rimmed glasses.

"Anything we need in the air force – airplanes, rockets, ammunition – the obvious stuff. And other things too," he hastened to add. "Tables, chairs, and computers. Furniture for living quarters, like televisions and electrical appliances, sofas . . ." His voice trailed off. He looked to the judge for approval.

Herzog, satisfied, nodded for Diaz and the interpreter to continue.

"What do you do there?"

"I'm an aircraftsman, fourth class. I do general maintenance."

Diaz strode up to the witness box. He confidently rested his arm on the ledge. "You also worked for a time at a unit at Davis Monthan called the 355 Supply Squadron?"

"I did."

"And who was the most recent commanding officer of that unit?"

"Captain Chandler, sir. Captain Wickham Chandler."

"Did you ever know an individual named Dwight Buscom?"

"Yes."

"Describe your relationship to Mr. Buscom."

"He was a buddy of mine." Moffatt shrugged. "We went through training together."

"Did Dwight Buscom work with you at Davis Monthan?"

"Yes, sir. For nearly two years."

"And where is he now?"

"Elmendorf Airbase, Alaska. He was transferred in May, right after completing his punishment detail."

"Punishment detail?"

"Yes, sir. In March, Captain Chandler went after Dwight for making a phony entry in the duty sheets. In May, he drew two weeks' punishment doing night watch at AMARC. I was on nights at the same time."

"You were on the punishment detail also?"

"No, sir!" Moffatt retorted self-righteously. "Regular tour."

"Was Wickham Chandler one of the duty officers on those dates?"

"Yes."

"Have you ever had any difficulties with the Tucson police?"

Moffatt hesitated, then, evidently resigned to his fate, inched onward. "Last December we was busted for coke. Simple possession," he added lamely.

"Was any one else arrested with you?" the prosecutor cajoled.

"Yes. Dwight Buscom."

"Did you tell your air force superiors about this?" Diaz ventured.

"No way!" The young airman seemed appalled at the notion. "If I did I'd be up for a dishonorable discharge."

"And that's the last thing you would want – isn't it, Mr. Moffatt?" the prosecutor suggested.

"Yes, sir," Moffatt replied.

"Could you tell us what happened to you because of your arrest in Tucson?"

The witness asked for water. A pitcher and glass tumbler were brought to him on a tray and the guard poured. Moffatt drank the glass empty, then wiped his mouth with the sleeve of his uniform jacket. The air conditioners grumbled in the windows. A few spectators started to whisper and were quieted by the guards.

Moffatt peered about the courtroom, a look of stony hostility etched into his face. Fuentes followed the man's gaze to its destination – Ramon Obregon.

The *federale* sat easily, humming under his breath. He calmly tapped a pencil on the tabletop. Then he suddenly snapped the pencil in two. The airman stiffened visibly at the sound, then slouched into his chair.

Moffatt coughed, a dry, hacking sound. He started to speak. His voice was raspy, shallow. He halted occasionally, whether to clear his throat or recall the evidence, Fuentes couldn't say.

"Captain Chandler spoke to Dwight and me on a Tuesday in February," Moffat began. "A few days after we'd pleaded guilty in the Tucson court. We'd finished dinner in the mess and were going back to barracks. The captain pulled up in his car and asked us to hop in. He told us he knew about the convictions. He said it was a bum rap, that he felt badly for us, especially since we had to keep it a secret from the base commander or get dishonorable discharges. He asked our help with a scheme he'd dreamed up, something to move stock out of the base warehouses. The way he was talking, we knew it wasn't something legit, even though he never came right out and said so. Let's face it, no commissioned officer ever talks business with an enlisted man. At least not in the air force I work in."

Diaz nodded sympathetically.

"We didn't bite that day," Moffatt continued. "Dwight was real reluctant. The next morning, Captain Chandler hit him with false entries in the duty log. Someone else had forged them. The idea of punishment detail really got Buscom's attention – and mine." The airman slouched back in his chair.

"Yes?" the prosecutor prompted.

"We met the captain later that morning. He explained his plan."

"Please outline this 'scheme' to the court."

The airman appeared to tremble. "Well you see, it's like this. Over time, me and Dwight had developed contacts in Mexico to get us cocaine, at a place called Coronado. In the first week of March we arranged to get some for the captain."

"Why?"

Moffatt faced his questioner with a look half bemused, half disdainful. The answer seemed self-evident. "We didn't have much choice, did we? He was blackmailing us."

"This was the first time?"

"With Chandler? Ya."

"How much cocaine did you supply to Captain Chandler?"

"A key."

Diaz arched his eyebrows. "Sorry?" he said loudly, and for effect.

"A kilo."

"And what did you use to pay for it?"

Moffatt wavered. "Stuff we'd stolen from the warehouse in the past," he allowed finally. "Things we kept hidden in the desert for a rainy day."

"So you'd stolen from the air force base before?"

"Only a little," Moffatt protested. "Nothin' big. Old televisions, fridges, computer hardware . . . ."

Diaz interrupted. "How long had you been doing it?"

"Maybe a year," the airman answered, his eyes shifting.

"And Chandler knew?"

"Ya." Moffatt nodded vigorously, as if he were the wronged innocent. "He seemed to know all about it. He even showed us some of the inventory sheets we'd altered."

"You always purchased drugs with the items you stole?"

Moffatt meekly nodded his head.

"Answer the question."

"Yes."

"You say you got Chandler a kilo of cocaine?" Another nod. "Describe the things you exchanged to get that amount."

"A thousand top-end Pentium chips. A few expensive computers." Moffatt screwed his face in concentration. "I think that was it."

"Did you make any profit from this deal?"

"No sir," Moffatt protested.

"Where did the drugs go again?"

"To Captain Chandler, sir."

"And what exactly did he do with a kilo of cocaine?"

"I don't know," the airman answered. "It wasn't my business after he got it." Moffatt hitched his sloping shoulders. "He was an officer."

"What happened after that first occasion?"

"Chandler asked us to do it again. He said it was cool and nothin' could happen 'cause we were in it together. He said that with the size of our inventory on base, we were going to do some big-time trading."

"And you allowed him to continue with these obviously criminal demands?" Diaz exaggerated his query with theatrical dismay.

"I didn't think we had much choice," Moffatt replied, forlorn. "He had us over a barrel."

"And?"

"We did what he wanted," the airman concluded with blind equanimity. "Then, a few days after our first buy, Chandler asked to meet our Mexican contact."

Diaz stopped in his tracks. His eyes sharpened. "You took Wickham Chandler, a commissioned officer in the United States Air Force, with you into Mexico to close deals with drug traffickers?"

"Ya." Moffatt's face dissolved into a grin. "I guess that's about right, now that you put it that way."

"When did the initial meeting with Chandler and your contact happen?"

"The beginning of the second week of April, a Monday."

"Describe it."

"Kinda simple, really. We drove to the usual spot in Coronado and introduced Chandler and a friend of his to our man. They went inside a building to talk. When they finished, we left. Two days later, we provided another trade – merchandise for drugs."

"How much was moved from the month of April onward?"

"A dozen kilos of cocaine, maybe more. I can't remember now."

"How many times?"

"Six, maybe eight trips."

"And you dealt only in cocaine?"

"No," Moffatt remarked. "Grass and hash, too." The grin evaporated. "And heroin."

Diaz let the last phrase settle slowly on the room.

"So you were quite diversified?"

"Pardon?" Moffatt scrunched his face into a huge question mark.

"Never mind," Diaz wearily dismissed the response. "You say Chandler met your contact on of the second week of April, a Monday?"

"Ya."

"From that point on, did you have any dealings with this Mexican 'contact,' as you've identified him?"

"No." Moffatt seemed genuinely affronted. "The captain told us he was going to be the new main man. That if he caught us back-dealing, he'd frame up charges so quick, we'd never know what hit us."

"And you believed him?"

Moffatt shrugged dumbly.

Diaz returned to his desk at a measured pace. He peered about the courtroom and then, certain the delay had achieved its intended impact, continued.

"Airman?" he asked sharply. "How did the drugs get across the border?"

Moffatt straightened his shoulders. "The Mexican people did waste removal. Oil sludge, stuff like that. They supplied tanker trucks to transport the sludge back into Mexico. The rigs had insulated compartments in the middle big enough to carry most of the hot goods we provided – undetected – in a single trip."

"Such units were never challenged at the border? Not even a routine check?"

Moffatt smiled, then shook his head knowingly. "Not too many people are going to check a tanker with a skull and cross-bones on it."

"But if, on the off chance the tankers were stopped...?"

"Then we'd bribe the officials," Moffatt remarked, as if it were the most natural thing in the world.

"Mexican and American?"

"Yes."

"Describe the items you brought into Mexico as barter under Chandler's direction."

The witness became restive. Then he calmly recited the criminal inventory. "Originally, we concentrated on computer hardware – motherboards, Pentium chips, stuff like that."

"Did Wickham Chandler ever pay hard cash for illicit drugs?"

"No, sir."

"Who decided what was to be taken from the air force depot at Davis Monthan?"

"Chandler always got a shopping list from his Mexican contact."

"Who was?" the prosecutor interjected.

"I don't know his name."

"Can you tell the court what he looked like?"

The American wavered. He fidgeted with his fingers.

"Perhaps I can help you," Diaz asserted sarcastically. "We'll work up to it, shall we?" The broad chamber doors opened. A court officer sauntered forward, pushing a dolly. On it rested a slide projector and tray. Responding to the prosecutor's whispered instructions, the custodian parked the device in the center of the room several paces to the left of the judge's bench. A second official carried a screen that he opened and placed at a respectable distance from the projector. The overhead lights were dimmed and windows were shuttered. The prosecutor turned on the projector.

The first slide appeared to have been taken at midday. A group of tin huts basking in honey-gold sunshine. Refuse. A Dodge pickup and a large aluminum-ribbed tanker trailer, the kind that carry fuels and such, were parked half in, half out of the picture.

The Dodge had Arizona plates. A pump-action shotgun nestled in a cradle behind the bench seat. The driver's door was open. Two men lounged near the truck, one on the running board, the other resting his arm lazily on the door bracing for the rearview mirror. The second man wore a scuffed baseball cap with the letters "A R O R C E" on it.

The two were smoking. Their faces were flushed, their clothing sweat-stained. They wore T-shirts and gym shorts. They seemed to be taking a break from some undetermined heavy exertion.

There was something highly unusual about the tanker. A few feet back from the stem of its cylindrical frame, the ribbing had been peeled back – five feet across and upward along the vertical rivets, to where it met the apex of the tubing – to reveal a huge compartment inside.

A mound of burlap bags nestled on powdered earth. A third male, tall and aquiline-featured, shifted a bag into the cavernous opening. He was also in a T-shirt and shorts. An indistinct figure filled the darkened niche.

Diaz blithely provided commentary with the restrained enthusiasm of someone showing home movies to uninterested neighbors.

"This was taken by a *federale* surveillance unit at an illegal drug transshipment point in Coronado on April 19 this year." He guided the airman onward to the inevitable truths. "Do you recognize the persons?"

Damien Moffatt peered at the screen for what seemed an inordinate length of time. Then he felt compelled to speak.

"That's a photo with me and Dwight – there – resting by the pickup," he explained. "I'm the one with the baseball cap."

"Yes," said Diaz. "And the other party?"

"The one lifting the stuff into the tanker hold is Captain Chandler."

"And what is that 'stuff' as you call it, Airman?"

"Heroin," Moffatt uttered in a flat voice.

"There's a fourth individual in these photos, isn't there?" Diaz probed. He directed the pointer to an indistinct shape barely visible inside the tanker's gut, a petite figure wearing cowboy boots and a white top with the image of a vermilion flamingo emblazoned on it. "Who is that person?"

Moffatt lowered his eyes to contemplate his feet. Miguel could see he was sweating.

A sigh of abdication. "Lieutenant Donovan."

"And is she in this courtroom?"

"Yes." Moffatt gestured lamely to the prisoner's docket. "The accused over there." His voice was a dispirited whisper.

"How did Wickham Chandler describe Maria Donovan to you?"

"As his girlfriend."

Fuentes pondered the response. The signs had pointed that way, and now he had his confirmation.

"Did she have any involvement with the narcotics?"

"Yes, sir," Moffatt explained quietly. "She was with Chandler when we met our contact that first time. When we loaded shipments in Mexico, she ordered us around more than Chandler, and Stateside, she took over the movement of the drugs. She acted like she was the boss . . ."

"A moment ago you said you moved hot computer technology into Mexico as part of this criminal enterprise."

"Yes."

"Did you ever transport anything other than what you've told this court today?"

Silence.

"Airman?" The imperious tone.

"Ya," Moffatt whispered. "Ya, we did."

"What were those items?"

Moffatt paled. He looked to Fuentes like a jackrabbit trapped in the headlights of an oncoming car.

"I asked you a question." The prosecutor raised his voice.

Silence swirling into a black, anxious void.

"Let's try it this way, shall we?" Diaz said impatiently. He clicked the advance on the projector. A second image appeared on the screen. Somewhere inside a shantytown, tumbledown metal framing rusted to apache gold. Shadows were shorter; the photo timer on the right corner indicated May 14.

There were three people in the photo. Fuentes identified Chandler, Moffatt, and Donovan dressed in packrat clothing and standing near some boxes. They were frame-frozen in an animated discussion. "PROPERTY OF THE UNITED STATES AIR FORCE" was stenciled on the sides of the boxes.

"What was inside the crates?" Diaz asked his witness with predatory sweetness.

Moffatt uttered a single word. "Guns." And then for clarification, "M-16s."

Miguel heard a collective explosion of breath from the gallery. He saw a *federale* by the door instinctively place a finger on the trigger guard of a semi-automatic. Obregon hunched forward attentively in his seat.

"Now you were asked a moment ago if you could identify the person who was your Mexican contact."

"Yes, sir," Moffatt croaked.

"Let's start by eliminating those we know." He took a pointer and tapped the images on the screen. Moffatt calmly identified them: Chandler, Donovan, himself.

"And Buscom?" Diaz wondered aloud. "I don't see him."

"That's because by May he wasn't around any more. He was transferred out at the end of April, right after he pulled night picket."

"Why?"

"It was during the picket we were able to move the rifles. Dwight was real touchy about it. He refused to help out, even with something simple like forklifting strong boxes to the tanker parked outside. He argued with Chandler over moving weapons. Didn't think it was right."

"Smuggling drugs but not guns?" Diaz muttered under his breath. "Commendable."

"Ya," Moffatt continued, ignoring the sarcasm. "They had a big fight that night. Almost came to blows. In the end, Dwight just left the warehouse and went straight back to his barracks. The next morning, he was history. Transferred to Alaska. Chandler knew he wouldn't talk, not with the stuff the captain had on us. "

"So what of you, Airman Moffatt?" the urbane prosecutor asked smoothly. "What sustained your loyalty to your captain?"

"It wasn't as if I didn't try, sir." The gawky airman sniffed with lame integrity. "That weekend, I phoned the captain at his home. Couple of times. Told him I wanted out, that it was too much, that I had a wife and kids. He laughed. Next thing I know, he's called the cops on me. They came pounding on my door, cautioned me about harassing phone calls."

"I see," the prosecutor commiserated.

"I don't need that kind of hassle, Mr. Diaz," Moffatt remarked mournfully.

"But you could have told the police the truth," Diaz offered, only mildly contentious. "You could have told them you were being extorted by Wickham Chandler."

Moffatt looked as if he'd just seen a creature from outer space. "Me, sir? They'd believe me over an officer in the United States Air Force?" He snorted with scorn.

Diaz shrugged. He took the pointer and moved it along the screen to a shaded image in the corner of the slide. A male.

"So who is this individual standing next to you?"

Fuentes could see the tiny muscles in Moffatt's jaw line tense. He surmised that if Adolpho Diaz was working off a cue card, the witness in the box had resolutely decided to forget his.

"Remember, you're under oath." Diaz balanced the passive provocation with one of his own.

Moffatt rustled in his seat. A slight twitch came to his cheek. He blinked his eyes apprehensively, then pursed his lips as if sealing them forever. Fuentes observed the quickening palpitations in the man's neck where the carotid artery coursed, faster, ever faster, becoming pronounced as his damning silence began to suffocate the room.

Miguel became acutely aware of the most parsimonious sounds. The clock ticking on a distant wall. The court clerk droning into the Dictaphone. Zenin whispering something to the other attorney, the rumpled American. The methodical scribble of words jotted by Herzog in longhand. An overweight spectator wheezing asthmatically nearby. Another scratching her arm.

"Mr. Moffatt?" Diaz pressured.

At that very moment, Judge Esubio Herzog received a hand-written note from one of the khaki-shirted guards lurking around the perimeters of the chamber. The judge read it, interrupted Diaz in mid-sentence, and, to the bewilderment of the entire court, indicated that he thought it might be a suitable time to recess for the morning. The accused would be taken back to the facility she'd been sequestered in for the trial, a secret and secure site in a nearby military garrison.

At precisely 10:38 a.m., Judge Herzog exited the courtroom. Fuentes remembered the time, because the officer in charge of the transport detail had inquired about it, just before he'd asked to borrow a pen to record the adjournment in an operational ledger because his own ballpoint had run out of ink. Miguel obliged with his jade-colored fountain pen. At that same moment, a *federale* courier beckoned him. He had an envelope in his hand, marked "Urgent!" The chicken-scratch scrawl was Asuncion's. Fuentes put it into a back pocket. He'd check its contents when he got outside.

The spectators were removed first. Three minutes later the hearing room was fully vacated. At precisely 10:43 a.m., the accused, Maria Donovan, was taken from the witness box under the close escort of four prison matrons, led through a doorway, and disappeared down a long, darkened corridor. There was no one left in the massive chamber. In the hallway outside, only two junior reporters were left, chafing for a story. Miguel avoided them.

At precisely 10:47 a.m., Fuentes exited the *Palacio de Gobierno* by a fire door. The outside air in the Plaza Zaragosa reeked of diesel fumes, overripe bougainvillea, and burnt cooking from food vendors camped in the plaza across the way. Heat-shimmer boiled the air.

A labyrinth of luxury buses and articulated trailers crowded the thoroughfare. Fuentes recognized the logos of two American networks, plus those of Mexican national television, on the parked rigs. Communication antennae sprouted insect-like from their rooftops. Heavy-duty wiring snaked out their bottoms, through thickets and up a circular drive before disappearing into the *palacio*.

He gingerly avoided the transmission cabling. The roadway was fringed with vegetation – hibiscus, chaparral ash, yucca – a once-beautiful proliferation intended to lend grandeur to a patrician setting. But the displays had grown thick with scrub brush and discarded litter from the plaza. The plants themselves were parched and yellowed.

A large Cummins dumpster hunched nearby, cylinders whining, mechanical arms raised to a bin lodged near the top of the circle. The truck had a bright magenta chassis with marmalade trim. Five fit men in immaculate white coveralls staffed it, each with a tidy red bandanna tied around his neck. Fuentes reflected that its cleanliness seemed out of place.

A horn blared. He jumped to the curbside just as a full-sized Chevrolet sedan passed, racing toward the *palacio*. The Chevy carried a male driver and escort, both wearing identical aviator glasses and designer suits, their inert features sporting the sculpted stupidity of career bodyguards. A moment later, a prison bus followed at the same breakneck speed.

The main entry to the *palacio* consisted of an ornate clay portico with a broad staircase on top. The Chevy came to a halt in the corridor, its motor running. Plainclothes federal guards swiftly surrounded the vehicle. The prison coach eased to a halt twenty yards behind.

Moffatt was escorted to the Chevrolet and placed in the back seat. A plainclothesman trundled on board at either side. The doors to the car slammed shut. It moved off. The prison bus inched forward. Donovan was led toward it. The bus stopped. Prison staff obscured her movements.

Fuentes removed the envelope from his pants pocket and opened it. The note was short, six paragraphs long, and scribbled in that jammed-finger style that was so uniquely Asuncion's. It was prefaced "Six Tampico Court: Town of Larendo, Mexico" and subtitled "Panama connection."

The able detective had done a commendable job of research, and the information he'd unearthed gave Fuentes serious pause to consider the playing field he was intruding on. It seemed that the Mexico City law firm that had so efficiently fronted Six Tampico had also incorporated Cheetah Enterprises, that hole-in-the-wall front that had afforded Humberto Guzman momentary credibility as he'd crafted the NEDEROIL swindle, nearly claiming Fuentes as its principal casualty.

Both businesses had been set up in the past nine months, within days of each other, and with identical cardboard principals authoring the deed. The symmetry didn't end there. Both firms also shared a Panama address for their work: 124 Passeo Liberation, Miraflores.

Miguel's eyes widened in amazement as coincidence briskly blended into that gray border country abutting conspiracy. While Cheetah Enterprises had done no more than announce plans to drill in the remote northern sectors of the Mar Muerto, the Larendo *maquiladora* actually owned an array of oil rigs energetically drilling offshore in the same sea, right off the State of Chiapas.

Felix had gone one step further, calling in a favor from an old police buddy in the Panamanian city of Balboa, just north of the canal. Miraflores proved to be the site of huge locks on the Pacific side. The Passeo Liberation? A gravel trail paralleling the waterway.

The corporate headquarters for the *maquiladora* was most intriguing of all: a size-ten shoebox in a confectionery store used as the mail drop for vessels traversing the Panama Canal. Asuncion's pal had also identified the individual who'd rented the post office box. A man named Humberto Guzman had traveled the passage in late May aboard a Liberian freighter named the *Cassandra,* a ship outbound from Havana to the Pacific Ocean. The ship had berthed on the canal next to the confectionery plant on the same date as the rental occurred.

The *maquiladora* already had one highly questionable death tied to it – a collection of embers once known as Eddie Bono.

Now Fuentes's personal nemesis, Guzman, was identified somewhere in this puzzle as an associate of the same firm.

He fumbled for a pen to make some quick notes. He needed to
know about the *Cassandra,* what its complete manifest and
passenger list was. And quickly! Felix's contact would surely
provide the best and fastest results to such unanswered questions.

It was then that Miguel realized he'd lent his pen to the prison
staffer. He turned to go back to the courthouse. Ahead, two of the
disposal crewmen ambled up the path carrying bundles of piping,
the kind used to create scaffolds. He noticed something curious
about one of the laborers. Rather than work boots, the man
appeared to be wearing expensive loafers and creased blue jeans.

A hollow *THRUMP!* The Chevrolet exploded in a rainbow of
glass, metal, and human tissue. Glass shards razored the air and
tinkled softly to the ground at Fuentes's feet. Damien Moffatt and
his escorts were as vapor in the air.

The disposal workers lifted their bandannas across their faces.
The pipe bundles they'd borne fell to the wayside like toothpicks,
to reveal trim AR-16 assault rifles. Without skipping a beat, they
began to barrage the area with a highly disciplined fusillade of
automatic fire.

The prison bus pulled hurriedly from the curb. At a signal from
one of the attackers, the garbage truck surged forward. Prongs
crashed into the bus's side, impaling it like a cheap child's toy.

The Cummins backed, then halted, readying for a second
thrust. The decrepit motor coach lurched back and forth, then
slowly rolled over onto its side.

Two attackers jumped from the waste-disposal truck and
raked the bus with gunfire. Beleaguered *federales* shot back as
they retreated.

BOOOMMMM! The gas tank on the garbage truck ruptured.
Brilliant cadmium flames haloed from the hulk of the cab. Pitch-
black smoke billowed into a cerulean sky.

Fuentes rushed instinctively toward the insanity, unholstering
his Glock and firing at intruders as he ran. In the plaza, people
scrambled for cover. Shrieks and screams rent the air, the brittle

resonance of children sobbing uncontrollably. Or was it grown men and women?

Ping! Ping! Snipers on rooftops. Miguel ducked behind the cement buffer of a tree planter. *Ping!* He wasn't certain if the gunmen were police or bandits. Or both. And with lead whizzing wildly about the white-hot day, he knew it didn't matter to anyone caught in the middle.

The rattle-rush-chatter of automatic weapon clips discharging. The *mee-maw* wail of emergency sirens – louder, ever louder. Every so often, sandwiched between shouting and screeching and shooting, an eerie silence.

One of the attackers was hit in the face. He lay, spouting blood, on the adobe tile. Miguel counted four, no five, uniformed shapes strewn on the ground closer to the *palacio*. The gunfire had not abated. Additional *federales* appeared from the building, encircling the insurgents and firing rapidly as they approached.

The remaining gunmen hid among the fauna. The dull pop of bullets into vegetation. The occasional gun muzzle emerging from behind a plant, a tree, flashing fire. *Pling! Pling! Thud!* A second attacker fell, twitching, into a bed of Brazil scrub, the side of his face sliced off.

In the confusion, Fuentes reached what was left of the bus. The metal frame looked as if it had been wrenched open by a giant can-opener.

Fuentes peered in and gagged, for there, amid the debris of broken glass and torn seats, were the remains of the prison guards. The hydraulic prongs of the disposal unit had cleanly severed the head of one. A second corpse had the rim of its head so abruptly detached by gunfire that brains stewed fresh in the skull. A third human of undetermined gender had died cupping spilled entrails. The uniforms worn by the corpses weren't blue. None of the dead was Donovan.

He hopped gingerly from the derelict. A bullet whizzed past his earlobe and pierced metal. He ducked. *Twang! Twang! Twang!* The rapid fire of a machine gun. Set against the stark background of plaza tile, his khaki uniform was morbidly inviting.

With great effort he crouched, rolled, then flung himself into scrub, grunting mightily from the sudden exertion. It wasn't a pretty maneuver, but then he wasn't trying to score points from an Olympic judge.

Cautiously, he scrutinized the plaza. A dozen bodies lay in the open space, some twitching, others still. Ruddy flames from burning vehicles layered thick black smoke into the sky above. A hundred yards away, using the slight protection afforded by pillars from the shopping colonnade, teams of *federales* regrouped, sending concentrated rounds in his general direction. Automatic salvos barked back at their position from a spot uncomfortably close to where he hid. Fuentes heard a feeble rustle in the brush, the scuttle of feet on stone. A flash of faded cobalt, then movement in an alcove. A figure sprinted toward the nearby cathedral. The immense doors of the aged church opened slightly, then shut with a muffled *bumpph*.

Carefully, Fuentes took up pursuit. He reached the building. It was musty inside. The ritual scents of Catholicism pervaded the oppressive air, the ancient mingling of beeswax candles, fresh-cut flowers, and incense. Through half-open transoms, he listened to the discordant symphony of a world gone totally mad.

Fuentes crept forward along a side aisle, his Glock drawn. His eyes had trouble adjusting to the dim light. The church was quiet. Suddenly he spotted them in a confessional: a pair of women's sneakers peeking out from under a coarse burgundy curtain. Petite shoes, cheaply made, the kind that prisoners wear. The kind Donovan was wearing.

Miguel approached ever so carefully, ever so quietly. His index finger moved from the guard onto the trigger. He stretched his free hand and grasped the fabric, felt its heavy twilled texture. He felt his chest tighten, tried desperately to control his breathing. He began to ease the material back. Slowly . . . slowly . . .

The next thing he felt was immense pain in the back of his head. And then . . . nothing.

25

Fuentes awoke to find he was lying face down on cold earth. The only illumination came from a flickering votive candle that played strange shadows on chalk walls moist with mildew. Piles of bones and human skulls lay in a corner next to a deck of decaying coffins. Bloated creatures with long tails and pink eyes scrounged about the skeletal remains. The room stank of rank waste and concrete. He felt groggy.

A male figure towered over him, clothed in a flak jacket and faded jeans; a powerful individual sporting an orange Iroquois cut and holding the black barrel of a Glock but a few inches from his forehead.

"Papagayo?" Fuentes muttered.

"You have an exceptional memory," the biker exclaimed in appreciation, "considering the circumstances."

Fuentes gazed about, confused. Behind Papagayo he spied an elfin creature. The candlelight muted her fine features. Maria Donovan.

"Where am I?" He winced at the tormenting throbbing in his neck.

"The cathedral crypt, *Jefe*," the woman obliged. "For now we're safe with the saints."

Fuentes tried to stand. The biker nudged him back to the earth with the forceful jab of a hobnailed boot.

"Be calm, *señor*. And you won't be harmed."

Fuentes decided to err on the side of caution.

"What's happening?" he mumbled. "What're you going to do with me?"

Donovan knelt at his side. "We need your help," she remarked simply.

"You need *my* help?" He focused on the patent absurdity of the notion. "You're standing trial for murder and you need my help? *Señorita!* You must be mad!"

The woman turned to her companion. "Play him the tape."

Papagayo took a tiny recorder from his jacket and brought the device close to Miguel's ear. He switched it on. Miguel listened to the phrases, to the grainy words that had become so hauntingly familiar: "Buy into NEDEROIL, Senator. This Friday. Big time. But sell everything before 1:oop.m. Before the sky falls."

The tape halted with an abrupt click. Fuentes firmed his jaw and hoped he hadn't betrayed any emotion. His mind was in turmoil. The voice belonged to Humberto Guzman, the oily-haired accountant with the bad skin – and the scruples of an alleycat. But how had Papagayo and Donovan come to have it? And for what purpose?

Donovan sighed, a soft, even sound like wind on a summer's night. She handed Fuentes a short printout, an article taken off the Internet from a small investment house in Tulsa. It announced the results of very recent explorations off the Chiapas coast. The findings were indeterminate but couched in a language that oozed latent wealth. In this instance, PEMEX had engaged in a joint venture with a small consortium. A few of its investors were even identified. They were players he could definitely link to the Larendo *maquiladora*. And with that realization Fuentes started, for they were also the same individuals who'd made millions through the NEDEROIL swindle.

"Whatever it was that meant you had to close the NEDEROIL investigation," Donovan began with a calmness that unsettled Miguel, "it was something so foul it necessitated the killings at Zita's. I don't think this foulness has ended. It may yet be causing the deaths of innocent people. I think, for a variety of reasons, that you've reached the same conclusion."

Miguel's head was spinning, his lips were dry as asbestos. "How can I afford to believe you?"

"At this stage of your career," the young woman replied glacially, "how can you not?" She sensed his distress. "Perhaps I should introduce myself. You know I'm a lieutenant in the United States Air Force. What you don't know is that I work for Colonel Bragg at the Office of Special Investigations."

Fuentes couldn't resist laughing. "You? Work *with* Bragg! Then I'm Emiliano Zapata!"

The tiny brunette shrugged her shoulders. "I gather that possession of this tape isn't good enough for you." The biker took another object from his pants pocket and deftly tossed it to Fuentes.

Miguel scrupulously considered the item. It was the lapel pin he'd given the American intelligence colonel, the one with the hand-painted seal of Coronado and the words *"Jefe de Policia"* scripted on the base.

"More?" Donovan asked with regal calm.

"Go on," Fuentes challenged defensively.

"You bought candies at the Davis Monthan exchange. A dozen. Eighty-five cents' worth. You were right to make the connection. They are my favorite – the kind Wick always bought for me."

"Good, Lieutenant," Fuentes allowed reluctantly. "You are very good!"

"And, of course . . ." Papagayo handed a slip of paper to Fuentes, "there was Tucson."

Miguel skimmed the notations. The format was conventional. Police mobile surveillance records. The dates and locations were more than familiar, as were the subjects – Fuentes and Asuncion. Both schedules were extraordinarily accurate; the log recorded their recent movements in the southern Arizona city to a tee. Fuentes's features were awash with disbelief inching reluctantly toward resignation.

Miguel screwed his face in abject confusion. "But the evidence is all there! Everything points to you as the murderer of four people!"

"No," Donovan explained. "The evidence you possess consists of a trail contrived to get me arrested and extradited to Mexico, nothing more."

"Contrived?"

"Yes. My OSI superiors were working on a calculated hunch that whoever killed Chandler would come hunting me, thinking that since Wick and I had been so close, I'd know his secrets and lead them to whatever they were after. We fabricated enough to place me before a Mexican court and, judging by today's entertainment in the plaza, right into their gun sights."

Maria Donovan stepped closer to Miguel. Her eyes were dark and hard. "Only I don't want to be drafted by their team any more."

"What changed your mind?"

"Instinct," the young woman remarked dryly. "For the entire proceedings, I've had essentially the same prison warders. Today, I get a new crew I've never seen before. And they don't cuff me. All the time I've been on trial, I've been routinely cuffed."

"An oversight."

She shook her head vigorously. "It was intentional. I believe the guards were bought off to leave me unshackled. It made it that much easier to get out of the bus when the shooting started."

Fuentes was puzzled. "How can you say the prison officers were on the take? All of them were killed in the exchange."

Donovan shrugged. "A business practice to cut down on unnecessary overhead. I think the plan was to free me to flee with the *bandidos*. And I might have gone along with it, too. There's just one little hitch."

"Which is?"

"I'm not yet one hundred percent certain what the *bandidos* are really after, either."

"You called them *bandidos,* how can you be sure they aren't rebels?"

Maria Donovan smiled. "Rebels don't wear Guccis and designer jeans, *Jefe,*" she said, with measured prudence. "Those bastards were in someone's pay. Someone very arrogant and very powerful."

Donovan turned serious once more. There's one other thing," she said, weighing the thought. "Last night, I got a surprise visit from a priest. The usual prison chaplain Father Lamas, only calls on weekends. This new fellow, who introduced himself as an associate of Lamas was slick – but for one item . . ."

"Which was?"

"He wore a clerical collar and crucifix."

"I'm sorry?" Fuentes said, perplexed. Then it dawned on him.

He nodded. In Mexico, clergy were forbidden by civil law from wearing priestly garb in public.

"He told me confession was good for the soul. I told him I didn't have anything worth confessing. He didn't seem at all pleased to hear it. Out of the blue, he told me that the hour of deliverance was nearly at hand and that I should be prepared."

"What?"

Donovan narrowed her eyes. "He said to be ready at eleven today."

Miguel heard water dripping somewhere in the distant darkness. "And I'm supposed to believe this story?"

Donovan shrugged. "It's true." She saw the raw suspicion on his face. "Look. Call Bragg when you leave here. With my blessing."

"No," Fuentes protested. "Not an American. It must be someone here. In Mexico. Someone I can trust to tell me what this is all about."

"Trust a Mexican in authority?" Papagayo broke out laughing. "You are joking!"

Miguel resisted the temptation to agree. He leaned against the wall and heard discordant sounds aboveground. Rifle fire. Sirens. Shouting. He felt his heart pounding, his breathing coming in apprehensive gasps, straining his chest; enormous pressure like an elephant lounging on his rib cage.

Faces flashed before him, faces filled with those smug expressions that clearly implied that power and truth were commodities to be bought and sold at whim by a select breed of people. Faces from his past. From his time in Mexico City. His time in the loop. When he was someone to be considered in the final equation. A force to be reckoned with. A dealer in the game. Faces that all looked remarkably like Obregon's.

It was at that precise moment that Miguel made up his mind. "*Señorita* Donovan?"

"Yes?"

He found a slip of paper in his pocket and etched a rough map on it. "Here's the key to my house. And directions."

The young woman's eyes softened. She grasped the key in

her hand. Her burly escort stood to one side and nodded silent thanks.

They broke into a trot down the passageway.

"Wait!" he called out to the rapidly disappearing figures.

They stopped in their tracks.

"Don't forget to feed the dog. His name is Salinas."

He thought he heard a faint ripple of laughter. And then they were gone, melding into the myriad tunnels that veined the foundations of the ancient church like faintly whispered prayers for the damned.

Fuentes hesitated, then slithered out of the bowels of the cathedral into searing daylight. He glanced up at the nearby clock tower. The whole nightmare had lasted, at most, twenty minutes.

Tuesday, August 7, morning.
Plaza Zaragosa, Hermosillo

26 The *plaza* was bedlam. Doctors and nurses had arrived from a nearby hospital. Working in teams, they attended to the wounded. A military helicopter buzzed overhead.

A police jeep screeched to a halt in the boulevard. The driver raised a forearm to shade his eyes as he anxiously canvassed the carnage. Fuentes heard his name called and made his way to the vehicle. The driver informed him that Obregon had requested his presence. Now.

They drove for an hour north of town on a cracked asphalt two-lane. The tires sizzled in the heat. Fuentes brushed beads of sweat from his forehead. His underarms were wet and clammy. He had difficulty breathing.

The driver gestured under the seat. Miguel fumbled about until he pulled out a sealed bottle of spring water. He offered it to his companion, who smiled appreciatively but declined. Miguel screwed off the cap and drank the clear, tepid liquid.

The jeep turned off-road past Benjamin Hill and made its way tenaciously north-westward. The route was little more than a miner's trail inching up-country. Deep wheel ruts, recently made, clawed into dry clay soil the tint and texture of burnt pie-crust. The grooves were well defined, the kind made by heavy machinery. A sharp turn this way, then another, and the land leveled off onto a mesa.

A thick copse of ironwood rose from the center of the plateau. Men in combat drab milled around in the stubbled shade, greased firearms at the ready. An occasional machine gun, a radio opera-tor; the indistinct definition of a secure area, running along the edge of the tree line.

The jeep halted by a brush break. Two MPs escorted Fuentes into the forest. They passed riflemen moving at the double in the opposite direction. The soldiers, armed with bandoliers of spare ammunition, sported shoulder flashes identifying them as para-troopers of the Presidential Guard. Miguel counted nine armored cars and half-tracks and an equal number of heavy-duty troop transports parked under tree cover, complemented by nets of dappled camouflage.

They came upon a clearing with tents pitched in a rough cres-cent. Unlike the more utilitarian ones surrounding it, the tent Fuentes was taken to was large and made of apricot-colored canvas, the kind found at small-town carnivals. Two paratroopers stood sentry at the entrance. They wore wraparound sunglasses that reflected Fuentes's movements with exaggerated symmetry. A regimental pendant fluttered from a long aluminum lance stuck into the earth. The guard on duty waved him through.

The air under the canopy was as close as two sweaty palms pressed together. A dozen uniformed men, arms folded in stud-ied patience, sat on field stools surrounding a makeshift table constructed of an old door frame resting on sawhorses.

The uniforms were split between *federale* and military. Miguel knew some of the police; the soldiers looked fitter than their civil counterparts. He identified a few majors, a colonel or two, some captains, by their rank badges. It was assuredly a respectable showing by the Mexican army, but he did not know why.

At their head, a cue-like pointer in his hand, stood Ramon Obregon. He'd changed from business attire to a canary-yellow jumpsuit, one with a multitude of zippers and shoulder flashes. It gave him the appearance of a South Vietnamese air marshal. Next to him, a flip-chart rested on a tripod. A blank sheet of paper covered the subject matter. Obregon motioned to the only vacant seat, and Fuentes dutifully took his place. It was then that he noticed that the chief *federale* officer in Sonora province wore high-laced riding boots and an equally stringent expression.

"Gentlemen," Obregon intoned imperiously, "now that you're all here, we can begin.

"Today's events do not reflect well on our professionalism. We lost five colleagues. The Department of Prisons – eight killed. There were eleven wounded, not counting civilians. On the plus side, we captured two intruders and killed the remainder. As you are all well aware, our principal prisoner escaped.

"Maria Victoria Donovan," Obregon rolled the name over his tongue. "Frankly, she's tedious, so I won't waste much of this session on her. We have more important things to worry about." He strutted before them. With a practiced sweep of the pointer, he flipped the chart to a multihued map of Mexico, one that high-lighted Chiapas, the troubled southern state abutting Guatemala, in phosphorus red.

"On New Year's Day 1994, members of the *Ejercito Zapatista de Liberacion National* – Zapatistas – occupied five towns in Chiapas, forcing residents to flee their homes. A virtual insurrection followed. Police and military were ambushed and killed. In Mexico City, bombs went off, and fifteen thousand troops were ultimately ordered into the state.

"As a result, massive demonstrations were staged for the consumption of the foreign press corps. As might well be expected, the international bleeding-heart lobby took over. American broker-age houses suggested that clients withhold investments until the Chiapas situation stabilized. The stock market plunged six percent in a single day, and the Mexican peso nearly died. The *presidente* at the time had no alternative but to declare a ceasefire and negotiate with the rebels. You are all aware of the outcome – housing, schools, roads, electricity, and increased political autonomy coerced from the Mexican state for Chiapas."

A grizzled colonel spat onto the ground.

"How does this concern us?" Obregon proceeded. "Well, the encampment you are in houses four battalions of presidential paratroopers and two hundred handpicked *federales,* deployed at the specific direction of the minister of justice. A few miles from here, senior government emissaries are negotiating with the Zapatista leadership. Our cordon effectively enables these discussions to take place without incident."

With a melodramatic flourish, Obregon flipped to a second chart. On it was written "Article 27." Nothing else.

"In 1917, after a civil war in which many died and the national economy lay in ruins, Article 27 became entrenched in the constitution. It has a definite purpose. It ensures that all natural resources in Mexico, including sub-soil rights, belong to the people. In the 1970s, the government modified Article 27 to give PEMEX exclusive rights throughout Mexico so that the nation – not a singular state, or group, or individual – would benefit.

"Our current *presidente* has chosen to embark on a drastically different path. Through discreet channels, he's let it be known that, in return for peace, the Mexican government will fundamentally amend Article 27." Obregon arched his eyebrows at the seeming absurdity of such a notion. "Gentlemen," he confided, "preliminary samples show that the ocean shelf extending along the Gulf of Tehuantepec and for six miles from the Chiapas shoreline holds the largest untapped oil field in the world."

There was an uneasy rustling as the reality of what the *comandante* preached sank in.

Obregon continued. "I'm personally aware that Justice Minister Rivera has asked President Estrada not to surrender such potential wealth to transparent blackmail."

The rustling stopped.

"Still, our president is tragically ..." – Obregon struggled with the wording – "less than firm. He is far too easily intimidated by threats of violence." Obregon's thin lips formed a leer. "Whenever Estrada sees a little glow on the grill, he wants to flee the kitchen..."

"You mean he's too busy baking pies in his designer oven?" an army captain interjected. Ribald laughter coursed through the room.

"Laugh if you will, but the Zapatistas have Estrada's number. Today's attack is a clear attempt to wring concessions from the oil talks by force. And you know what?" He let the words dissolve. "Given Estrada's fervor for peace at any cost, this brand of extortion has every prospect of succeeding. And when it does, a tribe of peasants – and the Zapatistas who manipulate them – will control a world-class reserve of oil that will be forever lost to the Mexican nation."

The tent was quiet. Obregon moved among his listeners with calculated poise.

"On March 23, 1994, in Tijuana, a laborer murdered the PRI's presidential candidate. A calling card found in the assassin's wallet connected him to an obscure group, the Association for the Committee of the People." Obregon perused his audience with hawk-like eyes. "Today, we have found similar cards on the corpses of the vigilantes at the Hermosillo courthouse.

"It is not my role to interfere with the wishes of our elected leaders." The *comandante* offered a thin-lipped grin. "They are, after all, infinitely wiser than we mere mortals." Polite laughter rippled through the tent.

The grin abruptly vanished as Obregon flicked the pointer sharply against his thigh. "But I will swear a thousand oaths to do my utmost to protect *el Presidente* from any harm he might face in Sonora. Even if he's too blind to appreciate it! And you will ensure he is well protected also!" Another whippet flick of the pointer. "Do I make myself clear!" An acquiescent silence. "Good." With a magisterial sweep of his hand, Obregon brought closure to this portion of the discussion.

"Now, as to Donovan," he continued. "Why did the rebels free her? To embarrass us? To destabilize?" A studied shrug. "No, gentlemen, I see a much more sinister agenda. I believe that the insurgents wish to undermine our very ability to exercise lawful authority in Sonora. I believe if we don't locate Donovan, she'll be tried by a puppet court and executed in a spectacular fashion by her captors."

THWACK! Obregon struck the flip-chart with his pointer. "I don't want to give these bastards the satisfaction of killing this woman," he glowered. "I want her to feel the weight of Mexican justice – not the bullet of a vigilante's gun. It is precisely for that reason that Maria Donovan must be captured. And captured alive."

A potent round of acknowledgment. Miguel could feel the anger and the energy. Obregon had his listeners in the palm of his hand.

The *federale* paused. "We've received a police report from a place called Cibuta near the U.S. border. The dumpster used today in the attack at Hermosillo was stolen last night from a truck stop. There are no solid descriptions. We have four eyewitnesses, including the driver, who seems too stupid even to be considered a potential collaborator.

"Which leads me to you, Fuentes," Obregon concluded. "I want you to investigate the theft. Find out anything that might bring us to where the *bandidos* are hiding Donovan. We've only got a short time before Estrada officially signs off on the agreement and completely relinquishes all rights off Chiapas to the native population. Use it well."

Fuentes meekly rose from his place and made his way to the tent door.

"Oh, Miguel?" The laconic command.

Fuentes dutifully stopped.

"A Very Important Personage is arriving in Mexico to witness this signing, and I don't want any complications. I particularly don't want this issue to deflect media attention from the official ceremonies at Santa Ana. Not while I'm in charge in Sonora. Understood?"

Fuentes nodded.

"Now, a driver from the motor pool will return you to town." The *comandante*'s magisterial gaze returned to the assembly. It was as if Miguel Fuentes, *jefe* of Coronado, no longer existed.

27

Though he'd never admit it, the Sonora occasionally overpowered Miguel with its ragged grandeur. Eight hundred miles long and four hundred wide, with magnificent brooding landscapes of creosote and rabbit brush, cactus scrub and candelabra cacti, the desert had come to rule his life and define his existence in ways that he was only now beginning to fully understand. And so it was, as he left the federal police compound at Hermosillo to journey along the back roads, homeward.

The black-and-white made steady progress over the brittle roadbed, growling past crumbling adobe houses with tar paper roofs and clapboard siding, and single-pump stations selling pirated fuel, stale food, and lukewarm soda. Stunted wooden crosses lurched out of the ground at roadside shrines. Occasionally, peasants with floppy straw hats and gnarled bodies shambled along the road skree, wearily lugging earthen jars and kindling bound with twine. Rich waves of heat pulsed through the air, while outcroppings of wild Mexican primrose danced in damask across a parched, shadowless land.

The Mustang was the only car on the road. In light of all that had happened in the past few weeks, Fuentes seemed the only sane person left in the universe. He sighed. Perhaps he was.

He reached the junction of San Cristobal just before eight. An eggshell aura softened a charcoal horizon and hinted at dusk. A sirocco wind played on the cactus. Fuentes purposely crisscrossed the dirt trails that delineated the tiny settlement. Then, satisfied that he was not being followed, he eased his vehicle to a stop at the bottom of the slope and walked up the steep hill to his home.

The screen door to his house was ajar. A tantalizing scent wafted outdoors – the aroma of chili peppers and beef.

The entrance hall had the look of careening bachelorhood about it. A clothes tree with unironed shirts and a pair of gray slacks suspended by the belt loops. A square table with a tempest of paper, unopened mail, magazines, and newspapers; atop them all, Salinas's leash and chewed-up Frisbee. On the floor, a confused jumble of sneakers, work boots, dress shoes, and sandals, a gym satchel with a sweaty jogging suit hanging out, a garbage bag full of dirty wash destined for the laundromat, a shopping tote with groceries unsorted, a twelve-pack of empty beer bottles. The passage was shadowy and cool, the living room in darkness. Salinas joyfully bounded out from one of the bedrooms to greet him.

Maria Donovan emerged from the kitchen, wiping her hands on a dishtowel. She wore a man's plaid shirt and khaki workpants cinched tight at the waist. She'd washed her hair and tied it with a shoelace. For the first time in quite a while, Miguel recalled that, from the moment of their first meeting, he'd found Maria Donovan very attractive.

"*El Jefe.*" She smiled shyly. "Welcome home."

The table was set for two. A crockpot of steaming chili resting on a striped towel dominated the arrangement. It was surrounded by a wicker basket heaped with sourdough buns and two black pots, one of yams, the other of fresh corn. Jars of green and red salsa completed the meal. A chilled bottle of beer rested beside Miguel's placemat; a tall glass of water brimming with ice nudged the other setting.

Fuentes removed his Stetson, tossing it expertly onto a vacant bench as he eased his chair back and sat down. He left his gunbelt on. The dog pranced about before settling at his feet. The animal seemed unusually relaxed with the new visitor.

"I compliment you on your choice of clothing," he said with a ready grin.

"The gentleman of the house has good taste," Donovan answered, returning his smile.

The meal looked quite appealing, and Miguel was hungry. He tucked a checkered napkin under his chin and filled a plate to overflowing with chili. He did the same for his comely guest.

Donovan handed him the basket of buns. He thanked her, took one, and expertly broke it open with his fingers.

"Are you still in command in Coronado?" she asked.

"For a little while yet." He took a bite of the bun. "At least with Obregon busy at your trial . . ." He paused, realizing how foolish such a comment had become. "It's hard to say now," he admitted. For a while they ate in silence.

"So tell me," Fuentes finally said. "Why am I harboring a desperado?"

"Because I'm not," she replied in a resolute voice.

Fuentes took a long slug of beer. "Explain, please. From the beginning."

Unruffled, Donovan began her tale. "Seven months ago, Tucson police received an anonymous tip about drug smuggling involving air force personnel."

"Moffatt and Buscom."

She nodded. "Tucson referred it to base security, who began a wiretap. No big deal. Drugs for stolen goods." Donovan sipped some water from her glass and continued in an even tone.

"Then the phone traffic went heavy – coded. The other side wanted assault weapons – M-16s – and lots of them. One hundred and ten to be exact. With ammunition to follow. That's why I was brought in from Washington. We arranged for Chandler to make the approach to Moffatt you heard about in court. I adopted a cover story making me his girlfriend.

"To gain credibility, we moved only small shipments. Wick stalled till we were sure it was the real thing. He told them guns would take time. It wasn't something we could do easily, not without drawing attention. All along, Buscom and Moffatt were arguing over our lines. Buscom wasn't happy with the idea of shipping M-16s. He quit after the first round. Moffatt was greedy for more deals, and he was angry at Buscom, ready to kill him with his bare hands.

"That's the real reason that Moffatt phoned Wick on the night the Tucson police intervened – not to plead for his family, but to let Chandler know he was willing to murder even his closest friend to keep the money flowing. That's why the captain had Buscom transferred. It was as much for his protection as to keep our alibi intact."

"So Chandler was clean?" Fuentes asked between mouthfuls of chili.

"Yes. He volunteered to help. He didn't have to. Wick said it was because his people were involved, and because, as an AMARC insider, he'd have instant access to any goods the Mexicans might demand. We even arranged the apartment at Sunrise so it looked like he and I were an item."

"And were you?"

"In appearance only, *señor*. I actually lived in a condo across from the base."

Fuentes toyed with a morsel of bread. "Tell me how the smuggling worked."

Donovan took the cotton napkin from her lap and abstractly began to fold it.

"All American airbases have environmental problems: fuel spillage on flightlines, tanker leakage, battery acid issues. At Davis Monthan, disposal is all too often ad hoc, lowest bidder gets the job, no questions asked. And, once waste leaves the base confines, it's considered to be effectively eliminated."

Fuentes spooned chili into his mouth. "What you really mean is: out of sight, out of mind."

"Yes. The Mexicans had been moving contraband out of Davis Monthan for some time before Chandler became involved. Still, it didn't hurt any when we ensured they got the disposal monopoly." She stopped pleating the fabric.

Twilight lingered beyond the screen door, a bleary mauve edging into ebony. A far-off train whistle echoed ethereally like a reed flute in an empty theater.

"They'd call in orders. Wick arranged to have items shuffled through the books using false invoices and inflated inventory counts, so the thefts weren't immediately spotted. Carrier rigs parked in the AMARC compound and were loaded by Moffatt and Buscom, at night, when no one was around. In the morning, they'd top up with environmental waste from elsewhere on the base.

"Even the border was no problem. For a 'charitable donation,' Mexican Customs wrote clean bills of health, sight unseen. In

Mexico, the syndicate used sophisticated routing. Coronado was the only constant hub. We'd be asked to coordinate our movements to arrive on the outskirts of town independent of the rig we'd loaded that day. We'd cool our heels while the tanker continued to the drop-off. Obviously, we were hostages if something went sour."

Donovan anticipated the next question. "We couldn't do surveillance. The trucks operated after dark and without lights. Helicopters were out of the question.

"The rigs always returned empty. The drivers probably dumped the sewage in the Sonora. At the Mexican end, we'd pack drugs into false compartments. Stateside, we'd discharge the narcotics in the desert. Once we knew Moffatt and Buscom were safely out of our way back at base, we had the drugs picked up by air force security and stored as evidence in the DEA vault in Tucson. We'd substitute the stash with phony loads so they wouldn't be the wiser."

"Drivers? There was more than one?"

"Yes. I don't recall repeats. I think they got their people from an agency, the type that don't ask awkward questions as long as they're paid in American dollars."

"Who arranged the contract with Davis Monthan?"

The young woman nodded her appreciation of the logic. "The document was signed by a broker in San Diego, who received his marching orders from a high-powered California law firm. It proved impossible for us to find the real owners. The trucks never had company markings or identifiers on them. The license plates.were clean, too."

"The Mexican handler?"

Donovan seemed perplexed.

Fuentes refreshed her memory. "Moffatt told the court he took you to a rendezvous in the second week of April – he thought a Monday – where you connected with a Mexican go-between," he prodded. "You must know his name."

Maria Donovan pondered a while, then concurred. She spoke with escalating certainty, like a climber finally getting a toehold on a particularly stubborn rockface.

"In the beginning, there was Luis. 'Louie the Louse' was the nickname Wick gave him. Luis had filthy fingernails and nose hairs he never trimmed. He was an older man – forty-five, fifty – not a bad guy, really. About the third visit in, Luis confided that he was only doing this because he needed money for his kids. He had five, including one with diabetes. His family was from a town called Camadero."

Donovan drank her glass of water and refilled it. Fuentes noticed she'd stopped eating.

"Telling us was Luis's big mistake. We never saw him again. The next time, we had a new driver. And each time after that. Later, we heard Luis wasn't working for them any more. One of the Mexicans told us. That's all he'd say. Myself? I think Luis was murdered for talking too much."

The house was quiet. Fuentes rose to let the dog out and invited Donovan into the living room. It was frugally furnished. A plaid sofa and two aged chairs. A portable TV sat atop a rickety stand; above it, a cheap print of mums in a vase. A pine table rested by a cubed window overlooking the crossroads. It was strewn with binders and a mountain of documents.

Donovan chose the sofa, Fuentes one of the chairs. He wasted little time getting to the point. "How does the stolen computer tie into this? The VAX 10 from Davis Monthan?"

Donovan was ready for the question. "Wick orchestrated that theft without our knowledge," she said frankly. "We don't know."

Fuentes's eyes opened wide in amazement. "I'm sorry?"

"We don't know." She ran a slim hand through dark hair. "We weren't scheduled to do a run into Mexico that week," she began cautiously. "Our last trip had been a shipment on May 14. We'd picked up eleven kilos of cocaine.

"At sunrise on May 21, I bumped into Wick at the main gate. He acted real defensive when we talked, said he was taking time off and heading up to the Grand Canyon to hike. Somehow he didn't sound right, so I trailed him into Tucson, where he switched cars at the rental place and headed south on route 19.

"I called Bragg on my cell. I couldn't track the rental without getting burned. Tucson PD had a spin team available, but they were too far back to take over the tail. Ultimately, a police helicopter locked onto Wick and watched him heading into Mexico."

The hand dropped to her lap, there to nestle with its mate. Donovan's voice dropped an octave. She grew more reflective. "The Tucson team stayed on him for me. He entered Coronado, parked his rental by the old Church of St. Lucia and went on foot into the Barrio. We figured it was to spook any tail. Ultimately, they placed Wick back in his car. He drove to Zita's, where he booked a room, and we set up obs.

"Later that morning, he drove to the El Toro. I decided enough was enough so I confronted him there. Right away I knew something was wrong – really wrong. Wick wasn't himself. He said he didn't want to see me, said it would jeopardize the whole thing. We had a big fight and I left. Later, I tailed him back to Zita's – we videotaped him entering his motel room." Donovan closed her eyes. "We were just a few seconds late."

Fuentes was too experienced to convey a response. If this performance was rehearsed, it was worthy of an Oscar. And he had no way to gauge its truth.

Donovan took a cassette tape from her pants pocket and went to a recorder resting on the mantelpiece. "We intercepted three incoming calls to his cellphone that day. One logged at 9:34 a.m., the second at 11:57, and the final one at 12:37 in the afternoon." She pressed the "on" switch.

The tape played, grainy; indistinct, a muffled crackling, then the abrupt silence of a line gone dead. "The first two are indecipherable, broken transmissions," she conceded. "But the third?" She raised a finger in anticipation. The audio quality was bad. With effort, Fuentes barely made out the words, a grinding out of vowels and consonants: "What's going on! My tech man says there's something really wrong with the program. He says what you told Bono a few minutes ago is crap! You're jerking us around, *hombre!* I'll meet you at the motel. One-thirty this afternoon. Be there!"

A ragged hissing signaled the end of the dialogue.

The message confirmed Fuentes's suspicions that Eddie Bono had been a mere errand boy in the fateful dance with death that followed. Yet Miguel now also had something he'd never possessed before. He had a "voice." However distorted, it was a voice connected to a body. A body connected to a name. And that might be traceable.

Donovan turned off the recorder and removed the tape. "Wick had his cell on 'mailbox.' We caught it all."

Fuentes whistled softly.

Donovan returned to her spot on the sofa. "The other side instructed us using mobile phones. Changing frequencies constantly, they gave our tech section fits. This time we were lucky. Three calls from the same site, the last two within a half-hour of each other. The techies honed in. A ring-back gave them the federal exchange for the State of Sonora. The speech pattern itself was doctored to disguise it."

"The federal exchange!" Fuentes felt a tantalizing shiver of expectation. "Does my government know this?"

Donovan hesitated. "In a way. Remember the DEA agent murdered in Guadalajara in 1990? The one who infiltrated the corrupt *federale* drug squads?"

Miguel nodded.

"We used a Mexican undercover operator to break that conspiracy – and we've got him now."

"Papagayo?" Miguel asked with surprised respect. "Who does he work for?"

"DFS," Donovan offered blithely. "The Mexican Security Directorate."

"But they specialize in political intelligence."

"Yes." Donovan sensed his confusion. "But we didn't go through customary channels." Her abrupt silence spoke volumes.

"So tell me," Miguel demanded wryly, "did you pick Papagayo because he was honest? Or because he was the best fit for your needs?"

"In Mexico the two are interchangeable, are they not?"

"Point taken. But wasn't there anyone higher you could have confided in?" he stumbled. "Perhaps in the Ministry of Justice?"

"Where would the level of trust be – who would I go to?"

"What you're saying is that you don't have faith in Mexico City."

"Your words . . ." Donovan countered.

"No, *señorita*," He shrugged. "It seems to be my reality. Like the cricket tells Pinocchio, 'Always let your conscience be your guide.'"

Fuentes vanished into the kitchen and returned with two crystal goblets and a decanter of red wine. He offered a glass to his guest; she accepted.

"Let's see if I've got this straight. First. You – an escaped convict on trial for murder – are seated in the living room of the chief of police of Coronado." A nod of agreement.

"Second. My government, through its senior and most trusted officials, has expressed a firm resolve to see you captured alive." A pause. "But they're not to be trusted. You think they have ulterior motives." A second nod, and the suggestion of a smile. He began to snicker.

"Third." By now Fuentes had to struggle to keep from laughing aloud. "A Mexican intelligence officer, who looks like the advance man for a freak show, operates covertly for American authorities, even though he himself is considered to be on the lower end of the Richter scale of honesty."

A smile had broken on what Miguel had come to acknowledge was a very attractive female face. A third nod and stifled giggle. Fuentes's reserve evaporated into open laughter. Donovan toyed with her wine glass.

"So what am I then?"

A veil fell over the pleasantness. An expression of profound sadness replaced it. "Right now, Miguel, you appear to be in the middle of a nightmare."

Fuentes grew somber. "I sort of thought the same. Obregon? Is he aware of what you're doing?"

" I don't think so." The young woman's disposition chilled noticeably.

"My compliments." He downed the wine in a single gulp and poured another glass. He offered more to his guest, but she declined.

"Tell me," he asked, relishing the irony, "now that I'm full-blown party to a conspiracy, why did you manufacture such an elaborate scheme?"

Maria Donovan accepted the oblique tribute with a graceful nod. "The investigation was airtight until the murders. From the very beginning, we'd funneled questionable profits into the bank in Bahia Kino. As far as the Mexicans were concerned, we were both *loco*. Why should they have thought anything else? Not only did we smuggle in whatever they demanded, we also kept the hot money in a place they could control with very little effort."

Her voice began to grow distant. "The explosion changed everything in a heartbeat. The decision was made to make me the prime decoy. The bank account was our lure. We felt that if I showed the wealth, that if I bought something flashy, they'd believe I was in up to my neck. And certifiably stupid to boot."

"The Hummer?"

"Full package. Bells and whistles, including sunroof. I picked it up just before the explosion. Buying it with hard cash so soon after Chandler's death gave me just the right profile – an out-of-control extrovert, growing careless, someone who might buckle under pressure. Then we reworked the condo on Sunrise to entice them to regard me as the prime beneficiary of Wick's murder."

"Which I did," Fuentes admitted.

"You had to," Donovan concurred. "There was no logical alternative. We deliberately left the boots and patrol jacket in the apartment to provide the grounds to get me arrested."

Fuentes nodded in frosty admiration. "I admit you wove a fine spider's web, but there's one thing you can't account for."

"And that is?"

Fuentes sighed, hollow weariness resonating through his frame. He strode to the pine table. Rooting through a mound of books and papers, he found what he was looking for. Then he went outside. A car trunk slammed. When he returned he was holding a three-ring binder and assorted documents.

Miguel tossed a computer printout into his visitor's lap. "Arizona driver's license history: Travis Victor Chandler, born 14 December 1940, Mobile, Alabama. Male, white, five-foot ten, one hundred and eighty pounds. Last known residence: Benson, Arizona . . ." He left the facts suspended for a moment. "For the record, Colonel Bragg states that Chandler Senior is in isolation in a military hospital in Frankfurt."

"And you don't believe it?" Donovan replied, her pretty face stamped with severity.

"No." Fuentes's countenance crimped as narrow as a desert lizard in a dust storm. "No, I don't. Nor do you."

He tossed a single piece of paper at the woman. "Don't bother to read it," he admonished. "I'll tell you what it says. Benson, Arizona. A report dated May 15. The day after Travis Chandler allegedly travels to Europe, someone slashes the tires of his Cadillac at a local shopping mall. They also deface the trunk by scratching two 'V's on it. No suspects. One day later, a pipe bomb explodes on the front porch of his home in Benson causing $6,000 in damage. Again, no suspects." A pause.

"Last week I checked with the local cop shop. They have no record of any of this. When I phoned the town newspaper, again no incident on record. Pipe bombs in a place like Benson? I think it would be front-page news, right up there with Mrs. Murphy's cat in a tree."

Donovan shifted minutely in her seat.

"In case you were wondering, I managed to get this by checking an independent source – the insurance bureau, this time in Phoenix. These things are filed regardless of who might want them purged" – Miguel snorted – "whenever money is concerned."

"Now for the fun part," he continued somberly. "Air Force dossiers I got from Bragg list Travis Chandler as a retired colonel, living contentedly on a full pension." He leaned over Donovan's shoulder and tapped the page with an assertive finger. "Yet the first incident gives his place of employment as recently as last month, at Fort Huachuca Military Base. The other one shows his current occupation as a computer consultant."

The silence in the room was deafening. He stopped tapping and gave the woman a sober, sidelong glance that left nothing to the imagination. "I believe you know more than you're telling me about Colonel Chandler. Much more."

"I don't understand what you mean," she snapped.

"I believe you do." Fuentes stretched slowly upright. His voice was as hard as burnished steel. "I think you know you've been intentionally obstructing a murder investigation because it suits the purposes of the American government."

Donovan bristled visibly. "I'm going to pretend I didn't hear that comment."

Miguel's face clouded at the threat. "And I'm going to pretend that you didn't remove documents from Benson City Police files that could provide critical evidence concerning several murders in Sonora."

Maria Donovan tensed. "And if I did," she glowered, "it's no concern of yours. We're in Mexico. Benson, Arizona, is in the United States of America. In case you hadn't noticed." She held her head high. "You have no jurisdiction over what I do. Or how I carry out my responsibilities."

"There I go, hearing that song again!" Fuentes sputtered in mock disgust. "There have been a number of homicides already, Miss Donovan. There may be more." His voice eased an octave. "May I remind you that you've been charged with four of them. And that you're on the run. Here. In Mexico." He reflected on the irony, then chuckled. "In case *you* hadn't noticed . . ."

"So what are you trying to tell me?"

Fuentes struggled to find the words. "I guess what I mean to say is that we need each other now, Maria. More than ever. Because the only way we can solve this, is together."

She nodded demurely. Her features appeared softer to him, her eyes gentler and more vulnerable.

Fuentes went to the dining room, brought back a kitchen chair and straddled it. He opened the three-ring binder and leafed through it. "Here's what I wanted." He pointed to the photo at the bottom of a page with two oblong snapshots on it. "There! The postcard. The one of the Alamo with the notation on the back!"

She didn't need to look at the binder. "IF THE WORST HAPPENS . . ." she said with a spontaneity that puzzled Miguel.

"You remember!"

Donovan blushed at her own abandon. "It intrigued us – a lot. We sent the card to Forensics, but we weren't very successful in determining the writer's origin or association with the deceased."

"J. J. Bramble?"

"Yes," she nodded. "He's a big zero to us."

I know." Fuentes vigorously nodded agreement. "Along with lab reports, Bragg provided me with thirty volumes of investigative binders. All with covering notes. Bedtime reading during your trial. I keep them locked in my car," he added halfheartedly.

"They've been helpful?"

"For the most part, not very. Except for the correspondence on the postcard."

"Why?"

"Because I believe it was sent by Travis Chandler."

Donovan tried hard not to look shocked. "But the card was postmarked May 17? By then Chandler was in Germany."

"Not necessarily." Fuentes spoke with the forbearance of someone accustomed to being misled. "Look at the cancellation." He tapped the circular imprint with a finger. "It went through the post office in Fronteras, just south of the U.S.–Mexican border."

The expression on the woman's face did not alter one iota. "That means nothing."

"Miss Donovan, Miss Donovan," he rebuked wearily. "Like your good colonel, you too are being far less than forthright. Look, for whatever reason, you have made up an incredible lie about one man's journey to Europe. And all the while, your own people have been madly trying to determine the whereabouts of your precious Chandler on the strength of a postcard that shows he might be somewhere in North America and not at all where you wanted him to be. Please tell me – why did you do this?"

Donovan was silent.

"Perhaps I can help you." He turned the page. "The events as they happened. On May 15, Travis Chandler's car is vandalized. A day later, his home is pipe-bombed. Then, on Thursday May 17, there's a curious confrontation at a 7-Eleven store near Magdelena, sixty miles south of the U.S. border. Around eight in the evening, two Mexicans confront an American male in his fifties entering a Cadillac parked in the lot. There's a struggle as they try to force him into a pickup with Sonora State license plates. He escapes. Shots are fired. The store's plate-glass door is shattered. No injuries, and the suspects flee. Yet, after all this, the male pays cold cash for the damage and wants the matter hushed up. The manager files particulars of the incident. Knowing Americans, he wants to protect himself against future litigation."

"Again," Fuentes smirked, "the insurance bureau strikes gold. The Cadillac has Arizona plates – they're recorded on the claim report. It was owned by Chandler. The middle-aged subject at the 7-Eleven matches the description we have of our man." Miguel seemed to be enjoying the disclosure. "Now tie all this into an NCIC check I ran that showed the Cadillac had been stopped by the Arizona Highway Patrol earlier on May 17, southbound near Tombstone, and, like the man says, 'We have ourselves a new ball game.'"

He inched forward in his seat. "A week ago, I had Asuncion visit the 7-Eleven. The manager says the *Yanqui* is a regular with a bungalow in San Ignacio, two miles from the spot. Chandler isn't around for a few months, then he sees the man steadily – three, four weeks at a stretch. Who knows? After the pace of life at Huachuca, maybe Chandler needs to recharge his batteries with some desert-type solitude.

"So next, my detective locates his place. Isolated. Off the road. Nearest neighbor is three miles away. Anyway, there's no one home. No sign of life. And no car.

"Now, old Felix is a stubborn sort. He returns to the 7-Eleven and checks around. Finds a pay phone in the store. Out of habit, he records the number." Fuentes began to speak excitedly. "You remember the digits scribbled on the sheet in the captain's study? Next to the starchart?"

Donovan nodded enigmatically, not quite certain where the Mexican was leading.

Fuentes grabbed a pencil and ripped a sheet of paper from a nearby pad. He furiously scribbled numbers on the paper, "1 1 2 6 2 5 2 3 2 3 2 9 0 5 1," and rhymed them off aloud. "I checked the Tucson sequence every which way from Sunday." He thrummed the pencil on the page. "Until I ran it backwards!"

Donovan found herself nodding.

"And then the numbers on the chart are the same as those of the pay phone outside Magdalena! Conclusion?" Fuentes stared into the young woman's face. "On May 17, Travis Chandler called his son from Mexico — specifically from the 7-Eleven by Magdalena. And do you know why?"

Silence.

"Here we face two options," he remarked drolly. "One: we have an American tourist visiting sunny Sonora with shots just fired at him, calling Stateside to make sure he's turned off the oven. Or two: we have a U.S. computer expert employed at a top-secret military installation who has just survived a series of rapidly accelerating attacks on his person by Mexicans, attacks which culminate in an abduction attempt. An expert we now can't find. An expert who, I believe, instinctively reached out to his son for help!"

"Of course," Fuentes couldn't resist, "since I've been so frank with you, you should be forthright with me, don't you think?"

"We ... we didn't know," Donovan stumbled. "We had no way of knowing he'd come south."

Miguel flipped the binder pages back toward the front. He thrust an index finger into the air with exaggerated resolve. "You acknowledge that he didn't travel to Europe?"

Donovan nodded.

"Remember the story you told me about Orpheus and his mission to free a wife from death?" Miguel stopped flipping. The page held only one snapshot — that of a corpse lying on a slab in mutilated repose. Wickham Chandler. "Meet Orpheus."

Donovan gazed at the morgue shot.

Fuentes continued. "For whatever reason, the syndicate needs a VAX and they've blackmailed Wick with his father's life to get them one. First, they try intimidating the old man in his hometown. Apparently, it doesn't work. Travis flees over the border. They locate him in Sonora and try abduction. He escapes and immediately contacts his son to alert him to the attacks. Wick panics and comes through by stealing the computer – anything to keep his dad alive."

"So you think Chandler surrendered the VAX?"

"No." Fuentes shook his head. "Because if he'd done it, they wouldn't have gone to the trouble to capture you. As far as the Mexicans are concerned, Wick and you are partners. They think you know where the computer is. And they've freed you to lead them to it. Now, the question is, can you?"

Donovan's features were a study in acquiescence. "With Chandler gone," she allowed with a shrug, "no more than you." She seemed to be considering her alternatives. "Then what of Travis Chandler?" she asked. "Is he dead?"

"No," Fuentes explained. "He's alive. For the Mexicans to succeed, he's got to be. The wrecked Caddy is a warning. It's the hook in Junior, the incentive to come across. With Dad out of the picture, that incentive is gone. I personally think Travis is alive and in hiding. He may not even know Wick's been murdered.

"There's more," Miguel allowed. "Once I knew the Caddy had crossed into Mexico, I was left with an obvious inconsistency. How did the car get back to the States and into the underground in Phoenix, where we saw it a few days later?

"I had U.S. Customs do computer runs on all incoming Cadillacs in the two-week time frame following Travis Chandler's disappearance. I didn't particularly care about the license. And you know what?" Fuentes's eyes fairly crinkled with mirth. "On Friday, May 18, at nine at night, a pirate tow truck carts a late-model Caddy into the U.S. at Nogales, headed for a GM dealer. Warranty work on the ignition. Same color, same year, different license plate. It's got paperwork from the owner authorizing the move, illegible endorsement and all. No one bothers to check VINs or anything like that. Hot cars don't move north. Still, the details are logged as per standard operating procedure.

"I had the license plate run. The car was allegedly reported stolen in Benson on the same morning as the confrontation at the 7-Eleven. Coincidence, Miss Donovan?" Fuentes answered his own question. "I don't think so. Seems to me to be part of a well-oiled conspiracy. And such conspiracies exist only for something extraordinary. Not assault rifles or even microchips. That can be done by riffraff or at government auctions. So what is this remarkable machine?" His eyes veiled. "What exactly does a VAX do?"

"Its capabilities are enormous. I can't tell you more."

"You don't tell me more, Miss," he lectured, "and you might find yourself talking to Obregon yet."

"You wouldn't dare!"

Miguel's stare needed no interpretation.

For a junior U.S. Air Force officer, Maria Donovan had experienced more than her fair share of unpleasant assignments and, in the process, tested the patience of more security heads and Judge Advocate General overseers than she cared to remember. But she couldn't recall seeing an expression on any of them that matched the bleak, impenetrable tenacity that she now confronted. If granite had a human countenance, it would be Fuentes's.

"The VAX was in transit to Fort Huachuca when it was stolen," she confessed. "The fort is a critical element of the U.S. Army's Battle Command Laboratory, along with Fort Leavenworth in Kansas and Gordon in Georgia. Huachuca concerns itself with electronic warfare. The VAX deals in virtual reality – the computer simulation of war games, specifically in an air environment."

"I beg your pardon?"

"It replicates air-to-air combat in a training module. People can sit before the machine, key on, and pilot a jet."

"That's nothing to die for," Fuentes snorted with skepticism.

Donovan suddenly seemed to have aged a millennium. "It is," she uttered finally. "The VAX can also override a live pilot to steer aircraft from the ground via remote control using what we call 'excimer laser radiation.' It can sabotage things, *Jefe*. Passenger airliners, military jets, you name it. It's also Very Top Secret."

Not a muscle on Fuentes face had moved. "And Travis Chandler is the inventor, isn't he?"

Maria Donovan wavered. "Yes. Yes, he is."

Fuentes rubbed his chin. "That tells me two things," he said, with the icy reckoning of someone wagering his last chip against the House at the end of a long and smoky night. "One, they need Chandler *and* the VAX. And two, they have neither in their possession – yet. Because if they did, they wouldn't need you. You can bet your life on it."

Maria Donovan pondered what Fuentes had told her. Gradually, her features stiffened to a look of cold acceptance.

"Sort of like a super video game, is it?" Miguel offered.

"Only if you like a game that kills by remote control with the ease of a delete button," she responded.

Fuentes nodded. "One last question."

"Yes?"

"What are you planning to do?"

"I don't know." She shrugged numbly. "But I just had an idea."

"Can you tell me what it is?"

"Listen, Miguel," Donovan said. "Given the circumstances, I think the less you know about my movements from here on in, the better it will be for your health."

Fuentes agreed. He excused himself and exited the living room. When he returned, he carried a pillow and plain wool blanket. A Smith and Wesson bull barrel was tucked snugly into his belt. He flopped the bedding down onto the sofa and gestured down the hall.

"You can have the bedroom. I'll be quite at ease here. Besides," he nodded to Salinas nuzzled up against the fluffy pillow, gazing at them with liquid brown eyes, "the dog snores." And he smiled "Keep the gun for the night." Miguel gave the handgun to his guest. "Just in case."

"You trust me?"

"More than Obregon."

"I take it that isn't a heck of a lot."

"It's enough to keep you alive." He turned away without another word.

Fuentes was roused from a deep sleep by the slamming of the screen door. He reached under the sofa and drew out a loaded revolver. The numerals on the neon wall clock showed that it was shortly after four.

Far beyond the bay window, a dented old moon emerged from a thick cloud chamber, casting a muted paleness over the desert. He heard the motorcycle gunning through the night. Then silence.

He found his bed made and a neatly handwritten note on the pillow.

> Will be in touch within the day.
> Take care of yourself.
> Love,
> Maria

Fuentes secretly hoped she meant it.

Wednesday, August 8, dawn.
San Cristobal

28 Fuentes worked the shaving lather feverishly with a brush, then applied it to his face. It felt cool to his skin. He picked up the razor and lifted it to his cheek.

The countenance he saw in the mirror looked haggard. For the first time in months, he felt that way, too. His temples were sprouting gray; worry lines that he'd always assessed as imaginary were now suddenly quite prominent. There was a puffiness about his eyes. Yet it wasn't just his physical appearance that was dismaying him.

Miguel Fuentes was more than a little uneasy with what he was doing. He'd never considered himself a conspirator; it wasn't in his nature. Still, there was enough that suddenly troubled Miguel about the "respectable" way of doing things, and where that had gotten him in life, that he was prepared to try the darker side – even if it involved playing a little of both ends against the middle. Just this once.

With tight, deliberate strokes he shaved off his mustache.

Ten minutes later, he was dressed. He went into the hallway, lifted the phone to call Asuncion, hesitated, then returned it to its cradle. No, somehow he didn't think it would be wise to speak on his telephone. Not after the visitor he'd had last night.

He planted the straw Stetson squarely on his head, the gunbelt tightly around his waist, and the Raybans snugly over his eyes. Then he strode out onto the patio above the crossroads to face his world.

The Mustang was covered in grime; the windshield and head-lights were matted with bugs. Fuentes would ensure it was spot-less before he arrived at his office. He always did, even though the money for the carwash invariably came from his own pocket.

After loading the trunk with his precious files, he turned the ignition and gunned the car out of the gully, barreling through the tollbooth and onto the highway to Coronado in a gush of fine platinum dust. With the murder trial now sidetracked, he had unfinished business to attend to.

Two black boxes were welded tightly into the gap between the front bucket seats: a Coronado police communications radio and a newer unit, recently installed by technicians in anticipation of the pending takeover. Fuentes clicked on the toggle of the town unit, but on principle left the second transceiver off. He had no interest in listening to the babbling of his *federale* brothers-in-law. Not until he had to.

He wondered if the new regime in Coronado would be as appreciative of the car as he'd been. Obregon would certainly want to upgrade the Mustang to a more dignified luxury model, more in keeping with a senior government bureaucrat. Angrily, Fuentes dismissed the thought. He still had the better part of a week left before officially handing over the reins of power. He'd be damned if he'd surrender both his integrity and his pride so meekly. The spider logo on the driver's door was now strangely comforting.

A shrill transmission on the town radio interrupted his musings. Unit Three – Coronado East – detailed to attend the Church of Santa Lucia and see the *padre*. The receiver crackled with static. Fuentes played with the volume dial and barely made out the details. Something about headstones being vandalized. Officer Commacho in Unit Three acknowledged.

This would make the second time in less than a year that graves had been disturbed. Miguel thought it more than a passing coincidence. Was it kids? Was it deliberate – something more sinister? The last time this happened, the padre had alluded to the occult, but Fuentes had dismissed the theory.

Miguel made a mental note to have someone interview Benito Alvirez. Alvirez was eleven years old and already had a record for stabbing another kid with a pencil and puncturing his lung to assert control over his dominion. Eleven years old and already the leader of one of the town's toughest street gangs. Benito might do something like this. Or order it to be done. In the meantime, Emilio Tomas Commacho – "E.T." as he was nicknamed – was one of Miguel's few good men. The line of investigation would be complete.

The police radio reported an accident down the tollway: a jackknifed tractor-trailer with no injuries, save for the trucker's pride. The mishap compelled Fuentes to chart a roundabout course into town, a backroad detour that added thirty minutes to his schedule and several stone chips to the paint job. The carwash would have to wait.

The day was sweltering; traffic into Coronado was incessant. After wending down the Passeo Bolivar, he made his way to Avenue Valencia and brought the Mustang to rest in a narrow laneway next to the police building. The town's garbage collection contract had been abruptly canceled three days before and the streets and alleys were already teeming with refuse.

He found solace in the fact that the brownstone housing the

policia looked as seedy as ever. There was a marked vehicle out front: a brand-new Crown Victoria. A highway unit. Miguel paid it no heed. *Federales* often passed through and occasionally stopped for shoptalk and refreshments. Fuentes encouraged the practice. It was better to know your enemy than to be blindsided by him.

He entered the office, grimacing as he was hit by a gust of frigid air. He smelled the same mildew smell and saw the same tattered posters for criminals long ago recaptured and flyers for children long ago lost to eternity. But something drastic had happened. The portable television atop the bookshelf was turned off. The door to the ComCen was ajar, the room piled to the ceiling with cartons. A flurry of torn magazines jammed a garbage pail. Stella sat primly in front of her desk, puffing furiously on a cigarette. She jabbed at her cuticles with a nail file. Smoke wreathed her head. Most important, there was no duty officer on deck to greet him; in fact, there was no sign of any of his staff.

The door to his private office opened. A tall *federale* sergeant in knife-creased khakis emerged, carrying a mass of manila folders. His Sam Browne and calf-high traffic boots gleamed. He sported a deep tan and, judging by his confident gait, a deeper ego. He couldn't have been more than twenty-four years old if he'd wanted to be.

"Can I help you?" He blocked Miguel's movements.

"My name is Fuentes, Sergeant. I'm the chief here in Coronado."

"Of course." The man's face was vacant. He did not move. Neither did he offer Fuentes the courtesy of an introduction.

Fuentes peered around at the empty hat rack, the silent television, and the bulwark of boxes. "Where are my men?" he demanded with mounting suspicion.

"Your men?"

"Yes, damnit it! My men!"

"Your dispatch is being centralized to our site in Hermosillo," the newcomer remarked in a patronizing manner. "This will be completed before the end of the week. Quite frankly," he sniffed, "we've had to make serious staffing changes to reflect that reality."

"What kind of changes?" Fuentes seethed.

"The usual ones that come with any restructuring," the *federale* replied with poised indifference. "Your patrol areas have been reconfigured. A few people salvaged by reassignment, the majority given their walking papers." He leveled his stare to match Miguel's. "We fired most of them yesterday."

"Fired?" Miguel stormed. "Which ones?"

The sergeant reached to the near wall and removed a clipboard from its nail. He handed it to Fuentes. Two columns of surnames were typed on a flimsy sheet. The words "Severance" and "Transfer to *Federale* Strength" topped the columns. There were twenty names below "Severance" and five on the right side under "Transfer." Only one of these – Commacho – had any potential. Ominously, Miguel's nemesis, Pluto Velas, was also listed among the few retained.

"You've decimated my command!" Fuentes shrieked in outrage.

The sergeant shrugged. "Come now, *Jefe*," he cajoled. "Tell me you wouldn't have done the same if you'd had the chance."

Miguel smoldered at the insult. Furiously, he perused the roll. One name was missing. "Asuncion?" he demanded. "Where is he?"

"I'm sorry? Who?"

"Felix Asuncion," Fuentes said impatiently. "My intelligence coordinator."

"Oh! We terminated his services yesterday."

"Why wasn't I told?"

"It's not for me to say. Take it up with the *comandante*."

"You haven't answered my question."

"Sorry." The sergeant's tone indicated that he was neither that nor respectful of his visitor's rank. "We thought you'd be involved in the trial for the rest of your time as chief. The *comandante* deemed it best that we make the changeover early rather than waiting till the last second."

"So you didn't consider the courtesy of a call before you dispensed with my people?"

"The *comandante* saw no need. I concurred." The young man didn't bother to mask a rising impatience. "Now if you'll excuse me, I have work to do." He turned on his heel to walk back into Fuentes's office.

"Wait! Where are my things?"

The sergeant halted in his tracks, then gestured to a trio of plastic garbage bags stacked against the wall. One of them leaked a sticky substance. "I think we packed them appropriately."

Fuentes opened the top bag in the pile. It held slimy chicken bones and rotting potatoes and yams, wrapped in the ink-stained shreds of an FBI diploma. He reached in to salvage the certificate. The bag burst from its weight. Torn paper scraps, photo remnants and shards of broken glass cascaded out.

"Do you call this 'appropriately?'" Fuentes fumed.

"Did I say that? Sorry. I meant to say 'approximately.'"

At that precise moment, something in Fuentes snapped. He grabbed the sergeant by the collar and pulled him downward with such force that their faces were mere inches apart. He crossed his collar tabs with a neat flick of his wrists, as if he were tightening a bow. The sergeant's features flushed crimson. A cheek muscle flinched. Veins on his temple grew prominent and pumped a furious tattoo. Miguel knew the telltale signs all too well.

"Now listen to me. Carefully. You might think you're taking over Coronado because Obregon told you so. Think again." He balled his right hand into a fist that loomed menacingly under the man's nostrils, and he felt his captive wince. "You're trained in self-defense. Tell me? How much force is required to drive nasal bone into brain tissue?" He left the threat unfinished. "You will call me 'sir' and mean it! Or I'll have those stripes!"

"Yes, sir," he gasped with difficulty.

Fuentes loosened his grip on the shirt. The man gave a hoarse cough as he rubbed his neck. His breathing was rapid.

Miguel walked to the threshold of his office and opened the door. "Now help me carry those bags back in here and let me get on with the business of policing this town."

"But, but ..." the sergeant stammered, "you have no men!"

"Then your people will have to report to me in their stead, won't they?"

"They could never do that!"

Miguel reached for his phone. He dialed a Hermosillo

number and, after informing the shocked secretary who'd vetted the call that he was still in command, was patched instantly out to Obregon.

"I'm back at my station with one of yours, Ramon. He's assisting me in the investigation." A calculated pause. Miguel held the phone away from his ear. A squeal of frenetic expletives from the receiver.

"And you are . . . ?" He peered coldly at the sergeant.

The young uniform muttered his surname: Jiminez.

"Yes, Ramon. It's Jiminez." More profanity. "He's one of your best?" A lopsided grin. "I sort of thought he was too." A trilling on the line. The grin was replaced by an expression of somber resolve. "You do want this done properly, don't you? Or should I come back to assist in your search for Donovan?"

A weighty silence. Then the chipmunk chatter once more. But less hectic.

"Good." Miguel had gauged his thrust well. "I'll continue to explore the truck theft from – as you so aptly put it – my 'current posting.' Yes? Good. My report will be submitted by six o'clock each morning, in triplicate, on *federale* format. To you. Oh, and Ramon? If the investigation is becoming a costing issue? Don't worry. Maybe we can do lunch when it's over. I'll buy. I know how tight your budget must be now that you're actually on the verge of taking over Coronado. I've been there, you know? Give my best to the Riveras."

Fuentes hung up and focused his attention on the man before him. "Now that we have our protocol cleared up, what were you in the middle of doing when I came in, Jiminez?"

"The dailies." The sergeant was now all attention.

Miguel held out his hand. The uniformed officer dutifully handed over the folders. Three vehicle accidents, one, a minor personal injury involving a bus, a peasant, and a burro with an attitude. Five persons held for drunkenness. Four minor assaults, with an informal resolution in one case and no suspects in the others.

But there was something else. Someone had shot up a second-story window at the Crisco Hotel, a downtown fleabag near the

Cameo Theater. At least twelve rounds of 7.62 ammunition had punctured the mattress and floor, ricocheted into the linen storage room below, and decorated the wall behind the bed. The sniper had probably fired from the roof of a four-story building across the street.

The shooting had occurred shortly after 4:00 a.m. There were no injuries or suspects. The room had been rented to an "M. Blanco," who'd checked in around 10:00 p.m. without baggage and paid by credit card. Thereafter, *Señor* Blanco hadn't been seen for the rest of the night. When the police had crashed through the door immediately after the shooting, they'd found it vacant. There was a vague description of the mysterious M. Blanco obtained from the desk clerk – Hispanic, dark hair, colored shirt.

"There was also a break and enter at the Environmental Protection Unit last night," Jiminez interrupted, offering another sheet.

Fuentes skimmed the ten-paragraph report. A brick tossed through plate glass and a suspected intrusion. The place hadn't been alarmed. And why should it have been? What right-minded person would pilfer air-quality statistics? There'd been a standalone computer on site. It had been smashed to pieces. According to Roberto Elliott, the regional engineer and head of the facility, the only items missing were a stereo tuner and petty cash from a desk drawer. Total loss, counting window and demolished computer? Under twelve thousand *pesos*.

A prostitute and her trick had been parked in a laneway adjacent to the facility. The john was otherwise occupied; the hooker – somewhat less attentive to the man's needs than he might have believed – had a better view of the street. At the conclusion of the performance, the trick proved reluctant to pay for services rendered. Police arrived in response to the sound of staged screaming and stumbled on a sea of broken glass from the break-in. A description of the suspect was negotiated as a tradeoff to satisfy the woman's pocketbook, if not her virtue. The burglar was a male Hispanic, slight build, dark hair, wearing a multicolored shirt.

Fuentes flipped back to the hotel incident. The two descriptions, though slight, were a match. Assuming it was the same man,

Fuentes wondered if the break-in and murder attempt were connected.

The break-in had happened shortly after two-thirty, according to a witness named Barragan, an elderly insomniac who lived above the insignificant government office and corroborated the prostitute's testimony. Two-thirty-six to be exact. So the thief had time to return to the hotel and risk becoming Swiss cheese.

Fuentes considered the environmental office break-in. The thief had escaped employing the same route he'd used to enter. He'd cut his thumb on a shard of glass, leaving a bloody smudge on the shattered pane. With such a bonus, the crime lab had readily matched the print. Renaldo Jaime Cortez, aka Renny the Rat.

Sergeant Jiminez anticipated the question. "U.S. Border Patrol intercepted Cortez two hours ago along the wire at Douglas, Arizona, attempting to enter the States. I've sent a car on a prisoner return to the Agua Prieta police post."

Fuentes nodded agreement. Because of Asuncion's meticulous briefings on criminal players in Coronado, Renny Cortez was a name well known to Fuentes. In his youth, Cortez had been arrested a number of times, mostly for break-and-enters. A frail teen with a game left leg, he'd been a stablehand at the local racetrack, tossing bales of hay and walking horses.

But his mind was always elsewhere – in a world of high stakes and easy money, a world where he lived by his wits and acumen, a world of petty crime.

Cortez had found break-ins too labor-intensive, a tedious investment of energy with high risk and doubtful outcome. So he'd found a niche, trolling the town market, lifting wallets. Renny subsequently acquired quite the reputation for light fingers. That is, until he was caught with the billfold of a PRI official. The victim was a person of substance; the judge was suitably austere and uncaring.

Sixteen months in prison had been the sentence, a year and change to break rocks and spirit. And that might well have been the end of Renaldo Cortez. But, as is so often the case in such matters, the period spent in custody altered his life. And not for the better.

Renny bunked with a career criminal whose specialty was illegal wiretaps, the kind that gave bedbugs a bad name. Then and there, Cortez made a conscious decision. No longer would he live on mean streets, dependent on his wits and the facility of his fingers. Instead he'd let the naked words of his prey serve his needs and those of his client, whoever that might be.

A correspondence course on electronics, coupled with a spy kit from a mail-order catalog, and Cortez was en route to notoriety. From divorce lawyers, to corporate idea pirates, to gang bosses intent on reining in out-of-control members, he found a ready – and lucrative – demand for his clandestine skills. So much so that shortly after their joint releases from prison, he was able to eliminate his principal competition by mailing an anonymous – and highly doctored – tape of a steamy tryst involving the man and a young *señora* to the woman's spouse. The husband, suitably enraged, promptly shot the aspiring Don Juan in the back, effectively ending his career – and life. Renny Cortez became a legend on society's darker side, one whose talents justifiably went to the highest bidder.

In the late Eighties, the pace of communications technology accelerated from a trot to a gallop and finally a leaping charge into the future. Renny's adaptability cunningly paralleled the dash. He shrewdly scored a menial job at a television station, sweeping floors and getting takeout for the crew. With diligence, patient reading of the manuals, and a spare key to the studio engineer's office, he acquired a thorough knowledge of the newly integrated world of sound and computer bytes.

His ancient Uher recorder was replaced with a laptop and workstation configured to deal with digital equipment, and his cumbersome spools with floppy disks. The investment in cash was over $200,000, but there really wasn't much of an alternative if Renny wanted to stay solvent in his chosen profession. Cortez had long ago accepted a truism that others had missed – that a man who could effectively re-word history was more important than one who could make it. And the words flowed like honey....

Fuentes mulled over the data. He placed a call to information, got a number Stateside, and spoke to someone for a short while, scribbling notes as he talked. Then he rose to leave. "I have some interviews to conduct to support *Comandante* Obregon's investigation, so I'll be out until late afternoon. When can we expect the prisoner?"

"It'll be a while, *Jefe*. Certainly not until after five."

"Good. Please ensure that no one speaks to him until I have the opportunity to."

Sergeant Jiminez hesitated. The break-in had scarcely been major. "Sir?"

"It's a small thing, Jiminez," Fuentes remarked with a crooked grin. "Just humor me, okay?" The grin evaporated. It was replaced by a stare that would melt asphalt. "I like to think I'm still in control." He smartly swung the gate, then stopped cold in his tracks. "In my absence, you'll do what is required of you?"

"I'm a professional, sir," the young man replied sanctimoniously.

"Now where have I heard that before?" Fuentes commented, more to himself than to his audience.

"I beg your pardon?"

The *jefe* of Coronado shook his head. "Nothing, son. It's nothing that you'd ever understand." He opened the door back to the streets and was gone.

Fuentes returned to the Mustang and jammed the comfort dials on the dashboard hard to the right so the air conditioner was on full tilt. He eased the driver's seat back into a semi-reclined position, inching the brimmed Stetson over his eyes. He then meticulously reviewed what he knew, or, at the very least, had been told.

The Cummins dumpster used in the kidnap attempt had been taken at gunpoint from the parking lot of a nondescript truck stop north of Coronado. Obregon had given him the particulars concerning the driver and the three witnesses.

Miguel was convinced that this avenue of inquiry would prove fruitless. True enough, the theft had probably occurred. If nothing else, it provided an alibi to cloak the identities of the culprits and their motives. The truck driver was likely legitimate, as were the witnesses. Co-conspirators to a crime don't usually remain behind to surrender their names and addresses to police.

But what could onlookers possibly have seen, other than a spiral of dust thick as talcum tunneling down the highway? Nevertheless, Fuentes would diligently interview each and every one of them. Out of the mouths of babes . . . .

Miguel reset the seat to upright and started the motor. The first subject – a reclusive dirt farmer – lived seventy miles away. The other independent witnesses were nearer Coronado. The driver himself dwelled in town. The entire exercise would take the better part of a day. And somehow Fuentes still had to squeeze in sufficient time to properly question Renny Cortez. But first, there were two people he had to visit.

Wednesday, August 8, mid-morning.
Santa Lucia Mission

29 Santa Lucia was a venerable mission church located on the eastern approaches to Coronado, out by the old town center, where it nestled in the sea of tangled shrub and mesa that passed for the playground of the nearby peasant Barrio.

Originally painted sunflower-yellow, time and uncaring elements had liberally peeled away the building's exterior to expose a frayed foundation of mottled adobe and decaying bedrock. Heavy oak doors, bleached a pallid beige by decades of fierce sunlight, hung stolidly from iron hinges, sealing the entrance. A finger-like steeple timidly probed an uncaring sky. The Angelus had faithfully chimed from a corroded bell for ninety-three years until petty complaints from a local labor cooperative to the municipal council had stilled the sound.

Fuentes found Father Ezequiel working in a tiny vegetable garden located in the shade next to the "rectory" – a dilapidated mobile home that had once been the field office of an American copper consortium. Soft mid-morning light tickled the starched calico drapes that hung from its tiny cubed windows. The door was ajar, and sounds of Chopin drifted placidly across the courtyard.

The priest seemed to sense Fuentes's arrival. He turned from his hoeing and grinned broadly, exposing a set of perfect teeth.

"Miguel. It's good to see you, though there are surely better circumstances. It's been, what – several months since you last came here to Mass?"

Fuentes muttered an embarrassed greeting.

"No matter." Father Ezequiel placed his hoe against a wheelbarrow and wiped callused hands on a nut-brown cassock cinched at the waist and draped loosely over his angular body. On his head, the *padre* wore the mangled baseball cap of his favorite team, the Chicago Cubs.

A wizened man, Ezequiel had been the pastor and sole cleric at Santa Lucia's for thirty-seven years. He'd lived to his present, mellow age on a stern diet of fibers and cheap cuts of meat, with only a tot of rum and occasional ice cream cone to remind him of the earthly pleasures he'd forsaken when he'd decided to call this arid land home. His cocoa-butter skin was patchy, cancerous some might call it, flecked from years of overexposure, but the priest didn't mind. If Brother Sun was to be his demise, it was the Will of God.

Ezequiel de Allende was a most unusual clergyman, even judged by Sonora's lengthy historical measuring stick. He was born in Madrid in 1928, to a father who was a corporate banker and follower of Opus Dei, the ultraconservative Catholic lay organization that shadowed General Franco's regime; his mother was the daughter of well-heeled Seville gentry, descended directly from the Royal House of Bourbon.

Ezequiel was an only child, a precocious extrovert with a brilliant future mapped out for him by his parents. For much of his youth, he politely followed the family cartography, graduating magna cum laude in chemistry from the prestigious University of Barcelona before entering his father's firm in a junior position. He quickly accelerated by dint of his own efforts, as much as those of his parent, and soon gained a reputation for skillfully turning a coin. After securing a number of significant contracts through a heady blend of innovation and sound business practice, Ezequiel was well on his way up the corporate ladder of success.

His personal life was likewise blessed. He was handsome, sociable, and much sought after by young women – and he was certainly well aware of it.

Yet, after a time, Ezequiel came to realize that something was lacking in his quest for self. So, it didn't surprise his parents when, after much introspection and soul-searching, he announced that he was becoming a priest. The family already had one archbishop and several monsignors in its lineage.

What did cause the de Allendes profound consternation was that their son would choose such an unassuming order – the Franciscans minor, rather than the mighty Dominicans, or their equally cosmopolitan contemporaries the Society of Jesus, the Jesuits.

When Ezequiel compounded that regrettable selection by opting for the missions of Mexico, his parents effectively disowned their offspring; his mother, who outlived his father by a full decade, recanted only on her deathbed to favor him in her will.

Returning to Spain to bury his remaining parent, Ezequiel showed that institutional poverty had not dulled his fiscal acumen. After leaving much of his inheritance in a trust for St. Lucia, he purchased enough school supplies to last a decade, a used Volkswagen minibus with a handicap ramp, an old farm tractor, a water irrigation system for the village, and enough garden tools and seed supplies to make each family in the parish virtually self-sufficient.

"Did my man come to investigate?" Miguel asked.

"Commacho?" The priest nodded. "Yes. He left an hour ago. He was very good."

Fuentes started to frame an apology. "I'm sorry I didn't attend myself. I'd have been here earlier but . . ."

The priest hushed him. "Not to worry. I heard of the explosion at Zita's, the senseless deaths. Such matters are certainly important enough to occupy your full efforts."

"May I see the spot, *Padre?*"

"Certainly, *Jefe*."

Ezequiel led Fuentes a short distance to the old graveyard and out among the rows. The old man walked gingerly, easing his weight on a twisted hickory cane.

The cemetery was massive, comprising several acres of land. An uneven stone wall girdled long columns of crosses and tombstones.

Santa Lucia was one of the oldest burying grounds in the State of Sonora. In the beginning, the town's élite had selected plots in the hard, unyielding earth surrounding the church. But as time passed, the building and its holy grounds fell into abject disfavor. In time, the plots declined from their once-elevated status to become an impoverished reliquary for Indians, half-breeds, and sinners.

As they walked past rows of anonymous markers, the mounds became gradually smaller, the flower memorials more profuse, the dates on the tombstones more touching. This was the last earthly abode of infants and stillborn babies.

It was at the farthest gravesite that Father Ezequiel halted. There was no need for words; Fuentes could see the damage for himself. The frame holding the memorial photo on the monument had been partially pried away from the granite, the glass shattered. Judging from tight gouges on the stone, it appeared to have been done with a sharp–edged instrument, perhaps a chisel or an army knife.

Miguel stood for a time in silence. "Margarita Gonzales?" he remarked finally.

The old man nodded. "Hasn't her family suffered enough?" His voice was as dry as cracked wheat.

Fuentes pursed his lips in thought. "When did you find it?"

"At dawn, when I was reading my breviary." Ezequiel paused. "Do you have any idea who'd do such a thing?"

Miguel shook his head in bewilderment. "No, *Padre*, I don't." His mind raced. Margarita Gonzales. The four-year-old killed during the Bolivar construction mishap. At the time the fatality occurred, rumors alleging large-scale corruption at the project had already been gathering momentum in the *cantinas*. The fact that an innocent had died because of what appeared to be criminal negligence hadn't helped matters one bit.

Community unease had been fueled by an aggressive young newspaperman who had parallel-tracked lukewarm police inquiries into the accident and related matters and had threatened to break the shocking news of what he'd unearthed, nationwide. Out of decency, the journalist had waited for the victim to be given a Christian burial.

On the day of the interment, it seemed as though the entire population of Coronado had emerged to pay their respects. With thousands of mourners converging on the church, it became one of the grandest services in the town's history. A PRI representative had attended the mass and laid the most exquisite wreath of white orchids on the grave. He'd also presented a beautiful letter of condolence to the bereaved family from the Office of the President of Mexico.

Though it hadn't been evident in their actions, Fuentes later discovered what the citizens of Coronado had been thinking in their hearts – that the Oshkosh and its load had been patently unsafe, and that the reputation of the developers had been deemed too important to jeopardize over as paltry a thing as a child's life.

Fuentes also heard what those self-same citizens muttered when it became known, that on the day following Margarita's interment, the inquisitive newspaperman had been involved in a single car accident along an isolated stretch of desert, an accident that left him in a coma. He died without ever waking.

Later, much later, Miguel learned that the gravestone had been purchased for the family by *Señor* Hector Rivera. As an act of contrition? No, that was impossible. Knowing the *delegado,* it was more likely another exhibition of his pervasive power. Fuentes also discovered that the Coronado police never conducted a strict mechanical inspection of the journalist's demolished compact.

Fuentes's predecessor – "Luppy" Lopez – disappeared four days after commencing an inquiry into the girl's death. Within a week, Miguel had been chosen to succeed him. He inherited a town near open revolt, for it was broadly rumored that the *jefe* had received more than his share of *mordido* – hush money.

Miguel lightly traced his fingertips over the grainy monument façade. His eyes caught something in the dry, jumbled earth. The glint of gold in sunlight. Intrigued, he dug around until he unearthed the source: a necklace with a Saint Christopher medallion affixed to it and one of its links broken. The metal was of good quality and clearly designed for an adult. He turned the medal to its obverse. The characters R. C. and a date – 60-09-27 – were inscribed on a smooth face.

"You have any workers in the cemetery, *Padre?*"

The priest shook his head.

"Then who digs the graves?"

"Volunteers. On the day before the interment."

Fuentes let the medallion twirl playfully in sunlight. "Any of them have names with the initials R and C?"

Ezequiel mulled over the question. "No."

Fuentes palmed the adornment, then deposited it into his shirt pocket.

"Did you hear anything last night?"

Father Ezequiel furrowed his brow in thought. "There was something. At around three. I was getting up to use the bathroom." The words tumbled out with the recollection. "The sound of men shouting. Angry shouts."

"And?"

"That's all I can say." A weak smile. "You get so used to it in the Barrio."

"Do you remember if the noise came from the cemetery?"

"Yes. From this direction."

They lingered a dutiful time before the grave, then walked back to the camper. The priest asked Fuentes to join him at a rusty table under a tree, away from the morning heat shimmer. They sat on three-legged stools.

Ezequiel vanished, returning with a squat earthen pitcher. He poured them both a drink, his liver-speckled hands trembling ever so slightly.

"Altar wine." He winked. "Unconsecrated, of course. I refined the blend. I might as well put my chemistry training to use, no?"

They drank the rich, carmine liquid. The music stopped.

Miguel heard the faint moan of a diesel engine, felt the coarse rumble of a far-off freight train. The eleven o'clock from Hermosillo north to Phoenix.

The old man offered more to Fuentes, who politely declined. The priest smacked his lips and served himself another.

"The garden is good?"

"*Sí*. Chili peppers, yams, potatoes. It meets my needs, and I have enough to share with the community." The priest lapsed into a comfortable silence.

A child yelled in the distant Barrio. A dog barked. Pots and pans clanked. In the sky, the insistent drone of ancient propeller planes – a DC-3 waggling its wings toward Chihuahua.

They finished their drinks. Ezequiel escorted Fuentes to the car and offered his blessing. "*A Dios,* my son."

Miguel crossed himself with a clumsy sweep of his hand, more out of courtesy than belief.

"And in the case of this poor child's grave," the priest offered, "may justice be done."

"As it will be, *Padre,*" Fuentes muttered. "As it will be."

As he left the grounds, Fuentes waved. He drove the Mustang hard down the roadway, heard the motor groan in protest, absently watched as specks of cinammon-colored dust flitted across his windshield.

He tried to focus his mind on the murder investigation. But the image of the damaged tombstone nagged at him. And whether he was aware of it or not, Miguel Fuentes was already beginning the lonely journey to places other than those the good *padre* yearned for: dark, solitary places where vengeance, not justice, dwelt.

Wednesday, August 8, noon hour.
Coronado

30

Fuentes honked the horn a few times, parked outside the street-level walk-up. When that didn't work, he tried the restaurant. Eng was alone in the kitchen, cutting up *bok choi*. After much grumbling, the restaurateur found the key he needed and let Fuentes in.

He took the steps two at a time, pausing at the top of the landing in the presence of the sorry spectacle that assailed his senses. The room reeked of filth and stale urine. Fuentes shuffled through strewn newspapers. He booted an empty vodka bottle, sending it spinning into a wall.

His detective was asleep. Even in repose, Ascuncion's countenance was beet-red, his jowls a crosshatch of veins. The Zapata mustache was caked with mucus and vomit. A dilapidated wine crate squatted by the bedside. A pair of dark aviator glasses perched atop it; one of the lenses was cracked. A set of false teeth resided in a cloudy glass.

"Felix! *Despiertate!* Wake up! It is almost noon!" Miguel prodded Asuncion with increasing vigor as it became apparent that words alone had no effect on the slumbering lump.

"Leave me alone, Eng," the sleeping figure slurred.

Fuentes called his name again.

Asuncion closed his fists and jabbed out instinctively, punching air. "Leave me alone, you Chinese bastard!"

Another nudge, this one not quite so playful.

The ancient detective started upright. He locked his elbows and wavered for a moment like an immense barrage balloon struggling against a headwind.

"Come, my friend," Fuentes beckoned. "We have serious work to do."

"Work?" Asuncion mumbled. "You don't work in Coronado any more, *señor.*" The detective spoke with a bleak gruffness. Fuentes paid no heed.

"I told you once before – I work here until I'm terminated."

Asuncion squinted at his unexpected caller, a sad, startled look on his face. "That can come in many ways, *Jefe.*"

"Not if I do what I must." Miguel loomed over the bed. "I need your help."

"You don't, boss," Asuncion responded with spiritless abandonment. "I heard about Hermosillo." He coughed wetly.

"You'll never get to the bottom of it, so why try? They already say it's a fix."

"Because," Fuentes countered with fierce pride, "if I don't, no one else will. Come!" he snapped. "I need you. At least for the next few days. Until my time is up."

"I'm too old." Felix dismissed him.

"My right hand is never too old, *amigo*," Miguel offered soothingly. "Or too useless."

"Obregon thinks I am," Asuncion responded in a plaintive tone. "He has no time for me."

"But I do." Fuentes went to the clothesline and picked out a pair of pants. He pitched them to the bed. Then he found Felix's beloved combat jacket on the floor, scrunched into a ball, two nearly white socks, and a maroon T-shirt with the words "Be All That You Can Be." He threw these items in the same general direction.

Asuncion sat slumped on the side of the bed, balefully regarding the pile of clothing arrayed before him. He fished false teeth out of the glass and maneuvered them delicately onto his gums. Then he dressed.

The rumpled detective rummaged under the bed and emerged with his beloved high-tops. He slid the sneakers on, unlaced. Then he stood, casually slipping the combat jacket over his pear-shaped frame.

There was one more item.

"The fridge?"

Asuncion nodded.

Miguel rooted around the rancid foodstuffs until he found the Glock wedged between a tin of Clamato juice and a rank head of Boston lettuce. The home-sewn shoulder holster had a layer of frost on it. The speed-loaders were in a bowl; the handcuffs in the freezer. Asuncion strapped on his weapon and cuffs.

They lumbered down the cramped stairs to street level. "I can't pay you a salary, you know," Fuentes admitted.

Asuncion shrugged. "There are some things more valuable than money," he avowed solemnly.

"Such as?"

A smile ransomed Felix's normally dour face. "Clean under-wear, *señor.*" Miguel broke into hearty laughter. For a moment, at least, all was right with the world once again.

He opened the passenger door to the Mustang and waited till his friend was seated. Then he got in, turned the key, and began to drive off into the filth and squalor that was Coronado.

The road was little more than a mule trail. Fuentes had the window partway down. Fine sand pellets driven by an elfish breeze tapped a vigorous tattoo on his grizzled cheek.

After a few minutes of silence, he broached the topic of the break-in. It was puzzling. Cortez hadn't been considered a burglary suspect in these parts for six years. His name hadn't even cropped up, certainly not during Miguel's short tenure in Coronado. Fuentes surmised that for Cortez to burglarize the *federale* office, it had to have been for a profoundly more serious purpose than to steal a stereo and rifle the petty-cash box.

And that's precisely why he now sought the benefit of the sage counsel seated next to him in the car.

After hearing Fuentes through, Asuncion closed his eyes and pillowed his swarthy head into the headrest. His face was calm, but his lips were moving. His eyelids fluttered, then stilled.

Some time went by. Suddenly the eyes opened. Asuncion appeared refreshed. He motioned to a pay phone a hundred yards distant and asked for Fuentes's credit card. "The cost of doing business, *Jefe,*" he shrugged as he lurched out of the seat and headed toward the phone booth.

"It took a few calls," was all he'd say on his return. And so the matter lay, for Miguel knew that if Asuncion had anything even remotely practical to contribute to the topic of Cortez and his activities, sooner or later, he would.

The out-of-town witnesses to the truck-jacking proved as useful as a unicycle to a centipede. The first, the dirt farmer, had difficulty remembering the stolen vehicle's color, let alone volunteering a useful description of its thieves. The second, a waitress, was only marginally better. She recalled men loitering around the Cummins, but when pressed wasn't certain if they were the actual hijackers or legitimate patrons. Fuentes probed further, and it became quite apparent that she hadn't even seen the theft. She'd told the police what she'd assumed they wanted to hear.

The third party, a tool-parts salesman, was best of all. And that wasn't saying much. He got the number of thieves right – but only because he'd peered intently at them as the huge truck bulldozed his dilapidated AMC Gremlin into an irrigation ditch. He offered that they were probably male. The observation didn't push the police inquiry much more successfully up the rope than the hot-winded comments of the other two.

The interviews took longer than Fuentes had expected, so, after sliding by Eng's for Chinese take-out – like most police meals, provided gratis – they returned to the office.

They found Renny Cortez to be the sole occupant of the holding cells. An exasperated sergeant, seething to return home to Hermosillo, quickly briefed them.

Fuentes peered into the cubicle holding their captive. Up close, Cortez seemed slighter than Miguel had been given to expect: five-foot three, probably less; a spare, uneasy frame garbed in a seedy Madras shirt and grubby slacks cinched in by a beaded Navajo belt. He wore a cheap wristwatch and lugged several gold chains around a spindly neck; one of them held a crucifix. His hair was creosote black, long and oily, and slicked back from bony temples to reveal wolverine eyes that were as probing as they were purposeful. A set of furry brows formed a skirmish line across a cramped forehead pitted with acne scars.

The rest of Cortez's face beat an industrious retreat to pronounced stupefaction: lips as meager as the shadow cast by a clouded sun, ill-mannered ears, a wavering chin with all the definition of quicksand. Impossible as it seemed, the mug shot had been overly kind. In real life, Renny Cortez had an impatience about him that curdled even these insubstantial features to a perpetual scowl.

The officer assigned the four-to-twelve detail was Pluto Velas. He was slow getting the prisoner's meal, so Fuentes and Asuncion retired to the *jefe*'s office and picked at the beef-and-rice concoction that skidded around their plates.

As he ate, Fuentes began to sort through some of his pending correspondence. A morning newspaper was crumpled roughly in the upright stacking tray, wedged between memos on fire routes and fuel allowances. Miguel idly opened it to scan the headlines. He spied a two-column story at the bottom of the front page, next to the weather map.

A 40,000-ton vessel owned by a Hong Kong shipping firm and crewed by Filipinos, the M.S. *Malinta,* had crashed full speed into one of the locks leading into Gatun Lake on the Panama Canal. The article described the lock chambers as being 82 feet high and 110 feet wide. The vital international seaway would be closed for repair for twenty-four hours.

Fuentes tried to imagine a ship capable of destabilizing a steel wall that imposing. The technique became crystal clear in the next paragraph. The man at the helm of the *Malinta* had been dead drunk, as had the senior officer on the bridge. Both were under arrest by Panamanian authorities.

Fuentes suddenly recalled a significant unanswered question. "Felix?" he remarked between chews. "Could you check something for me?"

"Sure."

"Remember the information you got from your police friend in Panama a few days ago? The tip about the Liberian freighter that Guzman traveled on through the Canal – the *Cassandra*? I need to know her passenger list and manifest."

Asuncion excused himself.

When he returned, he had the impish smile of a Cheshire cat. The ship was easy. In general terms, it was hauling heavy goods from Cuba to the harbor of Puerto Escondido in the Pacific state of Oaxaca. He'd have the complete passenger list and fully item-ized list of what was in the ship's hold humming across on the station's fax machine in five minutes.

But the grin on Asuncion's generous face was evidently reserved for something far greater. Fuentes suspected he'd also received other information that he'd asked for and was about ready to try it on for size. Felix whispered a few well-chosen words. Miguel's features brightened considerably at the news. He also handed his boss a plastic envelope with an object inside it and stenciled numerals along its sealed edge.

With what passed for dinner completed, they got up from the table to go and interview Cortez.

"Hey, *Amigo,* long time no see," Asuncion remarked harshly by way of greeting. He introduced Fuentes.

Cortez grunted. He paced restlessly.

"You know we found your prints at the entry?"

The tense pacing persisted.

"So what did you break into an environmental office for?" Asuncion challenged. "You suddenly develop a grudge against Mother Nature? Or maybe ..." He fixed his eyes on Cortez's. "Maybe somebody paid you to remove documents."

Cortez ignored him.

"Don't bull me with the silent treatment. We know you do a lot of stuff for Rivera. I hear you do his wires. There's also real solid street talk that the *delegado* wasn't too happy about certain files at the environmental lab ..." Felix intentionally left the rest unsaid. "Tell me, what did Hector Rivera want from that office?"

Cortez stopped pacing. "I did computer work for Rivera in the past, that's all." His dusky eyes darted about. "Upgrading a management system. I know nothin' about any break-in."

"Right," Fuentes huffed in disbelief. "We got your prints at the scene." He chuckled. "A stereo and loose change don't make thieves scramble like rabbits to cross the *Yanqui* border. But there's more to it, *hombre!*"

"I told you. I know nothing," Cortez squirmed.

Asuncion was unrelenting. "We have witnesses who can eyeball the suspect at the break-in. Olive pants. Madras shirt. Enough jewelry to crown a Brownsville pimp. The description matches you, my son."

Cortez traced an index finger up the length of a metal bar and down.

Miguel sighed in seemingly sincere disappointment. "You see, Renny, it's really sort of sad. I respect you, and you can't understand it."

The prisoner's eyes narrowed. He nervously licked his lips.

Fuentes scratched his forehead. "Let's see how this plays out, okay? A professional like you generally works high-end clientele. You're someone who tends to stay out of our hair. And that's fine by me. You don't bother us. We don't bother you." A grin flitted across his features. "Suddenly, you do a two-bit entry." The grin evaporated. "It doesn't scan, *hombre*. It's not your style."

Cortez's left eyebrow twitched. "So what if I did a small favor for a friend?" he remarked in a low voice, studiously avoiding Fuentes's probing gaze.

"A favor?" Asuncion snorted. "I don't think so! It's against your religion. You don't do anything that doesn't have a dollar sign on the front and at least five figures dangling on the end."

Fuentes took another tack.

"I just found out from my friend Felix here that the head of the environmental office, a rotten little scab named Roberto Elliott, bypassed four very senior people to snare the top environmental position in Sonora. I also found out that he recently moved into a ritzy condo that costs him three times his monthly salary, and that the lease has been covered by the *delegado*. Now, we all know that *Señor* Rivera isn't that generous. Not unless he has to be. Certainly not to environmental engineers …"

"Let's face it," Asuncion interjected. "Nothing happens in this town without Rivera's consent. Not even break-ins. Especially not at government offices. So it gets me to thinking that you're either running *for* Rivera or *from* him." The detective let it sink in. "We think you're running from him. You want to know why?"

Renny Cortez was expressionless. The finger-tracing stopped.

Fuentes took up the chase. "Early this morning, someone sprayed a hotel room here in Coronado with a ton of rifle lead – AR-16 variety. Lots of environmental damage."

Asuncion rubbed his cheek thoughtfully. "The description of the registered occupant of the room matches you. This 'occupant' – someone named Blanco – hasn't returned to the hotel."

Cortez shifted slightly on his feet. His face was stone.

"Nothing?" Fuentes smiled. He gave the prisoner a long sideways expression that said *Enough, this is serious.*

"Maybe this will get your attention. The shift sergeant tells me that within fifteen minutes of your arrival there were two callers asking about you and offering to post bail. Both male voices. Neither left a name. One phone traces back to a local punk who does errands for Rivera. The other is a pay phone on the street outside the *delegado*'s office. The callers seemed real anxious to get you out. But not anxious in the way friends might be, if you get my meaning."

Cortez sighed.

"That digital-intercept equipment cost a lot of bread, didn't it?" Asuncion commented out of nowhere.

Cortez started. "I don't know what you're talking about," he sputtered.

"You should!" Fuentes moved in for the kill. "Especially when the warranty form that the American computer firm has on file records your name and Rivera's business address."

"No way." Cortez gulped. He retreated in the cell.

"Yes!" Asuncion asserted with childlike merriment. "I confirmed it a few minutes ago. Two hundred thousand dollars worth of technology!" He chortled in open admiration. "With upgrades and a maintenance package. With your name and his address registered at the corporate headquarters in New Jersey! Guess one of the *delegado*'s secretaries goofed. In any event, Rivera obviously cares for his people. At least, while they have something to offer him. You do have something to offer the *delegado*, don't you, Renny?"

Cortez shrugged. Fuentes could see he was sweating.

"My guess?" Miguel gambled. "Elliott, the environmental guy, had dirt on Rivera that he passed on to someone more powerful than the *delegado*. Otherwise, right about now, Elliott would be rattlesnake roadkill on the tollway. Let's face it, Rivera doesn't reward a two-bit civil servant with anything – certainly not a promotion. Especially after being blackmailed by him. The way Hector Rivera thinks, Elliott should be thankful he still has a life, if you know what I mean.

"Another guess?" Fuentes continued, upping the ante. "Somewhere in all of this, someone crossed somebody else up. Big time. And that person is not too happy.

"Only you know if you have anything to tell us," Fuentes continued with frosty assertiveness. "You can rot in this cell till you make bail under my terms – which is never – or you can cooperate, and we can take you from here to somewhere in Mexico that no one will ever know about."

Renny Cortez seemed to shrink visibly.

Miguel reached into his pocket and drew out the gold medallion. He dangled it on his fingertips. "Is this yours?"

Cortez didn't move. Fuentes systematically observed the man's eyes. They were fixed on the ornament.

"It's a Saint Christopher. I found it at the grave of the Gonzales girl. Remember her? Crushed by a canister that tumbled off that runaway truck a while back?" A pause. "The thing intrigues me."

Miguel held the smooth side of the amulet close to Cortez's face so he might see the fine lettering. "The initials are R. C., Renaldo Cortez, perhaps? And the date – August 27, 1960? That's your birthday . . ."

Cortez commenced the tense pacing once more. Fuentes returned the keepsake to his shirt pocket.

Now it was Asuncion's turn. "Eh *Amigo?*" He baited the hapless prisoner. "We just checked over the property in your possession when you were arrested."

Fuentes held up a plastic pouch. Inside the pouch was a Swiss Army knife. "Want to bet this blade matches the scrapings on that kid's tombstone?"

What little blood there might have been in Cortez face drained away. Miguel could see his neck artery thrumming.

"Nothing to say?" Fuentes appeared genuinely disappointed.

"It was just a thought," he allowed affably. "Before someone who might not particularly like to see you alive comes around to ask after your health."

Fuentes was unrelenting. "Let me tell you how this plays out. You steal something for the *delegado* and go to a cemetery rendezvous to do the handover and get your money, just like he promises. But Rivera's goons ambush you. The *delegado*'s a businessman. He figures: why pay for something if you can get it for free? But you confuse the issue when you escape. One of his crew stakes out the hotel you're staying at on the off chance you'll go back there. It's four in the morning. The guy on the roof gets blurry-eyed and mistakes wind in the drapes for you shifting in your bed. Or maybe he imagines something. Who knows? Anyway, he sprays the room with ammo."

Cortez stopped pacing.

"Did we tell you the sniper used the rooftop of the very building that houses Rivera's offices? Or that his suite has a fire exit to the roof? Or that we know there were two outgoing calls from the hotel on your room phone that night, both to people we know work for him?"

The prisoner's face was now pale as death.

"No?" Fuentes sniffed. "Too bad."

The clock ticked on the wall. Louder and louder.

"So you hightailed it to the border, eh?" Fuentes remarked sarcastically. "Just like the Westerns! Hurray for Hollywood!" His voice dropped down to a trace. "But it doesn't matter one dry taco shell. Because you're right back here. And this is Rivera's territory!"

The silence started slowly and became long and harsh enough for an ice age to envelop them. Cortez shook his head. He just couldn't do it.

"You know what I think, *hombre*?" Fuentes shot like a marksman. "I think you were looking for something specific at the environmental unit – something that might help the *delegado* out of a jam. Something that involves computers."

"No," Cortez proclaimed furiously. "I never stole a computer from that office!"

Fuentes sighed. The prisoner's theatrics were wearing thin. "You don't have to steal one to find out what it knows, do you?" he said quietly. "Tell us what you took and maybe we can help you."

Renny Cortez looked as if he'd swallowed arsenic. His eyes flitted between the two men, seeking a shred of understanding and finding none.

A phone rang. Cortez started like a hunted rabbit. Asuncion answered it, and ripped several incoming sheets from a fax machine located on a nearby table. Banging the phone down roughly onto its cradle, he shouted the news to Fuentes and jammed the fax, unread, into the rear pocket of his pants.

Renny Cortez and his games had become instantly insignificant. There was a fire in the Barrio Santa Lucia! A big one! Over by the north end, the farthest and most inaccessible location from the tollway. And there was already a confirmed casualty.

When Fuentes and Asuncion arrived at the Barrio, the sky was still hot lava, but the worst of the inferno had been contained. Fire trucks were hosing down what remained of the blaze. Two dozen shanties had been destroyed. Ambulance crews were bandaging the injured. Three dogs, a few chickens, and a cat had been killed. There had also been a human fatality – a crippled recluse named Felipe Mitchell. A body bag held the human remains.

There were four police cars on scene parked in a gaggle next to the fire trucks; three *federale* patrol cars and a plainclothes unit – a dark, royal-blue Buick. Uniformed officers were busily holding back onlookers as two suits dispassionately strolled around the site.

Fuentes's attention was drawn to a commotion on the high ground near the main roadway. A marked car was halted, motor running, roof lights blazing. An agitated crowd had gathered around the vehicle. Miguel doubled his speed up the slope, Asuncion breathlessly in tow. He shoved past the spectators.

He saw young Jiminez standing a few feet from the police car astride a prone body, a drawn revolver in his visibly trembling hand.

The corpse lay face down in the clay. It wore a black flak jacket over faded jeans and had richly brocaded tattoos of snakes on both arms. Blood spurted from the carotid artery, but the flow was diminishing. There was another puddle under the midriff, a large, dark-crimson one. A knotted bandanna covered what appeared to be a shaved head. Fuentes recognized the orange bristle cut inching up the nape of a bull neck. Papagayo!

"You shot him?" he demanded of the sergeant.

"Yes!" Jiminez stammered, nearly hysterical. "I pull up to the fire. I spot two people running toward the highway. I remembered the description that *Comandante* Obregon broadcast about the two suspects wanted for the Hermosillo massacre!" The officer shuddered as if an electric shock had convulsed him.

"Two . . ." Fuentes's eyes narrowed. "The *comandante* indicated that there were two?"

"This one," Jiminez burbled. "And a woman. A tiny one, but she got away. I think she might have been the American – Donovan!"

"You idiot!" Asuncion barked. "How did she escape?"

"They had a motorcycle . . ." he muttered. "A Harley waiting by the roadside. I got my gun out to stop them. He blocked my path while she bolted. He came toward me – I, I had no choice!"

Fuentes crouched to one knee next to the body. His hand felt for a pulse. Out of the corner of his eye, he spied Asuncion making his way to the Mustang. He thought of Donovan. Of the precious few seconds she had gained.

In the distance, the motorcycle reached a crest and was silhouetted against a duned horizon.

"Felix!" Fuentes shouted as the detective reached the radio and took the mike off its cradle. "Felix! Wait!"

The detective turned to face his *jefe*. A long, lingering moment passed between them. Fuentes wanted to scream something, then caught himself. He forced another second through the eye of the needle. "Don't forget to broadcast on the *federale* band!" he yelled finally with an audible lack of enthusiasm.

Asuncion spun to follow the motorcycle, but it had disappeared.

Miguel rose, listlessly brushing specks of dust from his pant leg. The crowd was growing subdued. For no reason in particular, his gaze shifted to the emergency vehicles. The town's fire chief was leaning on the door of the blue Buick, chatting amiably with the sole occupant inside. The conversation ended.

The car began to pull away. Abruptly it stopped. The driver peered in Miguel's general direction as if seeking him out. Then a raised hand and a lazy wave. Fuentes tipped the brim of his Stetson, ever so slightly. He would not give Obregon the satisfaction of anything more.

Wednesday, August 8, 4:00 p.m.
Somewhere in the Sonora desert

31

The Aerospatiale Super Puma wallowed momentarily in the brisk head wind, its rotor blades spooling like eggbeaters. Then it descended, light as a feather, on a stopgap helipad – the hard clay of a schoolyard. The sole passenger in the helicopter sensed the abrupt bump of wheels touching down and peered out the starboard portal. A dust storm the texture and hue of paprika greeted him. Sprigs of tumbleweed swirled in the eddies. Visibility was almost zero.

He waited for the turboshaft engines to cut and the mammoth clipper blades to stop spinning. Gradually, a pathetic tapestry emerged from the flinty veil, empty sandboxes and forsaken swings surrounded a crumbling clay-brick structure.

In the distance, a boarded-up general store with tilting thermometer gas pump and a decrepit hotel faced onto the main street. A procession of tumbledown structures was arranged in irregular grids: clothing shops, a grocer, carpenter, three lawyers, and a government licensing office; their fading signage hinted broadly at a past prosperity. Cars and trucks were abandoned in the roadways. Further afield, a broad smattering of decaying adobe houses suggested what had once been a thriving town. But there was now no indication of human life.

"If desolation had a name," Obregon muttered sourly.

He peered at his watch. Only seventeen hours to go till the VIP

279

visit. The riding boots pinched his feet. His long tapered fingers clenched the attaché case with such force that his knuckles were a burnished white. He was seething with anger.

The call had come only a few minutes ago. The news was mixed. One of his teams had secured the VAX in the Barrio rubble. It was being rushed to his offices. The operation in the barren desert country around Querobabi had been far less successful. In a maneuver that had taken precious weeks, the entire area had been searched, including a dozen derelict mines. And? Nothing. Where in hell could the target have gone? How could he have disappeared so easily?

The pilot, his helmet's shield protecting him from the sun's glare, turned to Obregon. He looked like an insect. "We're here, sir. El Lupo."

Obregon nodded archly. Where else did the dunce think they'd be at? Damn military pilots! He would have preferred a police unit, but the ministerial aide had been unbending. It was the air force or walk. So here he was – the sole passenger. Ramon knew it was much less a compliment than a matter of control.

He'd had a flitting premonition that the craft might suffer mechanical failure en route to this meeting but calmed that fear by reminding himself that it was he who possessed the final elements to the equation. He and no one else. For what must have been the tenth time, he patted the attaché case.

The pilot again, acknowledging receipt of a message. He 10-4-ed into a clipped-on mike in the helmet. "The minister is expecting you in fifteen minutes ..."

A man was waiting in the schoolyard when the cabin latch opened: a trim, decisive figure in buff dungarees and open-necked vermilion shirt. Obregon noted the fine-tailored cut. With a dour face, the stranger introduced himself. Ramon didn't catch the name and didn't care. It was irrelevant. The man offered to carry the attaché case. He declined. The emissary soberly motioned for Obregon to follow on foot. There would be no transport. Anywhere.

They walked briskly onto what must have once been a principal thoroughfare. Obregon had an uncanny feeling. Somewhere in the broad and desolate distance, a signboard screeched on its hinges. The vehicles he'd viewed from the helicopter were, on closer observation, long discarded; there was no model newer than the early Sixties. Paint finishes had matted to a dull monochrome, and air had seeped from cracked tires to leave them rusty-rimmed and riveted to the hard-baked ground. A lizard crawled across the hood of a peach-and-ivory Studebaker.

Buildings screamed desolation. Doors had collapsed on their frames; piles of sand had swelled inward in unrelenting waves. Surely and steadily the Sonora desert was reclaiming its own.

Obregon cringed at the hiss of swarming flies. A dog lay in the roadway, ground to a pulp by what appeared to be the fresh tread of a heavy vehicle.

He peered into the scalding metal sky, raising a hand to block the sun. A pack of vultures hovered above. His eye caught something in the distance, a glint against a flinty horizon. Then a second dab of light, more calculated this time, flashing rhythmically along the ring of hills that encircled the ghost settlement. Black dots crept along the ridge top like ants moving across a mound of raw brown sugar. He sighed with relief. The security perimeter he'd placed above El Lupo was intact.

They reached the end of the street. The last building was the town's hotel – El Meridian. Its main doors and its windows were boarded up. Pumpkin and khaki paint flakes hinted at its original colors. Looming over it, incongruously, was a large wind vane. The device, a steel tripod encased in cement at its base, stood two stories taller than the Meridian and was as broad as the hotel was deep. A porcupine's quill of antennae bristled into the sky from the crown of the tripod, while a flurry of guide wires sprang outward along its torso like the spokes of an immense overturned umbrella, to secure it to earth.

Wordlessly, the man in the buff dungarees took Obregon to the rear of the structure. Numerous garbage bags and crated water dispensers rested along a wall next to a massive delivery door, the kind that permitted trucks to park in bays. Obregon estimated the access to be wide enough to support two parked vehicles at once. The ground was well traveled. There were tire treads – many and recent – and there appeared to be oil slicks left behind by large vehicles.

His mute guide opened a sealed hatchway carved into the entry. The passageway was pitch-black, stale, and uncomfortable. There was a nauseating reek of machine oil and the constant drone of dynamos.

After a time, Obregon found he could make out human shapes – at least four, all dressed informally. They eyed him with the practiced apathy of professional observers. "DFS? Mexican Security Directorate?" he commented to no one in particular. And as he fully expected, no one responded to the obvious.

The guide tugged at his sleeve. He was directed to a gaunt elevator, a wire cage with a sliding gate – the kind one would expect to find in an ancient silver mine. Three men entered with them. Another remained at ground level. Ramon held the attaché case protectively against his chest.

The elevator plunged with great commotion down a narrow shaft. Obregon felt his ears pop and yawned uncontrollably. The cage jiggled in space, gradually slowed, and then, with a jarring shudder, stopped. Harsh artificial light drenched their faces. Dripping stalactites hung like icing from black bedrock.

Obregon was led into an immense canopied chamber. Track lights bisected a granite ceiling. Whirling fans scalloped the hard air. Three passages extended like fingers – one to his right, two to his left. The one to the right was sealed by a solid iron doorway with the words "GENERATOR – KEEP OUT" stenciled on it in English. The remaining paths faded abruptly to darkness.

With some difficulty, his escort eased the iron hatchway open. They entered a well-lit conference room, furnished with a rectangular table and several chairs, all finished in matte black. The furniture was modern – stern Scandinavian, Obregon guessed, and not inexpensive. There was a door to one side made of expensive teak. It was shut. The walls were painted peach, and were bare, save for the base motif of the Mexican eagle rampant to one side and a large map of the world hanging the length of the farthest wall. Three television monitors dropped from brackets in the ceiling, staring blankly.

The door opened. A male in his mid-thirties entered; he was of above-average height, clean-shaven, with close-cropped hazel hair and a fine-boned face. He sported a two-tone windbreaker, powder-blue jeans, and Dockers without socks – jaunty attire more suitable onboard a Caribbean yacht than in this mysterious underground passage beneath the Sonora. He possessed the most piercing cat's eyes that Ramon had ever beheld and reeked with the heady assurance of well-heeled money.

Obregon rose respectfully. The newcomer gave a lissome wave of his hand. "Ramon," he remarked with studied polish. "It's good to see you, *amigo*. Come." He motioned to the seats. "Sit down."

"*Si*, Minister," Obregon did as he was told.

"How is my father?" the man asked.

"He is . . ." Ramon hesitated. And for all the right reasons. "Well, sir, he's doing fairly well. Everything considered."

Hippolito Rivera nodded but evidently had little real interest in his parent.

"There have been extremely serious developments in your father's company this past week," Obregon plugged gamely onward. "They say that the principal investors aren't happy with the *delegado*'s handling of certain sensitive matters, that they've moved to liquidate their investment and kill the firm." The *federale* gazed into the eyes of his host and suddenly realized he'd said far too much. "Though I'm not familiar with what they mean," he stammered. "Nor interested, sir."

"I'm intimately aware of these circumstances," the minister remarked acidly. "They involve issues of prudence and are nothing for you to concern yourself with as a police official, *Comandante*."

"Sir," the docile voice. In the presence of his betters, Obregon did as he was told.

Rivera glibly changed the topic. "You haven't been here before?" The *comandante*'s every gesture admitted as much.

"It's quite intriguing: an abandoned silver mine renovated during

HERMOSILLO

the Cuban Crisis. My great-uncle Remo was one of the original occupants. Like me, he was the justice minister, the first of various Riveras to hold that post." The young man became pensive. "Service to the nation runs in the family – as does initiative."

The minister's features relaxed. "It was my uncle's idea to construct the ghost town above us to keep away unwanted influences. He named it El Lupo. Don't ask me why." Rivera emitted a droll chuckle. "We offered it to the Americans when they needed to negotiate with Castro. But they had their own Disneyland."

Rivera fingered a control panel on the underside of the table. "Ready for the show to begin?" Obregon nodded.

The wall map lifted to reveal a window on a high-tech world. Obregon found he was peering into what appeared to be a media studio. Headphoned technicians hunched before a multibanked control panel. Above their heads was a row of television monitors. A test pattern beamed from each. The technicians were busily oblivious to their viewers.

Adjacent to the studio was a well-appointed boardroom with ponderous furniture and formal oil portraits of Mexico's historic figures. In the boardroom sat a middle-aged man in a high-backed chair. Obregon recognized him immediately – Emilio Estrada, *el Presidente*. Beneath a sparse thatch of sandy hair, Estrada's pouchy face was florid; his hands were tightly clasped in front of him. He appeared to be terribly worried.

Confronting the leader of the Mexican nation sat a larger man of indeterminate age but more evident composure. He wore peasant attire; his hair was jet black, long and unruly, and parted in the middle. Around his neck hung a necklace of stained beads. He clenched a corncob pipe in a strong jaw and toyed with a pencil, doodling on a legal-sized notepad.

"*Comandante* Bruno," was all Rivera said.

He pointed to the monitors. They showed a group of four peasants seated at a table glumly playing cards. "His bodyguards. Bruno doesn't trust us. The *comandante* supposes we have something up our sleeves." He chuckled. "Quite astute of him, don't you agree?" His laughter ended as abruptly as it had begun.

A reel-to-reel tape deck rested on a coffee table between the two men in the boardroom. It whirled like a Ferris wheel at a country fair. "They think they're collecting everything for the record on that machine. And *only* that machine," Rivera mocked. "It's part of the agreement."

"And aren't they?" Obregon asked with some perplexity.

"Of course." Rivera smiled a smarmy smile. "The room was swept for bugs by my people. I'm assured there aren't any devices inside." He touched another hidden button. Suddenly, Obregon could hear the *presidente*'s voice as clear as the summons of the Angelus bell.

"I concede the issue of offshore oil rights in the Mar Muerte, *Comandante*. I assure you that it will be in the agreement we sign tomorrow." The shrill, nasal twang, as if Estrada had a clothes-pin clamped onto his nose. "You know I'll do whatever is required to ensure peace in Mexico. I value – " His words were cut off in mid sentence.

Obregon saw Rivera's jaw muscles tighten, his face contort with displeasure. "Contrary to our president's misguided wishes," the justice minister slurred acidly, "I believe in the need to render an independent record of historic events as they transpire. Should something go wrong..." Another pause. "Which leads me to the reason you're here."

Obregon coughed. "Sir."

"You've completed the official arrangements for tomorrow?"

Ramon cleared his throat. "There are thirty thousand police and soldiers on the detail, from commencement to completion. According to hourly updates, the sports field is already one-quarter full, and we still have almost a full day before the principal VIP arrives in Mexico. We'll have a minimum of ten helicopter gunships in the air at all times while the official celebrations are held."

"More important," Rivera asked, "are our plans complete?"

"They are," Obregon replied curtly. "We'll employ a two-tiered approach. The first involved a highly advanced computer system. But in the unlikely event that it is somehow neutralized, we have an equally effective process of cessation." He opened the briefcase and removed a thin folio. From it he pulled out several scale maps of the town of Santa Ana, and more particularly the sport ground abutting it.

"*Comandante* Bruno stays in a heavily guarded motel in Magdalena de Kino. He will be flown into Santa Ana, landing at 0850 hours," he explained. "Our president resides in a rented villa four blocks from the rebel leader and will be choppered in by a different route, arriving at 0855 hours – promptly."

Obregon's manner was crisply methodical, as precise and tidy as his budgets. "The USAF helicopter carrying our principal visitor south from Phoenix will land at exactly 0900 hours. That gives the VIPs a little more than half an hour for the signing ceremony. After that, *Comandante* Bruno emerges a truly liberated man. And our president and his distinguished guests can affably settle down for a triumphal Mass of Thanksgiving. They tell me the music chosen is quite beautiful. Beethoven. Brahms. And of course," a wry smile, "Handel's *Messiah*."

"Your particular favorite?"

Obregon nodded. "It's the only canticle I would consider suitable for such an historic event."

"With modifications?"

"I believe a new and unexpected emphasis will be placed on the power of light to effect dramatic change," Obregon remarked enigmatically.

"Quite." Rivera appeared very satisfied.

He looked at the maps. Obregon gestured to a red crayoned line heading due south from the United States border and two more – one blue, the other green – starting at the northwest point of the diagram in the town of Magdalena de Kino. The streaks never overlapped, though the blue and green routes chosen were quite similar. All three ended in what was plainly the largest open space around Santa Ana.

Rivera looked up. "You have found suitable candidates to assist us?"

Obregon pointed to one of the monitors. It displayed a small room with perhaps a dozen peasants hunched over tabletops, playing poker. "I don't think that will be much of a problem." He smirked. "Whether they're dead or alive at the time is of no significance."

"Yes," Rivera concurred. "Isn't it wonderful that the pilgrims at Santa Ana will witness such a miracle."

"Sir?"

The justice minister eased languorously back in his chair. He glowed at the thought. "A few minutes before nine tomorrow morning, before the shocked eyes of one and a half million persons in the Santa Ana soccer field, and countless millions more worldwide, the president of Mexico will disappear. Forever."

Wednesday, August 8, 5:45 p.m.
Coronado freight yards

32 Shortly after six, with the sun blazing a tangerine gash in the dusky sky, they arrived at the last stop in their grueling odyssey – the lodgings of the truck driver, Paco Limas. The address given – the Coronado freight yards – had struck Fuentes as unusual.

He inched the Mustang into a rainbow-labyrinth of freight cars. The unit they sought rested on a feeder track. It carried the colors of the Atcheson-Topeka line. "DINER" was stained onto the sides of the coach in worn gold leaf. A dog tenuously leashed to a rotting train spar barked relentlessly at their approach.

A clothesline ran from an obsolete signal mast to a half-open portal. Two golf shirts, an odd number of socks, and some stained underwear clung to it. The remaining windows of the railway coach were plastered shut by a patchwork quilt of garbage bags held together by yellowed masking tape. An oil drum filled with trash made a much-used campfire, and the ground around it was littered with discarded bean cans.

They mounted a step up to the galley. It was closed. A moment's insistent banging. The door opened a crack. A man of indeterminate age and with no teeth emerged to slouch before them. He wore a sleeveless undershirt, filthy chinos, and a miserable disposition, born as much of aptitude as of loneliness. The tattoo of a cartoon Popeye graced his right upper arm. The name was misspelled in a way too subtle for its bearer to appreciate, but it brought a slight smirk to Miguel's face. The sunlight glittered on the blank rectangles of steel-rimmed granny glasses.

Asuncion gruffly outlined their reason for being there.

Limas nodded tersely. "I had nothing to do with it, *señors*," he answered, with a jumbled mixture of false bravado and fear. "On my mother's grave, I'm innocent." He spat a trail of chewing tobacco into space. It landed on the white gravel that carpeted the trestle side.

The discussion was excruciatingly awkward and slow. Two days ago, Limas had picked up the unit at a dealer's – Stateside. Yesterday morning, en route to the new owner in Mexico, he'd stopped at a truck stop outside Cibuta to take a leak. Suddenly, men wearing bandannas had pulled him forcibly from the cab. The three were carbon copies: hazel-eyed, sporting ball caps, shiny cowboy boots, and speaking in a confident monotone. Average everything. Your typical, off-the-shelf *bandidos*.

Was there a gun?

Limas vacillated, visibly torn between machismo and accuracy. "There may have been, *Jefe*," he blurted. Then, "No," he nimbly amended, and "There probably was." Otherwise he wouldn't have allowed this to happen. Ex–Mexican army – he would have taken them on if there hadn't been. All three. There could have been twenty-three for all it mattered, he spouted grandly. But for the gun. A Colt pistol it was. No – a Magnum! A large one! The kind that Dirty Harry brandished in the movies.

"I'm sure there was." Fuentes shook his head in none-too-subtle frustration, acutely aware that no firearm had been mentioned in the initial report.

Asuncion changed the topic. "Who do you work for?"

"I don't," Limas responded.

"Then how did you get to drive this truck?"

"I used to be military, got my ticket on transports. Deuce and a halfs. After I came back to Coronado, I rode steady doing the lettuce and tomato run into Texas. But business has really slowed down, what with American safety checks and all . . ."

Limas took a crumpled handkerchief from between his belt and the frayed elastic of his underwear. He blew his nose and with dainty swipes patted down red-rimmed nostrils. "One day at the pool hall in Coronado I get talking to a kid I know, a boy by the name of Melio – Tico Martin's son. He says someone they know wants drivers *pronto* and gives me a phone number. He said they paid real good . . . I needed the money."

"You have that phone number now?" Asuncion asked glibly.

"I think so." Limas rustled around a pants pocket until he drew out a scrap of paper. He gave it to the plump detective.

"So what happened?"

"I called and spoke to a guy, said I'd take the job. He mailed me a one-way bus ticket and thirty percent of the salary, up front. I was supposed to pick up the truck at a dealer in Tucson and drive it into Sonora. It was a nice unit. A big Cummins dumpster, gorgeous as a Cinco de Mayo float."

"Colors?"

"Bright red and orange."

"Any markings on the rig? Company labels? You know . . . ?"

"No."

"Describe the man's voice," Fuentes interjected sternly.

The trucker stared at Miguel. His glasses fogged over. He shook his head in the negative. "It was only a short phone call."

"Any background sound? Church bells? City traffic? Machinery?"

The facial cast remained.

Asuncion took over. "Did he tell you where to deliver this truck?"

Limas appeared more at ease with this approach. "Ya," he replied. He took the soiled polka dot handkerchief and swirled it over his glasses. "The town market in Coronado. Opposite the statue of Pancho Villa."

"And?"

"I was to hand the keys to someone and get the rest of my cash."

"Describe that person."

"They didn't say. Just that he'd make himself known."

"And the people you talk about?"

"Never met 'em." Limas chewed his lower lip.

Fuentes abruptly prodded, "Who's this Tico?"

"Tico? That would be Tico Martin. Lives in the mountains up by Cucurpe. Melio told me he used to run rigs regularly for these people. Until the accident. Then he got real sick . . ."

"What accident?"

"A few months back in Coronado. The kid killed by the loose cargo?" The man thoughtfully scratched a grizzled chin. "Tico was driver of the rig. A mother of a truck it was too – an Oshkosh. Haven't seen a unit like that since we transported heavy tanks in the army."

A taut sigh. "I should'a known better. Everyone warned me about Tico. There's a hex on the guy." The man's pupils darted from Fuentes to Asuncion and back, appealing for understanding and finding none.

Fuentes seemed perplexed. "A hex?"

Limas's eyes clouded over and became unreadable. "Go find Tico Martin," he muttered with mounting anxiety. "You'll understand. He don't work no more. Not after what he did." The trucker took out the handkerchief again and blew his nose, loudly this time and with great effect. "You'll understand. He's got *la raiha* – the curse," he concluded ominously.

"Cucurpe?" Asuncion asked.

"Ya. Southeast on the dirt trail, a mile from the tollbooth. The only shack at the dump." He eased himself back inside the comforting darkness of his meager home.

"Do you know the name of the company that hired you?"

Paco Limas grunted. The door creaked shut before they could ask more.

They radioed the nearest *federale* detachment and had the duty officer research the phone number. The results proved a mixed blessing. It'd been listed to an A. Alvirez and was disconnected. That was the good news.

The bad? Subscriber histories could be sourced, but only via

Mexico City, where all such records were kept on microfiche. The information might take four days to obtain. Even for this one? Fuentes wondered. "Well," the man confided dolefully through running static, "if it's really important, maybe three."

Wednesday, August 8, shortly before 6 p.m.
Phoenix, Arizona

33

He traversed the hotel room with the slow yet deliberate footfall of someone who realized that each step brought him ever nearer to his Maker. He was an old man now, with little vigor and a bad hip. He was resigned to it, even though his staff was loath to consider the inevitable.

He hummed a folk tune from the mountains of his native Poland. His official visit thus far had been strenuous, even troubling. The American media had not been kind, the public relatively indifferent to his presence. The arrival of the millennium and flippant talk of Nostradamus had tragically placed his Central European ancestry in the limelight far more than his Message of Peace.

He glanced patiently up to the grandfather clock. It was just before six. Dinner would be in exactly twenty minutes. He was fixed in his habits, faithful to his moods. The menu was his favorite: a hearty serving of potatoes, sausages, and cabbage prepared by his personal cook, Sister Malgorzena; it was a meal that he'd share with his constant travel companion and countryman, the stiletto-featured monsignor from Krakow who acted as his executive aide. They would also have three dinner guests this evening, two senior officials of the American government and a high-ranking member of the local clergy.

His eyes drifted to the Louis XV mirror that graced the adjacent wall. He shrewdly considered his image as others might gaze upon it, careful not to linger too long and stray into vanity. His hair was short-cropped, as he preferred. It was the same snow-white as his cassock. Though naturally stout of body, his physique was relatively trim. He watched his weight carefully, avoiding the pastries and rich desserts that now condemned many of his countrymen to stolidity more than solidarity. He was no longer limber of gait; he'd begun to use a cane to counter the hip problems that had required two operations. Skiing, once a passion, was now an extravagance.

In his late seventies, he slyly admitted to himself that he still cut a striking figure, but that was only to be expected. It was in his blood and destiny, for his lineage flowed through an ancient nation of warriors and priests, romantics all, perpetually queuing throughout the ages at the twin altars of martyrdom and melancholy, and doing so with hard-jawed panache.

Still, the sadness he now perpetually carried as his cross gave a hard glint to eyes tinged a bleached Baltic blue. His forehead was flushed, the temples ravaged by squalls. Crinkles that had before framed them with mirth were now deeper and harsher, as if the skin itself were weary of putting on pretense.

Outside in the hall, he heard muffled laughter, the characteristic commotion of armed guards changing shifts. Had he peered out from the closed damask draperies of his high-rise abode, he would have observed the many-tiered defenses that protected him from any number of potential assassins. Armored cars, barbed wire, and concrete barriers pretending to be planters. Snipers discreetly tucked away on rooftops. Roving helicopter gunships.

At last count, the FBI and his own Central Office of Vigilance had quantified the "serious risks" to his person at a mere eleven. But this being America, the land of the free and home of the brave, there were sure to be at least a hundred frenzied fools with varying degrees of competence and sanity who were pigeon-holed into the second and far more problematic cubbyhole of "potential problems."

He was the only occupant on the thirty-fourth floor of an opulent hotel located in the very center of this modern American city, and would be so for the duration of his stay. The State Department had also booked all the rooms three levels above and below, as they always did for Very Important Personages. The profound security precautions did not faze him. Not any more. Certainly not after the Failed Attempt.

At the coming of dawn, he would travel to another land, to another people. And perhaps change the course of history.

A restrained rap at the door. The monsignor appeared, black robe swishing, the enameled smile of a plaster saint frozen across his face.

"Your Holiness."

With a composed nod, the elderly man acknowledged the words that beckoned him into the dining room next door.

Here, in downtown Phoenix, Arizona, roughly fifteen hours away from what could well be the crowning jewel of his mission to the Americas, the two hundred and sixty-second Pope of the Holy Roman, Catholic, and Apostolic Church was sitting down to supper.

Wednesday, August 8, evening.
Somewhere in the northern Sonora desert

34 It was shortly after 8:30. Twilight lingered a pompous maroon as they made their way up a steep and rugged incline. Fist-shaped clouds aggressively fringed the distant mountains. It was a humid evening, the kind that drains enthusiasm and energy in equal parts from sane men and not-so-sane causes. Fuentes knew there might be rain by midnight and he welcomed it.

The hovel lay in a muddy mush of oil-slicked water, behind what passed for the local dump. The shack was roughly twelve feet square and covered in tar paper, its tin roof sagging. Three slits that might once have been windows were now boarded up with uneven lengths of plywood. An old fridge door leaned into the structure and served as its portal. A few feet from the entrance, a cardboard box filled with blazing votive candles rested next to a rusty oil drum. A squadron of flies flitted aggressively about the makeshift doorway.

As they neared the hut, the stench of rubbish initially masked the smell, but a breeze soon wafted the choking odor toward them. Fuentes recognized it, that ominous slaughterhouse scent that loitered in one's nostrils and on one's clothing for days, defying soap and water, coffee grounds, cheap Cuban cigars, and towering shots of bourbon. And it seeped out of the shack like beef stew gone putrid, cloaking them in its covenant of lingering death.

Fuentes took a handkerchief and tied it to shield his nose and mouth. Asuncion had already covered his face with a huge red bandanna.

With some effort, they inched the fridge door aside. The interior was as murky as an Aztec crypt; the air was sluggish, brimful of the sickly sweet stench of putrid flesh. Fuentes's eyes grew accustomed to the dimness. He sensed three beings. A portly male in a full-length white cloak with a monk-like hood shielding his face loomed before a thing that lay inert on a camp bed shrouded in rags. A black-shawled woman knelt in a corner of the room, shuffling rosary beads. She appeared lost in a trance.

Four large kettles sat at the foot of the bed, while a huge rusting cauldron squatted indolently in the center of the floor. The cauldron was crammed with wooden sticks.

"*Brujeria!* Witchcraft!" Fuentes whispered ominously, for he knew that the robed male was a masked *santero*, a priest observing a rite of Palo Mayombe, the primitive cult brought to the New World by African slaves centuries before.

The two men lurked in the darkness. Etched across the *santero's* mask were artificial scars, a cross-hatching of arrows, bows, Xs, and other symbolic markings, which served as his personal autograph and differentiated him from others of his kind. He was oblivious to their presence.

The *santero* removed a long object from a hemp bag. Fuentes shuddered. According to ritual, it would be a human tibia. Stripped of flesh, polished chalky smooth, this would become the priest's scepter, his *kisengue*.

Suddenly, the mystic let out a blood-curdling scream. "*Kadiempembe!* – To Satan, who devours souls!" In jumbled Afro-

Spanish incantations he screeched for "Olofi, the father of all gods" to exact his revenge for the death of the human lying before them – the remains of the man once named Tico Martin.

The woman whimpered. She clicked the rosary beads ever faster in gnarled hands. Fuentes suspected that one of the kettles might contain the severed head of a goat, another, the body parts of a dead rooster. In the remaining two kettles, a decaying turtle, twigs, coins, gold beads, and a plaster statue of the Virgin Mary would be swirling in a vile broth of blood, semen, and water. And who knew what other foul concoctions.

The *santero* reached into the bag, took out a rag doll, and doused it into the rich, scarlet liquid. He turned imperiously to the weeping woman. "I've spilled the blood of a freshly killed human onto this image, my daughter. Tonight, you must bury it in a Christian cemetery. If you do this, the persons who've cursed your recently departed husband with such untimely death will likewise die."

In that instant, Asuncion sneezed. He caught himself with an awkward gesture that brought his entire body bowling forward into what passed for light.

The priest started, as if snapped out a trance. Eyeing the intruders, he reached into the folds of the formless cloak that draped his body, pulling out a huge machete. The woman in the raven-black dress screamed.

The *santero* bolted at them, face grimacing like a clenched fist as he wildly waved the shiny cleaver above his head. Fuentes drew his Glock and fired. One. Two. Three. Four rounds. The widow fainted outright. Asuncion's weapon was still holstered.

The impact jolted the *santero* as if he'd just been struck by lightning. He crumpled to the ground like a marionette whose strings have been expertly severed by an indifferent master. His left foot knocked over one of the kettles, and the clay mask that had hidden his face tumbled to the ground.

Fuentes started, for he was gazing upon the lifeless features of Pluto Velas.

A dark, brownish mixture, the texture and consistency of gravy, oozed from the large kettle. Other contents slowly followed the

inevitable urgings of gravity: animal parts, rosary beads, and coins.
And finally, bouncing like a bowling ball from hell, a human head
– eyes gouged out, neck muscles dangling where it had been
severed from its torso. Fuentes recognized the contorted features
all too well – the remains of the prisoner: Renny Cortez.

They grimly approached the mummified torso. It was bathed in
a foul mixture of blood and feces. There was an opening near the
head of the thing, a gap, perhaps four inches by four in diameter,
where the macabre wrappings had eased back from their moorings.

Miguel looked around the room. A metal rod leaned against
the wall. He took it and jigged the sodden material back and forth
until the thing looming beneath it was exposed.

Fuentes retched behind his protective scarf. Even the stolid
Asuncion paled. For there, cradled in cloth, was the fiendish caricature of a human face, a purple mask the color and texture of an
overripe yam. The thing's orifices were closed, yet amber pus
dribbled freely from them.

Even as he choked back the urge to vomit, Fuentes forced
himself to unravel the layers surrounding the corpse. A peaty
odor like sulfur permeated the air.

The body beneath was naked. A male with the flaccid body tone
of late-middling years, its trunk was the same port-wine color as
the misshapen face. The stomach was bloated. A gridwork of veins
and arteries traced crimson across languid lavender skin. The left
forearm sported a military tattoo, with the words "Semper Fidelis
– *las fuerzas armadas de Méjico*" – and the year "1994."

Asuncion tugged at Fuentes's sleeve. He gestured to a
makeshift shrine, a five-inch by ten-inch black-and-white snapshot in an inexpensive frame propped against the foot of the bed.
A man and woman on a summer's night at some rural pig roast,
holding one another in mock embrace and smiling shyly toward
the anonymous photographer, it captured a happier time. The
man was wearing a tank top. On his forearm was a tattoo identical to that on the cadaver.

Inside the frame was an article from a regional daily newspaper. It was dated January 28 at Coronado and tersely related the

death of four-year-old Margarita Gonzales in a trailer mishap that involved discharged cargo. Attached by staples were a series of five company checks, each made out to cash. They were all drawn in a time frame from February through March, and from the same bank, a branch in Coronado. The authorizing inscription was illegible. Fuentes flipped them over. They were all endorsed with the same chicken scrawl: Tico Martin. He glanced scrupulously at the company name: Hercules Transport. There was no business address.

Fuentes and Ascunsion numbly exited the chamber and greedily swallowed the damp night air.

Severed heads generally started their journey connected to bodies, and in this respect Fuentes was not to be disappointed. Cortez's cannibalized torso, still handcuffed, was lying in a drainage ditch fifty yards away, next to a chainsaw. Bloody chunks of sinew stuck to the saw blades.

Velas's marked patrol car was abandoned nearby. His shabby uniform was crumpled into a ball on the front seat. Holster and gun rested atop the clothing, along with a jotted note with directions to the site. Fuentes recognized Velas's scrawl. An envelope containing several thousand *pesos* was also on the seat. Addressed to Velas in a woman's hand, it contained a want ad from a local tabloid promoting the services of a *curandero* – a folk healer – "skilled in Ochosi," giving the first name "Pluto" and a phone number in the Coronado exchange. On a sheet of paper, written in the same flowing script as the envelope's address, a woman named Nina pleaded for the life of her husband Tico, who "was being consumed by Satan in a *serape* of death."

Miguel knew *curanderos* were passive, innocuous shamans. They sold herbs that cured sickness of the soul – for them, the true root of disease and ill fortune. Incense to promote good luck. Scented soaps to wash away curses. Body oils that assured wealth and happiness. These were relatively benign items in a nation where such supernatural baubles were welcomed in the homes of even the most devout Catholics.

But Ochosi? That was a darker layer in the circles of hell.

Asuncion inspected the firearm. It hadn't been recently used. He glanced clinically to the alpha screen on the patrolman's paging device. It had stored three messages: two involved bets on horses, the third intrigued him: "2 am PROMPT 305 Fleet Garage. In emergency call 905 8138." The transmission had been sent within the past hour.

He showed the communication to Fuentes. A wary shrug. It meant nothing. Yet. Miguel called the *federale* station at Nogales from Velas's car. He related information of the murder and its macabre sidebars, prudently indicating that he'd stumbled across them while checking an unrelated "minor" matter.

The shift supervisor was nonplussed. Surely the *jefe* was aware that they had other responsibilities that were equally taxing. The imminent VIP visit to Santa Ana had drained their strength to the bone, and a month-long manhunt in the Querobabi area now involved over a hundred police and military personnel. "It's tough enough," the supervisor confided, "to run a unit in these days of budget restraint without having to chase one man across a hundred square miles of canyon at the whim of the new *coman- dante* in Sonora. And we still don't really know what the guy is wanted for! Imagine that!"

"Yes. Imagine that," Fuentes agreed accommodatingly.

Pressed, the supervisor affirmed that he would dispatch a crew of detectives sometime later that night. How late? They'd get there when they got there, he chided with refined rudeness.

Fuentes reminded the man that, as a matter of course, Ameri- can media monitored radio bands for drug enforcement plays along the borderline. Aggressive *Yanqui* reporters would unques- tionably pounce on this carnage, especially when it involved black magic spiced with a human head and a mummified torso.

As the man wheezed a reply, Fuentes cleverly played out his hand. Could someone at Nogales contact an answering service to shed light on the last item shown on Velas's pager? Oh, and could it be done immediately, if not sooner? Miguel smiled as he heard the muffled curse. Good.

They updated their memo books while sitting on a hillock on

the windward side of the hut. The lunatic widow lolling vacantly back and forth on her heels inside the shed would remain undisturbed. She wasn't going anywhere – in time or space. It took less than twenty minutes; there wasn't much to write.

Three police units, two unmarked, and an Ident. cube van arrived in short-winded haste from twice the distance – and a good five minutes earlier – than the ambulance crew dispatched to transport the woman to a holding facility for the mentally ill. Eleven uniformed men and a team of investigators soon secured the morbid scene.

A video team transcribed the vast and gory details to VHS, as gum-chewing identification officers stood lackadaisically by with tape measures and large white-bond notepads. An officer vomited in a drainage ditch. Another inanely posed for a photo grasping Cortez's skull by its hair like some prize game hunter.

A command post was set up at the rear of the cube van, complete with area search maps, flip-charts, and *federale* radio frequencies. It was under the provisional authority of a Nogales detective who seemed loath to supersede Fuentes as senior officer present, until Miguel commented that the Mexican stringer from a major American network was en route to interview the ranking policeman on scene. The detective traveled "smart" with a quick change of wardrobe and, it appeared to Fuentes, a remarkable transformation in attitude. Not only was he willing to take on the task, he was also able to effect it in a freshly pressed suit with a monogrammed shirt and bilingual calling cards to boot.

Within half an hour, Nogales had unearthed a mixed bag of news concerning the pager data. The bad? Pertinent information on the mysterious communication was sketchy. The answering service remembered a male with a head cold and nothing else. The good? Investigators sourcing the number hoped to have a firm answer from the phone company later that night, or perhaps sometime in the morning. Or more than likely, in the next three days via Mexico City, "where all subscriber histories are maintained on microfiche."

The incoming call to the command post was not unexpected. In fact, Miguel had forecast that it would come much earlier in the evening. This time, Obregon minced no words. In less than twelve hours the VIP visitor would set foot on Mexican soil. His escorted helicopter was scheduled to land at 0900. Fuentes had been given the assignment of positively identifying the truck thieves. He wasn't even close to doing so, and the *comandante* was nearing the end of his tether. Was Miguel incapable of even such a menial task?

Harsh breathing on the line. Well, was he capable or wasn't he? Fuentes hung up without responding to the ultimatum. It suddenly seemed so trivial.

Fuentes picked up a handful of soil and tossed it around his fingers, sensing its roughness. He'd been asked to investigate a straightforward truck theft and ended up with a cult murder. Yet both incidents shared an eerie strain.

The faceless people who'd arranged the shipment of the Cummins dumpster from the States were starting to look remarkably similar to those who'd owned the Oshkosh that killed the four-year-old Gonzales girl. Miguel's seedy predecessor had disappeared while conducting inquiries into her death, an investigation that Fuentes had always considered not only slipshod but also highly suspect.

It was quite apparent that they were onto something more.

Tico Martin had driven the Oshkosh and thereafter become mysteriously ill with an enigmatic disease. Renny Cortez, a professional criminal who normally wouldn't be caught dead committing a break-in, had done one in, of all places, a federal environmental office, where nothing of importance was even reported stolen.

Now both Martin and Cortez were dead. Tico's cadaver was a ghastly mess. Only hours ago, the same purple dye had tinged Cortez's fingertips. Renny had recently visited the child's graveside.

Fuentes gazed off. "Remember what that idiot Limas said about Tico Martin?" he remarked.

Asuncion nodded. "That he had the *la Raiha, señor.*"

Miguel let sand trickle through his hands. He got up and vigorously rubbed his palms. Then he turned to the detective, his eyes bright with defiance. "Yes. *La Raiba*. But you know what? I think that same curse has hit Renny, too. And I think it has a home."

"Where?" Asuncion eyed his boss quizzically.

"Where? In the graveyard of Santa Lucia."

Wednesday, August 8, night.
Santa Lucia Mission

35 It was nearing midnight. The desert sky was vaulted low; the moon a mere sliver; the horizon potash-black and unyielding.

Ancient tombstones lurched out of the ground like a potter's field of dinosaur spines. Most had toppled over; a few stayed erect, defying the ravages of time. A bat whisked by overhead, its paper wings rustling. It let out a shriek of annoyance. Far away, a lightning bolt slashed down the dismal sky. A few moments lapsed. Then, the charged resonance crackled the air.

They'd awakened Father Ezequiel from a sound sleep. He'd been intrigued enough by their proposition that he'd rushed to accompany them still wearing his green cotton nightgown and bedroom slippers.

They approached the burial site cautiously, careful not to disturb the grave. The old priest shone a pencil flashlight on it. The damaged stone stared blankly back. Fuentes contemplated the marker: the frenzied chips notched into the façade of the monument, the shattered casing still holding the child's photo by a single screw to its granite base. A wicked wind tousled his hair.

Miguel knelt and patiently removed the property bag from his back pocket, took the Swiss Army knife from of its plastic envelope, and flicked it open. He considered the various blades, finally selecting the broadest one, and brought it parallel to the chiseled incision. It was a neat fit to the grooves made in the rock.

As Fuentes eased back onto his haunches, he stumbled and drove the tip of the knife into the photo's casing. A square object tumbled from the seam.

"*Jefe!*" Asuncion gasped. Father Ezequiel arced the flashlight to the base of the grave.

Fuentes reached down, outstretched fingers blindly tapping the soil. Suddenly they stopped. "Here!" he shouted. The flashlight darted to the object in Miguel's grasp. It was a computer disk.

Asuncion and Fuentes glanced knowingly at each other. They had their proof. Now there was but one more thing to do. One more question to answer. And it lay six feet below.

The *padre* held out a hip flask. "Are you sure you don't want some altar wine?" First Fuentes, then Asuncion, grimly accepted the offer.

They'd brought along digging tools for the task. The earth proved to be loamy. Still, the work, which took the better part of a half-hour, was backbreaking. Asuncion wheezed asthmatically, soon leaving Miguel to toil alone. The priest stood above them, the pencil flashlight in his gnarled hand, his face severe and unresponsive. Fuentes's shovel contacted the top of the coffin. Five shovelfuls more and then he bent forward, feverishly dusting away dirt until he'd cleared the top. The pine box was split in places, mildewed, but still intact. A rank musk wafted from somewhere within. Strangely, a section of the surface seemed to have been disturbed, as if someone had punched a hole into the planking with a fist.

Fuentes steeled himself as the *padre* made a frenzied sign of the cross. With the tip of his shovel he pried open the crumpled lid. The decaying wood gave way and a low and evil hiss escaped the sarcophagus.

The thing lurking inside was tiny and shriveled into a corner, as if consciously avoiding the light. The *padre* suddenly turned away as Fuentes swallowed back rising bile. Behind him, a visibly shaking Asuncion mouthed gibberish in the guise of prayer. The fragile corpse had deflated with decomposition. Large, gaping holes cratered the body where carbon gases had exploded.

Its burial clothing was rotting and hung in tatters. What little skin that remained was stretched tautly across a less than four-foot frame like a festering membrane. Bone the color of nicotine stains poked aggressively to the surface at all angles.

Maggots paraded across a crushed forehead and into the eye cavities of what had once been a child. The pupils themselves had been eaten away. A worm wriggled through a gap where yellowed teeth met raw, puckered gums. Yet the skin tone itself was terribly wrong, even for a cadaver bloated by the heat of its confinement. It should have been bluish green, like stagnant sea water. Instead it was purple, as if stippled in a sorcerer's brew of hackleberry and juniper.

"May God have mercy," the old *padre* whispered. He crossed himself again. The flashlight arc wavered weirdly with the pious act. "What caused this desecration?"

"The death?" Fuentes responded. "The little girl was struck by a canister that fell from a truck. She died instantly."

"That explains the head wound ..." Ezequiel observed, with the same stoicism he might adopt to hear an octogenarian's confession. "But not the discoloration. What did this canister contain?"

"We never found out," Miguel admitted. "The canister was voided before we got to it. All that the investigators were able to seize was an invoice declaring that the substance being transported was propane."

"Propane?" Father Ezequiel shook his head. "I don't think so. More likely it was a carcinogen, and a volatile one at that. Only a PCB has such noxious effect on human skin. Do you know if this canister was sealed at the time of impact?"

Fuentes hesitated. "We believe so ..."

The *padre* furrowed his brow. "Perhaps you should reconsider your hypothesis. I suggest it was leaking badly. And I submit that the child was exposed to its contents ..." The priest waited for the words to sink in. "Come with me. I play more than checkers in the trailer."

The living area in the mobile home was modest. A kitchenette, and a sofa seat that opened to a single cot. A washbasin. Cupboards, drawers, and closets crammed the portions of the walls where there were no windows.

Father Ezequiel reached into a footlocker and brought out a laptop computer. "It has solitaire on the desktop," he admitted sheepishly. "For the nights I finish meditation early."

They eased themselves onto narrow kitchenette benches. The padre clicked on the machine and placed the floppy in the single port. The disk held two directories. They were sequentially numbered and appeared to have been entered around the time of the break-in at the federal government's environmental offices.

Father Ezequiel opened the first file. It contained a scanned document on "Republic of Mexico Ministry of Environment" letterhead sent to the attention of a firm called Hercules Transport. It notified the company operations manager of "Regional Office concern that vehicles and cargoes registered to Hercules are carrying suspect/hazardous goods from the United States of America into the Republic of Mexico and its Federated States." The letter went on to caution that "Immediate attention to this matter is essential for the continuance of your license to carry such goods on the Federal Highways of Mexico." The correspondence was relatively recent; dated in January of the current year.

The second directory held additional communications from the ministry: a total of thirteen letters addressed to Hercules, giving dates, consignments, and shipment routings from Arizona into Mexico, including licenses and makes of transporting vehicles. In some cases, drivers' particulars were also included.

In a perplexing twist, all the items in the second schedule were copied to Humberto Rivera in his capacity as PRI *delegado* for the State of Sonora. In each instance the signatory was Roberto Elliott, Environmental Engineer. In six letters, Elliott appeared to have been promoted, and was finally signing off as "Chief Federal Environmental Officer for Sonora."

Fuentes reviewed the documents one by one. He stopped short at an item dated January 28 concerning a shipment from Davis Monthan Air Force Base, Arizona, which purported to contain raw sewage. As he absorbed the details, Miguel's thinking moved rapidly into the deep and uneasy waters of true comprehension.

The tow unit had been an Oshkosh F 2365 Heavy Equipment Transporter, the only one listed in the entire file. The driver had been Tico Martin. There were three asterisks appended to the data, the expression "hot load!" and a dollar sign. Most important, this particular correspondence had been addressed to Hector Rivera as president and CEO of Hercules Transport.

Fuentes perused the other correspondence. Rivera's title did not appear elsewhere. He returned to item seven. "Can you print this?" he excitedly asked the priest.

Father Ezequiel removed a portable printer from a closet and hooked it up. The characters began to clatter gamely onto the pages.

Asuncion watched with childlike curiosity. "*Jefe!*" He suddenly shouted. "*Jefe!* Hurry!"

Fuentes rushed to the detective's side. There, on government stationery, was the official address for Hercules Transport – Six Tampico Court. The address of the *maquiadora* factory – the business sibling of Cheetah Resources – and that of Hercules were one and the same!

Guzman and Rivera! Miguel knew the mysterious backers of the Larendo *maquiadora* were test-drilling for oil off Chiapas. Felix's investigations had shown they'd successfully acquired the exploration site after Guzman's initial attempts to secure it had failed. More important, the documents also now established that Hercules was an integral component of Six Tampico Court.

Fuentes had known for some time that the rot in Mexico City ran deep. Now he could all but taste the fetor. Rivera had probably shepherded the Chiapas permits through the PRI hierarchy. The *delegado* had probably also been instrumental in manipulating the NEDEROIL episode to its lucrative conclusion. And why not? It was obvious that swilling at the money trough was an idiosyncrasy that fit quite nicely into Humberto Rivera's lifestyle.

But there had to be something else. Assuredly, the Tampico complex had claimed Eddie Bono's life, and now, with the ripening corpses of Martin and Cortez and the pitiable remains of Pluto Velas, it had abruptly snatched three others.

Fuentes was far from ignorant about what the PRI was capable of doing. It wasn't oil profiteering alone that he'd been deflected from. Such venality could have been assured without the stench of death tickling anyone's nostrils. For all the greed involved, seismograph results weren't generally the stuff that losers were murdered for in Sonora.

He thought back to the last call on Chandler's cell on the day he'd died; the one emanating from the federal exchange in Sonora. Could that enigmatic voice have been Rivera's? Was it he who had lured the captain to Zita's? Could the *delegado* have been the linchpin in a Mexican-American connection that traded drugs for guns and who knew what else? It was certainly beginning to look that way. In fact, it seemed to Fuentes that Hector Rivera, along with Humberto Guzman, had his feet firmly at the epicenter of the four murders at Zita's.

The air in the Mustang was sultry stale as they reentered it; the black silence of the Barrio enveloped them, portentous and overpowering. Fuentes had been torn between a journey to Larendo and one to the more gracious Rancho Rivera on the hilly outskirts of Coronado.

The next message on the police radio made up his mind for him. Notwithstanding the customary three-day delay in subscriber information, the Nogales detachment had been successful with the phone trace. The number on Velas's pager was confirmed. It was listed to *Señor* H. Rivera at Hercules Transport, Six Tampico Court, Larendo.

Thursday, August 9, after midnight.
Somewhere in the northern Sonora desert

36 The office building lay in self-assured darkness. Adjacent to it, at one of the five squat factory units that made up the site, a shipping bay was open. Though it was the middle of the night, the pace of work inside the industrial unit was unrelenting. Transport trucks were greedily loaded in the slips. Workmen in red coveralls and enameled safety helmets scuttled about, bathed in an unmerciful neon light that turned the interior into an otherworldly imitation of day.

Fuentes and Asuncion crouched behind a low brick wall. They'd left the Mustang a hundred yards back in the bend of the road and safely out of view.

The parking lot of the adjacent El Toro bar was half full. The jukebox spilled Lori Morgan into the night. Fuentes always liked "Something in Red." A long stack in the slanted roof at the rear of the saloon puffed milky smoke into the heavens. Bright light beckoned from a screen door. The sizzle of meat, clanging of pots, hastily barked orders, a dish clattering on a tile floor, the clamor of a twenty-four-hour fast-food kitchen drifted on a light breeze.

A windowless structure, four and a half stories tall and rectangular, abutted the manufacturing complex. A fire exit crept down its side. The ladder started at the rooftop and touched down at the desert floor. A series of massive garage doors, of the concertina variety, covered its front. The doors were shut. A sign above the doors identified the unit as "Fleet Garage – Building 305."

Then: a second buzz from Velas's pager and the keyed missive: "Reminder: 2:00. The American."

Three colossal trucks loomed near the fire-ladder, motors running, like dreadnoughts straining at anchor. A man shambled toward the vehicles, got in one, and drove it into a semi-enclosed washing area.

Fuentes glanced at his watch, then excitedly nudged Felix. Eleven minutes to the hour. It all fit! By disposing of both Martin and Cortez, Velas had effectively eliminated the two most serious threats to the *delegado*'s continued survival. Dead men told no tales – and certainly couldn't refer to their briefing notes. Even by Rivera's miserly reckoning, Pluto's depraved acts were probably worth Judas money. Only, unbeknownst to the *delegado*, there'd be someone else collecting.

Fuentes motioned to the solitary gate officer in the sentrybox by the entrance. The man strolled back and forth behind the candy-striped barrier, regular as a metronome. Asuncion raised a finger, then three, and made a circular gesture with his hand. Fuentes nodded. There were probably several more guards on the plant grounds. He spied a second in a far-off corner of the site aiming a searchlight at a rapidly moving object. It was a jackrabbit. The light never lost its target.

The plant was enclosed by a cyclone fence capped by thick sinews of barbed wire. There was one road in; the same one out, and it passed the sentrybox. The sentries seemed alert; they were certainly armed. For all intents and purposes, the facility was secure. Fuentes cursed under his breath. Less than ten minutes to go. How would they get nearer?

Bammm! A door slammed at the El Toro. A man bounded down the stairs at the rear of the saloon and out into the parking lot, holding a large thermal bag in one hand. He jumped into a Ford Escort. The car spurted toward town.

A second car idled in the lot of the El Toro, a rusty Chevette with a clapboard sign propped on the roof. Fuentes gestured Asuncion back to the Mustang. He had a plan.

They found a pay phone near a garment mill located on the outskirts of Larendo. The night shift was on break, lolling on the grass next to an open fire door. The company's name and phone number were daubed in colossal characters on a stucco wall girdling the factory: Bonanza Fabrikz. The rest was almost too easy.

They intercepted the Chevette as it entered the industrial complex that skirted the town. There was no other traffic on the road. The driver pulled over for the flashing police light. He waited obediently as the solitary policeman approached the car.

Driving delivery with an extra large pepperoni pizza, double cheese and four Cokes, he knew he'd have no difficulty explaining what he was doing at this late hour. But he was also shrewd. He always carried spare pizzas for hungry police officers. And money, should their appetites be more deeply rooted.

The driver didn't see Asuncion creeping up on his blind side, didn't expect the strategically placed blow to the base of his neck. Fuentes felt no remorse. Time was more important than protocol. One woozy delivery man was worth the price to enter Six Tampico.

The Chevette was too cramped for Felix, so Fuentes drove alone, leaving his partner in the hills with the Mustang. The car's interior reeked of anchovies. One of the headlights had burnt out; the remaining one cast an eerie sweep on the road ahead.

The gate guard was suspicious; there'd just been a delivery to the facility fifteen minutes earlier. The admission that he was new and the extra large pizza with double cheese left as a courtesy were sufficient to gain Fuentes admission to the grounds. Miguel calculated that he had, at most, ten minutes to find Rivera. Once he'd confirmed the *delegado*'s presence, he'd leave. There was no need to tempt the devil in his own domain. They'd stake out Rivera on the public highway, where he'd be fair game.

He parked the car to the side of Building 305 near the idling tractors, made his way to over the fire-ladder, and started to climb. He swiftly reached the top of the structure. A forest of aluminum ducts and exhaust vents confronted him. Construction tools littered the roof: crowbars, shovels, brooms, a tray for mixing concrete. Miguel crawled gingerly around them until he found a trapdoor. The sky above was awash with stars, the night air exhilarating. He wondered why he didn't just pack it in and live like a normal human being. The moment passed.

The door wasn't locked. Fuentes wrenched it open and peered into a spaghetti swirl of pipes and cables. Far below, pan lights hung by flex cords from unpainted steel beams. The fixtures cast tiny pools of light on the ground. Even from this height, the air seemed alive with the chalky haze of floating dust.

He found a catwalk and stealthily made his way down a rung ladder until he touched the workplace floor, sixty feet below. Banks of tools cluttered the walls, like pikes and staves would the armory of a Teutonic castle. A swaybacked calico cat darted across his feet. Otherwise, the premises were deserted.

The floor space appeared to have been designed for five extended service bays and a mammoth grease pit. A Reo occupied the bay farthest away. The other four were empty. The truck had fresh lettering stenciled to the driver's door: "Hercules Transport."

An immense cubicle, nearly as long as the building and half as high, dwarfed the Reo. The door was ajar. Above it was a sign: "PINTURA REPARACIONES" . . . "PAINT REPAIRS."

A pink-and-gray hardtop was parked inside. Miguel recognized the car as Rivera's Kaiser. He drew his gun and entered. The enclosure was dim and except for the antique vehicle, vacant. Polished deflector shields lined the walls and mirrored his every movement. A series of large air ducts hung suspended from the ceiling. A massive fume vent tapered down from its center.

Heavy paper completely masked the windows of the Kaiser. Fuentes touched the hood. It was still warm. Manufacturer's lettering on the wheel well identified the model as American. He recalled the paged message to Velas. He tried to open a door but they were locked.

He cautiously exited the chamber. Four offices filled the east flank of the building, and each had a frosted glass door. Only one office was open. Fuentes eased himself inside.

The floor was carpeted in garish mustard plush, the walls covered in pin-ups of nude women and muscle cars. Well-established grease stains marked the flow of traffic from the entrance to a mock mahogany desk resting on minarets of brick. Three car tires were stacked in the middle of the room. Beside them lay an elongated packing crate, heavy-duty, the kind used for consigned goods shipped by sea. Stenciled on its side were words in Cyrillic script and then the country of origin, Tajikistan, and the destination, Puerto Escondido, State of Oaxaca, Mexico.

Fuentes poked about inside. It was empty, save for a pictogram that displayed a man in military uniform holding a blowpipe in an exaggerated combat stance. The instructions, too, were in Cyrillic. There was a bold star on the front of the character's helmet: headgear of the kind once issued to Soviet soldiers. Wood frames used to secure the contents suggested that two items had been shipped, both tube-like and, by the thickness of the framing, both reasonably heavy. One of these objects was three times the length of the other. There were also remnants of threading tucked about the framework. It was crimson in color, and textured like carpet piling.

A teal-colored phone rested on the mahogany bureau, along with keys on a ring and a digital clock that showed the time: 2:07. Fuentes picked up the ring. It appeared to hold a car set: ignition, trunk, and duplicates of each. An identification tag with the name Humberto Rivera was taped to the loop. Miguel glanced at the phone. The number was 905-8138 – the digits on Velas's pager. He picked up the receiver. The line was dead.

He rushed to the darkened chamber, keys in hand, and opened the car door.

The interior was warm and smelled faintly of wrapping paper. The dome light revealed splatters of blood on the driver's seat and padded roof, as well as clumps of gray matter. The gore was fresh.

The glove compartment was jammed open. Inside, Fuentes found an oblong office envelope, the kind that usually conveyed tax returns and death certificates. Miguel carefully opened it. Inside was proof of payment for a return airline ticket, first class to Amsterdam, and invoices for a hotel room in a place called Hilversum, all in the name of Eduardo Bono and all dated early January. Miguel reflected on the information. The flight Bono took was three days prior to the day the Dutchman was discovered floating dead in the canal. He pocketed the envelope.

The rest of the interior appeared untouched.

Fuentes followed a red trickle along the concrete floor to the rear of the car. The trunk was ajar. He raised it, then stepped back, momentarily startled. Inside, trundled in heavy rope, lay the body of Hector Rivera.

The *delegado*'s eyes were bound shut by duct tape, the rear of his head shattered as if someone had crushed a watermelon with a mallet. Blood oozed out – a vivid, tar-like crimson. The entry point had been the mouth, the bullet, in all probability, a Magnum.

The deceased's hands were blotchy and bloated from the rope used to bind them. The skin on his arms held the paraffin cast of the newly dead. Fuentes sniffed the coarse aroma of feces.

Fuentes rested his hands on the trunk's frame. He heard a metallic click. A pocket tape recorder in the trunk had been tripped by the movement.

"*Que pasa*, Miguel!"

Miguel instantly recognized the voice. It belonged to Obregon.

"I was hoping you'd drop in tonight – certainly after my message. As you can see, Hector Rivera is quite dead. As far as the public is concerned, you will have committed this outrageous deed. Don't be surprised, Miguel! The forensic boys will see to it. The man has outlived his usefulness to us, and when he began to threaten my boss, what was I to do?

"By now you'll have figured out the reasons we can no longer allow you to stay alive. Quite frankly, you know too much for your own health. And ours. Remember what Flores taught us at the academy, my tragic friend? That policing is a science of precision and efficiency. After all of our discussions about efficiencies, to think it's precisely because you've become so efficient that you must now be eliminated!

"By daybreak, the official version will have you murdering the *delegado* after discovering he'd authorized your capture. By noon, you will have died in a fiery car crash on route 15 fleeing my *federales*. You shouldn't have hidden Donovan. A pretty piece of fluff, but not worth it. So? As of midnight, you've officially become a very wanted person. It's tidier that way – don't you think?

"The airplane tickets and hotel receipts in the glove compartment? They're quite legitimate. I found them sitting in there myself. You see, the Dutchman's murder was the *delegado*'s doing. As was the killing of the American at the motel. For that he used the maid to carry a parcel into the room. She had also been Rivera's mistress, but that never stopped him. Business is business. Of all people, I should know, shouldn't I? Consider these my gift to you. To put your mind at ease and celebrate the good times we had together. I owe you that much, my innocent, trusting partner. Now you can go to heaven, or wherever you feel comfortable, in the knowledge that you were right, all along. About NEDEROIL. About Rivera. About the whole thing. Not that it matters. Sorry we can't share a last bottle of wine. I have VIPs arriving at dawn. *Adios, amigo.* And pleasant dreams."

Abruptly, the huge doors slammed shut. Fuentes was sealed in the paint chamber. With a monotonous hum, lights flicked on in the ceiling and along the walls. The room suddenly became unbearably hot. Miguel frantically peered around. He would be baked alive!

He took his Glock out and started firing rounds into the reflectors: Nine. Ten. Eleven. One by one he shot out the reflectors. Glass cascaded around him. Miguel reloaded and kept shooting, furiously trying to neutralize the light shimmer before it turned him into a fried lobster. Two clips gone and the radiance was still relentless. There were just too many panels to destroy and too little time!

Suddenly another sound filled the chamber; a low, rippling *hisssssss* high above. Miguel peered up. A powdery cloud of vapor emanated from the rafters.

He rushed to the main doors and began to pound wildly on them – to no effect! He fired a round, then a second one into the steel seam that sealed the doors together. It was no use. The cloud drifted ever lower.

He rolled under the car. The fit was tight. He was only able to inch inward a small way. He coughed. His lungs were filling with vapor. He couldn't control his coughing. He lay, dazed.

Fuentes felt a nudge at his thigh; then another, this one more urgent. A set of feet. He groggily eased himself from under the chassis.

A petite figure confronted him, wearing oversized industrial coveralls and a bath towel wrapped so resolutely about its face that it gave the effect of a Berber tribesman in a dust storm.

The stranger hurriedly handed him a water-soaked cloth. He wrapped it around his nose and mouth.

"Come on!" the intruder urged in a muffled voice, gesturing to a strand of heavy rope dangling from the ceiling. "Hurry up! We haven't much time!"

Fuentes recognized the intruder's voice. Donovan!

He furiously made his way up the rope toward the ceiling. Near the top, a tight aperture created by a crowbar held a huge ventilation blade frozen in place. He inched warily through the gap that remained and found he was on the roof staring out at a sable sky.

He glanced down the cable. Donovan had passed unharmed through the menacing blade. She kicked the crowbar loose. The ravenous chop-chop-whine of the revolving fan commenced once more.

Donovan lowered the cloth from her face. She looked weary, but her eyes held their sparkle.

"How did you know I was here?"

"Later," she shushed and motioned to the fire exit. "We only have a few seconds before they figure out you aren't dead inside that chamber."

They made their way briskly down the ladder. Touching the ground, they scurried for shelter behind one of the Peterbilts. Its motor idled gruffly.

A klaxon wailed in one of the crane towers. Then another. Blazing perimeter lights switched on a hundred yards to the west. Fuentes heard the furious shouts of angry men; the banshee howl of revving vehicle motors.

"They've just discovered where I got in," Donovan explained.

A Jeep XJ spurted by, a whisper from their hiding place. It sported a roll bar with small-caliber machine gun mounted on it.

"Any bright ideas on how to get out?"

Fuentes's eyes darted about the enclosure. "You drive a standard?"

"Sure. I owned a Hummer, remember?"

"Thirty-five gear?" he thumbed to the towering Peterbilt cab. She shrugged. "You?"

"I won't know till I try . . ."

They clambered aboard the vehicle. The interior reeked of expensive leather and stale beer. The dashboard was as impressive as the cockpit of a 747, and only slightly less complicated.

Fuentes engaged the gears. The motor groaned, and the truck

lurched forward with an ungiving vibration, rear tires kicking up bits of loose asphalt.

He doggedly accelerated, targeting the main gate one hundred yards distant. A worker rushed out to block their flight, gesturing defiantly with a drenched mop. In seconds, the truck towered above the man. A dull crunch. A high-pitched scream, faint and failing. The mop bounced harmlessly off the windshield, trailing a soapy stain.

Fuentes didn't bother to eye the rearview. He fumbled about the dash, located the wiper-blade button, turned it on. One swish. Two. Three. The soapy window was clean again.

Thud! Thud! The passenger side mirror evaporated. Another volley. The insistent *clump!* of bullets lodging in the truck frame. A third volley demolished the driver's door window. Shivers of glass sprayed the air.

Ten yards. Five. As the guard dove for cover, the truck barreled through the barricades, and then Fuentes was onto the highway – number 15, the four-lane hardtop. He turned south and away from Larendo, back toward Coronado.

A Jeep Cherokee appeared from nowhere. It closed in on them from behind. Muzzle flashes twinkled like holiday sparklers from its opened windows. The Jeep moved to parallel the Peterbilt in the oncoming lane. Out of the corner of his eye, Miguel saw the front seat passenger raising a rifle. There was an expression of glassy expectation on the shooter's features. Now he knew how a condemned man felt facing a firing squad. Instinctively he jerked the steering left, then right. Then left again. The Jeep was hit broadside. It caromed off the roadway into the desert and cart-wheeled, coming to rest on its roof.

Miguel pushed the accelerator to the floor – 50, 60, 70, 80 miles per hour. The Peterbilt wobbled with the speed. They were entering foothill country. The road narrowed in this stretch to two lanes. It started to coil wildly. Fuentes braked, accelerated once more, braked again. The cab wobbled and wove uncertainly on its frame mounts. They traveled ten, perhaps twenty miles with a posse pursuing them like a pack of rabid dogs, moving closer one instant, then dropping back in a bend, yet all the while never able to come near enough to get a clear shot amid the spiraling landscape.

Then, abruptly, they were out onto flatlands again. Fuentes floored the gas pedal. The truck surged forward.

Suddenly, Fuentes felt the monster truck shudder. The steering wheel bucked wildly. A front tire had burst. Miguel struggled with the wheel. Brake. Pedal. Brake. He eased off the gas until he had a semblance of control, then switched off the headlights and veered from the roadbed, bounding into the charcoal desert. Fuentes forced the truck across the landscape like an incensed bull. They tumbled about inside the cabin like rag dolls.

The Peterbilt jerked atop the lip of a gully and skidded to a stop, half in and half out of a blackened crevasse. Miguel cut the motor. He and Donovan leapt out of the cabin and ran toward a stand of cacti, their shadows long on the desert floor.

The highway was visible a quarter mile distant, a velveteen ribbon dwindling to nothing. A Cherokee dashed by, then another, both with rooftop lights that glittered wintry blue. The second Jeep slowed suspiciously as it neared the spot where the truck had left the road. A searchlight scanned the scrub waste, but halted short of the abandoned rig. The beam then flicked off. The Jeep moved on, zooming westward like a lit-up pinball, until it was a mere speck on an inky horizon.

Fuentes rested a moment, gulping the air, tense with anxiety. The night was chill and slightly damp. All around was pitch black, wavering now and then into a semblance of shape; then back again to void. After a time, his eyes grew accustomed to the lack of light. Great lumps of bedrock, harsh and unrepentant, littered the land.

Fuentes turned to Donovan. "How did you find me?"

"I followed Obregon. I was hoping he would lead me to the VAX."

Miguel's eyes narrowed.

"When I left your place this morning with Papagayo, we thought we'd find the computer hidden in the Barrio."

"The old man?" Miguel interjected.

Now it was Donovan's turn to look surprised. "You knew?"

Fuentes shrugged. "I wondered why a person as important as Obregon would suddenly appear at a slum fire. And how he was able to have your descriptions broadcast so accurately on the police radio, especially Papagayo's – an individual he had never seen, and supposedly had no knowledge of. Then I saw Felipe's corpse and discovered he was the only person killed by the fire, and it all began to make sense." Miguel paused. "Remember how the old man played that computer game on the night we visited him?"

"Precisely." Donovan calmly closed the equation. "Wick thought Felipe's shack would be the perfect place to hide the VAX while he tended to Obregon. Why wouldn't he? Felipe routinely received contraband from the *Yanquis*. One more item would be nothing special to him."

Her voice trailed off to a whisper. "Obregon got to Felipe before we could. We found the old man dead and the VAX missing. A government SWAT team waited in ambush for us. We managed to escape into the Barrio. That's why they started the fire – to smoke us out."

"And to destroy all the evidence of a murder," Miguel added bitterly. "Not that they usually worry about such technicalities..."

"You don't appear shocked."

"Nothing that bastard does surprises me, Maria. It seems the *comandante* has enough pull to neutralize even the Mexican Security Directorate."

"So it appears..." The massive wilderness engulfed them in an awful silence. "But why the VAX?"

"That's what I've been asking myself," Fuentes conceded. "Initially I thought they stole the computer as collateral for something else." His jaw hardened with resolve. "Now I believe Obregon actually means to use the system himself. And that's why he may need Chandler."

Suddenly there was a sound in the gloom. Faint at first, then more distinct. Ratchety, clamorous. Coming from the north, from where they'd come from. A car, headlights off, wallowing over nearby *arroyos*. The clink-clatter of a loose frame; the grate-groan of defiant metal.

Fuentes heard a male voice. Cursing. Brusque. Then a solitary wail: "*Jefe!* Where are you? It's me! Felix!"

Fuentes rose cautiously from his hiding place. Then he rushed toward the car. "Here!" He feverishly waved his hands above his head. "Over here!"

The Mustang halted, then changed direction. It bucked stubbornly toward them and jolted to a stop a few yards short of their hiding place. Felix tumbled out, careful not to slam the door. He rushed to them, sidearm at the ready. His jaw dropped visibly. "Lieutenant Donovan?"

"*Si, amigo.* May I introduce Lieutenant Maria Donovan."

The bewildered expression stuck to Asuncion's frazzled features.

"I'll explain it later," Fuentes continued. "For now, let's just say it's another of Obregon's little games."

The detective nodded with exaggerated severity. "*Si, Señor,*" he mumbled, "it surely must be."

The surrounding silence suddenly became turbulent. The unrelenting *thrump-thrump* of helicopter blades. They dove for cover. A dense search beam singed the earth. A coal-black craft hovered above. In the distance, to the west, similar frosty shafts lanced downward from the cosmos. Fuentes counted three.

"Army reconnaissance," said Asuncion.

Fuentes nodded, acutely aware that the stakes in this game had risen exponentially.

They remained hidden until the helicopters blended with the remote horizon, then scampered to the Mustang. They slumped in their seats and sat there for a time, drinking in the stillness.

Asuncion spoke first. "After you didn't return to the rendezvous, I worried big time. Then I saw the Jeeps chasing a truck driving away from the compound. I knew it had to be you. Obregon was in one of them." He shrugged. "So I followed you. The *federales* have been broadcasting your description for the past twenty minutes, nonstop. They have warrants for your arrest. You and the woman."

"For the murder of Humberto Rivera." Fuentes sniffed.

"Yes." Asuncion looked startled. "How did you know?"

"I have the very best sources," Miguel commented dryly.

"And I have this, *Jefe*." Felix proudly took some crumpled fax pages from his back pocket and handed them over. "You remember the *Cassandra*?" He jabbed his fingers excitedly across the sheets as Miguel began to read. "Here!" He pointed gleefully. "Here you have Guzman on the passenger list!"

Fuentes wordlessly considered the information. There were only five individuals on the list, not unusual for a freighter. Three Danes, who by their shared surname appeared to be a family embarked on a holiday to the New World; an American, either a medical doctor or a scientist; and Guzman, holding a single cabin – 3 E – to himself.

Sheet two itemized the ship's cargo: a massive shipment of steel cable in transit from a mill in the Slovak Republic, and several hundred tons of brown sugar from Cuba.

Fuentes flipped to sheet three. It detailed the passengers' effects for the purpose of Mexican Customs, those things that had been stored in the *Cassandra*'s hold, either because of their size or weight, or their lack of entertainment value or functional purpose on the voyage. He skimmed the inventory.

The brief catalog confirmed his suspicions about the American, who'd listed three large tents, several tripods, and enough camping equipment for an assault on Everest and was probably, therefore, a research scientist. And the Danish trio, who, with three mountain bikes and several cases of granola bars and mineral water among their belongings, were undoubtedly off to save the rainforest from mankind.

And then there was Guzman. In the ship's hold he'd stored two container trunks of reasonable size and heft in which to carry his personal effects. But there was a most curious item – a long, narrow crate weighing approximately seventy-five pounds and listed as outdoor, all-weather carpeting: origin identified as Tajikistan. He recalled the box at Six Tampico.

The police radio crackled. "Tango Three to Tango One. Over."

"Tango Three. Go." Fuentes recognized Obregon's voice.

"Tango One. We have cordon sealed. Believe we have subject two clicks east of Altar, off number 2. Approval to move in. Over."

A delay. "10-4. Proceed and advise. Over."

"10-4." Conversation ended. The night was silent.

"You know what they're up to, Felix?" Fuentes asked.

The *sergente* shook his head. "No. But there's been an awful lot of radio traffic up by Altar in the past few minutes. Just before I sighted you. Something about 'Project Phoenix'?"

Fuentes started. "Project Phoenix? That scheme's supposed to be around Querobabi, well over forty miles away. There's nothing happening hereabouts. At least nothing the *federales* have told me about." Another helicopter vectored overhead through the night air, heading north-northwest toward the morose bank of hills.

Fuentes furiously pounded the steering wheel. "Altar, you say?"

"Yes."

Suddenly, Miguel bound out to the rear of the black-and-white. He opened the trunk, fidgeting about in the darkness. Then he gingerly closed it once more.

He returned to his seat holding scraps of paper; he pored over some notes and photos, then, satisfied, turned to his partner.

"Open the glove compartment, will you, Felix? And hand me the map inside."

Asuncion did as he was told.

Fuentes placed the item in his lap, then patiently unfolded it: a standard chart of northern Mexico, the kind sold at all PEMEX gas stations. "Where is this place – Altar?"

"It's a tiny town, just there." Asuncion jutted a stubby finger to the top corner of the parchment. "About twenty miles west of Santa Ana."

"Business activity?"

"A few abandoned copper mines, *Jefe*." A bewildered shrug.

Miguel lifted a leaf of glossy paper from the pile. It was a photo print of the foolscap littered with dots that they'd found in Chandler's place. He took a pen from his breast pocket and fleshed out the specks. They soon resembled a rough cross tilted leftward and, flowing from its tip, the contour of an isosceles triangle.

Fuentes pursed his lips. "Maria, remember what you told me about the diagram we saw in that apartment? What was it you thought our captain had an interest in?"

"Vega. The fifth brightest star in the summer sky."

"But what did you say about Altar?"

"*Altair*," she corrected him. "Not much."

"A pity," he commented dryly. "Because I don't think Wick Chandler cared as much about Vega as we thought. I believe his fascination all along was with A-l-t-a-r." He pointedly spelled the word. "Have you ever seen *Five Graves to Cairo*?"

"What is it?" Donovan raised her eyebrows. "A National Geographic special?

"No." Fuentes chuckled. "A war movie. A 1943 classic starring Franchot Tone, Erik von Stroheim, and Akim Tamiroff. Tone plays a British army corporal stranded after the fall of Tobruk and forced to pose as a waiter at a rundown desert hotel when the place is overrun by the advancing Afrika Korps. The manager is played by Tamiroff, fez and all. Anyway, the Desert Fox, von Stroheim, is barreling toward Cairo, with the English army right on his heels. He commandeers the hotel as his headquarters. Tone becomes a spy for the Allied cause, trying to determine where Rommel hides the stores he needs to fuel his panzer tanks in their dash toward the Suez. The riddle is solved when Tone discovers that Rommel has relied on an old map of Egypt, and before the war he secretly stockpiled caches where the letters E-G-Y-P-T are located on the parchment, all along 'the five graves to Cairo.'"

He unfolded the map. "Let's see if I'm right. Felix, get me a Kleenex. In the glove compartment." Asuncion did so. Miguel took a single sheet and unfolded it. He took his pen and painstakingly dotted the tissue to mirror the star formation on the photograph, then eased it onto the chart. The place names showed faintly through. He shifted the paper, first this way, then that, ever careful to ensure that the representation of the star Altair remained atop the dot marking the town of Altar.

Suddenly, he stopped. "Bingo!" An assertive grunt. "We have Travis Chandler's hiding spot!"

He stabbed the tissue forcefully in three places, so that the marks remained indelibly on the map.

"Look!" he gushed. "Old Travis couldn't have been more precise with directions if he'd been drawing a map to his home! The town of Magdalena is located on the PEMEX map precisely where Deneb is diagrammed on this chart. Coronado is spotted on Vega. And there!" – he jabbed the town of Altar – "there, roughly, is the old man's current position."

Donovan looked perplexed. "How can you be so certain?"

Fuentes grinned. "Because Chandler all but telegraphed it to his son in that postcard. In the film *Five Graves*, Tone plays a corporal named J. J. Bramble." Miguel flicked through the photos until he found what he was seeking, then euphorically handed it to Donovan. "What's the name on the postcard?"

Donovan glanced down at the inscription. "J. J. Bramble," she whispered.

"Two miles east of Altar, off Highway 2?" Fuentes mused. "Is that where our *federale* friends are scampering for Project Phoenix?"

Asuncion nodded vigorously.

Fuentes tossed the snapshots into the back seat of the Mustang, where they landed in a jumble. "Let's get going, *amigos!*" he enthused. "We have a breakfast date with the *federale comandante* for the State of Sonora. Only this time I'll be hosting!"

PART THREE
SANTA ANA

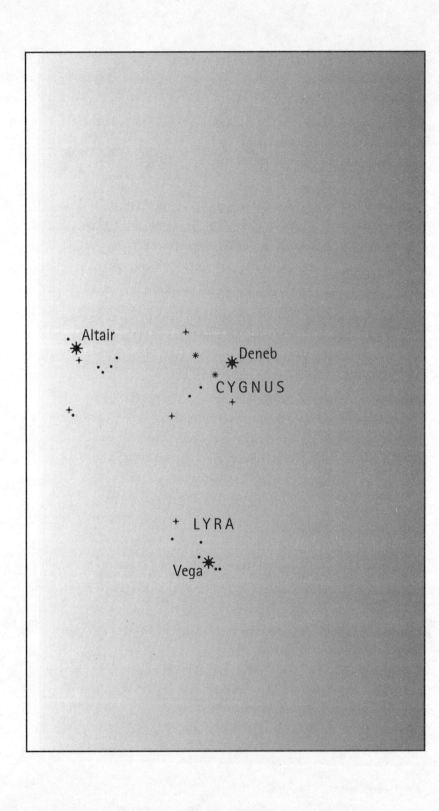

37

Miguel tightened his grip on the steering wheel as they moved warily across the craggy terrain. He left the headlights off and was careful not to touch the brake pedal. They ran parallel to the highway, staying several hundred yards away. At first they traveled slowly, wary of dust, but soon Fuentes stopped caring. He revved the motor. The Mustang buckled into a gulch, the front fender screeching in protest as it struck bedrock. The car rose resolutely back to the desert surface, then roared westward, gamely kicking up pieces of shale as it went.

The route Fuentes had chosen was deliberate. Their journey took about an hour but felt as though it might stretch into eternity. Springs and shocks seemed to collapse. The windshield cracked and the muffler roared exhaust from a rock puncture.

As they drew closer to Altar, Fuentes stopped the Mustang. The three exited the car and eased their way to a hillside lookout. What confronted them was a mine, well below ground level. Combat helicopters circled above. Fuentes prayed they would not pinpoint the Mustang – or them. Asuncion had astutely grabbed a pair of binoculars from the back seat to take along. Now he calmly trained the glasses on the bustling spectacle below.

Enormous halogen lights pierced the gloom, illuminating the tilting structures and pit entrance proper. Abandoned buildings lay in a crimped hollow between the two hills: a storage shed and multi-bay garage; canteen, change house, office, and an infirmary identified by a pallid pink cross daubed on a sagging roof. Outside the garage, a trio of derelict trucks squatted on rusted wheel rims. Fuentes guessed the operation had been abandoned at least a decade; in this part of the country, it had probably been a silver mine, and judging by the sheer variety of buildings and their methodical construction, a prosperous one at that. The name of the defunct firm was feebly stenciled on the change house wall: "Alamo Mines of Mexico, Ltd."

A provisional command post was set up beside the infirmary. It comprised a forty-five-foot military trailer, six personnel carriers, a trio of *federale* Crown Victorias, and a royal-blue Buick with its front doors ajar. A gaggle of army trucks were parked in an orderly fashion nearby. A platoon of helmeted soldiers scrambled up the slope toward the pit entrance. Shrill whistles blew. More men clambered out of the trucks to dutifully follow the first party into the tunnels.

Asuncion trained his binoculars onto the site and watched calmly as the dark fissure swallowed up wave upon wave of troops. Miguel estimated a rifle company was committed already, with a second poised to follow.

As this was happening, a tall, refined male eased himself out of the driver's side of the Buick. The man stood alone, sanguinely puffing on a cigarette as he contemplated the activity about him. He flicked the butt to the ground, then sauntered toward a group of immaculately garbed soldiers congregated nearby – senior command types, Miguel surmised.

"Obregon?" Fuentes wondered.

Without taking his eyes from the binoculars, Asuncion nodded. "*El Diablo* himself, minus tail and horns. It can be no other."

A slight figure, hunched at the shoulders, exited the Buick and ambled over to where the *comandante* stood, buoyantly chatting with the army cadre. The newcomer wore a bright apricot ball cap and a brown bomber jacket tightly cinched about his waist to ward off the night chill. He held a cellphone in his hand. Every few moments, and with the most lively hand gestures, he spoke into it. For some odd reason that Miguel couldn't quite place, the unknown man looked very familiar.

"Felix? Who's the new *hombre*?" Fuentes pointed. "The one in the ball cap."

Asuncion wiped beads of sweat from a grizzled cheek. His brow wrinkled in fierce deliberation. Then, suddenly, recollection wended its way across coarsened features. "What was his name, *Jefe*?" The *sergente*'s jowls jiggled as he shook his massive head. "That little fellow we met in the American colonel's office in Phoenix. The one with the red bow tie."

"Homer Styles?" Donovan blurted in disbelief.

"*Si!*" Asuncion nodded. "That's him!"

Miguel peered through the raven-black night toward his charges. "Maria? What do you know of this fellow Styles?"

The young woman crawled forward until she rested between the two. She crouched efficiently on her haunches. "I know he's a senior bureaucrat in Washington. And that he works with the Reconnaissance Bureau. I was introduced to him by Colonel Bragg the day before I met you for the first time."

"Reconnaissance Bureau?" Fuentes asked. "What do they do?"

"Satellite imaging." The young woman spoke with more than a hint of circumspection. "Military surveillance." Her voice faded away into judicious silence.

"Maria," Fuentes chided, "this is no time to play twenty questions. What do they do? Exactly."

Donovan glanced away, clearly uncomfortable with what she was about to relate. "They monitor communications from one of our satellites," she admitted finally. "From phone to fax to modem. Internationally."

"That's better," Fuentes remarked coldly. "Is that monitoring of hostiles? Or of friendly nations, too?"

She shrugged. "If you were to ask Styles, he'd tell you as far as his agency was concerned, there isn't any difference."

Fuentes contemplated what he'd just been told. "So why does Washington want to help Obregon find Chandler?"

"Politics makes strange bedfellows." Donovan sniffed.

"As does greed," Fuentes added up.

Donovan halted. "Maybe."

"*Jefe*," Asuncion whispered. "*Jefe!* I'm sorry for interrupting, but look!"

Below them, the soldiers had encircled Obregon and the American. A heated torrent of words appeared to pass between the two men. Suddenly Styles stormed off, obviously ruffled by the outcome of the exchange. He pounced on one of the army types and gesticulated irately to a spot halfway up the opposing hillside and quite some distance from the mine entrance, to a copse of stunted pine and, discernible within it, a blackened fissure in the rock.

The officer spun back to his peers. A megaphone appeared from nowhere. Harsh commands resonated sharply through the night. Three sticks of helmeted soldiers hopped out of the rear of the transports and maneuvered up the slope, toward the stunted pine.

"There!" Asuncion pointed. "There!" He gestured excitedly toward a solitary figure clambering along a rock cleft fifty yards east of the pine stand. Bold halogen beams relentlessly sectored the slope, yet somehow missed the man.

The figure moved along the hillside, then changed direction to make a sharply angled descent. Fuentes observed his progress. The climber was skillful. He cleverly used the darkness and ground cover to advantage. An army platoon in skirmish order drifted past his perch, yet he remained undetected.

Fuentes thought quickly. "Come on," he whispered gruffly. "I think that's someone I'd like to meet."

They tumbled down through the prickle bush into the valley below, giving the military encampment a wide berth. The commotion disguised their movement. Within minutes they were shielded by the merciful bulk of the surrounding foothills.

"Here!" Fuentes commanded as he peered up the sheer northern slope. "We'll stop here."

They huddled flush with the hill and waited.

Above them, they could hear the man's exertions, his feet on loose shale, the sucking noise of agitated breathing. Then, suddenly, he was upon them. Fuentes leapt at the bounding form and swiftly muzzled the runaway's mouth with his hands as Asuncion dove for the man's legs.

The three fell into a struggling heap. The stranger resisted with bleak determination. Asuncion grabbed him with a bear hug and tried to keep the man's hands to his sides. The stranger was tense as a tightly coiled spring. Miguel found he had to punch the man briskly in the side of the head. Once. Twice.

"Mr. Chandler?" Fuentes whispered furiously. "Travis Chandler?"

The eyes of the newcomer flickered with the tiniest inkling of confirmation.

"We aren't going to hurt you," Miguel offered. "We're not with them!"

The man scrunched his face. "I don't believe you," he gasped.

"We know about the postcard," Fuentes continued in a calming voice. "The coded message you sent your son. We know about the attempt on your life."

In an instant, equal portions of bewilderment and alarm flared across Chandler's features. He remained closemouthed.

"I'm the chief of police of a place here in Sonora called Coronado." Fuentes motioned to the others. "This is Lieutenant Maria Donovan of the United States Air Force. And my partner, Felix Asuncion."

Chandler's demeanor remained impenetrable, yet Fuentes felt the strain in the runaway's muscles ease just slightly. He helped the man sit up. Prudently he kept a grip on the newcomer's shoulder. Just in case.

"Your son is dead, sir," he offered at last.

"No. He can't be!" Chandler gasped. "Not Wick!"

Miguel waited a respectable spell. "I'm investigating his murder," he continued gently. "I believe it's tied to the disappearance of a computer from the depot at Davis Monthan Air Base."

"But I have e-mail!" the older man whispered with incredulity. "Wickham corresponded with me on a regular basis. As recently as today . . ."

"I'm afraid your son was murdered in Mexico," Miguel spoke with as much compassion as he could muster. "Back on May 21. Near Coronado."

Chandler's jaw firmed up. "Wick's alive," he avowed with blind determination.

Miguel played out his hunch. "If you really think that, why did you just flee the mine? Why didn't you wait for Wick in there? Just as you said you would in the postcard?"

An abrupt gush of compressed air. A helicopter gunship clipped by, scarcely one hundred feet above them. A robust beam clicked on from its belly and traversed the desert surface, before the machine coned up the far slope. A second craft echoed the pass over, then a third. Fuentes motioned his team to the ground. For his part, Chandler needed no coaxing.

They hid until the choppers were on the far side of the gully, loitering over the surging military assault.

"It's your call, Mr. Chandler." Miguel dusted himself off and eased back to his observation post. "We know you worked at Huachuca. We know someone tried to kidnap you in San Igna-cio." The ruthless race against time had made him unrelenting. "What was it? Blackmail?"

Chandler stared blankly at his accuser, then to the others, and back to Miguel again.

Beneath them, four troop transports had arrived, screeching to a halt. Another company of soldiers jumped out and charged up the opposite slope. Shouts. The shrill sound of raiding whistles.

Fuentes made up his mind. It was only a matter of minutes before the search grid expanded and caught them in its web. "Let's get out of here," he urged harshly.

Asuncion and Donovan started to move toward where the Mustang was hidden; still Chandler hesitated.

"Now!" Fuentes barked angrily. "Come on! Or do you want to end up dead like your son?"

Travis Chandler didn't stir. Donovan leaned toward the prone man and shushed Fuentes with a wave of her hand.

"You were a member of a Red Horse Unit, sir?" She gestured to a tiny signet ring on Chandler's finger. "A field engineer?"

The older man peered at her with cautious distrust.

"'O! For a horse with wings.' That was the unit motto, wasn't it?"

"Yes," Chandler responded warily.

"Shakespeare. The play *Cymbeline*." Donovan paused. "Did you ever serve in 'Nam with the 554th?"

The flinty edge of long-suppressed memory. A nod, more attentive now.

"My dad was a marine gunnery sergeant there," she continued. "Got decorated at Chiu Lai, 1966. Charlie'd laid an ambush for his platoon. His ARVN scout gave him the only escape route. Two of Dad's men weren't comfortable with having their lives in the hands of a stranger, and a Viet to boot. Dad had to make a snap decision."

"What did he do?" Chandler asked.

She rummaged around her pocket and found a small coin. She tossed it into the air, catching it in her palm. She covered the piece with another hand. "Heads you come with us, tails we'll be forced to kill you. Your call, sir."

Chandler glared incredulously at the young woman. "You surely can't be serious…?" he sputtered.

"Your call," she repeated coldly.

Chandler stared at the others, first at Asuncion, then at Fuentes. Their faces were expressionless. After the longest silence, he moved slowly to his feet and followed them into the dark desert.

They soon reached the Mustang and inched away in first gear, headlights off. Chandler sat motionless in the front seat. Fuentes pointed the vehicle due west, piercing the rich ebony envelope that the heavens yet offered. The tiny dash clock showed 3:27. An imprecise aura piqued the eastern horizon.

They journeyed without a word being said. Miguel had no notion of where to go or what to do. He just knew he had to take the Mustang as far away from this military operation as he could. And as quickly. He asked Felix to turn up the volume on the *federale* radio band.

He glanced over to his reluctant passenger. Chandler's right hand trembled as it rested in his lap. He smelled faintly – a tangy, sweet-sour odor. Fuentes was uncertain if it was from copper dust. Or panic.

"What's going on, Mr. Chandler?" Fuentes pressed. "Please tell me. We don't have much time before those soldiers realize you've escaped. And then they'll all be out here hunting us."

Chandler peered at Miguel with haunted eyes. His features held the look of a cornered animal.

"Mr. Chandler?" Fuentes repeated. "Sir? Remember what happened to your son?" Miguel switched gears. The car accelerated perceptibly. Pebbles pinged off the undercarriage.

Travis Chandler took a deep breath, then began. "For the past year, while Wick was at Davis, I was in charge of a major project at Huachuca …"

"The VAX 10?" Fuentes interrupted. "One was stolen at Davis Monthan, right about the time your son vanished."

Miguel gazed sternly at his passenger. Travis Chandler seemed to shrink visibly in his seat. The grim desert light had drained the man's skin to pale chalk. He sighed.

"I knew my boy was involved in a major criminal investigation. A high-pressured one. It's the sort of strain that fathers recognize when it affects their sons, even tight-lipped ones like Wickham.

"A few weeks back I get an anonymous death threat. Then a pipe bomb blasts the front off my home in Benson. Within minutes of the explosion, I get a phone call warning me not to contact local police or air force security. Or else.

"Wick panics. We agree that I'll hide in Mexico, at a *hacienda* we'd rented once by San Ignacio. Suddenly, bandits try to kidnap me outside Magdelena. Wick gets the ultimatum. Supply them with a VAX. And with me. And if not, they'll hunt me down and he'll have a dead father."

The Mustang's engine started to grind from overheating. Fuentes eased his foot off the gas pedal. He noticed that Chandler had calmed somewhat. The older man related the information more easily now, as if gratified to get an enormous weight off his chest.

Miguel was puzzled. "Why didn't your son go to base security? Surely they could have shielded you?"

"Why?" Chandler responded with a gaunt smile. "I wish I knew. Maybe Wick thought no one could protect me here in Sonora. Not the United States Air Force. And certainly not the Mexican *federales*." He gestured in the direction of the mine site furiously receding behind them. "Maybe Wick's bosses felt it was too risky to involve me in what he was up to." A hesitation. "Maybe I was considered expendable . . . ."

"By whom?" Miguel demanded harshly. "Your own son?"

Chandler's features steeled. "Does it really matter," he snapped, "now that Wickham's dead?"

The older man seemed very fragile and quite alone. He gathered up his courage and continued. "After the kidnap try, Wick and I stopped speaking by phone. Instead we e-mailed. I knew they'd search for me around San Ignacio, so I came down here. I sent Wick a coded postcard knowing only he'd recognize its meaning."

Chandler became brutally clinical. "For the past two weeks, I've corresponded with someone who signs off as my son, someone who I thought was Wick. About an hour ago, I was told – no, practically ordered – to stand by for new information. Then I was asked to authenticate my exact location.

"That was it!" Chandler sniffed. "Wick wouldn't do that. He knew where I was hiding. We'd camped here last year. Wick had made mention of the name: *Alamo*." A shrug. "I e-mailed some private thoughts about the anniversary of my wife's death. The reply was sympathetic. Too much so."

Fuentes arched his eyebrows. "Sir?"

"My wife died on Christmas Eve. Not the middle of June. It's a date you can never forget. Whether you're a husband – or a son."

Fuentes opened his window a crack. A faint wind tickled his hair. "What's down in the mine for them to find, *señor*?"

"My laptop computer," Chandler answered mechanically. "A few days' rations. A dirt bike I used to get supplies in from Altar."

"Anything involving the VAX?"

"That's all up here." Chandler tapped his head.

"What does this VAX look like, *señor*?" Miguel asked. "You know, the carrying case?"

Chandler paused before answering. "It's very bright and kept in a small neon-striped container so we can locate it easily in an emergency."

Fuentes hesitated. "What if I told you those people back there may have a VAX in their possession?"

Travis Chandler calmly considered the information as he

would a mathematical formula. "Then I'd have to wonder if there is anyone sufficiently skilled to operate it."

"Which is probably why they needed you so badly." Fuentes reflected on the solid walls of computer texts that lined a particular office in Hermosillo. "But if I said there might now be just such a person, a man I know here in Sonora . . . ?"

"I'm confused," Chandler admitted candidly. "To a novice, the VAX is intimidating, a virtual labyrinth. Even to an expert, it can be immensely sophisticated, even daunting. You say this person is brilliant with computers?" Chandler shook his head. "That may well be so, but there's much to master about a VAX in order to make it fully operational. It's not a video game, you know."

"I gathered that," Miguel acceded. "In all likelihood that's why they're still after you. They'd rather be safe than sorry."

"Quite." Chandler's face clouded in thought. "You say this man of yours is a genius?"

"Yes."

"Well," Chandler mused, "even a genius needs a purpose, a focus for his energy. The VAX 10 is very limited in its application. So, if what you say is true, and after all that's transpired, I'd be really concerned as to what this person might do with a VAX now that he's acquired it."

"As would I," Fuentes agreed. "As would I."

The Mustang bounced brutally down into a ditch, then righted itself with a low moan of metal on rock. Another army helicopter passed by overhead. Fuentes seemed to reflect on its movement.

"The VAX has the capacity to override the live pilot, am I right?"

"Yes." Chandler nodded. "It can guide an aircraft from the ground by remote control. At distances exceeding forty miles."

Fuentes let out an involuntary whistle. "Is it truly that powerful?"

"Sure is." Chandler smiled ruefully. "Almost enough to humble a Pope."

"I beg your pardon?"

"It's an old expression," Chandler admitted apologetically. "I hope it didn't offend you."

"No, no." Fuentes sat there for a time, tapping the steering wheel in a quiet, considered rhythm. Then he seemed to have made up his mind. He turned to Asuncion, who was uncomfortably crammed into the narrow back seat. "Felix? When is the Pope arriving in Mexico?"

"Why, today, *Jefe*. This very morning – "

"And where?" Miguel pressed. "At Santa Ana, isn't it?"

"*Si, amigo*." Asuncion nodded his head robustly. "I scanned the radio band outside Larendo. His Holiness will be landing at Santa Ana in the next few hours – at nine o'clock on the dot."

"Who is he meeting?"

"Who?" A droll chuckle. "Anyone who's anyone. Or wants to be. *El presidente*, the federal cabinet, a whole assortment of dignitaries ..."

"Does radio traffic suggest how the Pope is getting to Santa Ana?"

"By helicopter." Asuncion was puzzled by the question. "At least that's what the *comandante* indicated."

"You mean Obregon?"

"Yes." Asuncion nodded vigorously. "He radioed his men that he himself would ensure His Holiness had a bang-up welcome for his touchdown. Those were his very words."

Fuentes rustled around inside the glove compartment. The Mustang began to weave. It narrowly avoided one cactus stand, then another. The car brushed heavily along prickle bush. Suddenly, Fuentes popped upright in the driver's seat, his search complete.

"Maria?" He beckoned.

"Yes?"

"Here." He tossed an object over his shoulder to her. "You're a graduate of the Air Force Academy. Take this compass. There's a map there and an ocean of stars above us. Navigate."

"What?" Donovan replied, startled.

"You heard me, Lieutenant," Fuentes commanded. "Find me the fastest route to Santa Ana. We have a rendezvous with His Holiness."

38 As the svelte minute hand on the Oyster Mariner passed the numeral four, Obregon made the decision to break off and head for the command post at Santa Ana. The search in the mine would continue without him. There were four underground chambers still to be explored, and he had a hundred dull and docile men to do the exploring. Obregon would have preferred to capture Chandler then and there, if only to tap the man's computer knowledge when the crunch came. But there wasn't the time to do it. Besides, he'd managed to introduce himself to the VAX; it was in his hands now, literally.

The American spy satellite had tracked Chandler most efficiently. And, of course, once the man had made his inadvertent mistake, it had taken Obregon's American guest but ten minutes to pinpoint Chandler's exact location on the grid map, and less than a half hour for Ramon to bring his doggedly panting troops to bear.

The Americans were quite accommodating. All he had to tell Styles was that Chandler had the VAX, and they were off and running like bloodhounds after a fox.

Of course, the old fool had proved cunning. He'd sent e-mail to a telephone substation in Querobabi and ultimately fed it through to a switcher in Germany to blunt the scent. It had worked for a few weeks.

But the misdirection had ultimately backfired, for that one split second when human emotion had gotten in the way. That's all it had taken, a split second and he was in their web.

The Mexican air force helicopters hovering overhead would be freed up to join the official airborne escort at the American border. Protocol, after all, had to be observed.

A Huey would rush Obregon to Santa Ana and his appointment with destiny. Another would remain on standby at the mine site. If they located their prey, it could still dispatch Chandler to his side in less than fifteen minutes – whether he wanted to come along or not.

6:34 a.m.

The U.S. Air Force E-3 Sentry entered the stratosphere over the southwestern United States on a preselected route some time before the first hint of dawn. It had been aloft just over one and three-quarter hours. Powered by two CF6-80C2 engines with a thrust of 61,500 pounds, the E-3 now nestled comfortably at a cruising altitude of 50,000 feet, straddling the Nogales quadrant.

The rotating radar dome of the E-3 had the potential to range across two hundred miles. Combined with an intricate identification subsystem, the technology could detect, identify, and track all low-flying aircraft in that radius by filtering out signals from ground clutter that often confused less sophisticated radar systems.

The eighteen-member crew of specialists, lodged in comfortable captain's chairs, monitored the steadfast merging of a sea of tiny dots on their display consoles. The blips resembled large grains of white sugar across an indigo background. In reality, they scrupulously depicted the air forces of two nations as they maneuvered to safeguard the life of one man, an old and resolute Pole with a bad hip and a profound mission.

6:42 a.m.

Somewhere over Growler Pass, just west of the Papago Indian Reservation along the southern flank of the state of Arizona, a squadron of F-15 Eagles flashed across blue skies bearing south-southwest toward their specified station along the Mexican-American border. Based at Luke AFB, up by Phoenix, for just this mission, each fighter crammed an arsenal of Sparrow missiles, sidewinders, and internal Gatling guns under its slender wing roots. They possessed only slightly less firepower than might be necessary to bring on the Final Apocalypse. On this date, the flight was tagged "M – Michael," after the noble Archangel. Its task was to safeguard the direct spiritual descendant of Saint Peter.

South of the border, a smaller batch of silver Mexican Northrop F5 Tiger IIs from a military airbase outside of Mexico City had sortied three-quarters of an hour earlier on an identical task. For this extraordinary occasion, an ardent headquarters type had piously detailed the flight "J – Joseph" for the patron saint of Mexico.

Stylus-sleek jetfighters jagged across cloudless heavens creating a tapestry of vapor trails. At lower altitudes, two sticks of American A-10 Thunderbolts from Davis Monthan stolidly sniffed about the grim desert crevasses and moon-cratered landscape that flashed beneath their blunt bodies. The A-10s, or Warthogs as they were affectionately labeled by their crews, were considerably less glamorous than their pretentious sisters some 32,000 feet above. But they were also far more effective for any clientele that might lie in ambush along the desert floor.

In all, fifty-one fixed-wing aircraft from two nations had converged on the sixty-square-mile airspace atop the Sonora desert on this brilliant morning. They would be directed in their progress by a joint Mexican-American task force set up in the Cheyenne Mountain headquarters of NORAD, just outside Colorado Springs.

7:03 a.m.

Morning broke clear and fast above Phoenix as the gigantic Sikorsky S61-N lifted gracefully up from the cordoned-off hotel parking lot. The sun glimmered off its Plexiglas windows, blinding a cluster of suited dignitaries who waved their mannerly goodbyes from the asphalt below. Colored a chaste white, with a wide gold band painted across its body frame and the papal coat of arms scrolled just below the pilot's cockpit, it was christened "Papa One."

The S61-N was one of two such craft scheduled for use on this date. The other, in matching livery and with a similar gold band, carried the coat of arms of the Federal Republic of Mexico below the cockpit. It was scheduled to depart within the hour with its own noteworthy payload from a secret site in Hermosillo.

The stately Sikorsky could carry thirty passengers and a crew of three. On this occasion, its manifest showed a more discreet sixteen, including a Very Important Personage and his scarlet-frocked entourage. The helicopter held American military as well as assorted civil and religious notables from both nations.

Within seconds of lift-off, Papa One was enveloped in a tight cluster of U.S. Army Apache helicopters and a sweeping outer cordon of Marine Corps Super Cobras. In all, fourteen choppers droned purposefully southward through the ruby morning sky. From a distance, the enterprise resembled a swarm of bees, but no cache of honey would ever prove as valuable as this one.

The procession's inflexible progress was monitored by the AWACS aircraft sitting over Nogales, which implacably passed its findings on to the NORAD command center. All told, the 183-mile journey to the Santa Ana region would take Papa One exactly sixty-four minutes.

The schedule was tight and unyielding, the entire passage guaranteed to be trouble-free. No civilian traffic would be permitted to enter into airspace within two hundred miles of the armada from one hour prior to its Phoenix liftoff until one hour after the safe touchdown of Papa One on Mexican soil.

7:38 a.m.

At precisely that moment, a diplomatic handoff occurred in the air ten thousand feet above the invisible dotted line that marked the Mexican-American border. The U.S. helicopter escort out of Phoenix delicately peeled off to be replaced by Mexican choppers: six Sikorsky S-70 Blackhawks on the inside; nine Bell Hueys flanking the outside.

The pearl in the crux of the formation, Papa One, remained firm in its airspeed of 169 mph and in its direction, due south.

8:03 a.m.

The Mustang was now within three miles of the site and back on the main road, heading east, caught in a swelling tidal wave of humanity crawling toward Santa Ana. A golden haze wafted over the desert morning like the pall of incense at a Marian *novena*. Though the pace was slow, Fuentes knew it was safer this way than to be alone in the desert, where they might fall easy prey to probing government helicopters. Even so, he'd heard their descriptions and that of the Mustang broadcast every fifteen minutes on the federal radio band. He? Miguel Fuentes? Wanted for murder? Now a fugitive from justice?

Fuentes inched the Mustang forward along the roadway, pushing past grit-encrusted Ford pickups, ancient school buses, and rattletrap jalopies overflowing with pilgrims.

He wasn't certain what he'd be looking for at Santa Ana, but, thanks to Asuncion, he knew that it would involve the Pope, that it would happen at precisely nine o'clock, and, given the events that had transpired thus far in the day, that its effects could be profound. Probably deadly. But where among the hundreds of thousands of souls and acres of ground was he to begin looking? Fuentes glanced anxiously at the clock on the car dash. He had less than one hour in which to find out.

The location chosen for the papal mass was the municipal sports ground on the outskirts of town. Hard red clay that had effortlessly withstood a thousand soccer matches was being crushed into a fine powder by a myriad of urgent feet.

Fuentes estimated two miles to go. The Mustang progressed painstakingly around a bow in the road. In the distance, through gaps in the traffic, he could make out the modest outlines of the old village of Santa Ana: a church steeple, a creaking water tower, some storefronts, and, nearer to them, what seemed an ocean of lush flowers – saffron, pomegranate, and vermilion – but were, in fact, the peaks of umbrellas the faithful had brought with them to protect against the summer sun.

Red Cross infirmaries dappled the landscape toward the horizon like the tournament pavilions of medieval knights. The total number of clinics was outstripped threefold by sandbagged police posts, each with its own tent and giraffe-like radio antennae, and each housing a unit of *federales* toting shotguns.

Heavily armed troops manned checkpoints along the thoroughfares into town and redirected a legion of stuttering motor vehicles into parking corrals located in a sweeping circle along the remotest reaches of the site. From those locations, all pilgrims, save the infirm and the powerful, had to walk.

An immense canopy fashioned from pure white cotton dominated the field. Fully seven stories in height, it was so colossal that one could almost imagine the material put to worthy service as the mainsail of a China clipper. Within it rested an altar fashioned from rosewood and shaped in the style of a peasant's worktable. This unique sanctuary was clearly visible from all sides.

A giant gold crown capped the zenith of the edifice. Huge pieces of artificial glass, expertly fashioned in the shapes and hues of precious stones, studded the crown and gave it an awe-inspiring effect.

A no-man's land, fully one hundred yards wide, separated the altar from the first echelon of pilgrims. This zone was patrolled by helmeted soldiers resolutely strutting in pairs along its perimeter. The military were equipped with menacing Uzi submachine guns and correspondingly sinister attitudes. Toward the center of the restricted area, two enormous white bull's-eyes were spray-painted on the scorched bronze soil. Lush red carpets lined with white azaleas led from the circular imprints to the base of the altar.

A large tent had been erected to the west of the sanctuary. Gleaming highway buses motored patiently up to a slit in its side, and deposited volumes of white-vestmented priests, who then trooped off to a nearby parking area. At the other three points of the compass, massive aluminum bleachers surged outwards from the altar. Atop them, the rainbowed brilliance of a five-thousand-voice choir: the singers' gowns – red, yellow, and turquoise – billowed in a torrent of color. For the moment, their angelic voices were mute in expectation.

Cockleshell loudspeakers were strung atop huge, towering poles. All mewed a singularly bland rendition of *Ave Maria* orchestrated for strings – again and again – as a series of two-hundred-foot-high Jumbotrons, set randomly about the immense field, displayed collages fed to them by videographers detailed to the site: a wrinkled grandmother fingering a wooden rosary; a three-year-old *mestizo* boy slumbering in his mother's arms; a jowly businessman flipping through a gold-embossed Bible; a flock of Rayban-sporting nuns waving affably to the camera.

Another busload stopped at the tent by the altar, this one more touching than its predecessors. A dozen white-garbed clergy were removed from the coach by teams of *federales* and tenderly placed in wheelchairs, before they too disappeared into the shelter to prepare for the papal mass. The priests seemed docile to the point of indolence. Perhaps it was the barbarous combination of heat and humidity, Fuentes pondered. Or medication.

A pickup truck skidded to a stop behind the bus. Three workmen rushed out of the shade to greet it, dropped the tailgate, and lifted what appeared to be a section of rolled carpeting out of the flatbed. This they gingerly carried into the ceremonial tent. Curious, Miguel mused. Why would it be needed there? The camera switched once more, this time to a throng of school-uniformed children riotously waving papal and Mexican flags.

The visual images on the Jumbotrons were flawlessly choreographed to the strains of *Ave Maria*, as only a religious extravaganza could be. And in the manner of all things grandly liturgical, it had a time line. Clean digital numbering in the left bottom corner of each screen informed all that it was 8:16 in the morning.

The colossal throng surging to the altar was partitioned into manageable enclosures by a spider's web of heavy-duty roping. Crossing these at an angle were concentric circles; each with its peculiar color-coded entry scheme, with the sections nearest the altar reserved for the most distinguished of visitors.

There were twenty broad emergency lanes for essential services arbitrarily carved into the measureless human host. Miguel located one of them and locked in behind an army personnel carrier shunting sluggishly toward the heart of the field. Seen now from the air, he calculated that the Mustang would be perceived as just another municipal black-and-white rolling along among a hundred others also assigned to the massive security detail.

"*Jefe!*" Felix gasped. Fuentes started. A barber-pole barrier blocked traffic a hundred yards up the road. The personnel carrier jerked robot-like to the right, exposing the Mustang to view. Two paratroopers held the point. One of them had a field radio in his hand and was speaking into it. His facial expression was skeptical. He moved to his partner, a corporal, and pointed to the approaching police car.

"Get down," Miguel hissed. Chandler swiftly complied. Donovan did likewise. In the back seat, Asuncion needed no coaching. His revolver was out of its holster and resting in the darkened hollow of the console between the bucket seats. As he neared the obstruction, Miguel slowed his car to a crawl, pretending to negotiate between the rumbling military vehicle ahead and the sinuous sea of people that surrounded them.

Suddenly, a claxon boomed, loud as the foghorn on an Acapulco cruise ship. Miguel glimpsed into his rearview mirror. Out of nowhere, a Mercedes bus had crowded its way up to the bumper of the police Mustang. Ahead of them, the overworked military policeman began to aggressively flag Fuentes to one side. Another MP raised an automatic rifle to the ready position. Asuncion cocked his revolver.

"It's another load of priests in the bus behind us," Felix offered. "And probably very late."

Fuentes made up his mind. Without warning, he reached for the dash and flicked on a switch. A banshee wail filled the air as the police siren began to *mee-maw*. He stomped on the gas pedal and rushed the barrier, gesturing frantically for the two soldiers to raise the gate.

Twenty yards. Ten. At the last moment, the corporal flipped up the striped beam, stepped aside and grudgingly waved them through. They'd been lucky. They were just local *policia* – which meant they were less than nothing in the eyes of the army. Escorting a bus filled with burbling priests was about all they were deemed good for.

Fuentes kept his speed up as best he could. He flipped the sun visor down so that his face was obscured from view. Yet even inside the emergency lane and with the siren engaged, progress was painfully slow. The field was a living thing, and the devout continually surged over the rope barriers and across their trajectory. When they were certain that they were safely out of sight of

the two paratroopers, and then some, Fuentes swerved abruptly
to allow the bus to bully past.

Fuentes slowed the Mustang to a crawl, then halted. He
opened his window a sliver. The music had stopped, and had
been replaced by a low murmur. He vaguely made out the words;
thousands of people were reciting a rosary in unison.

They were now only five hundred yards from the altar. The
bus that had passed them was discharging its load of priests. Yet
a curious thing was happening. Here, among the common people,
and with no remaining checkpoints between them and the no-go
zone, all need for lawful order had evaporated. There was an
enormous, palpable tranquility in the audience.

Just ahead, a new apparition on the massive Jumbotrons. A fish-
eye shot of the throng in the sports field and spilling out far
beyond, a panoramic view taken from perhaps the very pinnacle of
the towering sanctuary, showing a sea of people so grand that only
God could count them. And then another shot, this one of massed
clergy strutting patiently about inside the shadowy confines of the
assembly tent. And a final exterior view of a three-hundred person
symphony orchestra seated on a makeshift stage in an open space
to the west of the altar, readying itself for performance.

Suddenly the scene shifted to a shot of a helicopter cruising
along in a brilliant cerulean sky, a snowy-white craft with gold
trim slashed across its fuselage and the papal coat of arms – the
crossed keys of Saint Peter – proudly depicted just below the
bubble cockpit. In a tiny, square window near the front of the
craft's cabin, a ruddy-faced passenger in crisp, ivory clothing: an
elderly, sanguine man, waving patiently back toward the camera.

A tumultuous roar went rolling through the crowd – a vigorous sound, intense as desert thunder in an August drought, joyous
as the first rain that flows from it – cresting, then ebbing, then
cresting once more as the man was recognized: "*Viva el Papa, Viva
el Papa!*" The field was suddenly electric with anticipation.

Lasers played nimbly across the upper surfaces of the ceremonial tent. The beams produced a bouquet of mountain roses, then
transfigured them into a hauntingly beautiful portrait of the

Virgin Mary, then back again. The man-made spectacle lasted perhaps a minute before the entire apparition was repeated.

Like all Mexicans, Fuentes knew the folk tale that was being evoked by the dazzling sound-and-light show. In the fifteenth century, in the hills of Tepeyac, north of Mexico City, it was said that a peasant named Juan Diego had seen a brown-skinned Virgin Mary bathed in a radiant aura. The Virgin desired that a shrine be erected to her memory at Tonantzin, a place where the Aztecs had long worshipped the Earth Mother.

The Virgin instructed Juan to go to the cathedral and relay this wish to Archbishop Zummarraga. The priest scrupulously demanded a sign to confirm that the visitation was indeed the Mother of God and not just the mad ramblings of a heathen.

Juan returned to the clergyman with his cactus-fiber cloak, or *tilma*, overflowing with rare roses of Castile. When the flowers fell from his mantle, they revealed a portrait of the Virgin. Our Lady of Guadaloupe, as she came to be called, became the patron of the peasants of Mexico and the object of much veneration.

And Juan Diego? He came to symbolize the complexity of the Mexican soul – its timidity and honor, dedication to God, and naiveté in the face of the temporal powers – often in ways quite removed from those originally intended by the Church.

Fuentes pondered his options. He had no idea where Obregon was or what his plans might be. But here, sitting in the middle of a field in Santa Ana, in a broken-down police car crammed with misfits and wanted persons, surrounded by a million innocents and the combined might of Mexico's army and its federal police force, he felt evil stirring.

"Well, My Lady," he whispered in near-despair. "What will it be today? A coat of flowers or a crown of thorns?"

He peered into the rearview mirror. "Maria? Do you want to take your chances and leave? You know you could still escape in this crowd with Mr. Chandler, and no one would notice."

Donovan chuckled. "Why would I leave you now, Miguel? Parked here, we have the best seats in the house."

The police radio came to life. Over the *federale* frequency came an American accent with the calm authority and bearing of a disciplined mind. "Heaven's Gate, this is Papa One. Am currently at Angels ten thousand ... bearing one niner-fiver. ETA to L-Zee, fourteen minutes. Firm at 0900 hours. Do you copy?"

"Papa One, this is Heaven's Gate ..." came the reply in Spanish-accented English. "That's a 10-4. We copy."

Asuncion vigorously tapped Miguel's shoulder. There! He pointed due north. Fuentes gazed into the haze. After a moment, several black flecks took form, as distinct as an insect swarm.

The Jumbotrons now showed masses of people tumultuously cheering, then the choir, then the symphony orchestra, and finally, the main altar, where priests were docilely forming up in long, orderly rows. Then – a multi-imaged collage of the four scenes, with the Sikorsky hovering, always at the center, seemingly transfixed in the sea blue morning air and, inside it, the placid man waving patiently from the small window behind the cockpit.

An elegant male tenor began a chant from somewhere in the massed choir:

> *Comfort ye, comfort ye my people, saith your God*
> *Speak ye comfortably to Jerusalem, and cry unto her*
> *That her warfare is accomplish'd*
> *That her Iniquity is pardoned.*
> *The voice of him that crieth in the wilderness;*
> *Prepare ye the way of the Lord*
> *Make straight in the desert a highway for our God.*

Fuentes instantly recognized the piece. It was the oratorio he'd heard in Obregon's office: the *Messiah*. The words were from the Bible, in English translation. The singer was joined by another, then another, and yet more, in an ever-mounting crescendo. Exquisite music filled the air, the pervasive resonance of lush strings and beautiful human voices.

> *Ev'ry valley shall be exalted*
> *and ev'ery mountain and hill made low;*

*the crooked straight
and the rough place plain.*

The melody became progressively more powerful. Lasers washing across the surface of the enormous canvas became instantly more striking, their colors richer, their lines of intersection more pronounced, as images of the flurry of roses and icon of the Virgin of Guadaloupe alternately seared the cloth.

And the glory of the Lord shall be revealed....

Gigantic screens captured a jubilant throng verging on delirium; a profusion of somber clergy, their robes flapping mutely in an unexpected desert zephyr; and the orchestra conductor, his severe red mane tossing tyrannically in rapture with the melody.

The symphony itself – violins, cellos, a brass section, and winds – and there, suddenly, at the upper corner of the screen, there near the large kettledrums, the tympani. There! Fuentes caught it!

In the very center of this outdoor extravaganza, where the sights and sounds were clinically orchestrated so that the E sharps and laser lights, the roses and the placid face of the Madonna, melded as one. There! Resting docilely on the stage next to the huge console that regulated the laser show and all other visuals, sat a trim, attaché-sized receptacle – striped lime and orange.

"What color did you say the container holding the VAX was?" Fuentes shouted with anxious anticipation.

"The box?" Chandler seemed perplexed. "The box was designed with bright scrolled pigments."

"Does it look something like that?" Fuentes gestured to the screen.

Chandler gasped as he eyed the gaily striped item. "That's it. The VAX!"

Fuentes leaned over to his detective. "The time, Felix?"

"Eight-forty-two, *Jefe*," Asuncion replied, nonplussed.

"'The people that walked in darkness have seen a great light ...'" Miguel observed quietly.

"*Jefe?*" Asuncion raised his eyebrows.

"It's a line from the Bible. The Book of Isaiah. 'They that dwell in the land of the shadow of death, upon them hath the light shined ...'" He paused. "It's also a stanza from Handel's *Messiah*. We've got to move."

The helicopter armada drew minutely closer, heading due south toward the large field. Viewing the jumbo screen, Miguel could now discern the crossed-key crest of the Holy See on the flank of the white Sikorsky. The escorting Blackhawk gunships threatened firepower. Down on the field, beige-coveralled ground crew rushed about to secure the two touchdown sites.

A new voice abruptly burst onto the police radio. This voice was speaking in Spanish, and repeating the phrases in clipped English: "Heaven's Gate? This is F – Foxtrot. Am currently Angels ten thousand ... bearing three-three-niner. ETA at L-Zee, seven minutes, thirty seconds. Firm at 0850. Do you copy?"

"That's a 10-4, F – Foxtrot."

And then yet a third voice. Spanish-speaking. Self-assured. Masterful. "Heaven's Gate? This is Eagle One. Am currently at Angels eleven thousand ... bearing four-zero-zero. ETA at L-Zee, twelve minutes. Repeat twelve minutes. Firm at 0855. Copy?"

"Eagle One." The same control in reply. "That's a 10-4. We copy."

Eagle One! Fuentes knew that code name all too well. It was reserved exclusively for the president of Mexico.

He hurried the Mustang. The words of the *Messiah* chorus burst inside the car, joyous, overpowering:

> *The Lord, whom ye seek,*
> *Shall suddenly come to His temple,*
> *Even the messenger of the Covenant,*
> *Whom ye delight in:*
> *Behold,*
> *He shall come,*
> *Saith the Lord of Hosts.*

Miguel scanned the horizon. Two flotillas loomed in the western sky, the first much smaller in size than the second. There were six craft in the initial swarm, a camouflaged Blackhawk chopper surrounded by a pride of royal-blue Huey gunships. An ivory Sikorsky, of the same class as that carrying the Pontiff, rested in the center of the second gaggle, flanked by seven military Blackhawks in matte-green finish. The choir sang on:

> *And he shall purify the sons of Levi,*
> *that they may offer unto the Lord*
> *an offering in righteousness ...*

The two aerial groups vectored hard eastward, then sharply south toward the field at Santa Ana, drifting down the same sloping route that the papal entourage was employing, but obviously preceding it by a good few miles. But for a small reef of hydro towers cutting east-west between the current location of the chopper squadrons and their impending touchdown, their pathway was clear.

The Mustang was moving forward quite quickly now. Here and there, soldiers standing along the roped-off perimeters to the emergency route had drawn their automatic rifles, hesitating to fire only because of the pressing crowd and their own ample astonishment at witnessing the unexpected – a decrepit black-and-white that had broken the security cordon.

"Time?" Fuentes shouted as the vehicle bounced and jerked wildly over the uneven bedrock. "I need the exact time!"

"Eight forty-eight," Donovan yelled from the back seat.

Thousands looked on, shocked and anxious as the police unit bulleted toward the open track surrounding the main platform. Paratroopers raised their Uzis. Some assumed a kneeling position and drew a bead on their target. Fuentes was certain the security forces had recognized the Mustang. He knew the only thing saving them from certain death was the immensity of the crowd that engulfed them.

349

"What are you doing, *Jefe*?" Asuncion screamed as he tumbled about in the back seat.

"The VAX!" Fuentes warned. "We have to get to the VAX before it does what it has been programmed to do!"

To the east, scarcely a hundred yards distant, the camouflaged Blackhawk carrying the unknown VIP briskly descended onto the landing zone. Hovering above it, at staggered heights, their port machine guns bristling, were the attendant Hueys. The Blackhawk touched down.

Several passengers disembarked from the chopper. A gaggle of armored cars, paratrooper strike teams, and federal agents formed a protective shield around them.

For a moment, Miguel caught the object of their swirling commotion, tall and noble, even in ordinary peasant garb, a corn-cob pipe held in a firm jaw, unruly raven hair parted in the middle. "*Comandante* Bruno," he whispered in disbelief.

And there at his side, moving with feline grace, was Obregon. As he ushered his charges toward the protection of a bulletproof glass enclosure by the altar, the *comandante* hazarded a glance in Miguel's direction. He barked orders. A team of soldiers broke from the armed swarm and shifted at the double toward the Mustang.

In the sky to the north, the first Sikorsky took shape, surrounded by the protective ring of armed Blackhawks. It hovered in a holding pattern as it waited for clearance to land. Eagle One, *El Aguila Una* – The President of Mexico. Further afield, the second Sikorsky, the one that carried the Pope, circled in ingenious evasive patterns with its accompanying gunships.

> *Oh thou that tellest good tidings to Zion,*
> *get thee up into the high mountain ...*

Directly ahead of them loomed the huge ceremonial tent, with a glistening gold-leaf crown capping its seven-story canopy. The majestic symphony orchestra; the mammoth choir. Then, suddenly, fireworks rent the air, and sparklers positioned in the halo above the Madonna whirled like hoops. The laser show increased in intensity; dusky roses melded on the canvas into the venerable image of Our Lady of Guadaloupe, then back again, in harmony with the orchestra's crescendos. Miguel marveled as fine laser filaments speared surgically up into image – ruby and turquoise, emerald and tan.

With reverent crowds shuffling uneasily behind and a ragged skirmish line of troopers awaiting their advance, Fuentes skidded the Mustang onto the exposed ground before the altar. Machine-gun tracers arced toward them like pieces of the sun falling from the sky. The left rear tire exploded. Miguel struggled with the steering wheel and slowed the car. He was only a hundred yards from the orchestra. Sixty. Fifty. Forty. The Mustang fishtailed. As if on cue, a sustained volley rang out, pockmarking the windshield.

"Duck!" Fuentes screamed. He instinctively twirled the wheel to the right, away from the shots, just in time to avoid another salvo. *Thwack! Thwack! Thwack!* The Mustang struggling to keep up torque. Thirty yards to go!

An army Hummer barreled into view to Miguel's left. He swerved out of its way. Glass shattered. A garbled shout. Fuentes glanced, horrified, to his passenger. Chandler lay slumped, blood oozing from a sniper's bullet to his forehead.

Suddenly, the rapid thrum of automatic fire walloped the rear of the Mustang. In the back seat, Felix collapsed into a pool of dark-red gore. Only the woman remained unharmed. Miguel steeled himself as nausea took hold.

Donovan grabbed his shoulder. "Not now," she commanded. "We must keep going! We're nearly there!"

An armored personnel carrier came at them, hitting the side of the Mustang and crushing it as it pushed it along. The car began to flip and roll. The two lifeless bodies flopped about aimlessly inside the cabin, mingling with fresh blood, crushed Dixie cups, and refuse. A persistent groan, like the sound of a huge can-opener, as the Mustang was wrenched apart. The car was impelled upside down, then back, landing on its axles with a loud crash.

Donovan lay partially atop the console; she pushed Chandler's lifeless body to the side. Fuentes shouldered his door; it held stubbornly shut.

The personnel carrier backed off, and then made another run. It plowed once more into the side of the police car. The car made one roll, coming to rest on the passenger side.

Miguel lay in a heap atop Chandler's corpse. He peered out at the world through the crushed windshield. Everything seemed insanely distorted from this position, as though seen by a lunatic through a child's prism.

Engine smoke and dust enveloped the interior. The pungent stench of feces and hot metal and human sweat surrounded him. The acrid haze grew denser.

Donovan started to cough. Miguel, gasping for oxygen, knew he had no choice. He crouched in the tight seat space and pulled Donovan behind him, then took his Glock and fired it rapidly into the windscreen. After a half dozen rounds, he flipped to the butt end of the pistol and hammered at the fractured glass until he had an opening.

The Glock flew out of his hands. He punched a passage through with his bare fists, dragging Donovan along. Smoke from the dying car curled up through the air.

Outside, he was engulfed in anguished cries. Women screamed, children wailed, and men cursed and shouted. Pilgrims stampeded through the ropes that had cordoned them into groups. Individuals too paralyzed to move were caught like dumb cattle in the stampede. Police used truncheons and fists to contain the near riot.

Fuentes peered through indistinct shapes, spitting particles of dirt from arid lips. He was standing less than twenty yards from the orchestra, perhaps ten from the location of the VAX 10. He and Donovan were as yet undetected in the filthy, swirling air. Miguel glanced at a Jumbotron: 8:53 hours.

Fuentes.

39 Fuentes's eyes were deliberately concentrated on the lasers piercing the morning sky. The image on the colossal panorama was now that of the Virgin of Guadaloupe, magnificently portrayed in azure and beige, ruby and jade. Laser lights lanced upward to the canvas, with the unerring precision that only the finest technology could bring.

Fuentes looked for patterns and found what he feared. One of the beams seemed errant. Fiery as an August sun, accurate as a hunter's blade, it inched immeasurably but steadily, off the canvas, out toward the north, out toward the second tier of helicopters shepherding the Mexican president's personal craft.

It was then that Miguel began to fully appreciate what was happening. It was also at that precise moment that Ramon Obregon glanced out from a bulletproof compound constructed behind the altar and spied Fuentes standing amid the clouds of dust. Their eyes met. Miguel could see wild fury on the *comandante*'s face. And he knew it was directed at him. And only him.

Suddenly Obregon did something both remarkable and telling. He bulled his way out of the protective bay onto the exposed altar dais, viciously shouldering past the assembled VIPs. Fuentes watched for a moment and knew exactly where Obregon was heading.

"The VAX!" Fuentes shouted to Donovan. "We've got to get to it!"

Security forces closed in on the site. Frightened people shoved and fought to escape the area. Some were trampled underfoot in those insane seconds. And yet, captive to the religious frenzy of the moment, for most of those gathered in the sports field, it was as if nothing had occurred.

In the confusion, Donovan and Fuentes broke into a mad sprint, heading straight toward the orchestra. Donovan ran well, she was soon a few feet ahead of Miguel. A suited *federale* tried to block their way. A straight arm from Fuentes and he was down.

The second swarm of choppers shepherding the Eagle hovered

in a pattern less than two miles away, near the line of hydro wires strung east-west across the horizon. The principal pilot in the formation was holding off from landing as he witnessed the melee below. He was radioing for instructions.

Six nautical air miles to the north, the commander of the papal airship harbored no such doubts. He hard-booted his Sikorsky west, then due north, moving at a steady clip toward the relative safety of the United States, with a timorous coterie of Mexican air force escort Hueys ragtagging behind.

This radical evasive maneuver was captured by the U.S. Air Force E-3 nestled some 50,000 feet in the ice-blue atmosphere over Nogales. But it wasn't the only blip on the radar screen for the specialists inside the pressurized cabin of the Sentry.

At that exact moment, Colorado Springs gave fresh instructions to the two-nation air cover that had brought the papal party to this crossroad in the cosmos. In the ensuing half minute, the dedicated squadron of American F-15s and their Mexican air force F-5 counterparts would be furiously revectored to the air quadrant that now hosted Papa One.

At the same instant, the two sticks of Thunderbolts heading back to Davis Monthan were redirected to close cover at airspace 600 feet over Mexican Sonora, to place themselves between the potentially vulnerable VIP and any proximate, though as yet undetermined, ground threat. Estimated time for completion for such a drastic logistical procedure? Three minutes, forty-two seconds.

As the five-thousand-voice choir started up again, the Jumbotrons showed a video of the Pope at St. Peter's Basilico. The sun flared down as the words of the *Messiah* thundered across the field in Sonora. Fireworks exploding in the halo around the Virgin had largely masked the gunfire. Most of the crowd was unaware that anything was amiss.

Fuentes peered uncertainly toward the horizon. He saw the laser locked onto the white Sikorsky that carried the Mexican president. The aircraft still dawdled along the hydro corridor. At that instant, Fuentes appreciated what was going to happen.

Gasping, he arrived at the orchestra area. It lay before him in a raised half-moon, with the string section at its heart, the wood-wind and brass positioned higher, and percussion instruments at its very apogee.

He bounded up a slender metal staircase, bulldozing past the astounded conductor. Donovan pounced onstage alongside him as they plowed through a forest of double basses, sending their thunderstruck owners sprawling. They clawed through banks of musicians toward the attaché case that was resting upright on the floor and was looped with a large bundle of cables into the master control console. It was the VAX 10!

Fuentes cursed aloud. They were running out of time. Obregon was virtually beside the VAX, less than ten feet from the console.

The time on the Jumbotron showed 8:54. The orchestra had ceased playing, yet it didn't matter. The enormous throng that filled the field to overflowing was in a catatonic frenzy.

Obregon reached the console. As 8:55 appeared on the Jumbotron, Obregon looked at Fuentes and pointed to the north, to the broad, blue open sky where the VAX's beam had locked on to the approaching Sikorsky.

The airship started to vibrate, slowly at first, then with ever-greater frequency. Its nose bucked turbulently downward, then up, then to one side. As its troublesome arc widened, the attendant Blackhawk escorts scurried to avoid its massive blades.

Fuentes peered furiously about the orchestra pit. He had time for but a single act. There was no margin for error. He grabbed the base of a music stand and raised the metal tube to his shoulder. Taking quick aim, he threw it spear-like at the bank of cables.

The speakers suddenly uttered a shrill shriek. The slew of lasers died. The Jumbotrons faded to black. The crowd gasped. Four thousand feet above, the Sikorsky sluggishly began to right itself.

A backup electrical system began to kick in and innocuous footage of the Pontiff blazed once more across the outdoor screens, bringing a measure of tranquility to much of the crowd. Fuentes anxiously looked for Obregon, but he had disappeared. He motioned to Donovan to follow him into the sanctuary.

The inside of the ceremonial tent was dark and stuffy. The air reeked of incense and earthy red clay. The temperature hovered at 100 degrees. Fuentes's eyes had difficulty adapting. He heard the metallic crash of a gate closing, the hiss of heavy machinery.

Shapes began to take on form. Seven stories of complicated construction supported the canopy: an intricate cross-lacing of aluminum beams arching upwards, all tethered together by black guide wire. It was akin to standing at the base of a miniature Eiffel Tower.

High above, a sequence of planks fitted diagonally across the metal bracing to form a level surface just below the peaked ceiling. The platform was proportionately sized so that there were, on all sides, several feet of clearance between it and the canvas skin. An elevator had been constructed from ground level to this height, and it now accelerated rapidly to the loftiest regions of the tent.

Obregon peered to ground level through the elevator's trellised gate. His face held a disquieting blend of abject frenzy and sublime confidence. The throaty clamor of the motor filled the space. Abruptly, the machinery stopped. Fuentes heard the sound of a metal door scraping open and the rapid staccato of feet pounding on wooden planking.

Fuentes and Donovan clambered up the braces toward the deck. Sweat poured off their faces. Finally, gasping, they reached the top. It was fully enclosed and capped by a peaked roof made of plywood sheets that dovetailed down and out, in all directions, like the apex of a pyramid. Miguel raised his head and peered tentatively across the length of the platform.

The walls were constructed of canvas and wood. Geometric shapes had been carved into them to hold pieces of prismatic glass. Each of the prisms was hinged so that it could be lifted up. Natural light flowing through them was a blend of sunlight-tinged topaz and lime and cobalt. Fuentes quickly recognized the mock jewels of the man-made crown.

The lookout platform held technical apparatus, including radio switches and remote cameras – this was the observation and security area for monitoring the multitudes below. A series of generator-operated ventilation fans shoved around what little tepid air there was.

The floor area was functionally partitioned into segments by canvas shrouds. Raising one, he observed the elevator resting in the central spine of the edifice. Its doors were open.

He raised the second tarp and for a moment couldn't believe what met his eyes. A dozen male bodies lay slumped about the deck like sacks of flour. Each had a bullet hole neatly drilled into his forehead. They all wore priestly garb, and some had orange-and-white polka dot bandannas knotted around their necks. Zapatistas!

In the corner facing north, Obregon crouched on one knee, as if genuflecting, before one of the opened portals. A rocket-launcher rested on his left shoulder. The device closely resembled the item depicted in the diagram Miguel had found at Larendo – the one in the box originating in Tajikistan that had been shipped by Humberto Guzman on the *Cassandra*. A half-rolled carpet, regal crimson, lay at Obregon's feet.

Miguel apprehensively gazed beyond Obregon, through the portal to the hydro wires, where a single white Sikorsky cautiously hovered amid a gaggle of jungle-camouflaged Blackhawks.

He heard the swell of music again, the choir gaining strength and power:

> *For to us a Child is born*
> *Unto us a Son is given*
> *And the government shall be upon His shoulder*
> *And His name shall be called wonderful,*
> *Counsellor,*
> *The Mighty God,*
> *the Ever Lasting Father,*
> *The Prince of Peace*

Suddenly, a dense violet flash spewed from the muzzle of the rocket-launcher, accompanied by a roar that engulfed the entire tent. It was as if someone had cranked open a doorway leading straight down to hell. Fuentes and Donovan dove for the floor, their ears ringing. Milliseconds later, the Sikorsky blew apart, sending a torrent of metallic confetti particles raining onto the earth below. The blast recoil tore through the tarpaulin behind Obregon, leaving a smoking hole.

"*Olah!*" Obregon bellowed as he raised his right arm in triumph. The *federale* calmly placed the rocket-launcher beside one of the prone corpses and peered out of the portal at the immense crowd, as if it were the most natural thing on earth to do after committing murder.

He casually opened his jacket and removed a gold cigarette-holder and similarly styled lighter. From the holder, he extracted one of his beloved Sofias. He lit the cigarette with a steady hand and sucked in the smoke through clenched teeth in covetous wisps.

Fuentes could hear the frantic tumult rising from the huge multitude, a large and mournful wail bordering on pandemonium.

Obregon turned to face them. His face was slightly flushed, yet he seemed strangely sedate. "I wanted you to witness this. You, like so many other pilgrims have had a very hard journey."

"You've just murdered those people aboard the helicopter in cold blood!" Fuentes raged.

Obregon reached into his coat pocket, removed a Glock pistol, and trained it on his accusers. "No, *amigos,*" he retorted. "I'm afraid that's not what history will record as having happened." He gestured to the corpses strewn about his feet.

"The good *padres* I've gathered here are actually Zapatista rebels, my friends." He did not try to mask his distaste at the word. "The public will be told they were part of a murder plot to assassinate the president of Mexico. Successfully, I might add. Though he doesn't know it yet, Bruno has conveniently provided us with his bodyguards. We've placed them here so that they'll be found with the incriminating evidence on their person. Their deaths will be viewed as a direct consequence of the gallant police action that followed the brutal slaying of our nation's leader."

With his Glock, Obregon offhandedly gestured to the distant black smudge where the Sikorsky had once been. "Bye-bye, *Señor*

Presidente," he chortled with a lopsided smirk on his face. His eyes had a glazed look to them.

"It would have been tidier and certainly more efficient if we'd used the VAX. That's why we sought it – 100 percent assurance and no chance of anyone important being implicated. But, it doesn't matter now. The launcher was surprisingly accurate from this distance, and the outcome proved to be the same. In the end, these bodies would still have lain here, along with the launcher." A shrug. "Face it, Miguel, your courageous effort went for nothing."

Donovan and Fuentes inched closer. Obregon caught the subtle movement. "Watch where you step. There are trip wires everywhere. I've set them to trigger on contact. One wrong step and …" A sly grin. "Poof!" He snapped his fingers.

"Why did you do this?" Fuentes asked.

"Why? Because that ignorant fool in the presidential palace in Mexico City was going to sign away offshore rights to some extremely valuable property in Chiapas, Miguel. My associates couldn't allow that to happen."

"Chiapas?"

Obregon nodded. "Correct. The oil in the Mar Muerto. Forget what that holy man from Rome says. Those filthy Zapatista savages have no more right to it than my dog."

"And so you committed cold-blooded murder?"

"I prefer to call the action a spontaneous diversion." Obregon smiled. "As far as the public is concerned, a team of Zapatistas will have killed the President of Mexico – not me."

"That's not rational." Miguel shook his head in dismay. "How would that help the Chiapas cause? Surely the peasants would have benefited the most from the offshore treaty."

For one small moment, Ramon Obregon looked strangely serene and remarkably compassionate. "In a few days, it will become public knowledge that *Comandante Bruno* has sold out his people for a piece of the backroom action." His voice grew weary. "After we spill that story, these corpses will soon begin to look like martyrs in comparison to Bruno. The public will conclude that this action was justifiable. Zapatista infighting to torpedo the treaty."

"The lies!" Fuentes snapped. "No one will believe this cover-up!"

"Why would I bother to lie now?" Obregon raised his voice in self-righteous disbelief. "I have no reason to. You can't harm this operation any more. What's done is done!"

"So what are you going to do with us?" Fuentes asked.

"Do?" Obregon sniffed derisively. "You should, by rights, be dead. I suppose I could expend a few bullets to make certain it happens once and for all . . . ." The *federale* seemed to relish the notion.

Miguel felt his back stiffen. He reached out to grasp Donovan's hand. It was cold.

"What do we do now, Miguel?" she whispered. She was trembling ever so slightly.

Fuentes steeled himself. "Close your eyes and tap your heels together three times," he remarked tenderly. "And think to yourself, there's no place like home ..." He stared at his tormenter and was surprised to discover that he no longer felt anything. No anger. No contempt. Just an empty, cold stoicism.

"I could kill you both ..." Obregon seemed to derive a certain perverse satisfaction from that specific notion. "Then again, I'd rather have the gratification of parading you in public. You – Fuentes – because since I've known you, you've been such an arrogant, hypocritical bastard. You deserve to be ridiculed by all of Mexico." He turned to the woman. "And you, Miss Donovan, because I sense it might be of benefit to me to have captured a wanted, and might I say, attractive criminal."

Obregon strode over to them, delicately avoiding the thin piano wire that traversed the breadth of the floor. Fuentes followed the thread to a box lodged against an electrical wall panel. He grimly imagined what hidden explosives it might trigger. He decided that madness such as this could be as calculated as it was cruel.

The *federale* was within inches of them now. Suddenly, Donovan spat at him. Obregon gasped, then swore, and passed a hand across the spittle. He drew back his hand to strike her. "You bitch!"

Then, the elevator doors opened and three large men stepped out, business-suited, glacial-featured, and wearing wrap-around sunglasses. They stood calmly, eyeing Obregon and his captives.

Confusion clouded Obregon's face. "Where is my support team?" he demanded imperiously of the newcomers.

"Waiting downstairs," the tallest of the three answered. His voice lacked tone and interest in his accuser. "The minister thought it would be best." Then, by way of explanation, he added, "We're from DFS."

Obregon grunted grudgingly. Hearing this, he knew better than to complain.

The ride to ground level was short, less then a minute in duration. Miguel considered his situation. Neither he nor Donovan had been handcuffed. But in these close quarters, it meant nothing. He wondered what lay in store for them.

The noise from the ceremony outside the tent had become quite ear-splitting. Hundreds of thousands of people were shouting in discordant ecstasy. The massive symphony and *Messiah* chorus was amplified by a sound system that roared to the very gates of heaven.

And then, intruding on this accumulated confusion, was the eggbeater chop of aircraft blades approaching at a low level, rapidly, from the north. Obregon looked bewildered. An incoming helicopter? After all that had happened? It couldn't be!

A hollow thump. They had reached ground level. Abruptly, the elevator gate swung open. There were perhaps a half dozen individuals standing in semidarkness awaiting them. One of the DFS agents stepped out first and directed Donovan to three shadows that fleetly took her away.

Obregon pushed the Glock into the small of Miguel's back. "Now, as for you," he hissed.

At that moment, a man stepped out from among the silhouettes, a slight man in his late forties with oiled brown hair, blotchy skin, and conspicuous eyes. He sported a rumpled off-white shirt and ill-fitting seersucker suit that hung from stooped shoulders like discarded clothes on a scarecrow. Somehow Fuentes thought he recognized the stranger, yet he couldn't quite place the face.

He didn't need to, because Obregon did it for him. "Guzman!" The *federale* gasped in astonishment.

"Gentlemen," the newcomer acknowledged with a diffident nod. He turned to his shadowed companions. "Arrest this individual!"

The order was carried out swiftly and smoothly. Obregon was instantly disarmed and handcuffed.

"Not me, you fools!" Obregon shrieked, struggling with his captors. "Him!" He nodded furiously toward Fuentes. "You want him!"

"No," Guzman chided. He smiled, timidly showing a row of stained teeth. "I'm afraid it is you who is under arrest, *senor*."

Obregon's face turned red with fury. "Arrest?" He howled. "You two-bit stock hustler! You have no power over me!"

Guzman stiffened visibly at the accusation. "Haven't they told you yet, Ramon?" he remarked tonelessly. "I've just been appointed your successor. I'm the new *comandante* for the State of Sonora."

"By whose authority?" Obregon sputtered. "Who?"

The slight, sullied man gave him a look of benign pity. "Who? By the warrant of the president of Mexico."

Obregon's face clouded. "That can't be! Estrada is dead!"

Guzman crooked an eyebrow. "I'm afraid you are mistaken, Ramon. President Estrada is in good health."

"Then who was in that helicopter?"

"Who? Why, your good friend the minister of justice, of course!" Guzman replied with sedate composure. "I'm afraid our president caught an unexpected case of motion sickness. It was strongly suggested that *Señor* Rivera might be available to take his place in the aircraft."

"Impossible!" Obregon asserted contemptuously. "This is a bluff!"

"Not at all." Guzman's eyes narrowed. There was more than a sliver of malice in them. "If you care to look down to the landing pad below us, it will soon become quite clear."

Obregon was rudely shuffled to a gap in the tent that over-looked the vast field. At that very instant, a large Sikorsky helicopter with a wide gold band across its body and an ornate coat of arms painted beneath the pilot's cockpit delicately touched down atop one of the bull's-eyes located by the main altar. The craft was immediately girdled by a horde of armed security personnel.

Moments later, as Obregon was escorted to a waiting armored car, a white-cassocked man with ruddy skin and a noticeably stooped back, born of carrying too many burdens for too long a time, tentatively descended from the Sikorsky and tenderly bent down to kiss the ground of Mexico.

And there, emerging to greet the Pope from among the pressing mass of dignitaries, strode Emilio Estrada, president of Mexico, ebullient, joyful, and very much alive.

Thursday, August 9, 9:10 a.m.
Santa Ana

40 At Guzman's insistence, Fuentes accompanied him back to the crown of the ceremonial structure for the commencement of the papal mass. A not-so-subtle escort trailed behind. There was nowhere else to go and no real reason to. Here, seven stories above a sea of zealous humanity, in a manner that was not so much invitation as injunction, Guzman cordially invited him to remain as his personal guest.

As the choir launched into the introductory hymn – Beethoven's *Ode to Joy* – Miguel learned why the Pope had returned to Santa Ana after what had first appeared to be his brisk retreat to the relative safety of Arizona. According to Guzman, His Holiness had been advised that several Mexican officials, including the minister of justice, had been killed when their helicopter had accidentally struck a high-voltage hydro pole on its final descent into the sports field. It was the Pope's own decision to return and pay homage to those unfortunates in his prayer for the departed. The signing of the treaty would now follow the Mass.

The Zapatista bodies? Fuentes wondered aloud as the choir chanted the "Gloria." What of them?

Guzman was mock serious in reply. Yes, indeed. Simply bodyguards that *Comandante* Bruno had brought to the confidential deliberations. A wry smile. The public would disingenuously be told that the twelve had perished in a fiery bus crash as pilgrims to the Santa Ana ceremony: "The deaths of the faithful, balancing the deaths of the mighty that had already darkened the day."

"So that's why they were dressed as priests?" Miguel pressed with halfhearted belligerence. Was Ramon Obregon right when he said they were Zapatista renegades rebelling against their *comandante*'s hypocrisy?

Guzman deftly avoided the query and made an observation on the beautiful music. It was Bach they were playing now, was it not?

Fuentes sat back and judiciously said nothing. He knew he had little choice.

The time came for the sermon. The Pope began his oration in Spanish. It was a lengthy one that utilized his fluency in six languages, including the obtuse and circumspect one of grand diplomacy. His Holiness lauded the president of Mexico for his insight in revisiting the Mexican constitution to achieve dignity and self-worth for the natives of Chiapas, and also the Zapatista leadership for its willingness to accept reasonable compromise on the tortuous road to lasting peace.

"Does Bruno know about the murdered men?" Fuentes whispered anew.

"No," Guzman replied frankly. "We want his signature on the treaty first. And we'll have it. I consider the death of the twelve the cost of doing business. Bruno will find out in due course. I think he'll actually be pleased they've been nullified. But that knowledge now – and out of context – might prove a little too awkward, even for Bruno. This deal is too important to be jeopardized by a dozen ignorant peasants with red mud between their toes and bedrock between their ears.

"Let's face it – in the next hour the Pope will witness an historic agreement to extend native land rights on the ocean shelf from the Chiapas shoreline. This covenant is good for the people of Mexico." He paused before he continued. "And others."

Miguel looked at his host quizzically.

"Come, come," Guzman reproached. "Even morality plays like this one depend on technology to carry them to success. By structuring the treaty very shrewdly, PEMEX will not be involved in the offshore drilling. Our liberal media friends will assume that the Mexican government has acceded to the will of the people of Chiapas for self-determination.

"The holding company that will actually control the drilling off Chiapas is a joint venture between a private Mexican consortium and its American counterpart, also a private firm. They will collect some 70 percent of the oil proceeds for the risks they endure. The remainder will be given to the poor of Chiapas. Naturally," Guzman continued ebulliently, "though it may not be apparent in public documents, both consortiums have a strong affiliation to principals presently here in Santa Ana."

"The president of Mexico," Miguel presumed bluntly.

An affirmative nod.

"*Comandante* Bruno ..." A second nod. And then a slightly more tentative foray. "And probably an influential American oil corporation with ties to Congress," Fuentes tossed in with considered cynicism.

"Of course." Guzman responded, as if it were all as natural as a desert sunrise. "Does it really matter to you which company?" he added with tenacious candor.

"No," Miguel said. "They all seem to have connections in Washington, don't they?"

"Now you're catching on, *hombre!*" Guzman laughed aloud. It was as if they were sharing an innocent joke between friends.

The Mass had reached the consecration of the bread and wine. Fuentes turned to watch the screens. The Pope looked old and frail, his face flushed and contorted with the effort. Miguel could almost feel the exertion it took the old man to raise the chalice above his head.

Fuentes politely waited for the prayer for the departed before he said what he really felt. "So this whole charade was nothing more than a struggle between PRI factions to decide who ultimately controls Chiapas oil."

A cavalier shrug. "I suppose you could call it that. Though I might be more sensitive to the political complexities of the piece."

"Suppose?" Miguel shook his head in disgust. "What else would you call it but a charade?"

"Me?" Guzman replied solemnly. "I'd call it free enterprise."

"Free enterprise?" Fuentes practically spat out the words. "All those deaths? All that sorrow? You really think the oil off Chiapas was worth so many innocent lives?"

Guzman pursed his lips. His eyes grew hard. He had tired of the game. "If not, Fuentes, perhaps you can tell me what is. We have fingerprints that connect you to the death of one of your officers – a man named Velas. And he wasn't nearly as valuable to anyone as Chiapas oil will be to Mexico!"

It was all Miguel could do to hold his anger in check. "That's extortion!" he growled. "You have nothing to implicate me. Nothing!"

"Extortion?" Guzman shrugged. "I prefer to call it good planning. Then again … planning is nine-tenths suspicion and one-tenth luck, isn't it?"

The choir began a chant, the "Pater Noster" – the Our Father. The enormous audience joined in, drowning out the choir with their fervor.

"You get my drift?" Guzman continued darkly, as he peered out at the millions. "The variance between suspicion and luck?" He turned and gazed into Miguel's face. "I think your notion of luck is not so strong a suit to hold as are my suspicions of you. Certainly from now on."

Miguel shrewdly made no reply. "What of Donovan?"

"She will never be seen in Mexico again."

"You can't just murder her!" Miguel bristled.

"Who said anything about murder?" Guzman tut-tutted. "If Donovan stays in Mexico, she becomes a hopeless encumbrance. The American government wishes to resolve this issue seamlessly. She will be relocated in a discreet manner. In any event, she has played out her role according to the script."

"I'm sorry?" Miguel interjected.

"You didn't know?" Guzman seemed taken aback. "After Chandler died, she was given great freedoms to ensure that the VAX got to Obregon."

"That much I've surmised," Miguel commented dryly.

"What you couldn't understand is that, after escaping from the courtroom in Hermosillo, she continued to coordinate her efforts with the Government of Mexico."

"Even after she told me she was on the run from *federales*?"

"She wasn't being all together untrue," Guzman remonstrated. "She was fleeing Obregon."

A silence. "Then she misled me," Fuentes remarked bitterly.

"No." Guzman stiffened. "Lieutenant Donovan had an important job to do. You were a vital ingredient in a larger equation. But you were questioning too much and too soon. As a consequence, Donovan was just being practical in her dealings with you."

"Practical?" Fuentes was seething inside. "And me? What of me?"

"You are a sensible man ..." Guzman responded bluntly. "You will do what must be done. For yourself and for Mexico." He shrugged. "There is no other option in life. For any of us."

Fuentes looked down over the field at Santa Ana. It was the time for the sacrament of Communion. In long, reverent lines from all directions of the compass, thousands upon thousands of poor and ordinary people moved forward to receive the host and renew their beliefs.

"I envy them their blind faith in goodness," Miguel mused aloud.

"Goodness!" Guzman snorted cynically at the spectacle. "What is goodness but something that makes us feel righteous about ourselves? Spare me the goodness, Fuentes." The nimble little man mechanically brushed dandruff off his shoulder. "Give me a strong dose of reality."

Miguel seemed perplexed. "You would term a grand fraud being perpetrated on the people of Chiapas a reality to be sought after?"

"I would," Guzman replied without batting an eyelash. "And I would be proud to. Much good will come of it. Our actions will give those pitiful *mestizos* down there in that godforsaken field more televisions, more dishwashers, more freezers. It will bring them schools and homes and prosperity."

Guzman paused, as if to reflect on what he'd said. His voice became gentler, his manner more conciliatory. "You know, Miguel," he offered, "consider this. At the end of the day, reality isn't so bad a thing to hang your hat on, in spite of how you personally might struggle against it. Embrace reality, *hombre*. It will stay with you long after everything you might believe in is gone."

Miguel gazed out at the vast expanse of humanity, at the altar and the rich and timeless ceremonies. He pondered the faces on the Jumbotrons – the children, the cripples, the elderly; the complex-featured men and ardent women. And in their deep and lustrous eyes he saw something far greater than what Guzman now offered him.

"Will reality replace such beliefs, *Señor* Guzman?" he countered in a cautious voice. "Will it really?"

Fuentes felt the heat swelter all around and found the sacred music wrapping him in a cocoon. He peered up at the vast desert sky above. It was pale blue, yet, for the first time in a long time, bright as hope.

Monday, August 13, morning.
Mexico City

41 The Human Resource wing at *federale* headquarters in Mexico City hadn't changed much since he'd been there to accept his assignment as the *jefe* in Coronado less than seven months before. *Señor* Ernesto still held court. He still smiled a crooked smile. And he still wore black.

On the good *señor*'s desk was a newly framed photo of his daughter lounging aboard her forty-five-foot sailboat. She wore a University of California T-shirt. She'd been accepted to Berkeley and in a few weeks would begin her first semester, studying modern languages and interpretive dance.

Señor Ernesto pensively scratched the scar on his right cheek. As a magnanimous gesture of gratitude from the president of Mexico, work would be found for Miguel.

Still, he must realize that there was still the contentious issue of harboring the *Yanqui* woman, his protests to the contrary. Surely Fuentes knew he'd publicly broken the law of the land. And that as an official of that law, he was honor bound to resign from the *policia* forthwith with no direct financial consideration offered, regardless of what Guzman might have implied. After all, the new *federale* police director for Sonora was a civilian and had no experience with operational matters. Nor could he be expected to understand such realities.

Miguel sat up in his seat.

Señor Ernesto coughed. He always seemed to when there was something stuck in his throat or gnawing at his conscience. The *señor* fluttered a meaty hand impatiently about the air between them, as if he were swatting at an insolent gnat. There was an option being offered should Fuentes wish to embrace it. His window of opportunity was small. He had twenty-four hours in which to make up his mind.

Or else?

The *federale* boss grunted ominously. He pushed a plain manila envelope across the table. It made a quiet rustling sound on the redwood desktop.

Fuentes contemplated throwing it back in the old goat's face. But the whim died as meekly as a trickle stream in an *arroyo*. He wordlessly took the envelope and set off for home.

Señor Ernesto informed him that he would be taken to the bus station. From there, he'd have to make his way alone to the cross-roads at San Cristobal. He would be provided with a compli-mentary one-way ticket. There were no police units available.

Fuentes picked up a cheap tabloid at a newsstand by the bus depot and read it while nibbling on a greasy beef *taco* he bought from a street vendor. There wasn't much of interest: baseball scores from the California minor league, a collage of candid photos from the past week's papal visit to Santa Ana. And splattered across the front page, a bold headline followed by the story of a high-ranking *federale comandante* who'd just been arrested for smuggling heroin into the United States.

The takedown had happened in Tijuana and involved eleven others snared in a joint DEA–Mexican police operation. Several kilos of the drug had been seized, detected in a shipment of sesame being transported by one of the largest firms in Sonora: Rios and Rivera, Ltd. The owner of this firm, a *Señora* Consuela Torres-Rios, wife of a senior PRI senator and personal friend of the president of Mexico, was also taken into custody.

According to the feature, the detained policeman had vigorously protested his innocence to anyone who might listen and, according to his attorney, he'd initially offered a sizzling exposé to the media – one that would conclusively uncover the foul underbelly of corruption resting at the very core of Mexican justice.

The police official had been shot dead in front of dozens of onlookers on his first appearance in a Tijuana courtroom. Less than five hours after his arrest and just a few minutes before his lawyer could get the exact details of the allegations out of him and to a syndicate reporter. The three gunmen got cleanly away. The accusations of corruption died with him.

The deceased was identified in the newspaper as Ramon Obregon, just four days into a new appointment as second in command to the Director of Personnel for the Federal Police of Mexico.

Miguel threw the newspaper into a trashcan along with what remained of his *taco*. For the first time he could remember, he didn't have much of an appetite.

In the end, Miguel never did return to the trim house that overlooked the paltry scattering of adobe huts and tiny cemetery. Late that evening, while he was still thirty-one miles distant from *El Presidio* – the Little Fort – it mysteriously burned down. His beloved dog Salinas died in the fire.

Arson? The investigator sent over from Coronado refuted the allegation out of hand. There were no suspects. And anyway, who in the area harbored a grudge against a minor ex-police chief? Certainly no one on their current files. No motive, no suspects. No case.

The official records put the cause of the blaze down as electrical. A short in the fuses. To Miguel it was a feeble epitaph for a fine animal. But he got the message loud and clear. That night, he stayed in the fleabag hotel by the bus depot in Coronado and slept with a chair jarred against the door and a loaded firearm under his pillow.

In the wan lemon light of dawn he opened the envelope and considered his fate.

The dispatch was short. Fuentes was being offered the position of security head for a small container firm in Veracruz. The pay was acceptable, though not grand – slightly less than what he'd last made as a policeman. Still, there was also a small apartment thrown in for a nominal rent situated near the main gate to the shipping yard. And a car.

Miguel understood the terms of engagement, though nothing was ever put into writing. Nothing had to be. All he had to do was forget what he had seen and heard. And believed. Perpetual silence was to be his part of the deal.

Just before noon, he phoned his acceptance of the offer into a voice-message machine in *Señor* Ernesto's office.

The apartment proved to be a walk-up above a pizza parlor. There were car keys on the card table in what passed for a kitchen. And a notation that the vehicle was parked out back in the alley, all gassed up and sporting a new jet-black paint job. The cosmetic makeover would be debited from his pay at source, for the next six months. He had no choice in the matter. The gas, lube, and filter were free. Courtesy of the local PEMEX dealer.

The car was a 1974 Mercury Monarch with chilli-pepper-red upholstery and shocks that swayed like fallen arches. It also sported three bullet holes inching upward from the rocker panel to the driver's side door. Fuentes didn't look to find out where the other bullets had lodged themselves. He likewise didn't bother to ask if it had ever had peach tassels.

Or why there was a rumpled note in the glove compartment

addressed to his predecessor, Mercedes Lopez – a typed note tersely reminding Luppy to attend a rendezvous to discuss "urgent business matters … Because Senor 'O' and the Familia are getting concerned ..."

Miguel never knew why he turned the single leaf over – perhaps it was instinct. Perhaps it was just the way things were meant to be.

There was handwriting on the back, a pinched scrawl, very familiar.

Three lines. That was all. There didn't have to be more to break what was left of his heart.

> Boss:
> Your cut from Ramon is the usual. $100 in U.S. bills.
> You'll find it waiting where you always want it.
> In the cemetery at Santa Lucia.
>
> Felix

Miguel stepped outside the car. There was a sudden rustling in the alley, a flurry of paper cups and newspapers. For an instant, the gust grew hot and stale; then it stopped, and the air chilled noticeably.

Silence.

An unnatural sound followed the wind's gust, a dense reverberation, rasping, sepulchral, with the cruel resonance of earth clumps thrumming onto a coffin.

Fuentes started. He crossed himself instinctively, glanced to where the sound seemed to have originated, then relaxed.

A rusting fire-exit ladder dangled drunkenly from one of the walls that bound the alley. One of its legs beat an imprecise tattoo against a derelict oil drum.

He eased back into the car and tenderly touched the vinyl upholstery. It was old and cracked and faded. The bucket seats were lumpy. In places, the springs poked through. The spot on the dash where the AM radio had once been was now no more than a messy labyrinth of loose wiring. The floor carpet was threadbare, nearly bald, and the front windshield had huge cracks zigzagging outward in the pattern of a spider's web. He smelled age in the car, and despair.

Outside the alley was quiet. The metallic *rat-a-tat-tat* of the ladder had mercifully stopped. Here, near the harbor, the salt air was stinking moist and drenched with foulness.

A split second. Fuentes pricked his ears and peered alertly about. There was something else out there now – an altered mood in the wind, an ebb and flow that carried with it all his pain and frustration and loneliness. There was something else.

Then he did something he hadn't done in years. He laid his head across the steering wheel of the Monarch. And cried.

And for a fleeting moment, just a moment, he thought he caught the sound of the Devil's laughter.